Mediterra

Red-hot, ruthless

Mediterranean Playboys

THE SPANISH HUSBAND
by
Michelle Reid

THE MILLIONAIRE'S VIRGIN
by
Anne Mather

THE ITALIAN GROOM
by
Jane Porter

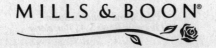

MILLS & BOON®

*MILLS & BOON and MILLS & BOON with the Rose Device
are registered trademarks of the publisher.*
Harlequin Mills & Boon Limited,
Eton House, 18-24 Paradise Road, Richmond, Surrey, TW9 1SR

MEDITERRANEAN PLAYBOYS
© by Harlequin Enterprises II B.V., 2004

The Spanish Husband, The Millionaire's Virgin and *The Italian Groom*
were first published in Great Britain by Harlequin Mills & Boon
Limited in separate, single volumes.

The Spanish Husband © Michelle Reid 2000
The Millionaire's Virgin © Anne Mather 2000
The Italian Groom © Jane Porter-Gaskins 2000

ISBN 0 263 84070 0

05-0504

*Printed and bound in Spain
by Litografia Rosés S.A., Barcelona*

Michelle Reid grew up on the southern edges of Manchester, the youngest in a family of five lively children. But now she lives in the beautiful county of Cheshire with her busy executive husband and two grown-up daughters. She loves reading, the ballet, and playing tennis when she gets the chance. She hates cooking, cleaning, and despises ironing! Sleep she can do without and produces some of her best written work during the early hours of the morning.

Don't miss Michelle Reid's latest sizzling story:
THE PASSION BARGAIN
On sale next month, in Modern Romance™!

THE SPANISH HUSBAND

by

Michelle Reid

CHAPTER ONE

CAROLINE was pacing the floor and becoming more agitated with each step that she took. She arrived at the window which led out onto the terrace, saw nothing of the beautiful view the elegant two-bedroom suite offered her of the famous Puerto Banus, and turned to pace back the way she had come, glancing impatiently at her watch as she did so.

Nine o'clock. Her father had said seven o'clock. He had *promised* seven o'clock. 'Just going for a stroll before I need to change for dinner,' he'd said. 'To check out the old place and see if it's changed much since we were here last.'

He loved Marbella. They'd used to spend most of their summers here once upon a time, so she'd understood his eagerness to reacquaint himself with the resort—but not his refusal to let her go with him.

'Don't be a pain, Caroline,' he'd censured when she'd instantly started to get anxious. 'I don't need you to hold my hand. And I certainly don't need a watchdog. Show a little faith, for goodness' sake. Haven't I promised to behave myself?'

So she'd showed a little faith—and now look at her, she mocked herself bitterly. For here she was, pacing the floor like a worried mother hen with every nerve-end she possessed singing out a warning of trouble!

He wouldn't let her down—would he? She tried to reassure herself. He had been so firm, so *needy* for her to believe in him that he wouldn't, surely, fall prey to his old

weakness when he knew how important it was to them for
him to remain strong?

Then where is he? A very cynical voice inside her head
taunted. He's been gone for hours. And you know what
he can get up to when left to his own devices for too long.

'Oh, hell,' she muttered as the agitation suddenly
reached whole new levels, and, in tight and angry surrender to it, she snatched up her little black velvet evening
bag and headed for the suite's outer door.

If she discovered that he had sneaked off to feed his
damned habit then she would never forgive him! She
vowed as she stabbed a hard finger at the lift call button
then stood waiting impatiently for it to come. Things were
bad enough already.

More than bad enough, she groaned inwardly. Or she
wouldn't even be here, her father knew that! He knew how
much she hated this place now, hated the whole morass of
painful emotions it evoked.

Seven years since their last visit, she recalled as the lift
doors slid open. Seven years since they had been forced
to leave beneath a dark cloud of pride-shrivelling humiliation and soul-destroying heartbreak, vowing never to return again.

Yet here they were, not only back in Marbella but staying in the same hotel. And once again she was having to
go and hunt her father out in the very last place on this
earth she ever wanted to step foot in!

The casino, she named it grimly as she walked into the
lift. The wretched in-house casino, where she was all too
aware of the damage her father could do in such a terri-
fyingly short space of time.

And how long had he been missing? she asked herself
as she pressed for the ground floor.

Two hours at least.

Her fingers stood out white against her black evening

bag while she waited for the lift doors to shut. In two miserable hours he could lose thousands. Give him a whole night and he would, quite happily, lose his shirt!

Like the last time.

A wave of sickness suddenly washed over her, sending her slumping weakly against the lift wall just as the doors began to close. A hand snaked out, compelling the doors to open again, and she found herself quickly straightening as a tall dark man of Spanish descent, dressed in an impeccably tailored black dinner suit and bow tie, stepped lithely into the cabin with her.

'My apologies for delaying you,' he murmured in smoothly modulated English, swinging round to offer her a smile. A smile that instantly arrested when his eyes actually focused on her.

'That's okay,' she replied, and quickly dropped her gaze so as not to encourage any further contact.

The lift began to sink. Standing tensely by the console, Caroline was stingingly aware that he was still studying her, but pretended not to notice. It wasn't a new experience for her to be looked at like this. She had the kind of natural blonde, curvaceously slender, long-legged figure that incited men to stare. And the stranger was good-looking; she had noticed that about him before she'd lowered her gaze.

But she was in no mood to be chatted up in a lift—if she was ever in the mood anywhere, she then added, bleakly aware that it had been a long time since she had let any man get close to her.

Not since Luiz, in fact, right here in Marbella.

Then. No. Abruptly she severed that memory before it had a chance to get a grip. She wasn't going to think of Luiz. It was a promise she had made to herself before she came here. Luiz belonged in the distant past, along with every other bitter memory Marbella had the power to throw up at her. And this tall dark stranger looked too much like Luiz to stand the remotest chance with her.

So she was relieved when the lift stopped and she could escape his intense regard without him attempting to make conversation. Within seconds she had completely forgotten him, her mind back on the problem of finding her father as she paused at the head of a shallow set of steps which led down to the main foyer and began searching the busy area in front of her.

This was one of the more impressive hotels that stood in prime position on Marbella's Puerto Banus. Years ago, the hotel had possessed a well-earned reputation for old-fashioned grandeur which had made it appeal to a certain kind of guest—a select kind that had once included both herself and her father.

But the hotel had only just been re-opened, after a huge refurbishment undertaken by its new owners, and although it still held pride of place as one of the most exclusive hotels in the resort, it now displayed its five-star deluxe ranking with more subtle elegance.

And the people were different, less rigidly correct and aware of their own status, though she didn't doubt for a moment that if they were staying here then they must be able to afford the frankly extortionate rates.

It was a thought that brought home to her just how much she had changed in seven years. For seven years ago she too would not have so much as questioned the price of a two-bedroom suite in any hotel. She had been reared to expect the best, and if the best came with a big price-tag attached to it then that was life as she had known it.

These days she didn't just question price-tags, she calculated how long she would have to work to make that kind of money.

In fact money was now an obsession with Caroline. Or at least the lack of it was, along with a constant need to keep on feeding that greedy monster her family home had become.

A frown touched her brow as she continued to search for the familiar sight of her father's very distinctive tall and slender figure among the clutches of people gathered in the foyer. For two hundred years there had been Newburys in residence at Highbrook Manor. But the chances of there being Newburys there for very much longer depended almost entirely on what her father was doing at this precise moment.

And he certainly wasn't in evidence here, she acknowledged as, with a grace that belied her inner tension, she set herself moving down the steps and across the foyer to see if he had left a message for her at the reception desk.

He hadn't. Next she went off to check out the lounge bars in the faint hope that he might have met someone he'd used to know, got to talking and lost track of the time. Again she drew a blank, and her heart began to take on a slower, thicker beat because she knew that there was now only one place left for her to look for him.

Grimly she set her feet moving over to a flight of steps set in their own discreet alcove that led the way down to the hotel basement. Walking down those steps took a kind of courage no one would understand unless they had known her seven years ago. By the time she reached the bottom she was even trembling slightly. For very little had changed down here except maybe the decoration, she noticed with a sickly feeling of *déjà vu*. The basement area still possessed its own very stylish foyer, still had a sign pointing to the left directing the guests to the hotel's fully equipped gymnasium, beauty therapy rooms and indoor swimming pool.

Still had a pair of doors to her right, which were as firmly closed as they always had been, as if to keep carefully hidden from innocent eyes what went on behind them.

But the sign hanging above the doors was not innocent. 'Casino' it announced in discreet gold lettering.

Her father's favourite playground of old, she thought with a small shiver. A place where compulsive excitement went hand in hand with desperation and the flip of a card or the roll of a dice or the spin of a wheel had the potential to make or break you.

If he had given in to himself and gone in search of excitement, then she was sure she was going to find him on the other side of those wretched doors, she predicted as she took a reluctant step forward.

'You will be disappointed,' a smoothly accented voice drawled lazily.

Spinning round in surprise, Caroline found herself looking at the stranger who had shared the lift with her. Tall, dark, undeniably good-looking—her stomach muscles flipped on yet another sense of *déjà vu*. For he really did look uncannily like Luiz. The same age, the same build, the same rich Spanish colouring.

'I beg your pardon?' she said, thinking that even her first meeting with Luiz had been right here in this basement foyer, with her hovering uncertainly like this and him smiling at her like that...

'The casino,' he prompted with a nod of his dark head in the direction of the closed doors. 'It does not open until ten o'clock. You are too early...'

Pure instinct made her check the time on her watch, to discover that it was only nine-fifteen. Sheer relief had her winging a warm smile at the stranger—because if the casino wasn't even open, then her father could not be ensconced in there, wrecking what small chance they had of saving their home!

And now she felt guilty. Guilty for mistrusting him,

guilty for being angry, guilty for thinking the worst of him when of course he wouldn't do that to her!

'Perhaps I could persuade you to share a glass of wine with me in the lounge bar, while we wait for the casino to open?' the stranger invited.

Caroline flushed, realising that he had misinterpreted her sudden smile, and the pick-up she had carefully avoided in the lift was back on track with a vengeance. The kind of vengeance that made him flash her a megawatt smile.

By contrast she completely froze him. 'Thank you, but I am here with someone,' she informed him stiffly, and pointedly turned back to the stairs.

'Your father, Sir Edward Newbury, perhaps?' he suggested lightly, successfully bringing her departure to a halt.

'You know my father?' she questioned warily.

'We have met,' he smiled. But it was the way that he smiled that chilled Caroline's blood. As if he knew something she didn't and was deriding that knowledge.

Or deriding her father.

'I have just seen him,' he added. 'He crossed the foyer towards the lifts only a few short minutes ago. He seemed—in a hurry…' That lazily mocking smile appeared again, making her feel distinctly uneasy.

'Thank you,' she said politely. 'For letting me know.' And she turned away from him once again.

The feel of his fingers closing around her wrist came as a shock. 'Don't rush away,' he murmured. 'I would really like to get to know you better…'

His voice was quite pleasantly pitched—but his grip was an intrusion and alarm bells were beginning to sound in her head, because she had a horrible feeling that if she tried to break free his fingers would tighten—painfully.

She didn't like this man, she decided. She didn't like his smooth good-looks or his easy confidence or the lazy charm he was utilising—while using physical means to detain her.

She didn't like his touch on her skin, or the itchy suspicion that he had been shadowing her movements since the lift, and had timed his approach to coincide with the fact that they were standing at the bottom of a flight of stairs well away from other people.

And she didn't like the uneasy sensation of feeling vulnerable to someone stronger than herself and clearly so sure of himself that he dared detain her like this.

'Please let go of me,' she said.

His grip did tighten. Her pulse began to accelerate. 'But if I let you go you will not learn *how* I became acquainted with your papa,' he pointed out. 'Or, perhaps more significantly, *where* I became acquainted with him…'

'Where?' she responded, aware that he was deliberately dangling the knowledge at her like a carrot on a stick.

'Share a glass of wine with me,' he urged. 'And I will tell you.'

And it was such a juicy carrot, she noted, one that was trying to make her go one way while every single instinct she possessed was telling her to run in the other.

At which point anger took over, for if he believed she was open to this kind of coercion then he was severely mistaken! 'I'm sure,' she replied in her coldest voice, 'that if my father thinks your meeting memorable enough he will tell me about it himself. Now, if you will excuse me?' she concluded, and gave a hard enough tug at her captured wrist to free it, then walked stiffly up the steps without glancing back.

But her insides felt shaky, and the nerves running along her spine were tingling, because she half expected him to come chasing after her. It was an unpleasant sensation, one that stayed with her all the way up that flight of steps and across the busy foyer into one of the waiting lifts. In fact it was only when the doors had shut her in without him joining her there that she began to feel safe again.

And her wrist hurt. Glancing down at it, she wasn't surprised to find the delicate white skin covering it was showing the beginnings of bruising. Who was he? she wondered. What was he to her father that made him believe it was okay to accost her like that?

It was a concern that took her into her suite and immediately across to her father's bedroom door with the grim intention of finding out. But, having knocked sharply and then pushed open the door, she knew she was going to be unlucky, when it became immediately apparent that he had already been here and gone again.

And the way his clothes had been discarded on the floor told her he had changed in one heck of a hurry.

So as to avoid her? Oh, yes, Caroline conceded heavily. He was trying to avoid her—which could only mean one thing.

He had fallen off the rails again.

In a fit of angry frustration she bent down to snatch up the pair of trousers he had dropped on the floor and was about to toss them onto the bed when something dropped out of one of the pockets. It landed with a paper-like thud on the toe of her shoe. Bending to pick it up, she discovered that she was holding what appeared to be a set of receipts, and with her fingers actually tingling with dread, she slowly unfurled them.

After that she didn't move, didn't breathe, didn't even think a coherent thought for long, long seconds. Then, with a calmness that bore no resemblance to what was actually taking place inside her, she began to check with the methodical intent of one well-practised at doing it, every pocket in every item of clothing he had brought with him to Marbella.

Ten minutes later and she was standing there in the middle of her father's room, staring into space like someone turned to stone. They had been here in Marbella for less than twenty-four hours and, going by the tally on the receipts, in that time her father had managed to gamble and lose the best part of one hundred thousand pounds...

Standing by the window of his hi-tech control room, Luiz Vazquez looked down on the casino floor of this, the latest acquisition in his growing string of deluxe hotels.

He could not be seen from down on the floor. The window allowed him to look out but did not let anyone look in. And behind him the really serious viewing was going on, via closed circuit television screens watched over by his eagle-eyed security staff. The window was merely a secondary source by which the casino floor as a whole could be observed.

Luiz preferred to check out the floor with his own eyes like this. It came from once being a serious gambler and trusting nothing he could not see for himself. Now things were different. Now he didn't need to gamble to earn enough money to live. He had wealth and he had power and a kind of deeply satisfying sense of self-respect that had taken a whole lot of earning and yet...

A frown brought the two dark silk strips of his brows together across the bridge of his long nose. Possessing respect in oneself did not automatically win you the respect of others. A salutary lesson he had learned the hard way, and one he intended to rectify very soon.

It was, in fact, his next major project.

Vito Martinez, the hotel's Head of Security, came to stand beside him. 'She's gone back to her room,' he said. 'He's just arrived in the casino bar.'

'Tense?' Luiz asked.

'Yeah,' Vito replied, 'humming with it. Ripe, I'd say,'

he added, the evidence of his on-the-street New York up-bringing more pronounced in the dry-edged judgement.

A single nod in acknowledgement and Luiz Vazquez was turning away from the window, his expression, as always, a tightly closed book—not surprising for a man who'd used to play poker as lethally as he had.

'Buzz me when he comes to the tables,' was all he said. Then he was walking out of the control room, his long, lean level stride taking him across the elegant cream and black marbled floor of this tightly secured inner sanctum, then in through another door, which he closed behind him.

Silence suddenly prevailed.

Where the other room had been alive with a busy hum of activity, this room was so quiet you could hear a pin drop on the thick cream carpet covering its huge expanse. It was a luxuriously furnished room, plain but dramatic, with its modern black lacquered and leather furnishings enhanced by the simplicity of cream-painted walls.

Like the man himself, the room revealed nothing of his true personality. Except, maybe, for the black-framed picture hanging on the wall behind a large black-lacquered desk.

In its own way the picture was as dramatically plain as everything else in here—nothing more than the faint gold outline of a scorpion clinging to a white background with its lethal-looking tail curving upwards and over its scaly body in preparation to strike.

But it made the blood run cold just to look at it. For, although it was Luiz Vazquez's chair that was situated directly beneath that lethal claw, it was not him the scorpion seemed to threaten—but whoever was unlucky enough to sit in the chair placed on the other side of the desk.

Its message was clear. Mess with me and I strike.

It was his mark—his logo. Or one of them, at least. But

once upon a time the sign of the golden scorpion had used to adorn everything Luiz Vazquez was involved in. He had since learned to be much more subtle. And he just kept this one picture around him for personal reasons now—and as a warning to anyone who was unfortunate enough to find themselves summoned to these private rooms, that the cool-headed, soft-talking Luiz Vazquez still had a vicious sting in his tail.

But these days he was known better for his new logo. The one which gave his string of exclusive, internationally renowned hotels their name and had earned him quite a reputation for quality service and comfort during the last ten years.

For this was an Angel Hotel. Angel as in Luiz *Angeles* de Vazquez. Angel as in good, honest and true.

The sublime to the ridiculous. And an example of what good marketing could do because all of his hotels possessed in-house casinos which were the real draw. The luxury his admittedly well-heeled guests enjoyed while they played was just an added bonus.

The scorpion was probably a far more honest representation of what Luiz Vazquez really was.

Luiz went to sit beneath that scorpion now, sliding his perfectly contoured frame into a thickly padded swivel desk chair before reaching down to unlock and open one of the drawers in the desk.

His fingers, so long and lean and beautifully co-ordinated that they revealed even more about the man's extraordinary powers of self-control in the way they did everything with such neat precision, took out the only item in the drawer and placed it on the desktop.

It was a leather-bound dossier, expensive but nothing particularly ominous about it. Yet he didn't immediately open it. Instead he leant back in the chair and began swinging it lightly while one set of neatly filed fingernails tapped an absent tattoo against the desk. His expression revealed nothing, as usual. Whatever was going on in that shrewd, sharp mind of his was being kept hidden beneath the curling black lashes that usually shrouded his eyes.

Beautiful eyes. Eyes of a rich, dark fathomless brown colour that sat in the sleepy hollows of an arrestingly handsome face. A full Spaniard by birth, though raised in America, he undoubtedly had the warm golden skin of his Spanish forebears, the high cheekbones, the nose, the rock-solid, firmly chiselled jaw-line, and the shadowy outline of a beautifully moulded mouth.

But, for all of its good points, it was still the face of a cool operator. Of a man reputed to possess no heart—or, to be less fanciful, to possess the heart of an athlete, able to maintain the calm, steady pace necessary to keep the oxygen pumping into his clever brain no matter what pressure he put it under.

The fingers suddenly stopped tapping and moved, sliding over the desk and across smooth leather until they could curl and flick open the dossier cover to reveal a thick wad of documents stacked inside. With a supple dexterity that had been trained into his fingers years ago, he began sifting through the papers until he found the one he was looking for. Removing it from the stack, he set it neatly back down upon the top, then simply went still, his eyes glowing with a sudden burn as he sat there looking at a seven-by-nine colour photograph of—Caroline.

She was without doubt extraordinarily beautiful. No one with eyes would ever say she was not. Hair the colour of ripening wheat framed the most delicately perfect face even Luiz Vazquez, for all his thirty-five years of worldly experience, had ever set eyes upon. She had the flawless white skin of a pale English rose and eyes the colour of amethyst. Her small straight nose was classically drawn, like the finely defined curve of her delicate jaw-line. But it was her mouth that held Luiz's attention. Soft, warm, pink and full—it was a mouth made to drive a man wild with pleasure.

And he should know, Luiz mused cynically. For he'd had plenty of experience of just what that mouth could do—and he meant to have some more very soon.

It was a prospect that had the burn in his eyes changing back to their normal inscrutable cool as he utilised yet another facet of his strong character. Patience. The man was blessed with unending patience when it came to goals he had set himself.

That next goal was Caroline. And he was so sure of success that in his mind Caroline already belonged to him. It was this kind of belief in himself which gave him the power to put her photograph aside and basically forget it was there while he set about reading through the rest of the papers in the bulky dossier.

They were mostly bills. Final demand notes, warnings of foreclosure on bank loans, property mortgages, and, most sinister of all, the long list of unpaid gambling debts—both the old and the very new. He read each one in turn, consigning every detail to his photographic memory before setting it aside and doing the same with the next one.

A light on the desk console suddenly began flashing. Reaching out, he stabbed at the console with a finger. 'Yes?' he said.

'She's on her way down,' Vito Martinez informed him. 'He's playing for big money.'

'Right,' was all Luiz replied, and another stab at the console brought silence back to the room again.

Turning his attention back to the papers in front of him,

he picked them all up—including the photograph—deftly re-stacked the pile, then shut the dossier and locked it away in its drawer before getting smoothly to his feet. Then, with a deft tug which brought white shirt-cuffs into line with the edge of his creamy white dinner jacket, Luiz Vazquez rounded his desk and strode out of the room.

Back in the control room, Vito Martinez was still standing by the window. Luiz went to join him, saw Vito's nod and followed its direction to one of the roulette tables.

Tall, lean, quite good-looking for his age, and, as always, impeccably presented, Sir Edward Newbury was playing big chips—and the expression on his face was a mere hair's breadth away from fever-pitch.

Luiz recognised the look for exactly what it was—a man in the last throes of civility. Sir Edward was hooked—overdosing, in fact, and ready to sell his soul to the very devil.

Ripe, as Vito had said.

Grimly unsurprised by what he was seeing, Luiz then shifted his attention away from Sir Edward Newbury as, with his usual faultless timing, he looked towards the casino entrance just as Caroline appeared.

And everything inside him went perfectly still.

Seven long years had gone by since he had last physically laid eyes on her—yet she had barely changed. The hair, the eyes, the wonderful skin, the gorgeous mouth with the vulnerable upper lip and cushion-soft lower one he knew tasted as delicious as it looked. Even the long and slender line of her figure, so perfectly outlined by the exquisite styling of her black dress, had not lost any of its youthful firmness—as his own body was in the process of informing him, growing hot around the loins in a way only this woman had ever managed to kindle.

'His weakness', he labelled the sensation. The Spanish

bastard's desire to possess the forbidden in this woman, who was an icon to class and breeding. Even her name was something special. Miss Caroline Aurora Celandine Newbury... Luiz tasted the name on his silent tongue. She had a family tree that read like a history book, a background education fashioned exclusively for the élite, and a stately home any king would envy.

These were the credentials that gave the Newburys the right to consider themselves noble, Luiz judged cynically. To be good enough to be accepted by them you had to be someone at least as special. Even now, he predicted, when metaphorically they were down on their knees and could not afford to be too choosy, quality of breeding would be the yardstick by which they would measure whether or not you were worthy of their notice.

Caroline looked very pale, he saw as he watched her anxiously scanning the casino in search of her wayward father. She also looked tense and severely uncomfortable with her surroundings. But then she never had liked places like this.

She caught sight of Sir Edward as the roulette wheel began to spin. Luiz watched her body stiffen, watched the strain etch itself onto her lovely face and her small white teeth come pressing down into that exquisitely shaped bottom lip as she made herself walk forwards. He felt his own teeth set hard behind the flat line of his lips as he watched her pause a couple of steps behind her father, then knot her fingers together across the flatness of her stomach as if she wasn't quite sure just what to do next.

Really, what Caroline would have liked to do was get hold of her father by the scruff of his neck and drag him by it out of there. It was the breeding that stopped her; Luiz knew that. In the laws of polite society one did not make ugly scenes in public, no matter how bad the situation. Even when you knew that your finances were already in Queer Street and that what your father was doing was nothing short of criminal.

Black. Even. Sir Edward lost, as he had been doing steadily since they'd arrived here in Marbella late yesterday.

As the old man made a gesture of frustration, Caroline visibly wilted.

'Daddy...'

Luiz could actually feel her wariness as she placed a hand on the sleeve of her father's tux in an attempt to make him listen to reason.

No chance, Luiz judged. The man was half crazed with gambling fever. Once it hit there was no quick cure. Sir Edward could not give up now, even if he lost the very shirt from his back, and more.

It was the 'more' Luiz wanted.

After an initial start of surprise, then a guilty glance over his shoulder, Sir Edward Newbury turned petulant, and, with a tersely uttered sentence, shrugged off his daughter's hand so he could place another stack of chips on the table. All Caroline could do was stand and watch as five thousand pounds sterling hovered in the balance between a ball landing on black or on red.

Black. Sir Edward lost again.

Again Caroline attempted to stop him. Again her pleas were petulantly thrust aside. Only this time Luiz found his hands clenching into tight fists at his sides when he caught the briefest glint of telling moisture touching lovely eyes. It was sheer hopelessness that sent them on a hunting scan of the crowded casino, as if searching for help where none would ever be found.

Then, without any warning, she suddenly glanced up at the control room, those incredible eyes homing directly in on him with such unerring accuracy that he caught his breath.

So did Vito. 'Jeez,' he breathed.

Luiz did not so much as move a single muscle. He knew she couldn't see him; he knew the glass did not allow her to. Yet…

His skin began to prickle, a fine tremor of response rippling through his whole body on a moment's complete loss of himself as he stared straight into those beautiful, bright tear-washed eyes. His throat had locked; his heart was straining against a sudden fierce tightening across his breastplate. Then her soft mouth gave a tremulous quiver in a wretched display of absolute despair—and his whole body was suddenly bathed in a fine layer of static electricity.

That mouth. That small, lush, sensual mouth—

'He won,' Vito murmured quietly beside him.

From the corner of his eye Luiz caught Sir Edward Newbury's response as he punched the air with a triumphant fist. But his attention remained fixed on Caroline, who was just standing there watching, with a dullness that said winning was as bad as losing to her.

Abruptly he turned away. 'I'm going down,' he told Vito. 'Make sure everything is ready for when we leave here.'

And neither his voice nor his body language gave away any hint of the burst of blistering emotion he had just been put through before he strode away.

'Yes!' On a soft burst of exultation, Sir Edward Newbury turned and scooped his daughter into his arms. 'Two wins on the trot! We've hit a winning streak, my darling! A couple more like this and we'll be flying high!'

But he was already high. The wild glint burning in his

eyes was frightening. 'Please, Daddy,' Caroline pleaded. 'Stop now while you're ahead. This is—'

Madness, she had been going to say, but he brusquely cut her off. 'Don't be a killjoy, Caro. This is our lucky night, can't you see that?' Letting her go, he twisted back to the table as the croupier was about to slide his winnings over to him. 'Let them ride,' he instructed, and Caroline had to look on helplessly as every penny he had won was instantly waged on one feckless spin of a roulette wheel.

A crowd had started to gather around the table, their excited murmurs dying to a hush as the wheel began to spin. Caroline stopped breathing, her tongue cleaving to the roof of her paper-dry mouth as she watched that small ivory ball perform its tantalising dance with fate.

Inside she was angry—furious, even. But she had been reared never to make scenes in public. And the fact that he knew it was a weapon her father was more than happy to use against her. It was the nature of his weakness to rely on her good behaviour while he behaved appallingly.

So much for sincere promises, she derided as she watched through glazed eyes as the wheel began to slow. So much for weeks and months and *years* of careful vigilance, when she'd learned that trusting anything he said was a way to look disaster in the face.

She was tired of it, wearied with fighting the fight at the expense of everything else in her life. And she had a horrible feeling that this time she was not going to be able to forgive him for doing this to her yet again.

But for now all she could do was look on, feeling helpless, locked inside her own worst nightmare in the one place in this world her nightmares could be guaranteed free reign. This place, this hotel—this wretched casino. All she needed now was for Luiz Vazquez to materialise in front of her and the nightmare would be complete.

Like lightning striking twice. She shuddered.

Someone came to stand directly behind her, she felt their warm breath caressing her nape, though she only registered it vaguely. Her attention was fixed on that tormenting little ball and the rhythmic clacking noise it made as it jumped from compartment to compartment in a playful mix of ivory, red and black.

And the tension, the pulsing sense of building expectancy that was the real draw, the actual smell of madness, permeated all around her like a poisonous drug no one could resist.

'Yes!' Her father's victorious hiss hit her eardrums like the jarring clash of a hundred cymbals as he doubled his reckless stake—just like that.

The gathered crowd began enjoying his good fortune with him, but Caroline wilted like a dying flower. Her heart was floundering somewhere down deep inside her. She felt sick, she felt dizzy—must have actually swayed a little, because an arm snaked around her waist to support her. And it was a mark as to just how weak she was feeling that she let that arm gently ease her back against the hard-packed body standing behind her.

This was it, she was thinking dully. There would be no stopping him now. He wouldn't be happy until he had lost everything he had already won—and more. She didn't so much as consider him winning, because winning was not the real desire that drove people like him to play. It was, quite simply, the compulsion to play no matter what the final outcome. Winning meant your luck was in, so you played until your luck ran out, then played until it came back again.

A fine shudder rippled through her, making her suddenly aware that she was leaning against some total stranger. With an abrupt tensing of her spine, she managed to put a little distance between them before turning within that circling arm to murmur a coldly polite,'Thank you, but I'm—'

Words froze, the air sealed inside lungs that suddenly ceased to function as she stood there, staring into a pair of all too familiar devil-black eyes that trapped her inside a world of complete denial.

'Hello, Caroline,' Luiz greeted smoothly.

CHAPTER TWO

HER heart flipped over, then began to beat wildly. 'Luiz…' she breathed through lips gone too numb to move while, No, her mind was telling her. She was hallucinating—dreaming him up from the depths of her worst fears—because this place and her father's madness were all so synonymous in her mind with this man. 'No.' She even made the denial out loud.

'Sorry but—yes,' he replied with a real dry amusement slicing through his lazy tone.

But it was an amusement that did not reach the darkness in his eyes, and the room began to blacken around its edges as yet another dizzying sense of pained dismay took the place of shocked numbness.

'Please let go of me,' she said shakily, desperately needing to put some distance between the two of them before she could attempt to deal with this.

'Of course.' The hand was instantly removed. And for some crazy reason she found herself comparing his ready compliance with the complete disregard the stranger in the basement had shown when she had made the same request of him.

A man who had reminded her of Luiz. A man she hadn't liked on sight, whereas Luiz she…

'Your father's luck is in, I see,' he remarked, his gaze now fixed on what was going on behind her.

'Is it?' Scepticism sliced heavily through the two short syllables, bringing his dark eyes back to her face.

But Caroline could no longer look at him. It *hurt* to look at him. For Luiz personified everything she had learned to despise about her father's disease. Obsession, machination, deception, betrayal.

Bitterness suddenly rose to almost completely engulf her. She went to spin away from him, but at the same moment the crowd began to surge in, jostling her in their eagerness to congratulate her father, wanting to demonstrate their delight in seeing someone beat the bank against all the odds for once. Luiz's arm came back, looping round her in protection this time against several elbows being aimed in her direction, and Caroline found herself being pressed so close to him that she would have to be dead not to be aware of every hard-packed nuance of the man.

Her heart-rate picked up and her breathing grew shallow. It was awful. Memories began to flood her mind. They had been lovers once. Their bodies knew each other as intimately as two bodies could. Standing here, virtually imprisoned by the crowd closing round them, was the worst kind of punishment that fate could have doled out to her for being stupid enough to agree to come back here.

It was a knowledge that filled her with a kind of acrimony that poured itself into her voice. 'Still playing games for a living, Luiz?' she shot at him sarcastically. 'I wonder what the management would do if they found out they have a professional in their club.'

His dark eyes narrowed. And it was because she was being forced to stand so close to him that she felt the slight tensing of certain muscles—like a dangerous cat raising its hackles. 'Was that your version of a veiled threat by any chance?' he questioned very carefully.

Was it? Caroline asked herself, aware that all it would take was a quiet word in the ear of the management to have Luiz very quietly but very firmly hustled out of here. But—

'It was merely an observation,' she sighed, knowing that

she had no right to criticise Luiz when her own father was just as bad.

'Then, to answer your *observation,* no,' he replied. 'I am not here to play.'

But Caroline wasn't listening. A sudden idea had hit her, one that had her heart leaping in her breast. 'Luiz…' she murmured urgently. 'If I had a quiet word with the management about my father, would they stop *him* from playing any more?'

'Why should they?' His mouth took on a derisive twist. 'He's no professional, just a man with a vice he has turned into an obsession.'

'A suicidal obsession,' Caroline extended with a shiver.

The hand at her spine gently soothed her. And what was worse was that Luiz didn't say a single word. He knew her father—knew him only too well.

'I hate this,' she whispered, wishing she could just creep away and pretend it wasn't happening. But she couldn't, and somehow, some way she had to try and stop this madness before her father ruined them completely.

'Do you want me to stop him?' Luiz offered.

Her eyes flicked up to clash with his. 'Do you think you can?' she murmured anxiously.

In response Luiz simply lifted his gaze to where her father was emerging from his sea of congratulations. 'Sir Edward,' he said.

That was all. No raising of his voice, no challenge in the tone. Just the two quietly spoken words. Yet they carried enough impact to cause a small cessation in the buzz of excitement taking place.

And the fine hairs on the back of Caroline's neck began to tingle as she sensed her father spinning around. She couldn't see him because Luiz was keeping her pressed against him, but in the following long seconds of tense silence she certainly felt the full thrust of her father's shock.

His recovery was swift though. 'Well,' he drawled. 'If it isn't Luiz. This is a surprise…'

Eton-educated, brought up to be always aware of his own worth, Sir Edward Newbury's King's-English accent was a pitch-perfect blend of sarcasm and condescension that made his daughter wince.

Luiz didn't wince. He just offered a wry smile. 'Isn't it?' he agreed. 'Seven years on and here we are again. Same time, same place—'

'It must be fate,' her father dryly tagged on.

And fate just about covered it, Caroline was thinking hollowly. Ill fate. Cruel fate.

'I see your luck is in tonight,' Luiz observed. 'Taken the bank to the cleaners, have you?'

'Not yet, but I'm getting there.' Her father sounded different suddenly. Enlivened, invigorated.

At which point Caroline made herself turn in the circle of Luiz's arm to witness for herself the covetous gleam she knew was going to be in her father's eyes. But she also saw the childlike pique that took hold of him as he skimmed his gaze over her face. He knew very well how badly he was letting her down tonight, but was belligerently defiant about it.

It made her heart want to break in despair.

'How much do you think you've managed to win so far?' Luiz questioned curiously.

Sir Edward didn't even give his winnings a glance. 'Bad luck to count it, Luiz. You know that,' he dismissed with a shrug.

'But if you're feeling really lucky, then perhaps you could be tempted into a private bet with me?' Luiz suggested. 'Put the lot on the next spin,' he challenged. 'If you win, I'll double the amount, then play you for the lot

at poker. Fancy the long shot?' he added provokingly, ignoring Caroline's protesting gasp.

Their curious audience was suddenly on edge. Caroline
simply went cold. Luiz called this *stopping him?* In all her
life she had never felt so betrayed—and that included the
last time Luiz had betrayed her trust in him.

'No,' she whispered, her eyes pleading with her father
not to take Luiz on.

But he wasn't even aware of her presence any more.
And she knew exactly what he was doing; he was busily
adding up his present winnings, doubling them and doubling them again, then playing Luiz at a game even she
knew Luiz was lethal at, and seeing all his problems melting away in one sweet lucky night.

'Why not?' He accepted the challenge, and as his daughter stared at him in dismay he turned and, with a brief nod
of his head to the waiting croupier, coolly instructed, 'Let
it all ride.'

And the wheel began to spin once again.

Behind her Caroline could feel Luiz watching things
over the top of her head. In front of her, her father stood,
outwardly calm and supremely indifferent to the eventual
outcome even though their lives, in effect, stood hovering
in the balance. And all around it was as if the whole casino
had come to a breathless standstill while everyone watched
the game play itself out. There wasn't a person present
who believed that Sir Edward could win on the same colour for a fourth time.

Caroline certainly did not believe it. 'I'll never forgive
you for this,' she told Luiz, and shrugged herself free of
his grasp.

He let her go, though he remained standing directly behind her. And, like everyone else, they stood watching as
the wheel began to slow, allowing that wretched ball to
bounce playfully from slot to slot.

It was torture at its worst. She had known they should not have come here, had told her father over and over again that Marbella was the last place on earth they should look for salvation.

But he hadn't listened. He was desperate, and desperate men do desperate things. 'We have no choice!' was all he'd said. 'The finance company that bought up all our debts is based in Marbella. They refuse to speak to us unless we show up personally. We have to go there, Caroline.'

'And your gambling debts?' she'd hit out at him angrily. 'Do they have their greedy hands on all of those too?'

He'd flushed with guilt, then gone peevish on her as he always did when caught by his own inadequacies. 'Do you want to help sort this mess out or not?' he'd challenged harshly.

She had, but not this way. Not by banking everything they had on the spin of a stupid roulette wheel.

The dizziness returned, the blood seeping slowly out of her head as if squeezed by that steadily slowing wheel. Then, quite suddenly, it stopped. Silence hit the room. No one moved for the space of a few tense breathless seconds—until Sir Edward said, very calmly, 'Mine, I think.'

Without uttering a single word, Caroline turned and walked away, leaving the melee to erupt behind her.

How much had he won? She didn't know. When would he play Luiz? She didn't care. As far as she was concerned the whole miserable thing was well and truly over. She'd had enough—more than enough—and she never wanted to step foot in a place like this again.

She even felt a real disgust with herself for being talked into coming here at all. She should have known he couldn't keep his word. Should have known he didn't really care what happened to them so long as he could get his kicks.

The casino doors swung shut behind her. Eyes bright, mouth tight, body stiff with tension, she walked towards the stairwell with the intention of going back to their room. But suddenly she knew she couldn't do that, couldn't just go back there and await the next instalment in her father's quest for utter ruin. And on an impulse she didn't think to question, she found her feet were taking her across the basement foyer and towards the pair of doors that stood opposite the casino.

She'd half expected the swimming pool room to be locked at this time of the night but it wasn't, she discovered, though the lights had been turned down to their minimum, so only the pool itself was illuminated, showing glass-smooth cool blue water—and not another person in sight.

Without really considering her next actions, Caroline stepped out of her shoes, unzipped her dress and draped it over the back of a nearby chair, then simply dived cleanly into the water.

Why she did it, she didn't know, and cared even less that she had dived in wearing bra, panties and even her black stockings and suspenders. She just powered up and down that pool like someone intent on winning a medal.

She was performing her fourth lap when she noticed Luiz sitting in the chair next to the one on which she had placed her dress. The cold cut of her eyes completely blanked him as she made a neat rolling turn then headed back down the pool.

He was still there when she made her sixth cutting crawl through the water, still sitting there on her eighth. By the tenth her lungs were beginning to burst and she had to pause for breath. Crossing her arms on the tiled rim, she rested her brow against them and stayed like that until the panting began to ease.

'Feel better for that?' Luiz questioned levelly.

'No,' she replied, and at last lifted her face to look at him. 'Do you, for playing the voyeur?'

'You are wearing more than most women do who use this pool,' he casually pointed out.

'But a gentleman, on noting the difference, would have had the grace to leave.'

'And we both know that I am no gentleman,' he smilingly tagged on as if on cue.

Had she been cueing him to admit that? Caroline asked herself. Yes, she accepted, she had. It pleased her, for some reason, to make Luiz admit to what he was.

Or wasn't, she amended. 'Where's my father?'

'Counting his winnings, I should imagine.' His shrug demonstrated his complete indifference. 'Are you ready to get out of there?' he enquired then. 'Or are you expecting me to strip off and join you?'

'I'm coming out,' she decided immediately, not even considering whether or not his suggestion was a bluff. Past experience of this man's dangerous streak made her sure that he was quite capable of stripping to the skin then joining her without hesitation.

And she had no wish whatsoever to see Luiz Vazquez strip. Didn't need to, to know exactly what he looked like naked. Just as he didn't need to see her remove the black silk bra, stockings and panties to know exactly what was hiding beneath, she added grimly as, with another neat roll, she took herself underwater to swim to the nearest set of steps.

By the time she rose up again Luiz was standing at the edge, waiting with a large white towel stretched out at the ready. Where he had got it from Caroline didn't know, and found that once again she didn't really care. It was as if her brain had gone on strike where caring was concerned.

So she climbed up the steps and calmly took the towel

from him with a 'Thank you' murmured politely, and no hint of anything else in her tone.

He noticed the absence of emotions, of course. 'You're being very calm about this,' he remarked.

Caroline wrapped the towel sarong-wise around her body. 'I hate and despise you. Will that do?' she offered, bending to squeeze the excess water out of her hair.

He grimaced. 'It's a start. Do you want me to get another towel to dry your hair with?'

Finger-combing the wet tangles, she tossed back her head to send the chin-length bob flying back from her face. The swim had seen off most of her make-up other than her mascara, which now stood out sooty black in a naturally porcelain-white face.

'I want nothing from you, Luiz,' she told him. 'Because your idea of a favour is to cut off the outstretched hand.'

'Ah…' His own hands slid smoothly into the pockets of his black silk evening trousers. 'The hand I cut off, I have to presume, belonged to you?'

She didn't want to talk about it, so she turned away. Spying her dress on the chair, she went to pick it up. 'I'm going to my room,' she announced, walking towards the pool house door. 'Goodbye, Luiz,' she added coldly. 'I would like to say that it was nice to see you again, but I would be lying, so I won't bother…'

It would have been the perfect exit line too, if Luiz hadn't spoiled it. 'Haven't you forgotten something?' he prompted lazily.

She stopped, turned, and frowned at him in puzzlement. He was still standing more or less where she had left him, tall, lean, superbly presented against a backcloth of shimmering blue, and sexily dark and disturbing enough to make any girl's heart squeeze.

Caroline's heart gave that terrible little squeeze. And she

despised herself for being so susceptible to him, knowing him for what he was.

'Your purse and your shoes,' he kindly pointed out to her, and went to collect them from where she had left them, the purse thrown down on the chair, the shoes kicked carelessly beneath.

The shoes he casually held out towards her, dangling them from their straps on long lean fingers. Tight-lipped she took them, but when she went to reach for her purse Luiz slid it smoothly into one of his cream tux pockets.

'Give it back to me, please,' she commanded.

But he just offered her a lazy smile. 'With that prim tone you could be my headmistress,' he mocked.

'How would you know?' she hit back. 'The way I remember you telling it, you rarely bothered to attend school.'

His soft laugh was appreciative, but his tone held something else entirely when he added, 'Oh, I've known a few stiff-backed, cold-eyed females in my time.'

Which instantly reminded her of all the state institutes he had lived in during his childhood. And her inner eye was suddenly seeing a dark-haired, dark-eyed, lonely little Spanish boy who, even at the tender age of nine, had known exactly what it was like to rely only on himself for survival.

How many confidences had they exchanged during that long hot summer seven years ago? she wondered as a disturbing little ache took up residence in her stomach.

And how much of what he'd told her had been the truth? she then added cynically. And how much merely words calculated to earn her soft-hearted sympathy—while he quietly and calculatedly fleeced her father across a green baize table?

'What's the grimace for?'

Huskily intimate, disturbingly close. She blinked,

glanced up, found he had shifted his stance slightly and
now had a shoulder leaning against the crack between the
two doors. It was such an obvious blocking tactic that
Caroline was instantly on her guard.

'My bag please, Luiz,' she insisted, ignoring his question to hold out the hand from which her shoes now dangled from her own slender fingers.

He in turn ignored both the command and the outstretched hand. 'Did you know that your eyes go grey
when you're angry?' he murmured.

Messages began to sting through her blood. Sexual messages. 'My bag,' she repeated.

He sent her a spine-tingling smile. 'And your mouth
goes all prim and—'

'Stop it,' she snapped. 'This is childish!'

'Exciting…' he argued.

She heaved out a breath that was supposed to relay irritation but only managed to sound fraught. And her outstretched fingers began to tremble, so she closed them into
a fist and returned them to what they had been doing,
which was keeping her towel in place.

'I'm beginning to catch cold standing around here like
this!'

And sure enough she started to shiver, though whether
from cold or from something else entirely she refused to
let herself consider. But, whatever the reason, it diverted
Luiz away from his lazy teasing. And, with a swiftness
that completely threw her, he straightened from the door
to whip off his jacket then settle it around her wet shoulders.

The oddly gallant gesture sent her defences crumbling.
Tears flooded into her eyes. 'Don't play him, Luiz,' she
pleaded huskily.

'Here,' he prompted, taking her dress and shoes from

her fingers. 'Feed your arms into the sleeves then get rid of that wet towel…'

It was a refusal to listen in anyone's books. Despair wriggled through her while she obeyed him without thinking and pushed her arms into the sleeves of his jacket. The silk lining was warm against her cool damp skin, the scent of him suddenly swirling all around her.

'I thought you were going to help me,' she choked. 'But all you've done is make matters worse!'

'Madness only responds to the prospect of more madness,' he answered quietly. 'The only way to stop him tonight was by giving him a good reason to stop. So we play in an hour, away from the hotel, because I am not—'

His words were cut off mid-flow when Caroline reached up to press both hands to his shirt-front in pained appeal. 'Please don't do it! How can you want to do this to me all over again?'

But Luiz wasn't listening. Instead he was staring down at the place where her hands lay spread across the fine white linen covering his breastbone. His own hands came up to cover hers, and suddenly she was made acutely aware of hot flesh, of the prickly evidence of very male body hair, of the hard pack of muscle and the solid thump of a living heart beating steadily beneath it all.

A heart she knew could rage out of control when he was in the throes of passion. A silk-fleshed body she could remember moving against her own. And that thick crisp mat of chest hair sweeping down like an arrow, aimed directly at his—

Her mouth ran dry. The sex was back. That burning, pulsing, nagging ache that was tugging her senses into life. His hands moved, leaving her hands so he could slide his fingers beneath his jacket, and the towel suddenly slid to the floor. Skin touched skin. Caroline arched on a gasping response.

'No,' she groaned when she dared to let her eyes make contact with the burn now taking place at the back of his.

Luiz didn't answer. It was too late anyway, because he'd closed the gap and was kissing her—kissing her like a lover—fiercely, deeply, and so very intimately that she was utterly shattered by how beautiful it was.

I've missed him, she thought, and felt the tears return. I've missed the power with which we affect each other, the passion we can generate with just a simple touch. Her fingers moved, drifting up his shirt and to his face, where they traced each contour with the fever of a blind woman Braille-reading her most treasured possession.

He responded with a sigh that shivered through both of them, and he brought her into even closer contact with him, close enough for her senses to fly when she felt the throbbing evidence of his pleasure.

And she knew it was crazy, but in these few brief sensual moments, she knew that Luiz belonged to her. She owned him. She *possessed* him. If she said, Die for me, Luiz, he would die.

But, more than that, as incredible as that might seem, she would also die for him.

'Luiz…' she breathed into his mouth.

The soft breathy sound had the most powerful effect on him. On a low growl, he literally submerged her in a hot and hungry flood of heat that completely consumed her will to fight.

If she'd ever had any, she derided herself. Luiz was her weakness, just as gambling was her father's. Once you acquired an addiction it remained with you for life. Starve it for years and it would still erupt at the first tiny, tempting sip. And she was certainly sipping at her addiction, she admitted as she fell into the kiss with all the urgency of starvation, tasting him, touching him, needing him, wanting more!

His hands caressed her and she let them, his mouth devoured hers and she allowed it to. She could taste mint on his breath and on the moistness of his tongue, and feel the deep throb of his heart beneath her restless fingers.

Something gave between them. She hardly understood what it was until her breasts were swinging free and Luiz's hands were taking possession. After that the whole thing became a banquet at its most ravenous. He deserted her mouth to go in search of other delights, and she tossed back her head and simply preened with pleasure while he licked and sucked and teased her breasts.

It felt perfectly natural to lift up one long silken leg and hook it around his lean waist for balance as she arched to offer him easier access. But the action brought her into even more intimate contact with the hard masculine core of him. And after that she became lost in a burning bright kaleidoscope filled with touch and feel and sound and scents that were so entrenched in her psyche because this man had been her first lover. The one who'd taught her to feel like this, to respond like this, to need like this!

Her *only* lover—though she hoped to goodness that Luiz couldn't tell that was the case. Couldn't tell that she was responding this wildly and this helplessly because he was the only man ever to make her feel like this.

And while it happened it didn't seem to matter that he was also the man who'd completely shattered her once, betrayed her so badly that she had never been able to recover. Her father didn't matter. The game didn't matter. The knowledge that Luiz could only hurt her again didn't matter.

In fact she was so lost in what he was doing to her that when the knock sounded on the pool room door she could barely comprehend what the sound meant. Until Luiz straightened abruptly, thrust her leg away, then clamped her weak and trembling frame to his own pulsing body before reaching out to open the door a crack.

At which point the shock waves of what they had been so close to actually doing, began ricocheting horribly through her system. Seven years with no contact, she was thinking dizzily, and they'd fallen on each other like a pair of hungry animals at the first opportunity they had been handed.

It was all so utterly, shamefully vulgar that she buried her burning face in Luiz's throat and hoped to God that the person knocking on the door was not her father.

A man's voice she had never heard before, but which had the same American drawl as Luiz, said, 'It's all arranged. You have half an hour.'

'Okay,' Luiz acknowledged gruffly, quickly shut the door again, then with a firmness that utterly shook her, he put her from him.

It took her a few moments to realise what was happening, but one glance at his coldly closed face and she knew that the passionately out-of-control man she had been kissing had suddenly turned back into her enemy.

'What's arranged?' she asked tautly.

'What do you think?' he replied.

He meant his game with her father, she realised. Even after what had just erupted between them he was still going to play him.

'Here...' Bending down, he picked up her dress where it had fallen to the floor at some unknown point. 'Put this on; you're dry enough. We have things to do and you can't leave here looking like this.'

Looking like this... Through glazed eyes Caroline stared down at herself, saw the pulsing tightness of her distended nipples, her flushed skin, her long white thighs still trembling from the way he had made her feel. Even Luiz's jacket was no longer where she'd thought it was.

He was shrugging it back onto his own broad shoulders with what was a callous disregard for her raw sensibilities as she stood there almost naked in front of him, feeling completely humiliated and cheap.

Instead of burning up with undiluted passion she was now icy cold with dismay. The nausea arrived, attacking her throat and forcing her to swallow thickly a couple of times before she dared let herself speak.

'I hate you,' she whispered.

'Not as much as you would like to, I think,' was his reply.

She was completely demolished by it, because it was such a dreadful truth. Slipping back into her dress took the concentrated effort of just about every brain cell that hadn't been atomised. As she shimmied the black crêpe up her body, she noticed her bra lying on the tiled floor and wanted to crawl away in shame.

Luiz bent to scoop it up, stuffing the flimsy piece of silk into one of his pockets before turning her around to do up her zip. She moved like a rag doll, unable to think, unable to speak, and just stood there while he bent to feed her feet into her strappy black shoes.

He straightened again, then waited while her shaky fingers attempted to smooth some of the creases out of her dress. And the tension sizzling between them was dreadful. Not once did either attempt full eye contact. Not once did either of them attempt to speak again after that last telling comment of his.

When she eventually went still, in an indication that she had made the best of herself she could under the circumstances, Luiz opened the door, then stood back in a grim gesture for her to precede him back into the basement foyer.

The stranger she had encountered in the lift was standing talking to one of the dinner-suited bouncers. He glanced up as they appeared and was suddenly riveted. Caroline didn't even notice him; she was too busy being repulsed by the feel of Luiz's hand resting on her back as he escorted her to the stairwell.

She didn't want him to touch her now. She didn't want Luiz anywhere near her. Her chin was up, her head held high and her body erect—but her eyes were blind and inside she felt as if she were dying.

The moment they reached the upper main foyer, she stepped right away from him.

'Where are you going?'

Already two blissful steps away, Caroline paused but didn't turn. 'If you want to ruin my father a second time then go ahead,' she invited coldly. 'I certainly can't stop you—but I don't have to watch you.'

After that, she began walking again.

'But we haven't finished.' His hand came out to capture one of hers. And without another word he began trailing her across the foyer towards a door marked 'Private' that seemed to open magically as they approached it.

Frowning, because she just didn't understand what was happening here, she found herself inside yet another foyer that had her high heels tapping on black and cream marble. Luiz led her across to another door, which he opened by hand this time, gestured her to precede himself inside, then quietly closed the door behind them.

It was an office, Caroline saw. A very elegant black and cream office.

'What is this place?' she asked warily.

Stepping past her, Luiz walked across the room towards the desk, then placed himself behind it. 'My office,' he answered, bending down to unlock and open a drawer.

'You mean…' Her eyes flickered around the room. 'You mean, *you* actually *work* here?'

'Work here. Live here…' He placed a heavy leather-bound dossier on the desk in front of him. 'This is *my* hotel, Caroline,' he added levelly.

CHAPTER THREE

HIS hotel...? Caroline gave a small shake of her head. 'But this is an *Angel* Hotel,' she stated. 'Part of the *Angel* Group!' And the Angel Group was huge. Not just because of the string of deluxe hotels it owned throughout the world, but because it had other, much more powerful interests wrapped up in its multinational package.

Lifting his dark head, Luiz just looked at her. It was all it needed for the penny to drop. *Angel* as in Luiz *Angeles* de Vazquez, she was suddenly remembering. But it was the *Angel* in the Angel Group that was slowly filling Caroline with a new sense of dismay. Because it was also the group which had very recently acquired a bank in London that the Newbury family knew very well.

'Oh, my God,' she breathed, as full enlightenment finally began to dawn. 'It's you we have been summoned here to Marbella to see about our debts, isn't it?'

He didn't answer. But then he didn't really need to when confirmation was already written on his lean dark face. And she could only stand and watch as every image she had ever built in her mind to form Luiz Vazquez slowly cracked, then shattered right there in front of her until she could no longer see Luiz the exciting lover. Or even Luiz the ruthless con-man who'd fleeced her father of tens of thousands of pounds.

'What is it you want?' she whispered fraily as the shattered pieces that had once been Luiz settled back into their new order of things. And now she was seeing Luiz the ice-cool operator, whom, it seemed, had only gone up and up in the world while she and her father had gone steadily down.

'I want you to come and sit down,' he said. 'We haven't got much time. And now that you understand just why you are here we may as well get down to business...'

Business. The word sent an icy chill chasing down her spine. As she walked across the room towards him on legs that were shaking badly Luiz sat himself down, opened the dossier, selected a piece of paper from it, then slid it towards her as she sank into the chair placed opposite him.

'Tell me if you agree with what's written on there,' he invited.

Eyes flickering in an effort to get them to focus, heart slowed by the weight of what was unfolding in front of her now, Caroline pulled the piece of paper towards her, then picked it up in trembling fingers and forced herself to read.

Finely listed, tightly lined, it was a very precise inventory of every penny she already knew they owed—and a whole lot more that she actually hadn't known about, but she couldn't doubt their authenticity when the names of all her father's favourite London haunts were inscribed next to them.

And the bottom figure was so utterly repellent that her skin began to crawl. 'Could I have some water, please?' she breathed.

Without a single word, Luiz got up and walked over to a black-lacquered sideboard. He returned in seconds to place a frosted glass of iced water down in front of her, then just as silently returned to his chair while she picked up the water and sipped at it sparingly.

'We can't pay you, Luiz,' she told him, once she'd found enough voice to speak. 'N-not all of it anyway.'

'I know that,' he returned.

She swallowed thickly, and took a couple more sips of

water before making herself go on. 'If you refuse to play him at cards tonight, then the money he won in the casino plus some money I have of my own should clear a small part of this.' But not all, she added with a silent bleakness. Not anywhere near all...

'The planned card game and this are two separate issues,' he informed her. 'And I never—ever—mix business with pleasure, Caroline. Understand me?'

Understand? No she didn't! 'But we have the means to clear s-some of this, Luiz!' she cried, tossing the wretched debt list back at him. 'And you want to play card games just for the hell of it? Where is the business sense in that?'

Sitting back in his chair, Luiz didn't even deign to watch as the piece of paper skidded across the table then floated down onto his lap. His face was inscrutable, his manner relaxed. 'Where is your own block of money coming from?' Smooth as silk, he kept the discussion fixed to his own agenda.

Her breath shuddered on an overwrought sigh. 'None of your business,' she muttered, then got up and paced tensely away from the desk.

'It is if you borrowed from Peter to pay back Paul, so to speak,' he pointed out. 'Which would only make the bottom figure here worse, not better.'

'I have money left over from my mother's bequest,' she told him reluctantly.

'No you don't.'

'What—?' Stung by his quiet certainty she spun to stare at him.

Instantly she felt under attack. It was his eyes, and the knowledge of truth she could see written in them.

'Your mother's money went on paying back debts years ago,' he informed her. 'After that you spent the next few years selling off the family heirlooms one by one, until there were very few left worth selling. Then came the quiet period when your father behaved himself for a couple of years—or so you believed. When it all started up again, you resorted to selling off small plots of land on the far edges of your family estate to wealthy businessmen who were looking for somewhere to build a country retreat. But the council eventually put a stop to that, quoting the rape of country heritage law or some such thing.

'So what's left to sell, Caroline?' he asked. 'The ancestral home, which is already mortgaged to the hilt? Or the few heirlooms that are left—which probably belong to the bank already, on paper at least? Or maybe you were thinking of paying me back with the commission you earn working for those London-based interior designers who pay you peanuts for your considerable knowledge of all things aesthetic, to hunt out pieces of artwork and various *objets d'art* to decorate the homes of their wealthy clients?'

It was like being pummelled into the ground by a very large mallet. She had never felt so small in her whole life.

'What next, Caroline?' He pummelled her some more with the soft pound of his ruthless voice. 'What could you possibly have left that would appease any bank holding a debt the size of yours? Yourself, maybe?' he suggested silkily. 'Are you thinking of prostituting yourself to the highest bidder so that Daddy can keep on feeding his addiction because he can't help himself?'

'Stop it!' she choked. 'Just shut up—*shut up!*' She couldn't listen to any more! White-faced, totally demolished, she stared at him in blank incomprehension as to why he was being so cruel. 'How do you know all of this? Where did you get your information? How long have you been compiling that—' she waved a shaky hand at the thick wad of paper sitting on the desk in front of him '—dossier on me?'

'Information can be bought any time, anywhere, so long as you have the money to pay for it.'

'And that makes it all right to pry into my life?' she cried. 'Why, Luiz—*why?*' She just didn't understand it! 'What did I ever do to you to make you want to pursue me in this h-horrible way? It was you that once used me, remember!' she added painfully. 'You slaked one of your lusts with my body, night after wretched night, then went off to slake your other lust at a card table with my father!'

'I don't want to talk about that,' he gritted, and he was suddenly on his feet. Tense—like her. Angry—like her. As bitter as hell—like her.

'Oh, that's rich!' Caroline scorned him. 'When it comes to *your* faults, *you* don't want to talk about it! Yet you've just taken great delight in listing *my* faults and failings— and even had the gall to call me a prostitute!'

'I made it an option, not a fact,' he corrected. But he looked pale—pale enough for Caroline to know that she had touched a raw nerve somewhere inside his ruthless soul.

'And we both know who sold himself for the pot of gold, Luiz,' Caroline persisted angrily. 'We both know that your motive for keeping me in bed with you was so I couldn't be keeping an eye on my father!'

'All right, let's have that one out,' he decided, swinging round the desk to begin striding towards her.

Caroline wanted to back off, but hell could freeze over before she would let herself do so. He arrived, big and threatening, right in front of her.

'You think I prostituted myself for the pot of gold seven years ago.' She *had* hit a raw nerve, Caroline confirmed. 'So let's just see which one of us can delve the depths this time. Here's the deal, Caroline. Take it or leave it,' he announced. 'Sleep with me tonight and I won't play your father.'

Sleep with him? He was lucky she didn't wing her hand at his face! 'Well, if that isn't mixing business with pleasure—what is?' she spat at him in disgust.

'No—no,' Luiz argued. 'This is called mixing pleasure with pleasure.' And he was even smiling, the black-hearted devil.

'Go to hell,' she told him, then spun on her heel with the intention of walking out of there as fast as she damn well could.

'The offer holds only as long as it takes you to open that door,' Luiz fed swiftly after her.

Her footsteps stilled, though her heart-rate didn't, it raged on right out of that door and onto the next flight out of this awful place! She converted that rage into a different kind of action by wheeling back round to face him. Luiz didn't need words to know what she was thinking. And his answering shrug spoke for itself.

'Everyone has a price, Caroline,' he taunted silkily. 'I am just trying to ascertain your price, that's all…'

'I'll never forgive you for this,' she breathed.

'By that, are you trying to tell me that it would *hurt* you to go to bed with me?' he questioned smoothly.

From feeling chilled she went hot—hot with discomfort. Because, after what they had just almost done in the pool room, there was no way she could pretend that sleeping with Luiz would be anything but a whole lot of pleasure!

A light suddenly began winking on the desk console, saving Caroline from having to make the worst decision of her entire life.

Luiz swung back to his desk, sat down in his chair again, then reached out to flick a finger at a switch. 'Yes?' he prompted.

'It's time we were leaving,' the same deep voice Caroline had first heard through the narrow gap in the pool room door informed him.

His eyes narrowed thoughtfully on Caroline. Quite un-expectedly she began to shake so badly that she just had to sit down. The chair she had just vacated was nearest. Almost stumbling over to it, she lowered herself down as Luiz murmured a quiet, 'Two minutes, Vito…' and cut the connection.

Too long spent riding a roller coaster of too many shocks and worries had shaken her insides to pieces. She stared helplessly at Luiz, and knew he was waiting for her to voice her surrender to him out loud.

On a sharp stab of pain she flicked her eyes away, be-cause she couldn't bear to look at him *and* give him that surrender.

It was then that she saw it. 'Oh, good grief,' she gasped. She had only just noticed the scorpion crawling down the wall behind him. The picture was so life-like that she ac-tually reared back in the chair to take instinctive avoiding action. 'Luiz—that thing is hideous!'

'But effective,' he smiled.

It was then she remembered that the first business he had ever owned outright had been a small nightclub in New York called, as he had informed her rather deridingly, The Scorpion, and bought from an old friend whose de-teriorating health had forced him to accept a quieter way of life. Within two years Luiz had sold the club on to a big inner-city developer for the kind of money that had allowed him to give his own life new direction. 'And I haven't needed to look back since,' she recalled him say-ing to her with quiet satisfaction.

But the scorpion itself must still linger on in his affec-tions for him to have it hanging there on his wall. Or was there more to its being there than mere affection? Was it a warning that this lean, dark, smoothly sophisticated man had another side to him that was as lethal as the scor-pion's tail?

Glancing back at him, she found him watching her with the kind of mocking twist to his mouth that said he knew what she was thinking and was wryly amused by it.

'A scorpion stings its victims quick and clean, Luiz,' she murmured unsteadily. 'What you are proposing here is neither clean nor quick.'

'Unparallelled sex between two people who excite the hell out of each other? I should hope not.' He smiled, picking up the dossier to replace it in its drawer.

Then he was suddenly on his feet. 'Right,' he said briskly. 'Let's go…'

Let's go? Caroline's skin began to prickle as a fresh burst of alarm went chasing through her. 'But I haven't agreed to do anything with you yet!' she protested.

'Decide later,' he said as he came striding round the desk towards her. 'We haven't got time to deal with it right now.'

With that, Caroline found herself being lifted firmly to her feet. Her options, she realised, had dwindled to nothing. Time had seemingly run out. Without another word, Luiz was escorting her from the room and they were outside in the silky warm darkness before she realised what they were doing.

A top-of-the-range black BMW stood purring at the front entrance. Luiz opened the rear door and urged her inside before going round to climb in on the other side of the car. The moment the door shut the car was moving, driven by a man who was hidden behind a shield of smoked glass.

'Where are we going?'

'You'll see,' was the very uninformative reply she received.

It was late, but outside, beyond the car's side window, the resort was still alive with people out to enjoy themselves with a visit to one of Marbella's elegant night-spots or just simply taking a late stroll along the yacht-lined waterfront.

It was years since she'd been able to do what they were doing, since she'd felt carefree enough to want to.

Years and years of self-restraint, of living under a thick grey cloud with no hint of a silver lining. Years playing watchdog to her father's sickness, because she knew that if she didn't look out for him then nobody else was going to do it.

'He's fine,' Luiz murmured huskily beside her, reading her mind as if it already belonged to him. 'Stop worrying about him.'

Caroline heaved out a soft deriding laugh at the remark. For when had she *not* worried about her father? He had been a good old-fashioned rake in his heyday, and marriage hadn't really changed him. Though she thought— *hoped* that he had at least remained faithful to her mother.

No, she told herself firmly. Her father had been no philanderer. A rogue and a gambler, yes, but he'd loved her mother. If anything, all his old weaknesses had only re-emerged after her mother had died and he'd missed her so badly that he'd had to look for forgetfulness somewhere.

Or at least that was how it had been in the beginning. Now…? Her eyes glassed over, blocking out the need to look for the answer to that question because she already knew it.

The car began to climb out of the bay and into private villa country. Caroline recognised the area because she'd used to know so many people who owned holiday homes here. This had been her playground, a place for fun and carefree vacations away from the restrictions of boarding school during the long summer breaks. She'd used to have as many friends here as she had back home in England then. Now she could barely remember a single one of them, and could only shudder at the memory of her last disastrous visit to Marbella.

The car made a sudden turn to the right, driving through a pair of open gates and up the driveway to a private villa. Built on one level, it sprawled hacienda-style right and left of a stone-built archway which took them into a central courtyard.

As soon as the car stopped at an imposing wide framed entrance, Luiz was out of the car and coming around to her side to help her to alight.

'What is this place?' she asked, glancing furtively around the whitewashed vine strewn walls that were now surrounding them. But what really captured her attention was the fleet of other cars all parked up here. Cars meant people, and people meant—

'Luiz!' she protested in dismay when he caught hold of her hand and began pulling her in through the entrance. 'What's going on here?'

'A party,' he said.

Caroline began to wonder if she was losing her sanity. He had just put her through one of the worst evening in her entire life, and now he was casually dragging her off to a party?

'No way,' she refused, tugging to a standstill. 'I don't want to party. And I certainly don't want to do it looking like—this!'

He turned round to look at her, and something very hot suddenly burned in his eyes. 'You look sensational,' he told her huskily.

Sensational? She almost laughed in his face! 'That's the best lie you've told me to date!' she scoffed. 'I've just been swimming. My hair is a mess and I have on no make-up. My skin smells of chlorine and I'm not even wearing a bra!'

He just smiled a sinfully sexy smile and murmured, 'I know. I was there, remember?'

The smile had her floundering—floundering because it was pure *old* Luiz. The one who'd used to smile at her just like that when they'd been passionate lovers and so very at ease together that she would have cut out anyone's tongue if they'd tried to tell her he was using her for a fool!

It played oddly on her defences to remember that. Made her want to relax her guard and smile back at him, be the old Caroline, from when life had been wonderful and she'd been in love and thought she didn't have a single care in the world.

Her hand twitched in his—reacting to secret wishes. His own fingers tightened, as if he thought she was trying to get away and he was making sure that she didn't.

'Luiz...' she pleaded, responding to that glimpse of the man she used to know.

It was like watching warm living tissue turn to stone. 'If you are going to start begging, then don't,' he advised. 'We went way beyond the point where it could be of any use to you to do so, a long time ago.'

When had that point been exactly? she wondered, taking his verbal slap-down with a wince she didn't even bother to try and hide. When they'd been kissing each other into a frenzy in the pool room, perhaps? The twist to her mouth mocked the suggestion, because the man who had all but completely devoured her had recovered too quickly and too well to be vulnerable to anything—including the begging voice of the woman he'd held in his arms at the time.

In his office then, when he had cruelly and efficiently slayed her with words? No room for begging there, she thought grimly. No room for anything but bitterness and anger and pain and...

'Negotiations are over, I take it,' she clipped.

He gave a curt nod. 'All I want from you now is a simple yes or no to my proposition.'

'Your blackmail, you mean,' she countered thinly.

'Okay, blackmail.' He gave an indifferent shrug to her play on words, and took her into a large white hall constructed almost entirely of marble.

A pair of narrow hallways led off to the left and the right of her, linking the separate wings of the villa, she assumed. But it was to one of the rooms directly off this main hallway that Luiz took her.

'Who does this house belong to?' she asked tartly. 'Only I suppose I should know just whose hospitality I will be offending, coming to their party looking like this...'

'Then you don't need to think about it,' Luiz answered pragmatically. 'Since it is me you will be offending.'

In a night of hard shocks, this was just another one to help keep her knocked permanently out of kilter, she supposed, remembering the Luiz of seven years ago telling her smilingly that he lived out of hotels. 'Homes are for families, and I don't have one,' he'd told her casually, but she'd seen the bleakness in his eyes when he'd said it, and known that inside he hadn't been feeling casual at all.

It was a memory that brought with it another question that almost blew her mind apart. 'You're not married now, are you?' she choked out.

His answering burst of laughter took them in through the door and offered no warning whatsoever of what she was about to come face to face with.

Her heart dropped with a sickening thump to the pit of her stomach. The roller coaster ride of emotion she seemed to be on swung her through yet another violently swerving dive. Admittedly, it was a beautiful room, furnished in the very best that was tasteful in Spanish architecture.

But it wasn't the room that held her frozen. Or even the blanket awareness of a couple of dozen people turning in their direction—though their sheer elegance was enough to have her shrinking back to half hide behind Luiz, while sheer vanity sent her fingers up to self-consciously touch her tangle-dried hair.

No, being aware that she must look as if Luiz had just plucked her out of the sea like a mermaid and decided to bring her along here for her novelty value was not what was filling her with a dizzying dismay. It was the sight of a green baize table waiting at the ready, barely three feet away from where she stood, with a solemn-faced croupier standing nearby, counting different coloured gambling chips into neat stacks on a separate counter.

'Where is he?' she whispered, her voice thickened by the actual reality of what Luiz had set up here.

He didn't even try to misunderstand the question. 'In one of the bedrooms,' he replied. 'Taking a rest before the evening begins.'

Begins… The word played back and forth across her frozen senses, her glazed eyes barely seeing the waiting party of people now, even though they were standing there in expectant silence, obviously waiting for Luiz to introduce her.

But Caroline didn't want to be introduced. In fact she felt positively sick with revulsion at the very idea. Because if they were here, and that table was there, then they were all no-good gamblers like her own wretched father. Like the man standing at her side.

And it was decision time, she realised starkly. Now, before this situation got any worse!

Without any further consideration of what she was about to do, she slid herself stealthily round until she was standing directly in front of Luiz. 'All right,' she breathed into his left shoulder.

'All right, what?' he quizzed, aiming a puzzled frown down at her.

'All right. I'll sleep with you,' she whispered. Cold fingers took a fierce grip on his sleeve. 'Now,' she added tautly. 'We'll go and do it right now...'

CHAPTER FOUR

HIS sudden tension suggested that she had just managed to shock him. Caroline didn't care. She wanted out of this room and she wanted her father kept out of it too.

Hard hands suddenly grasped her shoulders, the slender bones almost snapped under the tension she was placing them under. 'Caroline—'

'No!' she interrupted with a choke that was almost a sob. Her mouth was quivering, she couldn't seem to stop it, and her throat was hot and tight. 'Negotiations are over, you told me,' she reminded him. 'You wanted my answer. Well, you've got it. So now get me out of here!'

His chest heaved on the sigh that shot from him; his fingers increased their grip. 'You fool!' he muttered, then, on a complete change of manner, said sardonically to their audience. 'My apologies, but I seem to have inadvertently embarrassed my companion. Please, go on enjoying yourselves while I take her away and attempt to make my peace before I bring her back again.'

The answering rumble of surprise and consternation flicked at her like the stinging tip of a whip. Luiz was smiling back at them through violently gritted teeth. His hands left her shoulders, an arm returning to clamp around them instead. Then he walked her stiff and quivering frame back through the doors, letting them shut behind them.

He was furious with her for causing that scene. Caroline knew that, but had gone way beyond the point where she could do anything about it. The knowledge of what she had just agreed to was clinging like a tight steel band

57

around her aching chest and stopping her from uttering a single word in her own defence.

With a grimness that made her feel like a child being marched off by a stern parent, Luiz took her across the foyer and along the opposite hallway. At the other end was a door that opened into a large bedroom furnished with the same stylish elegance as the other room, only this room had a king-size bed occupying prominent position instead of a card table.

The door closed them in. Caroline stood just in front of it with her head held high and waited to find out what was to come at her next.

Would he order her to take all her clothes off and climb into the bed? Or was he going to offload whatever it was he was keeping severely damped down inside him before he ordered her out of her clothes?

She couldn't see his face because he had his back to her, but she could certainly see his tension. And on one level she was rather satisfied to see that she seemed to have managed to rock the unrockable poise of Luiz Vazquez.

He moved at last, breaking the throbbing silence with a short heavy explosion of air before dipping his hand into one of the pockets of his cream tux. It came out again with her evening bag, which he tossed onto a nearby chair. She'd forgotten he even had it. Next came her black silk bra—which she had forgotten about also. But she was now painfully reminded of their passionate interlude in the pool room as she watched that item land on top of the bag.

He removed his jacket next. It landed on the bed. Broad shoulders, tanned neck, bright white dress shirt made of a fine enough linen for her to see the darkness of his skin showing through. Her heart began to stutter. Her throat went dry. The steel band around her chest tightened its grip a little more. He swung around to look at her appraisingly, making her sharply catch her breath.

She couldn't speak. She was too stressed out to speak. But even if she'd been able to she knew that she wouldn't. She had played her last card. Whatever was left was for Luiz to play.

'You have fifteen minutes to do whatever it takes to make you face my guests without the expression of horror.'

The command utterly threw her. She had expected anger, she had expected seduction, she had even expected a heavy mix of both! But she hadn't expected to feel the slap of his icy contempt.

But her chin tilted even higher, amethyst eyes glinting with a defiance that hid whatever she was feeling inside. 'But I don't want to face your guests in any way,' she stiffly informed him.

'Nevertheless,' he drawled, 'it is what you are going to do.'

'They have nothing to do with what we are here for!' she protested, breaking free from her steel casing when all Luiz did was swing away again, to stride across the room towards a long line of floor-to-ceiling cupboards.

'And it wasn't your friends that filled me with horror,' she added as she followed angrily in his footsteps. 'It was that card table standing there ready and waiting, like a stage prop, for you to play out some hideous act of destruction on my father!'

'You are still assuming that I am going to win, then,' he remarked, opening one of the cupboard doors.

Her footsteps stopped. 'Whether you will or not no longer comes into it!' Despite the anger, her anxiety was beginning to show in the faint tremor of her voice. 'We made a deal where if I sleep with you, you don't play him!

You proposed it, Luiz!' she reminded him. 'And I just agreed!'

In the process of withdrawing a fresh dinner jacket from inside the cupboard, Luiz glanced at her anxious, defiant face, flicked a similar glance at the waiting bed, then smiled the kind of smile that could freeze a fast-flowing river. 'I just upped the ante,' he told her softly. Then calmly shrugged himself into his jacket while Caroline just stood there dumbfounded.

'I d-don't understand…' she stammered. 'W-what do you m-mean?'

Smoothly, he repeated it for her. 'I just upped the ante.' With a deft tug he pulled bright white cuffs with black and gold cufflinks into view. He worded it differently. 'The deal has just changed.'

'But—you can't do that!' she protested.

He looked at her. 'How,' he oh, so tauntingly enquired, 'are you going to stop me?'

'But—I've already agreed to your sordid little deal,' she cried out in complete bewilderment. 'What else can you possibly want from me, Luiz?'

'That's it.' He nodded, as if she'd said something memorably fortuitous. 'Sordid,' he explained. 'I've decided that I don't want sordid.' He moved briskly to check out his bow tie in the sleek gold-framed mirror hanging on the wall above a rosewood tallboy. 'In fact sordid doesn't suit my plans at all, which is why I've decided to up the ante.'

'To what, for goodness' sake?' she asked in pure frustration.

His fingers stilled against the bow tie. Via the mirror he looked at her. Via the mirror his cold, dark inscrutable eyes captured hers. And Caroline found herself holding onto her breath in a way that starved her brain of oxygen during a pause that seemed to go on for ever—before he answered her with the silk-voiced simplistic use of a single word that completely blew her mind.

'Marriage,' he said.

Seconds, minutes—Caroline didn't know how long it was that she just stood there staring at him, as if he was on one planet while she was on another.

Then she gave a shaky laugh. 'You're joking,' she decided.

But his deadly smooth, deadly calm, deadly serious expression told her that this was no joke. He meant it. Marriage. Luiz wanted marriage. To her.

Without a single word, she turned and walked back to the bedroom door. This had gone far enough, she was telling herself grimly. And it had gone on long enough. Now she was—

'We have been here before, Caroline, but I am quite happy to act out the scene again if you need me to do it...' Luiz's voice slid snake-like after her. 'So, walk out of that door and I *will* play your father tonight at poker...'

Her fingers curled around the brass doorhandle, actually gripped and began to turn it before she lost the will. Slowly she turned, weakly she leaned against the door now behind her, defeatedly she stared across the room to where Luiz was now propped up against the rosewood tallboy, with his ankles crossed casually and his hands resting comfortably in his trouser pockets.

Tall, dark, undoubtedly the most attractive man she had ever met in her entire life, he exuded self-assurance from every supremely relaxed pore.

The self-assured kind of man who wanted his pound of flesh, for some utterly obscure reason. 'I suppose you have a good reason for making this proposition?' she prompted shakily.

His lashes flickered, hiding dark brown eyes as they slid over her. 'Yes,' he confirmed.

Caroline's mouth tightened. 'Am I to know what that reason is?' she asked.

'Not until you agree to do it,' he replied. 'And maybe not even then, depending on *how* you agree to it.'

'Then how would you *like* me to agree to it?' she enquired ever so, ever so sweetly, beginning to pulse with anger at the way he was making her pull answers out of him.

A smile touched his mouth, a very wry smile that acknowledged her sarcasm. 'Well, a simple *yes* would do for starters,' he drawled. 'But to hear you say yes because you simply can't imagine the rest of your life without me in it would be absolutely perfect.'

Since the chances of that happening were less than nil, she didn't even bother to remark on the suggestion. 'And what are the chances of the ante going up again before you're finished with me?' she asked instead.

'Finished with you?' Curiously he picked up on the word, then gave a shake of his head. 'In this case, my ever being *finished* with you doesn't apply,' he told her. 'I may sound like a fully emancipated all-American guy,' he said, thickening his accent to suit the remark, 'but remember that I *am* Spanish. And, being Spanish, I marry once and for life. So take that on board while you make your decision,' he advised her. 'I want your *life* Caroline,' he spelled out. 'And, because I have raised the stakes,' he added, 'I will not only *not* play your father tonight, but I will also agree to pay off all his outstanding debts, get your home out of hock and ensure that it remains that way for the rest of your life. At the same time I will take over your watchdog role with your father.' He seemed to decide that covered it nicely. 'Does that sweeten the deal a little for you?'

Sweeten it? It made it positively compelling, she thought with heaviness that took her that little bit closer to defeat—though if she had any choices at all she wished someone would point them out to her. 'If this is for life, then why me?' She frowned, wishing she understood what was really going on. And she knew there just had to be something going on that Luiz wasn't talking about.

'Why not you?' Luiz countered with a shrug. 'You are beautiful, you are well bred, and you would enhance the arm of any man,'

'A trophy, in other words,' she likened bitterly.

'If you like.' He wasn't going to argue with that belittling description. 'But honesty forces me to add that I still fancy the hell out of you or you wouldn't be standing here at all, believe me.'

His dry smile made her flinch. But she received the message well enough. *Be glad I do still fancy you, Caroline, or you would now be standing in deep trouble somewhere else entirely.*

'Yes. I will marry you,' she said, that briefly and that simply.

To give him credit, Luiz didn't try to draw out his victory. 'Good,' was all he said, then, straightening his lean frame away from the tallboy, turned to slide open the top drawer.

Standing there, watching him, Caroline thought she saw the merest glimpse of a tremor in his hand as he took it out of his pocket to open the drawer. But by the time he turned, with a clean handkerchief in a hand that revealed only super-sure steadiness, she decided that she must have been mistaken.

'You now have ten minutes to make yourself feel better about meeting our guests,' he said, with a subtle alteration in the possessive that didn't pass Caroline by. 'Bathroom through that door.' He indicated. 'Clothes in the cupboards. I have a few phone calls to make.'

With that he began walking towards her, looking the

cool, calm, inscrutable Luiz Vazquez who utterly scorned the idea that anything so weak as a tremor could dare to touch him.

She was blocking the door he obviously wished to go through to make his precious calls, but for the life of her Caroline couldn't give another single inch to him by stepping meekly to one side.

He reached her, stopped. Her heart began to thump. Taller than her, wider than her, darker than her in every way there was, he intimidated her on levels she had not known existed before she knew him.

His eyebrows arched. 'Is there something we missed?' he prompted, softly mocking her stubborn refusal to budge.

She had to swallow through a terrible tension before saying what was on her mind, but she was determined to say it anyway. 'Didn't you hurt me enough seven years ago without continuing this vendetta you seem to have going for my family?'

His hand came up, touched her pale cheek, and the skin beneath began to burn as if branded. 'Seven years ago you would not have needed to ask that question,' he murmured.

'Seven years ago I thought you loved me,' she replied huskily. 'But it wasn't love, was it, Luiz? I was merely there, and easy, which provided you with a bit of light amusement in between all the really serious stuff.'

He smiled an odd smile. 'Is that what you think?'

'It's what I know,' she insisted—even now, seven years on, still able to feel the bitterness of learning that eating away at her.

His dark head came down, making her stiffen and tingle when he brought his lips into contact with her ear. 'Then how can you bear to have me touch you?' he whispered in soft, moist, sensual derision—and dropped his fingers from her cheek to place them over her breast where the thin fabric of her dress did nothing to disguise her instant response to him.

With a jerk she stepped sideways and right out of his reach, hating herself and despising him so much that she could barely cope with what was now tumbling about inside her.

Luiz said nothing, but then he really didn't need to—which was the real humiliation as he simply opened the door she was no longer guarding and stepped through it.

Left alone, it was all she could do just to sink weakly into the nearest chair. Instantly she felt something beneath her, and reached down and plucked out both her bag and her bra. The flimsy piece of black silk dangled like a taunt from her trembling fingers, reminding her why it wasn't on her body.

It was still slightly damp. On another thought she got up and walked over to the bed, where Luiz had dropped his discarded jacket. The moment she picked it up the clean scent of him began to completely surround her. Her eyes were still glazed but her other senses were working just fine, she noted grimly. For touching this jacket was like touching Luiz. Smelling him, feeling him, wanting him—wanting him...

The jacket, like her bra, was damp, which was obviously why Luiz had changed it for another one. Damp around the pocket, where he'd stuffed her bra, damp around the shoulders from when he'd placed it around hers.

A sigh whispered from her that was so bleak and hopeless she was glad there was no one around to hear it. Seven weeks loving him, she thought sadly. Seven years hating him. And probably only seven seconds back in his presence and she had been fighting a losing battle against the way he could make her feel.

It was awful, like coming face to face with her own

darkest secret. For hate was merely the other side of love. Weren't the romantics always saying that?

Which left her with what to comfort herself? she wondered as she dropped all three items on the bed and turned her back on them. She didn't know—didn't think she wanted to know.

The clothes he had told her she would find in the cupboards happened to be her own clothes, which brought home even harder the amount of calculation he had put into all of this. He had been very sure of himself, very positive that she would end up here with him, one way or another.

In fact everything she had brought to Marbella with her was now residing in this room. Except for her father, she added—then instantly began to worry about him, maybe wandering about this villa like a loose cannon searching for some explosive excitement.

The prospect had her hurrying to change. She spent less than five minutes in the well-equipped bathroom, showering away the effects of her swim and then hurriedly blowdrying her hair before she applied a quick, light covering of make-up and went to decide what she was going to wear.

Luiz arrived back as she was slipping her feet into high patent leather shoes. Her chin-length bob was soft and shiny, her make-up underplayed, and her dress was made of dark purple silk crêpe, with a neckline that scooped down to caress the soft swell of her breasts and skimmed rather than clung to the rest of her curves.

Dramatically simplistic it its design, still the dress did things for her that made his eyes glint beneath the heavy shading of those long lashes he so liked to hide behind.

'I'm impressed,' he said. 'I didn't think you could do it in the time allocated.'

Caroline just sent him a coldly dismissive look. 'Is my father awake yet?'

'It's almost midnight, Caroline,' Luiz drawled back lazily. 'The time people usually go to bed, not think about getting up.'

'People don't usually throw parties this late, either,' she pointed out.

He smiled at the curt censure. 'I'm an owl.'

'So is he,' she countered. 'Where is he?'

'In the kitchen playing blackjack with the chef,' he replied laconically—then, at her look of slack-jawed horror, he grew angry. 'For goodness' sake!' he bit out. 'It was a joke!'

Some joke, she thought painfully.

Luiz strode forward; a hard hand grabbed one of hers. 'He's comfortably ensconced in the main salon enjoying the company of my guests!' he told her impatiently. 'Will you lighten up?'

Lighten up? she repeated furiously. She was tired, she was stressed, she had just gone through some of the worst few hours in her entire life—and he was now demanding that she *lighten up?*

'If I had a punch worth throwing I would probably hit you,' she whispered.

With a heavy sigh, Luiz pulled her towards him, and it showed how bad she was feeling that she let him hold her against his chest. 'He's fine,' he assured her huskily. 'And he will stay fine now that I'm looking after him—I thought you understood that.'

'He's an addict, Luiz,' she stated with heart slaying honesty. 'They don't get cured overnight.'

'I know,' he said quietly.

'Does *he* know?' she then asked sharply. 'About this deal you and I have just made?'

'He knows you are here with me, but that's about all.'

Which made just one more problem she still had yet to confront, she thought heavily, and moved right out of Luiz's arms. His eyes narrowed on her weary profile, but he didn't try to detain her.

Instead he moved back to the door, then stood waiting for her to join him. Caroline did so without uttering another word. As they walked side by side back towards the main salon she thought she could actually feel the vibration of her own body it was so beset by nerve-tingling tension.

'Do I get to know who any of these people are before I have to meet them?' she asked without much hope of an answer, since he was very economical with those.

'Nervous?' Luiz questioned as they crossed the foyer.

'Yes,' she confessed.

'Then don't be.' He sounded eminently confident of that. 'You are about to meet my family,' he told her. 'Not a firing squad.'

His *family?* 'But you told me once that you don't have any family!' She stared at him in disbelief.

He just smiled another odd smile. 'I don't,' he said, but the sudden cold glitter that struck his eyes sent a chill chasing down her spine.

'Enigmatic as ever, I note,' she drawled.

He responded with a different smile. 'My secret weapon,' he admitted.

But not his only one, she thought as she felt his hand make contact with the small of her back as the other hand reached out for the door. His touch stung through her like an electric power source, making her spine arch fiercely.

Her reaction made him pause, his features hardening. 'Just remember who you are and *what* you are to me when we walk in there,' he warned very grimly. 'It is very important to me that you give a good impression of a blissful bride, not a resentful one.'

Refusing to look at him, Caroline said nothing. But her chin dutifully lifted and her expression became smooth as he pushed open the door to the main salon.

The first thing her eyes went to was the green baize table, which she was relieved to see had been deftly covered with a white linen tablecloth on which several bottles of champagne now lay, chilling on a bed of ice. And the croupier, who had been stacking coloured chips earlier, now stood polishing fluted champagne glasses with the innocence of a waiter.

The next thing she allowed her eyes to take in was the room full of people. What she had seen only as a couple of dozen blurred faces the first time around, now became two dozen separate individuals who were, almost without exception, Spanish.

'Highborn' and 'haughty' were the mocking words that came to mind to describe the way they were looking back at her. Which then made her think that if these people were related to Luiz, then he had to come from some very rare stock. Some young, some old, some distinctly curious, some noticeably cautious, she noted. But what struck her the fiercest were the waves of antipathy she could feel bouncing off them, even though she could sense they were trying hard to hide it.

They don't like Luiz, she realised on a blinding flash of insight. They might be here in his home, enjoying his champagne and his hospitality, but they resent it for some baffling reason.

Which served to further confuse a situation that was already muddled enough.

Then, at last, she noticed her father, standing slightly apart from the others and seemingly not at all pleased, by the look on his face. He was frowning into the whisky glass he held in his hand instead of bothering to glance their way, as everyone else had done the moment the doors had opened.

She knew what he was thinking. He was thinking—When the hell, with all these people around, am I going to get my game of poker? Because that was the way his mind worked when he was in the grip of his personal madness.

Well, he is about to receive a rather nasty surprise! she predicted with no sympathy for him whatsoever. He had let her down tonight, let her down so badly that it was going to be hard for her to forgive him this time.

This time—she repeated. How many 'this times' had there been over the last ten years?

And how many more were there going to be? Plenty, she predicted, despite Luiz's grand promise.

'Really, Luiz.' A rather large-boned lady, wearing a very regal magenta silk gown, decided to break the silence with haughty censure. 'I am too old to be indulging in late-night parties. Do you see the time? Do you realise how unforgivably rude you have been, summoning us all here then leaving us to kick our heels while we await your pleasure?'

'My apologies, Aunt Beatriz,' Luiz murmured, seeming not to notice the contempt in the older woman's tone. 'But I was so sure you wouldn't want to miss this particular party once you knew the reason for it.'

'Reason—what reason?' Still cross, but curious, the aunt fixed him with a stern glare.

'A celebration,' Luiz replied—deliberately, Caroline was sure, titillating everyone's senses with carefully chosen words. 'Of my incredible good fortune…'

The moment he said it Caroline's chest felt tight again, responding to what she knew was about to come. Luiz's hand slid from her back to her waistline, but whether it was offering warning or support she wasn't certain. And her father's head came up, eyes that were more grey than amethyst fixing sharply on his daughter.

'In the full tradition of the Vazquez family,' Luiz was saying smoothly beside her, 'I have brought you all here to introduce you to Miss Caroline Newbury. The lady who has just promised to be my bride—and my future Condesa...'

After that kind of announcement it was difficult to say who was more utterly dumbfounded. His family or Caroline herself. Caroline was certainly swinging dizzily off balance yet again—because to be Luiz's future Condesa meant that Luiz had to be the Conde!

Her heart gave a thudding kick, sending shock waves rampaging throughout her whole system. As she watched, having no ability left to do much else, she saw two dozen faces drop. It was terrible. The whole situation was utterly terrible. Not so much for her but for Luiz. Did none of these people have a single nice thing to say to him? Could they not at least pretend delight at his news? They didn't know that Luiz wasn't head over heels in love with his newly betrothed!

And further back, standing apart from the others, was her father, his expression completely frozen. He had caught on quickly, Caroline realised. He might be self-obsessed most of the time, but he wasn't stupid. He knew that if Luiz was announcing his intention to marry his daughter, then she had sold herself to him for the price of her father's debts.

'No.' She saw his mouth form the denial, and tears began to clog her throat.

Then one voice—just one voice in a wilderness of silence—sighed and said, 'Congratulations.' A woman about her father's age stepped forward. 'And to think we all thought when you had us gather here tonight that you were about to surrender your title and go back to America!'

Hoped, Caroline grimly corrected as she felt the atmosphere in the room change from hidden hostility to forced elation in one violent swing. After that they were buried beneath a sea of congratulations, and she found herself struggling to keep up with the names and the embraces being thrust her way. Champagne corks began to pop. The waiter-cum-croupier began handing out glasses for everyone to share a toast.

While still standing apart from it all was her father, Caroline noticed anxiously. He was staring at her as if a veil had been ripped from his eyes and he was seeing clearly for the first time in years. It frightened her, that look, as did the way his face seemed to be getting greyer with each passing second that went by.

'Luiz—my father,' she murmured, an inner sense warning her that something dire was about to happen. But even as she caught Luiz's attention, she saw, to her horror, her father's fingers let go of the whisky glass so it dropped with a thud to the carpet. 'No, Daddy. No!' she cried out as his face began to distort and his hand went up to clutch at his chest just before he began to crumple.

CHAPTER FIVE

THE rest became a blur, a cold, dark, muddy blur, where Luiz leapt from her side to catch hold of her father just before he hit the ground. The croupier-cum-waiter leapt also, and between the two of them they managed to get his limp body onto one of the sofas, while Caroline just stood there, lost in the fog of one terrifying shock too many.

I did this, she was thinking over and over. I've just killed my own father. She couldn't move a single muscle, while someone else—a perfect stranger to her, though she must have met him just now amongst the confusing melee—strode briskly over to the sofa and knelt down to examine her father.

The way Luiz immediately deferred to him was telling her something she was incapable of understanding just then. But she watched as if from behind a pane of glass as the man's long fingers checked the pulse in her father's neck before he began quickly untying his bow tie then releasing the top few buttons to his dress shirt.

'Vito—my bag, from my car, if you please,' he commanded.

The man who'd jumped to her father's aid along with Luiz now quickly left the room, and an arm came carefully around Caroline's trembling shoulders.

It was the lady in magenta. 'Be calm,' she murmured gruffly. 'My husband is a doctor. He will know what to do.'

'H-he suffers f-from angina.' The information literally shivered from Caroline's paralysed throat. 'He sh-should have pills to take in h-his pocket. Daddy!' she cried out, as at last she broke free of her paralysis and went to go to him.

But Luiz's aunt held her back. 'Let Fidel do his job, child,' she advised. Then, with a calmness that belied everything happening around her, she relayed the information Caroline had just given her to her husband, the doctor.

Luiz's head shot round, his dark eyes lashing over Caroline as if she had just revealed some devilish secret aimed specifically to wound him. She didn't understand. Not the accusing look, or the blistering anger that came along with it. And he was as white as a sheet—as white as her father was frighteningly grey!

The slide of pills found, the doctor quickly read the prescription printed across them. By then his bag had arrived at his side and he was demanding Luiz's attention, instructing him to take off her father's jacket and roll up his shirtsleeve so he could place a blood pressure pad around his arm. While Luiz was doing that, the doctor was listening to her father's heart.

It was all very efficient, very routine to him, probably. But to Caroline it was the worst—very worst thing she had ever experienced in her entire life. She'd done this, she was thinking guiltily. She had done this to him by not insisting on breaking Luiz's deal to him in private and in her own less brutal way.

But she hadn't cared. Not until she had seen his face just now. She had been angry with him, and bitter, and had actually wanted to shock him into seeing what he had finally brought her to!

But what she had brought him to by far outweighed what he'd done to her.

'He is beginning to come round,' Luiz's aunt murmured.

The doctor was talking quietly to him and Luiz was still squatting beside them, his dark face honed into the hardest mask Caroline had ever seen it wear. And everyone else stood about, looking and feeling helpless, while right there in the middle of a beautiful cream carpet her father's glass still lay on its side in a pool of golden liquid.

She saw one of her father's hands move, going up to cover his eyes. He looked old and frail and pathetically vulnerable lying there, and as her heart cracked wide open she shook herself free from the comforting arm and went to him.

'Daddy...' she sobbed. She felt Luiz glance at her, then grimly straighten up to make room for her to take his place beside his uncle. Her hand went out, the fingers ice-cold and trembling as they closed around her father's then gently pulled his hand away from his eyes. 'I'm so sorry,' she whispered thickly.

'It was a shock, that's all,' he answered weakly. 'Didn't expect it. Forgot to take my pill today. My fault. I'll be all right again in a few minutes.'

The doctor was waiting with blood-pressure pad at the ready once the pill had been given a chance to take effect. Caroline flicked him an anxiously questioning look and he answered it with a small nod. Relief flooded the tears into her eyes.

Her father saw them and his grey face looked weary. 'Don't weep for me, Caroline,' he sighed. 'I have enough to contend with right now, without adding your tears.'

'But it's all my fault,' she choked. 'I should have warned you about Luiz and me. It was—'

'Supposed to be a pleasant surprise for all of you,' Luiz grimly put in, still aware of their audience, and protecting his damned deal from the risk of exposure even in the face of all of this, Caroline realised bitterly.

Her father seemed to understand and accept that. His tired eyes lifted to Luiz. 'We need to talk,' he murmured grimly.

'Not tonight, though,' the doctor decreed. 'For tonight you will be staying as my personal guest in my private hospital.'

And even as he spoke the sound of a siren whined its way into the room, curdling Caroline's blood and making her cling tightly to her father's hand. But what really worried her was that her father didn't attempt to put in a protest.

His eyes fluttered open. 'Don't look so stricken.' He smiled at her wearily. 'I plan to be a thorn in your side for a long time yet.'

'Promise?' she insisted with the kind of painful seriousness that had those who witnessed it lowering their eyes.

'I promise,' he ruefully complied. Then to Luiz, who was standing behind Caroline, 'Not quite the response you were looking for, I think,' he drawled.

'No,' Luiz quietly agreed.

'Does she know yet?'

'Know what?' Caroline put in sharply.

But on a wince her father closed his eyes again, and all conversation came to a standstill as the doctor began pumping up the blood pressure pad wrapped around his arm.

Two medics entered the room then, and Luiz was gently drawing Caroline to her feet, to make way for them so they could do what they had to do unencumbered. But the moment the medics began to move her father onto their mobile stretcher she was back at his side. The rest of the people in the room had slithered off into the ether. She neither saw them nor wanted to see them.

The drive to the hospital was undertaken with the minimum of fuss. Caroline travelled with her father in the ambulance while Luiz followed behind in his car. After that everything became a worried blur again as they waited while her father was put through several examinations before Luiz's uncle Fidel eventually came to pass on the reassuring news that it had not been a heart attack as such. 'But his blood pressure has remained a little high,' he added. 'So I am going to keep him in here overnight, just to keep an eye on him.'

With a sinking sense of profound relief, Caroline leaned weakly against the wall behind her. But when Luiz attempted to touch her she shrugged him off abruptly. 'I'm all right,' she said.

'You don't damn well look it,' he argued gruffly.

Ignoring him, she looked at his uncle. 'Can I see him now?' she asked.

'For a few moments only,' she was told. 'He is sedated, so he will not know you are here.'

They did stay for only a few moments, for as the doctor had said he was asleep, but his colour was much better. Caroline stood by his bed gently stroking his hand for a few minutes while Luiz looked on in silence from his position at the bottom of the bed. Then, with the helplessness that came from knowing that she could do nothing more by remaining there, she allowed Luiz to take her away.

They didn't speak as they walked through the hospital, but then they had barely exchanged a single word since the whole horror had begun in Luiz's drawing room. They reached the exit doors to find Luiz's uncle was waiting for them.

He glanced gravely from one face to the other—seeing too much maybe; Caroline wasn't sure. 'He is going to be fine,' he assured her gently. 'It really was only a small scare.'

'Yes, I know...' Nodding, Caroline fought yet another battle with tears, then impulsively stepped up to embrace Luiz's uncle. 'Thank you for being there,' she whispered simply.

'It was my pleasure,' he replied, but his attention was

fixed on her own drained pallor. 'Take her home,' he said to Luiz. 'Make her go to bed, and don't allow her to come back here until lunchtime at the earliest.'

They left almost immediately after that. The black BMW was waiting in the car park. Luiz had driven himself to the hospital, Caroline discovered when, after seeing her into the front passenger seat, he climbed in behind the wheel.

His expression was closed, and he still didn't speak as he set the car in motion. Outside it was dark and very quiet now, the hour one of those ungodly ones where even the owls Luiz likened himself to had retired.

'I want to go back to the hotel,' she said—and received no answer. Turning her head to look at him, she saw only that closed cast of a profile. 'Luiz...' she prompted.

He changed gear and turned the steering wheel to take them off the main road which would have taken them back into Puerto Banus. He had the long, brown, skilful fingers of an accomplished magician, she found herself thinking stupidly. And she knew she was only letting her mind notice his hands because she didn't want to get into another heated row with him.

Yet she couldn't let the subject go. 'I don't want to face all those people again,' she told him.

He decided to answer that one. 'They've gone home.' His voice was quiet, flat, utterly devoid of any inflexion when he added, 'The party, I think you would agree, is well and truly over.'

'Did it ever get started?' she shot at him tartly. If 'party' was the right word to cover whatever it was Luiz had been hoping to set up tonight. In truth, the man's motives baffled her. His family baffled her. One moment they'd appeared hostile and resentful, the next too ecstatic to be real.

'They don't like you,' she said continuing her thought pattern out loud.

'They haven't had time yet to make up their mind,' he answered levelly.

Caroline frowned. 'What does that mean?'

'It means I've only been an entity in their lives for a few months.' In profile she caught the slight hint of a grimace. 'Since my father died, in fact,' he tagged on, 'and it was revealed that he had left his estates, his money and his title to the bastard son they'd all preferred to pretend never existed.'

Sitting there beside him, Caroline took her time absorbing this information, because it helped explain so many other things about Luiz that had been a mystery to her until then.

'Did you know about him?' she questioned softly.

'Yes,' he said.

'Always?'

'More or less,' he replied. Economical and to the point.

'But he never acknowledged you until recently,' she therefore concluded.

Luiz turned the car in through the gates of the villa and drove them beneath the arch into the courtyard. As the engine went silent neither tried to get out of the car. Caroline because she sensed there was more information coming, and Luiz because he was, she suspected, deciding how much he wanted to tell her.

'He tried, once,' he admitted. 'Seven years ago, to be exact. But it—didn't come to anything.'

Seven years ago. Seven. Caroline's lungs suddenly ceased to work. 'Why?' she whispered.

Luiz turned to look at her, his closely guarded eyes flickering over her pale, tired, now wary face, and it was like being bathed in a shower of static. For, whatever he was thinking while he looked at her like that, she knew without a single doubt that his thoughts belonged seven years in his past and most definitely included her.

Then he flicked his eyes away. 'He wasn't what I wanted,' he declared, and opened his door and climbed out of the car, leaving Caroline to sit there, making what she liked of that potentially earth-shattering statement.

Was he was talking about her? Was he talking about them? Was he talking about seven years ago, when he must have been here in Marbella to meet his father and had instead got himself involved with an English girl and her gambling father?

Her door came open. Luiz bent down to take hold of her arm to help urge her out. She arrived beside him in a fresh state of high tension, trembling, afraid to dare let herself draw the most logical conclusions from her own shock questions.

But Luiz couldn't have meant that *she* had been what he had wanted seven years ago, she decided, or he would not have fleeced her father dry at the gambling tables the way he had done.

'Come on,' he murmured gruffly. 'You've taken enough for one night.'

Yes, he was right; she had taken enough, she agreed as a throbbing took up residence behind her eyes. She didn't want to think any more, didn't want to do anything but crawl into the nearest bed and fall asleep.

The house was in darkness. Luiz touched a couple of wall switches as they entered and bathed the hallways in subdued light, then led the way to the bedroom.

Once inside, she didn't seem to have energy left to even undress herself. Luiz watched as she sank wearily down onto the edge of the bed and covered her aching eyes. After a few moments he moved across the room to begin opening cupboards, then she heard his footsteps crossing the cool marble floor towards her and something silky landed on her lap.

Drawing her hand away from her eyes, she saw her own

smoke-grey silk nightdress. With a cool disregard for her utter bone-weariness, he pulled her to her feet and aimed her towards the bathroom. 'Wash, change,' he instructed.

She went on automatic pilot, and came back a few minutes later to find that Luiz was no longer there and that the bedcovers had been turned back ready for her to crawl between. She did so without hesitation. She was just sinking into a blissful oblivion when the door opened and he came back in.

The distinctive clink of ice against glass brought her gritty eyes open in time to watch him place a jug of iced water on the bedside table, along with a couple of glasses, then he strode off to shut himself away behind the bathroom door without uttering a single word.

Caroline lay there, not sure if she should be jumping up and making a run for it while she had the chance, or whether she should just give in to everything and let him do whatever it was he had planned to come next.

She didn't run, was too tired to run. And his *next,* was to reappear wearing nothing but a short black robe that exposed more of his tanned skin than it covered. He brought the clean scent of soap into the room with him— and a heightening of tension because he looked so damned sexually sure of himself, the way he obviously thought he could climb into this bed with her—and naked, by the looks of things!

'I won't sleep with you,' she informed him flatly.

He was hanging his clothes away in the cupboard when she spoke, but he paused, glanced at her. 'Sleep as in *sleep?*' he asked. 'Or sleep as in make love?'

'Both,' she replied. 'And I don't know how you've got the arrogance to think that I would.'

He didn't answer that one straight away. Instead he went back to what he had been doing while Caroline followed his every movement with a heart that was trying hard not to beat any faster.

It didn't succeed very well—especially when he turned towards the bed and began to approach. And his face was wearing that hard, implacable look she didn't like very much. Bending down, he braced himself with one hand on the pillow beside her head and one right by her curled-up knees. He looked very dark, very dangerous—and very, very serious.

'Let's just get a couple of things straight, Caroline,' he suggested quietly and chillingly. 'As far as I am concerned our deal still stands. If you decide not to go through with it, then you know the consequences. They haven't changed because your father was taken ill,' he pointed out. 'But,' he then added, 'if you decide to keep your side of our bargain, then I will expect you to convince your father, and everyone else for that matter, that I am what you want more than anything else in your life. Understand?'

Yes, she thought dully, she understood. Her choices here were still non-existent. 'If anything happens to him,' she said thickly, 'you know I'll never forgive you, don't you?'

He allowed himself a small grimace at that. 'I think I had already worked that one out for myself,' he replied dryly.

'And if you try to touch me now, tonight, I shall probably be sick.'

This time it wasn't a grimace but a weary sigh, and his dark head came closer—close enough for her to feel the warmth of his breath caress her face. 'If I touched you now, Caroline, you would probably burst into tears—then cling to me as though your life depended on it,' he taunted softly.

And to prove his point he brushed his mouth across her mouth. Sure enough, even as he straightened away, the tears were flooding into her eyes.

And she didn't feel sick. She felt—vulnerable. Too vulnerable to say another word as Luiz reached out to flick a switch that plunged the room into darkness. A few seconds later there was a rustling of fabric before she felt the other side of the bed depress.

He didn't attempt to reach for her, didn't try to cross the invisible barrier that ran down the centre of the large bed. She fell asleep still struggling with a mix of emotions ranging from the bitterly resentful to the wretchedly disgusted with herself—because he was right, and she did want to cling to him.

She awoke during what was left of the night, though she wasn't sure what it was that had woken her. But in those few drifting moments before she remembered just where she was, she was only aware that she was lying on her stomach, sprawled diagonally across the bed, feeling so sublimely at peace with herself that it came as a shock to realise that not only was it Luiz's bed she was lying in, but that her cheek was pressed up against his satin-smooth shoulder and her arm was lying across his hair-roughened chest.

And, worse, he was awake. She knew he was because he was lying there on his back, letting his fingers stroke feather-light caresses along her resting arm. It wasn't a sexual gesture; she knew that instinctively. More an absent stroking, as if he was lying there maybe staring into the darkness, lost deep in his own train of thought.

It was nice.

So nice in fact that she didn't really want to end it. Though she didn't know if she could simply go on lying here pretending to be asleep when she wasn't, because already she could feel her pulse-rate picking up, feel the even tempo of her breathing alter.

It was a long time since she'd last felt the warm strength of a man lying beside her. Seven long lonely years, in fact.

And even then it had been *this* man. This same dark, sensually attractive man, with the same clean, slightly musky scent that was so intoxicatingly familiar.

It seemed ironic now, to find herself in this situation when it was Luiz who had spoiled her from wanting to go to bed with another man.

He released a small sigh. Caroline wished that she could do the same, only she knew it would give the game away. Then her defences would have to go back up, the tension would return, the need to keep on fighting him.

The sigh escaped anyway, so she tried to use it as an excuse to slide away, as if in her sleep. Luiz moved at the same time, his fingers tangling with her fingers at the same moment that rolled onto his side and towards her. She wasn't quick enough to close her eyes, and it was like looking into a mirror and seeing her own sombre mood reflected back at her. Only his eyes were dark—as dark as the night still surrounding them.

He wanted her, she could see the need written there. And the mirror was in knowing that she wanted him. Too late to pretend. Too late to run and hide. He knew just as she knew. It was that simple, that final.

With the use of their tangled fingers he drew her up against him, and even as she felt the aroused heat of his body pushing gently against her his mouth was hungrily capturing hers.

And—oh, but it felt good, like finding something she had been mourning the loss of for too, too long. And perhaps because she didn't fight him, didn't even try to protest, he savoured the kiss, almost as if he was feeling the same way about it as she.

Or maybe it had more to do with the lateness of the hour, their slumberous state, the relaxed warmth with which they had come together, or even that all-encompassing darkness itself.

Whatever, this kiss was like no other kiss they had ever shared. It was slow and it was deep and it was unbelievably tender. And it went on and on and on, until she felt as if she were floating, lost to a beauty so profound that she had to reach up with her free hand and cup his cheek—just to check that he wasn't a mere figment of her dreamy imagination.

Her fingers found lean, taut flesh that rasped lightly with a five o'clock shadow. She touched his cheekbone, his nose, the corner of his mouth where it covered her own mouth, heard his low groan as if her exploration moved him.

Gently rolling her onto her back, he came with her, untangled his fingers from hers and began to touch her face in the self-same way. But the kiss began to alter, subtly at first, then with a deepening of sensuality that quickened the senses.

Linking her hands around his nape, she held him, and his touch begin to drift on a gentle exploration of her throat, her shoulders, and finally the satin-smooth slopes of her waiting breasts. As he brushed a caress across tightly budding peaks she gasped her response into his mouth. One of his hands began to dip low over her ribcage, and as she arched in response to his so-light caress he reached up, caught hold of one of her own hands and fed it onto his body.

It was a command for her to match his movements. She remembered it from the last time they'd come together like this. Luiz had been her tutor in the art of arousing a lover. What he made her feel, he wanted to feel; what he did to her to make her go wild with pleasure, he expected her to do to him.

But that had been seven years ago, and seven years of abstinence had made her unsure of herself. Her fingers fluttered uncertainly against his hair-roughened breastbone, found one small tight male nipple and began a tentative rolling of it between thumb and finger which had him groaning thickly. He wrenched his mouth from hers so he could string a line of heated kisses across her cheek and down her throat until he found and fixed on one of her own tightly drawn peaks.

She cried out. It was such a wildly exhilarating sensation. He muttered something she didn't catch, ran his hand down her body, lifting eager nerve-ends to the surface of her skin as he did so, then caught hold of the hem of her nightdress and deftly slipped it up and over her head.

With the silk gone, his fingers began tracing the sensitive flesh along her inner thigh. Her mouth fixed on his shoulder; his returned to her breast. She could feel the heat of him, the burning, burgeoning power of him, pulsating against her hipbone.

His hand was beginning to trail ever further upwards, and she knew that if he touched her where he intended to go next then he would expect her to touch him the same way. But—

'Luiz…' she breathed, needing something—reassurance maybe, or even a reprieve. She wasn't really sure.

'Shh,' he commanded, deep, dark, tense with arousal.

Did he think she was about to call a halt to it all? she wondered. But that was as far as it got—a question forming inside her head—before he literally sent her toppling over the edge as, with needle-point accuracy, he located the very life-force of her.

It threw her into a paroxysm of gasps and whimpers. No warning, no mercy. She hovered precariously on the very edge of orgasm, and as if he knew it Luiz uttered a soft curse, caught her mouth again with a hard, hot, urgent kiss that mimicked what he was doing to her. Then he was covering her body with his own and positioning himself so he could enter her with a sure, sleek thrust.

Delicate tissue unused to this kind of intrusion tensed on a moment's protest at his potent demand. Then she sighed softly, slowly relaxed the tension out of her thighs so that she could draw him in deeper. He responded with a husky groan. After that it became a powerful example of intimacy at its most intense level. Mouth close to mouth, breast to breast, hip to taut hip, they began to move as a single entity. Her hands clutched at his silk taut back while his held her possessively beneath him. Her breath shivered from her parted lips to mingle sensually with his. And with her eyes captured by the burn in his everything else was temporarily forgotten. Past betrayals, present mistrusts—nothing else seemed to matter but what they were feeling.

And feel it they did—together—together so perfectly that when her breathing grew shorter and her body more anxious he knew the exact moment she was about to leap, and drove them over the edge with a fierceness that was completely soul-shattering.

Afterwards, when it was eventually over and Luiz lay heavy on top of her with his face buried in her throat, there was even something perfectly shared in the way neither seemed able to move or speak. Nevertheless, Caroline was glad of the darkness to hide away in when Luiz did eventually find the strength to move. Rolling onto his side, he took her with him, holding her with arms that gave her no room to escape.

'You're mine now,' he said, and that was all.

Caroline didn't even bother to answer. For it didn't take genius for her to work out that she had always been his, even during seven years of never setting eyes on him.

CHAPTER SIX

THE next time she woke it was to find a voile-defused daylight eddying around her. She was alone, she realised, lying sprawled naked on her stomach once again, amongst a sea of tumbled white linen, with her arm thrown out in a way that told her exactly what it had been thrown across until that warm male body had slid stealthily out from beneath it.

Her heart performed a dramatic flip, the memory of the previous twenty-four hours enough to hold her still with her eyes closed tight while she tried to come to terms with knowing just how easy she had been for him.

It was scary. Because even as she coped with the inevitable clutches of shame that knowledge brought with it, she was also aware of a gentle pulsing deep inside that was warm and soft and infinitely sensual as delicate muscles searched for the silken force which had given them so much.

'Luiz...' she breathed, then wished she hadn't, because even whispering his name was a sensual experience.

I should hate him, she told herself. I *want* to hate him for doing this to me again. No wonder it all felt so very scary.

A light tap sounded on the bedroom door then, jolting her into a sitting position in the middle of the bed. She had just managed to scramble a white sheet around her nakedness when the door came open and a young woman appeared carrying a breakfast tray.

She was smiling shyly. *'Buenos días, señorita,'* she murmured politely. 'Don Luiz instructed me to waken you in time to meet him at the hospital at noon.'

Noon. Hospital—her father! Oh, dear God, how could she have forgotten him as thoroughly as she had? She was about to leap from the bed in panic when the little maid added, '*El señor* also say to tell you that your *papá* is well, and will be discharged later on today.'

And as Caroline sat, needing long seconds to take this reassuring information in, the girl walked forward and put the tray down on a small table, then turned to enquire if there was anything else she wanted.

'Er, no—thank you,' she answered politely. But as the young maid walked back to the door, a sudden thought hit her. 'Did *el sēnor* leave the address of the hospital?' she asked. 'Only I forgot to make a note of it in the panic last night.'

'He has placed Señor Martinez at your disposal,' the maid explained. 'He will know where he is to drive you.'

With that she was gone, leaving Caroline to wonder just who Señor Martinez was. The maid seemed to think that Caroline already knew.

She soon found out an hour later, when, dressed casually in soft doe-coloured trousers and a pale pink V-necked top, she stepped into the villa courtyard and found the croupier-cum-waiter and now chauffeur standing waiting for her by the black BMW.

'Good morning, Miss Newbury,' he greeted politely. Deep-voiced, smooth-toned, he had the same pleasant American drawl as Luiz.

Which made him—what, specifically? she wondered as she watched him move to open the rear door of the car for her. Luiz's personal bodyguard? His jack-of-all-trades assistant? His friend?

The very suggestion of Luiz possessing a genuine, slap-on-the-back kind of friend made her smile as she sank into squashy soft leather. He wasn't the type. Luiz was a man who stood alone and softened his guard for no one. Even when he made love he did so with a silent intensity that protected the inner man.

She shivered, not liking it. Not liking what he had been able to expose in her while keeping himself hidden. So, he enjoyed making love with her, she acknowledged with a shrug. She would have to be a fool to have missed the power behind the passion with which he had taken her. But he'd done it in silence. And even his climax had been a disturbingly silent thing that had kept whatever he was experiencing locked deep inside him.

So Señor Martinez couldn't be Luiz's friend, she concluded, because to a man like Luiz a friend would be seen as a weakness.

And, likewise, Señor Martinez didn't look like anyone's idea of a friend, she mused as she watched him settle his bulky size behind the wheel of the car. He had the cold face and tough body of a ruthless terminator—with a hint of the savage thrown in to add extra sinister impact.

All of which she was given the chance to consider only as long as it took him to set the car engine running then send up the partitioning piece of glass.

Shut out and shut in, she thought, and grimaced. Maybe they were brothers after all.

Her father's room was on the second floor. Her feet trod spotless laminated wood flooring and she became aware of an increase of tension as the moment came closer when she was going to have to face her father with the truth— it was no use trying to pretend.

He knew too much—knew her, knew Luiz, and he knew himself. It was being that aware of all involved parties that had put him in here in the first place. What she didn't want was to risk the same thing happening again once he'd heard the full story.

So, nervously she approached the room he had been allotted. The door was standing open; beyond it everything looked clean and neat. She saw Luiz first, standing gazing out of the window. With the sunlight streaming in around him he looked bigger and leaner and more intimidating than usual.

A force to be reckoned with, she likened with a small shudder. And had no concept whatsoever of how prophetic that thought was as she took a moment to brace herself, then stepped into the room proper.

He heard her and spun round, then went very still, watching her face as she glanced expectantly at the bed and began to frown when she found it empty. The room had its own bathroom. She looked next in its direction, saw the room inside was also empty, then finally—reluctantly—flicked her eyes towards Luiz.

'Where is he?' she asked, sounding afraid even to herself.

'It's okay,' he said. 'He hasn't had a relapse.'

Relief made her mouth tremble. 'Then where is he?' she repeated.

There was a lot to be said for having the sunlight behind him, she found herself thinking as she waited for an answer. At least with his face thrown into contrasting shadow she couldn't tell what kind of expression he was wearing, didn't have to guess what he was thinking as he stood there looking at her for the first time since they'd shared his bed.

'Luiz?' she prompted when she realised he still hadn't answered her question.

'He isn't here,' he told her quietly.

Isn't here? Isn't where? Her frown grew more puzzled. 'You mean—he's gone for more tests or something?'

The dark head shook and he took a couple of steps towards her. The moment he did it Caroline was having to fight the need to start moving back. It was the loss of the sun to hide his expression and the sudden awareness of his physical presence that intimated her.

He was dressed in much the same way that she was, in casual trousers and a plain tee shirt. But it wasn't clothes that made the man inside them. It wasn't designer labels or that air of subtle wealth he carried with him that made her insides draw tightly inwards in sheer self-defence.

She was too vulnerable to him, she realised helplessly. Too easily diverted by things that held no place in this room.

'He's gone home,' he told her. 'To England,' he added almost reluctantly.

'Home? England?' She repeated stupidly. 'But he can't do that!' she cried. 'He isn't well enough to travel! I need to see him!'

Luiz took another couplé of steps towards her as she spun round in a full circle so her dazed eyes could check the room out again, as if she expected him to miraculously appear and prove Luiz wrong.

But her father didn't appear. And as she made herself look back at Luiz the sickly suspicion that this was just another part of his overall plan, to separate father from daughter, began to take a firm grip. 'You've sent him away,' she breathed.

'He's gone home to put his house in order,' Luiz sombrely replied.

But she shook her head. 'You made him go so we can't get together and spoil your plans by coming up with an alternative solution to our problems.'

'Is there an alternative?'

Gently put, smooth as silk, the question pierced her like the lethal prick from a scorpion's tail. 'Then why has he gone?' she demanded, her heart beating so fast that she could hear it hammering inside her head.

'Guilt,' he told her bluntly. 'He couldn't face you, so he left before you could get here...'

Deserted her, he meant. Ran away, he meant. Left her here to face the rotten music alone, he meant!

It was too much. She couldn't bear it. She turned to leave, but not quickly enough to hide from Luiz the flood of hurt tears that burst into being. His hand snaked out, caught her shoulder, stopping her from walking away.

'Try to understand,' he murmured huskily. 'He saw himself last night for perhaps the first time. He saw the mess he had made of his life—the misery he had made of yours!'

'So he ran,' she mocked. 'How brave of him!'

'It was for the best, Caroline,' Luiz insisted. 'He wants to put his own house in order. Don't condemn him for at least wanting to try before he can bring himself to face you again.'

'In that case, let him swing for his own wretched debts!' she responded in swift and bitter retaliation. 'Find someone else to marry you, Luiz!' she flashed. 'Because I am now taking myself out of it!'

With an angry shrug she tried to free her imprisoned shoulder. All that happened was that the hand turned into a grip of steel.

'I am still *paying* for him to put his house in order,' Luiz inserted with deadly precision.

Caroline sucked in some air, held onto it for as long as she could, then let it go again with such violence that it escaped as a sob. 'So am I, it seems,' she whispered then.

'It is what we agreed,' Luiz confirmed.

And in her mind's eye she had an image of her father, running away like a frightened rabbit while Luiz stood viewing his departure from his lofty position in his eagle's nest, happy to let one tasty meal go because he still had another set cleanly in his sights.

Then she shuddered, and stopped thinking right there, because she just didn't want to know how she was going to describe herself. But still the apt description of a lamb being led meekly to the slaughter managed to fill her head.

And if cynicism could be measured in fathoms, then Caroline knew she was now plunging the very depths as she made herself turn to face him.

'Do you ever lose, Luiz?' she asked him.

His grim mouth flexed on a twist of a smile. 'Very rarely,' he answered honestly.

She nodded, and left it at that. After all, what was there left to say? She was here because Luiz wanted her here. Her father had gone because Luiz had wanted him gone.

'So what happens now?' she asked eventually, knowing the question told him that she was right back on track— just as Luiz wanted.

'Now?' he said curiously, his dark eyes fixed on her beautiful but cold amethyst eyes set in an equally beautiful but coldly composed face. And the twist to his mouth became more pronounced. 'This is what we do, right here and now,' he drawled—and with only that outwardly innocent warning he caught her by the chin, pulled her face up towards him then kissed her—hard.

She just hadn't expected it, so the rush of heat that attacked her nerve-ends had taken tight hold of her before she managed to find the will to pull away. Luiz let her go, but only because he was willing to do so, she was sure of that.

And still smiling that twisted smile, even though he had just used that wretched mouth to kiss her utterly senseless, he tapped one of her burning cheeks with a taunting finger. 'Now that's warmed you up nicely,' he noted smoothly.

She wanted to hit him. He knew she wanted to hit him. Standing there toe to toe, breast-tips to muscle-padded chest, he held her furious eyes with devilishly mocking ones and just dared her to do it!

It was a skin-blistering few moments. Neither moved, neither spoke, neither seemed even to breathe. Tension gnawed and antagonism pulsed—along with a slice of something else that further infuriated her.

Sex was its name. Hot sex, tight sex. Sex that plucked at the angry senses until they sang like an out-of-tune violin. And suddenly she could feel the fine lining of her body begin to ripple in an agonising parody of what happened when he was buried inside her. It wasn't fair. Her senses had no right to betray her like this! It wasn't fair that her breasts were stinging, their tender tips tightening into hard, tight, eager nubs against his wretched breastbone.

'Marriage to you is going to be one hell of an adventure,' he murmured—and effectively brought her tumbling back down to earth with a resounding bump.

She should have shattered. She would have preferred to shatter rather than have to continue to stand here knowing that he knew exactly—and in detail—what she had been feeling.

'I hate you,' she whispered, and spun her back to him with the intention of stalking stiffly away. But her exit was ruined by the sudden appearance of the doctor, Luiz's uncle Fidel.

'Oh,' he said, looking much as Caroline must have looked when she'd first walked in the room. 'Your father has left already?' he asked.

'There was a spare seat on a flight to London he didn't want to miss,' Luiz informed him. 'He has business that needs his immediate attention if he wants to be back here in time for our wedding next week.'

Next week? Caroline tensed. Long fingers came to clasp

her shoulders in a physical warning for her to watch what she said.

'I pray you will both survive till then,' his uncle said sagely. 'If you are to eat at the castle, Luiz, then make sure you take a food-taster with you. For if Consuela could have her wish it would be to see you six feet under the soil rather than have to watch you take what is left of her life away.'

Caroline didn't understand a single word of what was being said. Except that she and Luiz were, it seemed, to be married in a week!

'Don't worry about your father, child,' Fidel said smilingly, obviously reading her expression as one of anxiety for her father. 'He was fighting fit when I saw him this morning. And he will not forget to take his medication again after experiencing the shock he had last night.'

The doctor's beeper began sounding then, cutting short any more discussion other than for him to step up and give Caroline's cheek an affectionate peck before turning briskly away with, 'See you both at the church, God willing!'

Then he was gone, scooting away as abruptly as he had arrived.

'What did he mean, you need a food-taster?' she asked in his uncle's wake. 'And what castle—what wedding?'

'The wedding you should have been expecting,' Luiz drawled. 'The castle is the one I inherited along with my illustrious title. And the food-tasting quip was a joke—though not a very funny joke, I will admit,' he conceded.

It hadn't sounded like a joke to Caroline. In fact it had sounded like a bit of very serious advice! 'I wish you would tell me what is really going on here,' she bit out angrily.

'Feuds and fortunes,' Luiz replied laconically, and halted any further discussion by leading her out into a corridor that had too many other people walking about to allow for private conversation.

Vito Martinez was standing by the car waiting for them as they came outside. 'Any messages?' was Luiz's instant enquiry as they approached him.

'Nothing that can't wait,' the other man answered with a telling glance in Caroline's direction.

It niggled her to catch that glance. Just as a lot of other things were now niggling her. 'You two should think about joining the Secret Service,' she snapped out tartly, and climbed into the back of the car without waiting for a response.

A few seconds went by before Luiz eventually joined her. Car doors slammed, the engine fired and behind his protective shield of glass Vito Martinez set them all into smooth motion.

'Vito meant no offence,' Luiz said quietly.

Caroline twisted her head to show him amethyst eyes turned smoky grey with anger. 'Tell me, is that Vito the croupier, Vito the waiter, or Vito the chauffeur you are talking about?' she asked sarcastically.

'It is Vito my security chief and most trusted employee,' he replied very levelly, but it was a silken warning to watch her tongue.

Caroline was feeling too fed up with the whole darn situation to watch her tongue. 'Oh, I see, Mr Versatility, then,' she mocked. 'Does that mean he's the one that pulls out the toenails of your enemies for you in between making sure that sick old men catch flights out of a country you don't want them to be in?'

'Vito did not chauffeur your father to the airport; he chauffeured you to the hospital, if you recall.'

'Ah, he has assistants, then.' She nodded understandingly.

The steady gaze hardened fractionally. 'You, I think, are gunning for a fight.'

He was right; she was.

Luiz's eyes narrowed. 'Be very—very careful, *querida*,' he warned.

'Stop the car,' she demanded.

Why she said it Caroline certainly didn't know—but without hesitation Luiz leant forward and pressed a switch that sent the glass sliding downwards.

'Stop the car, Vito,' he commanded. The car came to a smooth halt.

Caroline was out on the side of the road before she'd had a chance to realise she was there. It was crazy. The whole situation was crazy! She didn't know what she was doing here in Marbella! She didn't know what she was doing letting Luiz Vazquez control her life! And she certainly didn't know what she was doing standing here looking out over the Bay of Malaga beneath a burning hot summer sun—shivering like a block of ice!

She heard Luiz's feet scrape on loose tarmac but didn't turn around. She felt his closeness when he came to stand behind her but didn't acknowledge he was there. Her eyes were hurting, and so was her head. And, lower down, that band of steel was encasing her chest again.

'In the hours since we met, you've tricked me, blackmailed me, kidnapped me and seduced me,' she told him in a tight little voice. 'You've helped me put my father into hospital, then had him neatly spirited away. In short, you've layered shock after shock after shock on me, in some neatly worked out little sequence aimed, I think, to keep me constantly knocked off balance. And you know what, Luiz?'

'What?' he prompted.

'I haven't got a single shred of an idea as to *why* you've decided to do this to me!'

He didn't reply—had she really expected him to? Caroline asked herself bitterly as she swung round to look directly at him. His lean hard face was giving nothing away—as usual. And as she stood there, letting the silence stretch between them in the hopes that it would force an explanation out of him, she found her mind scanning back to their seven-week romance seven years ago, looking for clues as to why he was treating her like this.

But the only thing she could come up with was the ugly scene they had had on the night she'd left Marbella for good. Luiz had been standing there, much as he was now, tall and tense, while she'd flung accusation after accusation at him.

'How could you do it, Luiz?' she could hear herself sobbing. 'How could you take everything I had to offer you then leave my arms to go and win money from my father in the casino night after night?'

'I don't suppose it has occurred to you that it was your father who was trying to win money from me?' he'd bitten back coldly.

His attempt to shift the blame to her father had only infuriated her more. '*You're* the professional!' she'd cried. 'You told me yourself that you used to make a living from gambling—whereas my father is just a gullible fool!'

'He's an *addict,* Caroline,' Luiz had hit back brutally. 'A compulsive gambler who is therefore willing to play *anyone* so long as he plays!'

'Well, he says he played you,' she'd told him. 'Are you telling me that he lied?'

'No,' he'd said heavily. 'He didn't lie.'

It had been the death of a beautiful love affair, she recalled as she came swimming back to the present. She had walked away. Luiz had let her go. And not a single day had gone by since when she hadn't closed her eyes and seen his ice-cold expression as she'd left him standing there—and wished more than anything that things could have been different.

'This has nothing to do with the past, but with the future.'

Luiz spoke so suddenly that she had to blink a couple of times before she could realise that he was actually answering the question she'd put to him before she'd gone floating off into memories.

'I need a wife to secure the final part of my inheritance,' he explained. 'And, having come to terms with the fact that I have to have one, I have decided that I would prefer that wife to be you. Does that make you feel any better?' he taunted lazily.

No, it didn't. She went pale. 'I'm just a convenient means to an end, then,' she said, seeing just how *conveniently* vulnerable to persuasion she had been for him. He hadn't even had to woo her, just make her an offer she couldn't refuse.

'As I am to you,' he pointed out coldly. 'Which seems pretty fair all the way round, don't you think?'

She found herself stumped for an argument because, put like that, he was right! Luiz waited, though, ruthless devil, until he was sure she was not going to throw him yet another tantrum on some other quickly thought up charge.

Then, 'Can we go now?' he requested, oh, so sardonically. 'Only I have a lot of things to do before we leave here in the morning.'

Leave...

He was doing it again! Knocking her off balance with yet another one of his little surprises! 'Leave for where?' she gasped out.

'Cordoba,' he replied, then turned on his heel and strode back to the car.

Caroline followed—did she really have any choice? she

angrily mocked herself. 'What's in Cordoba?' she demanded, the moment she was back inside the car.

'A small valley in the mountains that goes by the name of Valle de los Angeles,' he explained as the car began to accelerate. 'And there in the valley stands the Castillo de los Angeles, which belongs to Luiz Angeles de Vazquez, Conde del Valle de los Angeles...'

And if she thought she'd plumbed the depths of cynicism in her own way a while back, then Luiz was now demonstrating what little she knew about cynicism at all.

'There, *el conde,*' he continued in the same nerve-wincing tone, 'will wed his betrothed in the church of the Valle de los Angeles, as is tradition for all condes del Valle de los Angeles. Then he will carry his bride off to his impressive *castillo*—just in time to banish the resident wicked witch before he ravishes his new Condesa.'

'Wicked witch?' she quizzed, picking out the only part in the acutely sarcastic agenda that managed to completely baffle her.

'*Sí.*' He nodded. 'Doña Consuela Engracia de Vazquez—the present Condesa del Valle de los Angeles.'

'The lady your uncle mentioned earlier,' she remembered.

'*Sí,*' he said again. 'Tío Fidel is a very shrewd man,' he allowed. 'He is also the only member of my family that you can safely trust,' he then added, more seriously. 'It will be wise of you, *querida,* to mark that I said that...'

CHAPTER SEVEN

Mark it, he'd said...

But twenty-four hours later it was Luiz who seemed to be marking what he'd said, Caroline noted, as the closer they got to Cordoba, the more uptight he became.

Sitting beside him, she stared at the forever-changing vista beyond the car window and wondered what it was that was eating into him today. He should be happy, she mused testily. After all, he'd got himself one very meek and obedient passenger here, who hadn't put up a single protest against his arrogant take-over of her life—well, not since her performance out on the Marbella road yesterday, anyway.

But then she hadn't been given the opportunity to protest about anything else, she reminded herself. Because as soon as he'd delivered her back to his villa Luiz had shot off again with his security chief, and she hadn't set eyes on him until he'd come to collect her for this journey this morning.

And he had arrived dressed for travelling, in a light-weight black linen suit and white shirt, looking almost as uptight as he did right now!

'Are you ready? Is that your case? Do you think we can go, then?' Terse to the point of rudeness, he had barely given her chance to reply. And other than for a quick down and away glance at the dusky mauve skinny top and cream tailored skirt she had chosen to wear for the journey, not once had he allowed himself to make full eye contact with her.

Because he'd known that to do so would give her an

invitation to start speaking her mind again. Something Luiz obviously didn't want. Something Luiz obviously *still* didn't want, since he'd maintained that barrier throughout the whole time they had been travelling.

Maybe he was afraid she was going to start demanding to know where he had spent last night, she mused with an acidity that stung in her blood. Because he certainly hadn't spent it with her, in his own bed. And he might be refusing to look at her, but she had certainly looked at him enough to notice the signs of a man who hadn't got much sleep!

She had, she recalled smugly. She'd slept like a baby and hadn't even missed him until she'd woken up this morning to find the place beside her was still as smooth as it had been when she'd fallen asleep!

Liar, a tiny voice in her head said. You woke several times and worried because he wasn't there. You missed him too! Which makes the lie all that more pathetic!

'Damn,' Luiz muttered, bringing the car to a sudden stop. 'I think we just missed the turning…'

Slamming the car into reverse gear, he began driving them back the way they had just come, past a junction sporting a road sign indicating that a place called Los Aminos was off to the left.

He stopped the car again, uttered an irritated sigh and reached for the glove compartment to extract a road map, which he then spread out across the steering wheel and began to frown at.

Caroline frowned too. 'Don't you *know* where we're going?'

'No,' he replied.

Blunt and gruff, it didn't really encourage more questioning. But she was confused. It didn't seem likely, knowing his gift of near photo-perfect memory, that he could have actually got them lost!

'How often have you made this journey?' she asked, condescension feathering her tone.

A long index finger was following the wavy red line that cut a path through from Marbella to Cordoba. A sudden vision of that same finger tracing circles around her navel sent an injection of heat directly to her thighs. It was shameful. She despised herself.

'I haven't,' Luiz said.

It took a moment for her to take that answer in. Then she noticed that the finger had stopped at a road junction. This road junction, Caroline supposed, glancing up at the sign, then back at the map to see that indeed the finger was touching this precise point on the map.

'You mean you haven't done it from Marbella before?' she finally decided.

The finger began moving again, mesmerising her when she knew she shouldn't let it, as it traced a line off to the left that went skirting around Cordoba.

'I meant I have not been there—period,' he clarified, bringing the finger to a stop at a tiny dot on the map that bore the name Valle de los Angeles.

The remark came as such a surprise that it had her turning in her seat to stare at his grimly taut profile. 'Why not?' she demanded.

He didn't answer. Instead he began neatly folding up the map again, and just let the silence fill with the same tension they had been travelling with before he'd lost his sense of direction.

'Luiz?' she prompted.

'Because I knew I wouldn't be welcome, okay?' he launched at her tightly.

'But it belongs to you!' she exclaimed.

'What does that have to do with being made welcome?' Leaning across her, he put the map back into the glove compartment.

Sudden enlightenment hit. 'The one who might poison you,' she murmured softly. 'The resident wicked witch—your father's widow?'

'You bet,' he replied, shifting the car into gear.

'And she—resents you?' She tried to put it kindly, but still Luiz released a scornful laugh.

'Wouldn't you resent the man who has usurped your own son's position in the family?'

His father had *another* son? Luiz had a half-brother? While she sat there absorbing this latest piece of news, Luiz spun the steering wheel and set them moving into the left-hand fork in the road. A long and dusty winding road lay ahead of them. With a surge of power Luiz accelerated along it. Top-of-the-range plush as the car was, custom-built for quality performance with optimum comfort as it was, the BMW could do nothing about the kind of atmosphere its occupants created for themselves. It proceeded to throb with a hundred questions one of them wanted to ask, mingling with answers the other was clearly reluctant to provide.

In the end Caroline plumped for the most pressing question. 'Why you instead of him?' she queried.

'Because I am the bastard and he is not?' Luiz mockingly questioned the question.

Caroline flushed slightly at his blunt candour. Luiz might be possessive of his privacy now, but he had not been seven years ago. He had been very open then about his life as a fatherless child, living in a run-down tenement in the backstreets of New York with a mother who had struggled to make ends meet. She knew his mother had died when he was only nine years old and that Luiz had lived out the rest of his childhood in a state institution.

'I was chosen because I possess a lot of individual wealth and the family itself is practically bankrupt.'

In other words, his father had named Luiz as his successor out of expediency rather than desire, she realised. It was no wonder Luiz sounded so bitter and cynical about the whole thing.

'And your half-brother and his mother?' she asked. 'Where does it leave them in all of this?'

If it was at all possible, his expression turned even harder. 'Out in the cold, as far as I am concerned. As they have kept me out in the cold for most of my life.'

No wonder he had left it so long without bothering to go and meet his inheritance face on, she grimly concluded. For Luiz was not a fool; he knew what he was going to find waiting for him. Which left begging just one more question she couldn't leave unasked.

'Our marriage?' she prompted. 'What has it to do with all of this?'

For a moment she thought he wasn't going to answer. His mouth was tight, his eyes shot through with a hard glitter as they followed the snaking line of the road ahead. Then, 'Our marriage is the means by which I put them in the cold,' he replied. 'For by my father's decree they may continue to live in the castle only until I marry.'

His ruthless streak was showing again. And Caroline was beginning to feel sorry for Luiz's new-found family. She had a horrible feeling they had no idea what kind of man it was who was coming to meet them today, or they would have packed their bags and got out before he arrived.

'Ever heard of the word forgiveness?' she advanced huskily.

'Forgiveness is usually only given to those that want it,' he replied.

Slick and shrewd though his reply was, it still made her shiver. She fell silent after that. And they didn't speak again throughout the miles they ate up until they entered the sleepy little village of Los Aminos.

'We'll stop here for some lunch,' Luiz decided.

Caroline didn't demur. She was beginning to feel stiff and thirsty, and a break for lunch was a preferable option to keeping on driving towards she knew not what.

Luiz found a little café with wooden tables set outside beneath a faded blue awning. Pulling into the kerb, he climbed out of the car, then stood stretching taut muscles while he waited for Caroline to join him. The inn wasn't what you would call a fashionable place, but the basket of bread and bowl of crisp salad they were served were fresh and tasty.

She asked for a Coke, and Luiz did the same, then they sat sharing the lunch between them as if they did this kind of thing all the time. But the silence was still there, pulsing between them.

Reaching for another thick chunk of bread, she asked, 'How much further?' in an effort to break the deadlock.

'Same again,' Luiz answered briefly, while reaching for some more bread himself.

She huffed out a weary sigh that turned into a yawn. The day was hot and the air was humid, and she had lied about sleeping well last night, so now she was beginning to feel the dragging effects of hardly any sleep at all.

'Tired?' Luiz asked.

'It's the heat,' she blamed. 'And the travelling. Where did you sleep last night?'

And she could have bitten off her tongue the moment she caught the sudden gleam in his eyes. 'Missed me, did you?' he murmured silkily.

'No,' she denied. 'I slept like a log.'

'Well, I missed you,' he told her huskily.

Warily she glanced up, thinking he was just teasing— but he wasn't. And the atmosphere between them suddenly took a violent change. He was looking at her as if he was seeing her sitting there naked.

She looked away again quickly—but not quickly enough to stop her insides from coiling tightly, and she could feel a sensual tingling between her thighs.

'We could go somewhere,' Luiz suggested.

Caroline almost choked on her bread. Was he saying what she thought he was saying? She picked up her Coke and gulped at it in an effort to disperse the bread.

'You only have to say yes...'

Oh, for goodness' sake! she thought. 'No, Luiz!' she whispered hoarsely. And made the mistake of looking into his eyes again.

They were on fire. He wanted her. And he wanted her now! 'Stop it,' she breathed, feeling her cheeks begin to glow, and sent trembling fingers on a wild foray of the salad bowl—only to meet his fingers halfway, because he was reaching for her.

It was like making contact with a high-voltage cable. Caroline snatched her hand away on a sharp gasp; Luiz did more than that—he released a low, short, explicit curse, then lurched angrily to his feet.

It a state of near shock, because she didn't know what had happened between them, she watched him dig into his pocket for some money and toss it onto the table before reaching out to grab her hand.

And this time there was no snatching it back as if the contact was too electrifying to tolerate because Luiz wasn't letting go. He turned and began striding off down the sun-drenched and dusty street, trailing her behind him like some recalcitrant child he was taking off to be smacked.

She wanted to protest—demand where he thought he was going, when the car was parked the other way! But the sheer ferocity etched into his lean face was enough to keep the words locked up tight in her throat.

Suddenly he stopped dead, tightened his grip on her

hand and turned to walk her inside the foyer to what turned out to be a small hotel.

'Luiz—no!' she managed to gasp out at last, when the disturbing suspicion of what he was intending began to take horrifying shape in her head.

He completely ignored her. It was as if the devil was driving him. His face was taut, his jaw set, and she felt her cheeks suffuse with hot self-conscious colour as he grimly began negotiating the price of the hotel's best suite—on an hourly basis.

It was awful, the most embarrassing situation she had ever experienced in her life! The concierge kept on sending her brief but knowing little glances, and she didn't know where to put herself as Luiz placed a wad of notes on the desk, scrawled his signature in the register, then accepted the key the concierge was holding out to him before turning towards the stairs.

'I can't believe you're doing this!' Caroline choked out as he began striding upwards, pulling her with him.

He didn't even bother to answer, his expression so fierce that she began to quail inside her shoes as he led her along a narrow landing then unlocked a door and swung her inside.

The hotel was small and very simple; the room—darkened by closed shutters over the window—was nothing more than a bed, a table and a couple of chairs set on floorboards, and there was no air conditioning to help take away the suffocating heat. But by the time he had closed the door behind them she couldn't have cared less what the room was like. She was out of breath, feeling a nerve-tingling excitement that didn't go down well with how she knew she should be feeling in a situation like this!

'What the hell has got into you?' she demanded, managing to get her hand free at last.

Again he didn't answer, but then he didn't really need

to, because she knew what had *got into* him. In fact it was written all over his hard-boned, muscle-locked face!

With a growing sense of awareness she stepped warily away from him, only to watch in a kind of wide-eyed fascination as he shrugged out of his jacket and tossed it aside, then began pulling his shirt off over his head.

The two items landed on a chair. His bronzed torso expanded, then relaxed, as if removing those garments had been a matter of life or death.

Fire and ice, she found herself likening, as she waited breathlessly to discover what was going to come next. The fire was in his passion, the ice the medium he used to keep the other suppressed. It was a dynamic combination, one that set some secret engine she hadn't known she possessed humming throughout her entire system. She had never experienced anything like it. But it held her completely captivated as she watched the passion melt its way through the ice until all that was left was a blistering intent that began scorching her flesh.

'Luiz, this isn't—' Funny, she had been going to say, but he reached for her, caught her wrists and used them to draw her body against him, then fed them around his neck.

Burning eyes became hidden beneath sweeping lashes as he lowered his gaze to where his fingers began to undo the tiny buttons down the front of her top.

It was all so intense, so very macho that she didn't know whether she was feeling fiercely excited by it or just plain scared. But she didn't attempt to get away from him—which was an answer, she supposed. And as his hands brushed the top aside, to reveal the flimsy thin silk bra beneath, her spine arched slightly in feline invitation for him to touch what he had uncovered. Yet when he did touch her he did it in a way that completely snagged her breath. Because it was not the sensually possessive caress she had been expecting. His hands simply needed to touch her like this.

'Why?' she whispered. She just didn't understand this man one iota. He could be so cold, so utterly ruthless with his demands. But this was different. This was—compulsion.

'I need you,' was all he said. Then his mouth was crushing hers apart, and nothing else seemed to matter after that. Their clothes disappeared in hurried succession, their flesh coming together in an intoxicating mix of hunger, heat and sweat.

The bed waited, and as they folded down onto its soft mattress the smell of fleshly starched linen came wafting cleanly round them. It was a smell that seemed to make it all perfect, somehow, though Caroline didn't know why it should.

As time made deep and sensual inroads into the afternoon, without them being aware of it passing, they forget where they were supposed to be going—or maybe they chose to forget. It didn't seem to matter. It was hot and it was steamy and it was a much more appealing journey, one that explored the senses to the exclusion of none, allowed no room for inhibition. It pretended that this was good and right and absolutely the only thing in the world either of them should be doing.

So they made love all afternoon, slept a little in an intimate tangle of limbs, before rousing to begin making love all over again.

'Why, Luiz?' she dared to ask him again, when they'd quietened. 'Why are we here like this?'

'You're always asking me *why*,' he complained, nuzzling his mouth against her throat.

'Only because you keep hitting me with the unexpected,' she told him.

'Well, I thought the answer this time should be obvious,'

he said with a grimace. 'You're so beautiful you make me ache,' he murmured deeply. 'And so damn desirable that I can't even control myself long enough to get us from one place to another without having to stop off in the middle of the journey to do—this…'

His mouth took hers in the kind of kiss that sent any further words spinning off into oblivion. But she knew that, no matter how good for her ego his answer had been, it wasn't the real reason why they had ended up here in this bed, making love like this.

She had triggered something back at the lunch table when she had given away the fact that she'd missed him in her bed last night. She only wished she could understand what that something was, because then maybe she could begin to understand Luiz.

Eventually they reluctantly decided that they should be moving if they wanted to reach their destination before dark. Caroline went off to shower in the tiny bathroom they had discovered down the corridor. When she came back it was to find that the sun had left this side of the building and Luiz had opened the shutters and the windows to allow some warm but fresher air to filter into the room.

He was standing over a small breakfast-type table on which, she was surprised to find, rested a wooden tray with what looked like a plate of sandwiches and a tall jug full of iced water.

'Mmm, the hotelier in action, I see,' she remarked lightly.

He glanced round, grimaced a smile at her, then turned back to the two tall tumblers he was in the process of filling. 'We didn't really do lunch justice,' he said. 'And, knowing the Spanish habit of eating late in the evening, I thought we might as well have a snack before we leave.'

The ice chinked as it fell from jug to tumbler, and drew

her across the room. She hadn't realised she was feeling so thirsty until she heard that irresistible sound.

'Thank you,' she said, accepting a glass from him.

'The sandwiches are only cheese and ham, but help yourself,' he invited—then turned to go and take his turn in the bathroom, leaving Caroline to gulp thirstily at the water as she took another interested look around her.

What had only been quite seductively mystical shadows in the room before had now taken on rather interesting shapes with the light streaming in. The pale green painted walls wore the patina of age, and the polished floor had thick hand-made rugs thrown upon it. The bed was one of those big old heavy things you had to hitch yourself up to sit upon, and the two bedside cabinets had a pair of matching table lamps on them that would probably fetch a tidy sum in today's post-war collectors' market.

Which was her professional head talking, she acknowledged with a wry smile as she chose a sandwich then sat down in one of the two leather club chairs that flanked the little table. For she liked the two lamps exactly where they were, so to start thinking of how much they would fetch at auction, only to be carried off elsewhere, was not where she wanted her mind to go right now.

In fact she liked the whole room in general, and was aware, when she thought that, why she did. This room would always stay in her memory as the place where she finally found peace with her own feelings for Luiz. She loved him, she wanted him, she needed to be with him, no matter how he'd used her in the past or was using her now, in the present.

And if Luiz never came to love her back, at least she knew without a single doubt that he wanted her—passionately. She could live with that. She could *build* on that.

He arrived back in the room freshly showered and

dressed again, and her stomach gave a soft curling quiver
in recognition of the way she was feeling about him now.

Picking up a sandwich, he took the other chair and
folded his long frame into it. 'Not quite a palace,' he
drawled, glancing round them.

'Nice, though.' She smiled. 'I like little out-of-the way
places like this.'

'As opposed to five-star air conditioned luxury?' he
mocked.

She nodded, still smiling. 'This place has soul,' she explained. 'It has secrets hidden in its darkest closets.' Not
to mention my own secret, she mused ruefully. 'It has stories to tell of things long ago. These chairs, for instance,'
she said, reaching for her tumbler. 'Who sat in them first?
Who spilled their pot of ink on this wonderful table?' she
pondered, stroking a loving finger over the black stain.
'Was it a woman? Was she writing a farewell note to her
secret lover, so blinded by her own tears that she knocked
the pot over? Or was it a man?' she then suggested, her
eyes darkening subtly as she wove stories in a way her
father would have recognised, because she had always
done it. But for Luiz this was new, and it held him riveted
as he watched her softened face and listened to her dreamy
voice. 'Was he so engrossed in writing his one big novel
that he spilled the ink in distraction?'

'Both things could happen just as easily in a five-star
hotel,' Luiz pointed out dryly.

But Caroline shook her head. 'If this table had had ink
spilled on it in one of your hotels it would have been
replaced with a nice new one before you had a chance to
blink. No soul in that, Luiz,' she told him sagely. 'No soul
at all.'

'So you like all things old and preferably flawed.' He
smiled. 'Is that what you're saying?'

'I like *some* things old and *sometimes* flawed,' she

amended. 'I also like new, so long as it tells a story. I like *interesting,*' she decided that said it best.

'Well, I think I can probably promise you *interesting* where we are going,' he said.

And suddenly the cynicism was back. Impulsively Caroline reached for his hand across the table. 'Don't, Luiz,' she pleaded. 'Don't spoil it.'

He glanced down to where her hand covered his. His expression remained cast in stone for a while, then he released a small sigh, turning his hand to capture hers, and got to his feet, pulling her up with him.

His mouth was gentle on hers—seeming to be offering an apology. But when she made a move to deepen the kiss he withdrew, and his expression was still closed when he said, 'We really have to be going.'

The afternoon of near perfect harmony, she realised, was over...

CHAPTER EIGHT

Leaving Los Aminos behind, they began another twenty miles or so of driving before they would reach their destination. As the car ate up the miles so the scenery changed, from sprawling plains into rolling hills at first, then eventually into a more rugged terrain, where the hills took on the shape of forest-covered mountains.

The quality of the road they were travelling on changed also, narrowing to little more than a single car width as it wound them upwards on a steep climb that hugged a mountain face on one side and left sheer drops into deep ravines exposed on the other.

'How much further?' Caroline asked, beginning to feel as if they had been climbing for ever.

'The next valley,' Luiz replied. And his tension was back, in the clenched jawbone, the white-knuckled hands gripping the steering wheel.

He didn't want to come here, she silently reiterated. He didn't want to be this person who had to meet with people who were already programmed to hate and resent him.

And there was a hint of ill-omen in the way the air on the mountain suddenly turned colder, raising goosebumps on her arms she rubbed at with a small shiver.

Instantly Luiz touched a switch that changed the air conditioning from cold to warm. 'You should have brought a sweater,' he said.

'If I'd known where we were coming, perhaps I might have thought of that myself,' she smiled ruefully.

'There's a car rug on the back seat if you—'

'I'm fine,' she softly assured him, wishing she could say

116

the same about Luiz. But he was far from fine, she observed worriedly. For the higher they climbed the more tense he became.

'You could always make the grand gesture and pass everything over to your half-brother then just walk away,' she gently suggested.

His dark head shook. 'That isn't an option,' he stated.

'Because you feel he owes you for the years you had nothing while he had everything?' she posed.

'Because it just isn't an option,' he repeated in a tight voice that warned her that she was prodding what was really a very dangerous animal, the way he was feeling right now.

On a sigh, she took the hint, and fell silent. They were driving between the tall peaks of two mountains now, still hugging the side of one while the other stood guard in the distance. And really, Caroline observed, if they didn't reach the valley soon then the only place left for them to go would be off the side of the mountain, because surely they couldn't climb any higher?

Then—without warning—it finally happened. They rounded a deep bend, suddenly found themselves driving through a split in the mountain—and there it was.

The most beautiful place Caroline had ever seen in her entire life.

'Oh, Luiz,' she breathed, while he seemed to freeze for a couple of taut seconds, before bringing the car to a stop.

After that they both sat there and just stared in breathless awe at what had opened up in front of them.

The Valle de los Angeles… It could not possibly be anything else, Caroline decided. And they'd caught it at probably one of its most perfect moments, with the late sun pouring fire down its lush green slopes to brush everything on the wide valley bottom with a touch of sheer magic.

Directly below them blushing white-painted buildings stood clustered around a tiny church sitting in the centre of the village square. From there, and running parallel with the valley, snaked a gentle stream with a narrow dirt road running beside it through line upon line of what looked like fruit trees planted in uniform rows.

And there, standing out like the place from which all fairytales were conceived, stood a white-walled, red-roofed castle, complete with battlements and cylindrical towers, and even a drawbridge beneath which the stream ran while the dirt road stopped in front of it.

'This is perfection,' Caroline whispered.

Luiz stiffened sharply, as if the sound of her voice had woken him from a daze. But he said not a word—not a single word. He just put the car into gear and set them moving again—with a whole new level of tension sizzling around him that kept Caroline's tongue still.

Going down into the valley was not as hair-raising as it had been climbing up to it. Instead of teeth-tingling sheer drops on one side they were zigzagging down through a series of carefully cultivated terraces that spread out on either side of them. It was all so lush and green and obviously fertile that it was no surprise to find herself recognising just about every fruit-bearing shrub and plant imaginable growing here.

The road eventually brought them out in the valley bottom, just behind the village. Driving through the village itself was another experience entirely. People were out, strolling or just chatting to their neighbours, while dogs barked around the feet of playing children. It was like entering another world. Nothing about the place seemed quite real. Not the dark-eyed, dark-haired simply dressed people or their immaculate white homes with their brightly coloured painted doors and shutters.

And the sense of unreality deepened when everyone went still and stared as they drove by.

Oh, my, Caroline thought, they know who we are! Or at least, she amended that, they know who Luiz is. And she felt the hairs on the back of her neck began to tingle as she watched them stare curiously in through the sun-tinted car windows at Luiz's stern dark profile.

'Do I start referring to you as *el conde* now?' she asked in a shaky attempt to lighten the tension.

'Try the Vazquez bastard,' Luiz gritted.

And that was the point when she began to lose her patience with him, because while Luiz was busy seeing himself as the Vazquez bastard, he was blinding himself to what these people were seeing when they looked at him.

They were seeing the lean, dark, arrogant profile of one of their own. They were seeing their own black silk hair and olive-tinted skin and dark brown eyes that stated, quite plainly, Here is one of us. Their expressions were not deriding or hostile, or even vaguely contemptuous, they were simply curious.

If anything, it was the glances *she* received that brought other forces to the fore. For what was she to these people? She was a pale-skinned, blonde-haired utter stranger, with eyes the colour of amethysts. Nothing even remotely familiar about the way she looked to them.

When the road opened up into the village square, with the sweet little church in its centre, the people all jumped to attention—except for one young man, who ran across the square then into the church. Mere seconds later, a priest in his simple black robes appeared in the opening. Very tall, very thin, and with a shock of white hair framing his lined face, he watched them pass by with a solemn shrewdness that made Caroline's insides tingle.

'Is this the church where we are expected to marry?' she asked in a choked little voice.

'Yes,' Luiz replied.

'Then don't you think we should have stopped and at least passed the time of day with the priest?' It was censure and anxiety rolled into one question, because she didn't want to offend these people, and she was sure that once Luiz had got over whatever it was that was slowly killing him he wouldn't want to think that he had offended anyone either.

Luiz shook his head. Not once did he let his eyes divert from the way ahead as he grimly kept them moving across the square and through the next gauntlet of curious spectators.

He didn't even relax when they left the village and began to pass between the neatly tended fruit groves. Orange groves, lemon groves, peach and apricot groves. 'How can a place like this be bankrupt?' she questioned on a fresh bout of awe. It was all so rich in everything that life could offer.

'Through the extravagances of its previous owners,' Luiz informed her cynically.

He had to mean his own father. 'Nobody *owns* something like this,' Caroline objected. 'They are merely guardians, whose responsibility it is to take care of it all during their term of office. And if they can't see what an honour and a privilege that has to be, then they deserve to lose custody.'

'Spoken like a true lady to the manor born,' Luiz derided. 'Maybe I should just cut my unworthy losses and sign it all over to you.'

'And you can mock me all you like, *el conde*,' she sniped right back, 'But if you can't grasp the concept of what I am saying then maybe you should do just that.'

'Lecture over?' Luiz clipped.

'Yes,' she sighed, wondering wearily why she bothered to take him on like this. The man was impervious to any-

thing anyone said that didn't suit his own view of things!
'I've finished.'

'Good,' he murmured. 'Because I think we've arrived,
and I am beginning to feel like hell…'

As surprise admissions went, that one really managed
to strike at the heart of her. She turned in her seat, saw
how pale he had gone, saw how clenched his face muscles
were and automatically looked where he was looking—
and felt everything inside her shudder to a resounding halt.

For while they had been sniping at each other they had
come to the end of the fruit groves and driven over the
drawbridge, beneath a wide archway cut into the white-
washed wall that surrounded what she supposed must be
the castle's private enclave.

She had never, ever seen anything quite like it. From
up on the mountain it had all looked pretty stunning, but
from down here, on the valley bottom and this close up,
the castle was nothing short of enchanting, with its white-
washed walls blushing in the dying sunlight.

It was all so outstandingly—dramatically—beautiful.
Even the formally laid out gardens they were now passing
through took the breath away. The driveway opened up
into a wide cobbled courtyard with a statue of Neptune
spouting water into a circular pool, guarding the huge
arched entrance into the castle itself.

Luiz stopped the car. Without a word they climbed out,
then just stood gazing around.

'It's a folly,' Caroline murmured softly.

'Hmm?' Luiz's dark head swung round to frown a blank
look at her.

'The castle,' she explained. 'It's not what it appears to
be.'

'What makes you say that?' He seemed to have a struggle to get his voice to work, but once he had spoken some
of that awful strain eased from his face.

'Look around you,' she invited. 'There is absolutely no reason for anyone to build a fortified castle down here in the valley. The mountains themselves are the only protection needed down here. If you'd wanted to protect what was yours, you would have built up there, where we came in through the pass in the mountain. This...' she gave a nod of her head towards the castle '...was built to satisfy someone's eccentric ego. A folly,' she repeated, looking frontward again. 'But a beautiful folly...'

And if his family were guilty of bankrupting themselves due to their personal extravagances, she added silently, then at least it had not been at the expense of their exquisite home.

Luiz's home now, she extended, looking across the top of the car at this man who was such a complicated mix of so many different cultures that it was no wonder he kept most of his real self hidden—he probably didn't know who he actually was himself!

'We're being watched,' Luiz murmured.

'Mmm,' Caroline replied. 'I know.' She had felt the eyes piercing her flesh from behind leaded glass windows from the moment they climbed out of the car. 'So, what do you want to do now?' she asked. 'Bang on the door and claim ownership? Or do we take the more civilised approach and wait until we are invited in?'

But even as she put the two lightly mocking suggestions to him the great door behind Neptune was drawing open. Her heart skipped a beat. On the other side of the car she heard Luiz's feet scrape against gravel. Without thinking twice about it, she walked around the car and went to stand beside him.

As she did so a man appeared in the doorway, small, thin and quite old, his expressionless face giving no hint as to whether they were to be made welcome or simply grudgingly allowed to enter the castle's hallowed inner sanctum.

'It looks like it's showtime,' Caroline said softly.

'Looks like it,' Luiz agreed, and although he reached out to catch hold of her hand, as if he needed to feel her presence for moral support, she was relieved to see that the implacable Luiz Vazquez was back in place again and the other, tense and uncomfortable one had been firmly shut away.

Together they walked around the fountain and up to the door. With a slight bow of his dark head, the man murmured, 'Welcome *señor—señorita,*' with absolutely no inflexion in his voice whatsoever. 'If you would kindly come this way?'

The man stepped to one side in an invitation for them to precede him inside, and as the door closed quietly behind them they found themselves standing in a vast hallway built of oak and stone, with an eight-foot-wide solid stone stairway as its main feature. The rough plastered walls were painted in a soft peach colour, adding warmth to what could quite easily appear coldly inhospitable.

Caroline felt her tummy muscles begin to flutter. Beside her, Luiz's fingers tightened their grip on hers. He was used to big reception halls. He was used to standing in beautiful surroundings. But this was different. This was his past meeting head-on with his present. Even she, who had always known the place where her roots were planted, was acutely aware of how significant this moment must be for him.

Yet his voice was smooth and as calm as still water when he turned to speak to the old man. 'And you are?' he enquired, sounding every inch the noble Conde. Considering what she knew he was feeling inside, Caroline was proud of him.

'Pedro, sir. I am the butler here,' the old man replied—

and there was respect in his tone. He for one wasn't condemning Luiz for being the Vazquez bastard. 'Please,' he invited. 'If you will follow me…'

He began leading them across a polished stone floor past two suits of armour that were guarding the stairs. There were artefacts scattered about this hall that made Caroline's head whirl as it went into professional mode.

Maybe Luiz knew it. 'Enough *soul* here for you?' he questioned lazily.

'Interesting,' she shot back with a smile, then moved a little closer to his side when Pedro opened a pair of huge wooden doors and bowed them politely inside.

'Señor Luiz Vazquez and Señorita Newbury,' he announced, to whoever was waiting for them. And Caroline hadn't missed the fact that the butler had not referred to Luiz as *el conde* once since they had arrived.

If Luiz noticed the omission, he didn't show it. His expression was relaxed, his grip on Caroline's hand secure, and his stride was as graceful as always as he strode into what turned out to be a beautifully appointed drawing room, with a huge stone fireplace that almost filled one wall—where a woman stood, awaiting their arrival.

Black-haired, black-eyed, slender and petite, she was wearing a silver grey silk suit that was as steely-looking as the expression she was wearing on her face as she stared directly at Luiz, while he stared coldly back.

For a long, dreadful moment after Pedro had quietly retired, closing the door behind him, nobody uttered a single word while these two main protagonists studied each other, and Caroline stood witnessing it happen without taking a single breath.

Then, 'Welcome,' the woman said.

'Tía Consuela,' Luiz replied stiltedly.

Caroline hid the urge to frown. Tía? she was thinking. Why was Luiz referring to this woman as his *aunt?* Surely if she was anything to him then she was some kind of stepmother?

'You look like your father,' the woman observed.

'And you have a look of my mother—though you look in much better health than she did when I saw her last.'

Incisive, cold enough to freeze the blood, it was also a puzzle solved for Caroline. This woman was Luiz's mother's sister. It was no wonder his grip was suddenly biting into her fingers. What had gone on here thirty-odd years ago?

Feuds and fortunes, he'd said, she recalled suddenly. And she began to get a sense of what had probably happened, most of it revolving round two sisters, one man, and all of—this…

The slight hint of pallor had touched the other woman's face. But her eyes did not waver. 'Serena was a romantic fool, Luiz,' she responded. 'You will not make me feel guilty for picking up what she so stupidly trampled upon.'

At which point Caroline did actually wince, as her fingers were crushed almost to the bone. Fearing that Luiz was about to do something violent, she burst into speech. 'Introduce me, Luiz,' she prompted lightly.

For a second she thought he was going to ignore her, then he complied, tersely. 'Caroline, this is my mother's sister and my father's widow, Consuela de Vazquez,'

'Hello.' She winged a bright smile across the room towards his stiff-faced aunt. 'I'm so excited about coming here. The castle is so beautiful, isn't it? But I don't think it's as old as it would like to be,' she said, knowing she was babbling like a fluffy blonde idiot, but she didn't care so long as she could overlay the cold hostility threading through the other two. 'It wants to be eleventh century, but I would hazard a guess at only sixteenth century.'

'Seventeenth,' another voice intruded. 'In a fit of pique, when his biggest rival for the hand of a certain lady won the lady's heart because of the size of his home, our ancestor came home here to the valley and built himself his own impressive structure—then married the lady's younger sister. History has a habit of repeating itself in this family—as you will soon learn, I predict.'

Caroline had frozen where she stood, the voice familiar enough to send her floundering in a sea of confusion as a tall, dark, very attractive man appeared from way down at the other end of the long drawing room.

He paused and smiled at her stunned expression, and—completely ignoring Luiz—went on in that same light, self-assured way which had repelled Caroline so much the first time she'd met him.

'Felipe de Vazquez,' he announced himself. 'At your service, Miss Newbury.' It was the man from the lift in Luiz's hotel in Marbella. 'We never did get around to introducing ourselves, did we?' he added with a lazy smile.

'Señor,' she acknowledged. And it was only entrenched good manners that made her accept his outstretched hand.

His fingers closed around hers, cool and smooth and infinitely polite. 'Felipe, please...' he invited. 'We are going to be related very soon, after all...'

Instinctively her other hand tightened in Luiz's and she moved a small fraction closer to him.

It was strange in its own way, but as she found herself making comparisons between Luiz's bone-crushing grip on one of her hands and his half-brother's light clasp, on the other, she knew which grip she felt safer with. But then she was remembering the last time she'd met the man, and the suspicion she'd had then that if she'd tried to break away his grip would have tightened painfully—a sensation that was attacking her again right now.

'Felipe,' she acknowledged politely, and used the moment to slip her hand free and place it flat on Luiz's chest. It was such an obvious declaration of intimacy that no one,

not even Luiz, missed that fact. 'Luiz, isn't this a coincidence?' She smiled, keeping her tone light with effort. 'I
met your half-brother in the hotel only the other evening,
and had no idea he was related to you.'

'Yes,' Luiz drawled. 'What a coincidence.'

It was too soft, too smooth, too lazy to be nice. She
knew Luiz, knew the way he worked, the angrier he got
the quieter he became.

Did Felipe recognise that? she wondered, when his dark
eyes eventually moved to clash with his long lost half-
brother's eyes. 'So we meet at last.' Felipe smiled ruefully.

At last? The words hit Caroline like a punch to her solar
plexus. Because surely if she had first seen Felipe at the
hotel then Luiz must have known he was there?

Obviously not, she concluded, when Luiz replied dryly,
'Not before time, maybe.'

The atmosphere suddenly became very complicated as
a confusion of rather unpredictable emotions went skittering around all three of them.

There was ice—a lot of ice. There was curiosity. There
was mutual antagonism born from an instant burst of sib-
ling rivalry where both men carefully judged the weight
of the other.

She wasn't sure which one of them actually came out
on top in that short silent battle, but she certainly knew
which one of them held the position of power—no matter
what the mental outcome.

'Welcome home, Luiz.' With a slightly wry smile that
told her Felipe was acknowledging the same thing, he conceded the higher ground to his half-brother. 'May your
next twenty years be more fortuitous than your first
twenty…'

It was such an openly cruel thing to say that even his
mother released a gasp. So did Caroline, her fingers curling

tensely into Luiz's shirt in sheer reflex, as if she was trying to soothe the savage beast before it leapt into action.

But Luiz, to everyone's surprise, laughed. 'Let's certainly hope so,' he agreed. 'Or this place could be in deep trouble—as we all know.'

Tit for tat. Cut and thrust. Luiz had won that round. And he hadn't finished, not by a long shot. 'Which reminds me,' he went on in the brisk cool voice of a true business tycoon, 'I have a lot I need to get through here before our wedding takes place next week. So can we start with a tour of the place, before I settle down to some good old-fashioned household accounting…?'

CHAPTER NINE

CAROLINE was sitting quietly in the window of her allotted valley-facing guestroom when a light tap sounded at her door. For a few precious moments she seriously contemplated not answering.

It had been a horrible few days. Days filled with wariness and tension and eyes watching everything she did and everywhere she went as if they were worried she might decide to run off with the silver!

On top of that, Luiz had taken on the mantle of responsibility here as if it was just another new acquisition in his multinational group. He was quiet, he was calm, he was cool and he was exceedingly businesslike. People—staff, mainly—were already in complete awe of him. They scuttled about like little rabbits earnestly eager to make a good impression. And, all in all, the changes he had put into place already were enough to make the average person gasp.

But this wasn't a business proposition, was it? It was a home—though admittedly a very unusual home. But how did you attempt to point something like that out to a man who barely acknowledged your existence?

Luiz wasn't talking to her. He was angry about something, though she didn't know what. It was difficult to find out when he seemed to have locked himself away inside a suit of armour that wouldn't look out of place in the castle hallway!

She had an itchy feeling his mood stemmed from the fact that she'd met his half-brother before he had. He'd quizzed her about that chance meeting. No—*grilled* her was a better word.

'Where did you meet? How did you meet? What did he say? How did he say it?'

When she'd grown angry and demanded to know why it was so important, he'd simply walked away! Five minutes later she'd seen him standing in the castle grounds with a cellular phone clamped to his ear. Whoever he had been speaking to had been receiving the lash of his angry tongue. Even from up here in this room, looking down into darkness, she had been able to see that.

Since then she had hardly set eyes on him, except to share meals across a dining table with others there to squash any hope of meaningful probing into what was rattling him. They even slept in separate rooms. Now if that was a simple case of maintaining some old-fashioned values here in this time-lock of a valley, then Caroline could understand and accept that. But his cold attitude towards her on every count hurt, even though she kept on telling herself that it shouldn't.

The tap sounded again. On a sigh she got up, and went to answer it. It was one of the little doe eyed maids. 'Excuse me, *señorita*,' she murmured. 'Doña Consuela send me to tell you that the *padre* is here wishing to talk to you?'

The *padre*. Her heart sank. 'All right, thank you, Abril. Will you tell him I'll be down in a few minutes?'

Where was Luiz? she wondered heavily as she crossed to her bathroom. But she knew where Luiz was—or least where he wasn't, she amended. Because Luiz certainly wasn't here in the valley. In fact, Luiz had flown off in the helicopter that had arrived to pick him up early this morning and hadn't been seen or heard of since.

The helicopter landing pad was just one of the changes Luiz had brought into being since they'd arrived here.

He'd had ten men from the village clearing a spot over in the far corner of the garden before Caroline had even got out of bed on that first morning. Another addition he'd had put in at incredible speed was the telecommunications mast erected at the top of the valley—to improve satellite reception, he'd explained over dinner. Apparently you couldn't run a multinational group without good communication.

Shame he didn't apply the same principles to his personal life!

But he didn't, so she now had to go and face the *padre* without knowing a single thing about the wedding proposed for next week, because Luiz hadn't bothered to discuss it with her!

It was going to make her look really good in the *padre*'s eyes if he discovered that he knew more about it than the bride herself!

I'm going to kill you very soon, Luiz Vazquez, she promised him silently as she checked over her cream skirt and lavender top—which were beginning to look a little the worse for wear now, along with the other things she had brought to Spain with her.

When she'd left London she had packed for a three-day short break in a hotel. She had *not* packed for parties in villas and cross-country travelling, or exploring the many admittedly interesting rooms inside a castle!

She found the *padre* waiting for her in the small sitting room the family tended to use during the day because it opened directly into the garden. Tía Consuela was waiting with him, but once she had introduced Caroline to Padre Domingo, she left them alone.

In truth, Caroline felt sorry for Consuela. In the last few months she had lost her husband, seen her own son being disinherited of everything she must know he had every right to consider his, and was about to lose her right to live in the home that had been hers for the last thirty-odd years. Yet the way she had remained on here, taking whatever Luiz wanted to throw at her, had in Caroline's view been rather impressive.

Personally she couldn't have done it. Pride alone would have sent her running for cover well before her estranged nephew could show his face. But, cold and remote though she always was, she had answered all Luiz's intense, sometimes acutely detailed questions about the running of the castle, and was quick to refer him on to those who knew more about the running of the rest of the estate.

While her son did nothing, offered no information and kept himself very much to himself by riding one of his beautiful Andalusian horses out each morning and not coming back until it was so dark that he had to.

Felipe had gone from charmer to brooder in a couple of very short phases. And he might have remained on here, like his mother, but unlike her he did nothing to hide his simmering resentment.

Not that Caroline could really blame him for feeling like that. For, no matter what legal right Luiz had to be here, Felipe, had every excuse for feeling angry and bitterly betrayed by his father.

She just wished she could like him more on a personal level, then maybe she could become a kind of go-between for the two half-brothers, give them a fine line of communication which might help bring them closer together.

'Señorita Newbury,' Padre Domingo greeted her smilingly. 'It is a great pleasure to make your acquaintance at last.'

Taking his proffered hand, Caroline smiled in answer. 'I called to see you yesterday but missed you.'

'I was visiting a *compadre* in the next valley.' He nodded. 'We like to get together once a week to—compare flocks. But I was sorry to be out when you called.'

Pleasantries over, it was a bit difficult to know where to go from there. so she covered her own feeling of awkwardness by inviting him to sit down. 'Can I get you a drink?' she offered. 'Tea, coffee—or something cooler, perhaps?'

But he shook his white head and with a slight wave of one beautifully slender hand invited her to sit before he would allow himself to do so.

'You liked our little church?' he enquired when they had both settled into Louis the Fifteenth chairs still wearing their original upholstery.

Caroline smiled. 'It's the prettiest church I've ever set foot in,' she answered honestly. 'But then this whole valley is the prettiest I've ever stepped foot in,' she added with a warm twinkle in her eyes.

'But very isolated,' the father pointed out.

'Part of its charm,' Caroline immediately defended, with that same teasing twinkle.

'And also very—Catholic…'

Ah, she thought, losing the twinkle. 'Is that going to be a problem?' she asked. 'Luiz and I marrying in your church with me not being a Roman Catholic, I mean?' she went on, thinking silently—where are you Luiz? You should have seen this problem arising!

In his neat black robe with its round white collar the father eyed her thoughtfully from his thin, wise face. 'Is it a problem for you?' he countered eventually.

'Only if you expect me to make a sudden conversion,' she answered candidly.

'No.' He shook his head. 'I do not expect that sacrifice of you—as I would hope your English church would not expect the same thing of Luiz if the situation were reversed. See, we are emancipated here.' He smiled then. 'Even in our sleepy little valley.'

'But there is a problem?' Caroline prompted shrewdly. It was written in his thoughtful stare.

'The problem is more one of—sincerity than religion,' he murmured slowly, and when Caroline began to frown in confusion he seemed to come to a decision. 'Let me be blunt, Miss Newbury,' he said. 'It has come to my attention that you and Don Luiz are intending to exchange sacred vows with each other which may not be exactly truthful, and indeed are merely a means to a rather sinister end...'

Sinister? Caroline picked up on the word and pondered it frowningly, suddenly very wary as to where the priest was going with this. 'Are you trying to suggest that every marriage in your church has been a perfect love-match?' she questioned, aware that if any culture was known for arranging loveless marriages, then surely Spain had to be it!

'In this particular case, it is only your marriage to Don Luiz that I am concerned with,' the priest replied smoothly. 'You met for the first time only five days ago, I have been led to believe. Within hours of that meeting Don Luiz was announcing your intention to marry and your own father was collapsing due to the shock. It has also been suggested that your father is in debt to Don Luiz for a rather large amount of money which may well be the motive behind this—arrangement.'

'Suggested by whom?' Even as the full weight of his words came as a bit of a blow Caroline's hackles were rising—and it showed in the sudden glint in her amethyst eyes.

'The source of my information is not really important,' he dismissed with a wave of one slender hand. 'My concern here is really for you, *señorita*,' he explained. 'I came here today with serious concerns that you were being—coerced into the marriage for reasons beyond your control.'

'Are you trying to tell me, that you are refusing to marry Luiz and I?' she challenged, coming stiffly to her feet. She simply had not been expecting him to question their sincerity like this.

Inherent good manners made him rise to his feet also. 'No,' he denied. 'Don Luiz is the new *conde* here in this valley. If he tells me to marry him to a lady gagged and chained to his side, then I marry them.' He shrugged, adding with a wry smile, 'There, the old ways are not quite dead, heh?' And now it was his turn to flick her a twinkling smile.

But Caroline was in no mood to twinkle back at him. 'Then let me put your mind at rest,' she said coolly. 'Your information is wrong,' she declared. 'Luiz and I have known each other for seven years. We have been *lovers* for seven years.' Which was not quite a lie, even if it wasn't quite the truth. But in this situation it served her purpose very nicely to make that point.

Surprised though the priest undoubtedly was by her correction, it didn't faze him. 'But have you *loved* Don Luiz for seven years?' he threw right back.

Love? Caroline repeated to herself, and smiled a half-smile that was more rueful than cynical, though she had a feeling it should have been the other way round. 'I've *always* loved Luiz,' she responded dryly. 'But if you are going to ask me if he feels the same way about me,' she added, 'then please don't.'

'Then of course I will not,' he instantly conceded, and with eyes which conveyed a gentle apology for making her feel compelled to add that final remark, he gently touched one of Caroline's hands. 'Forgive my intrusion into what you clearly feel is your private business. But I had to be sure that you cared for Don Luiz before I could carry out his father's last wish.'

His father's last wish? Her eyes grew curious, but the

priest had already turned away and was walking across the room to where a rather bulky attaché case she hadn't noticed before lay on a table by the door.

'I am now going to place something into your care *señorita*,' he explained, 'that I must make you promise to guard with your life and show to no one…'

For some obscure reason, watching him open the attaché case as he spoke those words made her feel suddenly afraid. 'If it's something that will hurt Luiz, then you can keep it,' she told him.

'I commend your desire to protect him,' he replied, turning with what looked like several thin ledgers in his hands. 'And—yes—these will hurt Don Luiz if he ever sees them. He is, of course, the one exception to the promise I am about to make you swear. Can you read Spanish as well as you speak it?' he asked suddenly.

Caroline nodded. She had spent most of her summers since she was a small child right here in Spain, and that meant that Spanish had become her second language.

'Then, having read these—' he indicated the ledgers '—I will leave it to your discretion to decide whether you think he needs to know all that has been written in here…'

He began to approach her, and it was all Caroline could do not to snatch her trembling hands behind her back. For whatever it was he was about to give her, she knew she didn't want. He saw it in her face and paused two steps away.

'These are the diaries of Don Luiz's *papá*,' he informed her. 'Left in my care long before Don Carlos was taken ill. They explain why Don Luiz inherits all and Don Felipe very little. They explain why Don Luiz has been his *papá*'s beneficiary for the whole of his thirty-five years. So take them,' he urged. 'Read them and understand—for Luiz's sake, please, *señorita*…'

Sombrely he held them out to her. Reluctantly Caroline

accepted them, her fingers turning cold as they closed around the diaries; worse her heart felt as if it had turned to stone. She didn't know why, didn't understand what any of this was about. But she knew one thing as surely as she knew her name was Caroline: these books were dark things—dark and awful things.

'I'll read them,' she promised.

The priest nodded in silent understanding of the expression on her face and simply turned without another word to take his leave. But as he reached the door he paused, glanced back at her, still standing where he had left her in the middle of the room with the books clutched between tense white fingers.

'You know, *señorita*,' he murmured thoughtfully, 'it is, I think, quite a curious coincidence that you should have known Don Luiz for seven years. For it was also seven years ago that he first agreed to come here and meet his *papá* for the first time, only to abruptly change his mind. The reason he gave for that change, was that he had met the woman he was going to marry. Courting her, it seemed, was more important to him then than meeting his father. He did, though, promise to wed her here, in the church of the Valle de los Angeles, as was tradition. It seems he is about to keep that promise, hmm?'

He smiled. Then, before she could remark on that fresh piece of shock information, he was turning away again. 'Read the diaries, Miss Newbury. And learn about the man who loves you as much I think as you love him,' he advised as he left her alone.

Hours later she wished to God that she hadn't read the diaries. She wished to God that the whole Vazquez family had kept to their old ways and stayed right out of Luiz's life.

She hid the books away in her room on the top of a great oak wardrobe that stood against a wall. Then she went outside into the afternoon heat and paced the garden, lost in dark thoughts filled with heartache and betrayal, and the cruel sacrifice of one innocent child for the sake of another.

'History repeating itself,' Felipe had called it. Luiz had called it feuds and fortunes. Caroline called it unforgivable. And if Luiz knew only half of what she had just discovered via those diaries, then it was no wonder he had shut himself away inside an invisible suit of armour since coming here. This family was poison to anyone who touched them. Which brought to mind yet another remark made by his uncle the doctor. 'Take a food-taster with you,' he'd advised. He too knew that there was poison in this beautiful place.

The only bit of good she had gleaned from those diaries had been confirmation that the priest had been telling the truth about Luiz's intentions towards her seven years ago. But even that truth had its poisonous side.

For, if Luiz had loved her then, why had he gone from her arms directly to a card table to try and bankrupt her father night after night?

When the sound of a helicopter came whirring over the mountain, she wished Luiz had stayed away. She was still too upset, too confused. She needed more time to think, to absorb, and decide how much she was going to tell him about what she had learned today—if she was going to tell him anything at all.

Yet as the helicopter landed on its newly prepared site she found herself standing there waiting for him. As he stepped down onto solid ground her heart began to fill with a multitude of emotions she just couldn't separate.

Dressed in a dark grey business suit with needle-sharp tailoring, bright white shirt and a steel-grey tie, he looked the true tycoon, the true nobleman. In fact no one looking at his lean, dark, proudly arrogant profile would believe he had spent the first twenty years of his life living literally from hand to mouth.

He also looked sombre, she noticed, as if the worries of the whole world had suddenly descended upon him. She knew the feeling, since she was experiencing the very same thing herself.

The fault of this valley? Was the fatal flaw in its beauty its need to taint all that came here?

Fanciful though she knew she was being, she knew suddenly that she needed to be close to him—very badly. She also knew that she needed to get away from here, if only for a little while, to think, to regain some perspective.

So the moment he was free of the helicopter's lethal blades she began walking across the lawn to meet him. He saw her coming towards him and stopped and stared, as if he was seeing his life's dream, before those heavily defended eyes were hiding as usual.

And for no other reason than because she needed to, she wound her arms around his neck and kissed him urgently. His surprise was evident in the moment of tension she felt grip him, and for a couple of horrible seconds she thought he was actually going to thrust her away.

Then his arms looped around her—tightly enough to crush her against his hard-packed body—and he began to kiss her back with a hunger that easily matched her own.

It was like finding herself after being lost in a dark place for days upon end. Whatever else was between them that didn't make sense, this always—always—felt so very right.

He broke the kiss. She would have been content to remain right there, kissing him like this for ever. But those dark eyes of his were frowning down at her, probing the whitened pallor even the kiss had not managed to dispel. 'What's wrong?' he demanded. 'Who has upset you?'

Caroline just shook her head. 'I missed you, that's all,'

she told him huskily. 'I've been missing you for days, though you didn't seem to notice.'

'I noticed,' he murmured gruffly. 'I just thought it was better if I gave you time to yourself to—come to terms with all of this…'

'All of this' being the fairytale castle standing behind them, that had suddenly become a very haunted castle for Caroline.

'I don't need time to come to terms with it,' she denied. 'I have something similar of my own in England, if you recall—though I admit it isn't as grand as this. But— Luiz…' Despite trying to, she couldn't keep the strain from creeping into her tone. 'Can we get away from here for a little while?' she begged. 'Just you and me, somewhere— ordinary? Can that thing fly us out—just for a couple of hours? Please?'

'You don't like it here,' he sighed.

'I love it here,' she insisted, knowing it was a lie and that at that precise moment she hated this valley and everything in it. 'I just need some time away from it for a little while. Is that too much to ask?'

'No.' He was still frowning, because he knew she wasn't telling him the entire truth, but one of his hands flicked a staying motion at the pilot aimed to make him keep the engine running. 'Where would you like to go? To Marbella?' he suggested. 'We can be there in—'

But Caroline was shaking her head. 'There's this little place I know. A secret place,' she whispered confidingly, and her eyes began to warm with sensual promise. 'It has the softest bed on this earth, I think. No air conditioning and a bathroom down the hall. But it has the most wonderfully cool and crinkly starched cotton sheets on the bed, and there won't be a frosty face in sight…'

He was gazing down at her as if having to convince himself that she was suggesting what it seemed that she was. And Caroline's breath snagged in her chest while she waited for some kind of response.

Agreement or rejection? He was so unpredictable, burning hot, turning cold. Pounce and retreat. Trying to pre-empt his response was impossible, she acknowledged as his silence began to sew fine threads of tension beneath the surface of her skin.

Then a sleek brow arched, mockery spiked his eyes. 'Is this your ladylike way of inviting me for a dirty weekend, by any chance?' he questioned sardonically.

Put like that, it sounded so brazen that she felt her cheeks go red—then she caught the beginnings of his lazy smile and she smiled too. 'I suppose I am,' she admitted. 'Though if you prefer the company of your family,' she added innocently, 'then I am open to compromise...'

His dark head went back and he started laughing. It was the best sound she had heard in days. Her heart literally swelled on the pleasure of it, and he was still laughing after he'd captured her hand and walked her back towards the waiting helicopter.

Neither saw his half-brother watching them from the shrubbery. Neither saw the malignant glint in his eyes as he watched them lift off and fly away.

They were dropped off in a clearing just outside Los Aminos and walked into the village hand in hand. They must look an odd kind of couple, Caroline decided wryly, with Luiz in his razor-sharp suit and her in her simple cream skirt and lavender top.

The hotel proprietor was the same, and his eyes rounded as they stepped through the door. At the appearance of an exorbitant amount of money, the round-eyed look changed to one of obsequious respect which produced the same key to the same room with exactly the same bed.

'I'm even wearing the same clothes,' Caroline whispered to Luiz as they climbed the stairs hand in hand.

'And the same pink bloom on your cheeks,' he added teasingly. And as the bloom deepened on her first realisation of what she had actually dared to propose here, he shut the door with one hand and reached for her with the other.

They didn't go back to the castle that night. It was a wonderful warm, enchanted experience, where Caroline felt as if she had found the lover she had carelessly lost—not once but twice, when she thought about the last few lonely days.

They made love as if there would be no tomorrow. They touched and kissed and caressed each other as if this would be their last opportunity. It was all very hot, very serious and intense.

'You were my first true love,' she softly confessed to him at one point.

His eyes turned black in their sleepy sockets. 'And you, believe it or not, were mine,' he replied.

But—no, she couldn't accept that. For a man who loved someone didn't take her family for every penny he could squeeze out of it, she thought sadly, and to bury the sadness she took his dark face between her hands and brought his mouth crushing down on top of her own.

Maybe he sensed her sadness, maybe he saw it just before she buried it away. Whatever—something thrust him onto a whole new plane of passion. It was devastatingly rich, and left her floating in a place of boneless satiation from which she didn't return for ages.

When she eventually did decide to open her eyes, she found herself curled into Luiz's side with her cheek resting on his shoulder; it was growing dark outside.

'We didn't tell anyone we were leaving,' she remarked—without much concern for the omission.

'I sent the pilot back to make our excuses,' he replied. 'They are to expect us when they see us.'

He sounded so arrogant then, so much the lord of his valley that she released a soft chuckle. The sound brought his hand to her nape so he could make her look at him.

'That was the first sound of genuine amusement I've heard from you since we met again,' he told her huskily.

'What did you expect?' She pouted. 'When you've done nothing but blackmail and bully me!'

It was supposed to be a tease, but Luiz didn't smile. Instead his eyes remained darkly probing. 'I didn't bully you to get you here tonight,' he quietly pointed out.

'No,' she agreed. She had been the one doing the bullying this time.

'Are you ready to explain to me now what happened today to make you want to run away like this?'

So he knew she hadn't been telling the truth back at the castle. She turned her face down again, and began watching the way her fingers were drawing whirls into his chest hair.

'I had a visitor,' she said, deciding to come clean with the truth—or part of the truth anyway. 'The village priest,' she explained.

Luiz had gone still; even his heart seemed to have slowed beneath her resting cheek. 'And...?' he prompted very quietly.

'And he wanted to know if our planned wedding was a sham.' She smiled.

'Was he threatening not to marry us?'

Clever, quick Luiz, she thought. 'No,' she denied. 'In fact he assured me that if *el conde* came to his altar with his bride chained and gagged he would marry them.'

'Then what was his point?'

Now there was a question, she thought, and on a soft rueful laugh she sat up, to run her fingers through her tangled hair. 'His point was, I think,' she began slowly, choosing her words with care, 'to make me aware that

certain—rumours were circulating the valley about the sincerity of our feelings for one another.'

'Rumours?' he repeated.

'Mmm.' She nodded. 'Apparently it is being said that
you and I met for the first time only a few days before
you brought me here as your bride…'

'And you said—what?'

He hadn't moved a single muscle since this had started,
and Caroline now had her back towards him, so she
couldn't see his face. The worst thing about Luiz, she told
herself grimly, was his annoying ability to speak without
giving a single hint as to what he was thinking.

'I told him the information was inaccurate,' she said.
'That we had known each other for seven years. Then I
lied a bit,' she added with a shrug, 'and told him we had
been lovers for seven years…'

Only it hadn't felt much like a lie when she had said it,
she recalled. In fact it was probably closer to the truth than
anyone would believe—in her case at least.

'To which he said what?'

'You're very good at this,' she remarked, turning her
head to level him with a dry look.

Two sleek black brows rose in enquiry. Her stomach
muscles leapt. He's such a sexy devil, she thought helplessly.

'The Spanish Inquisition,' she explained. 'In fact you
remind me of a dripping tap. You just steadily and relent-
lessly drop your questions until you get to know what it
is you're after.'

'To which he said—what?' he repeated, and there
wasn't a single alteration in those black holes for eyes.

She looked away again, and a heavy sigh whispered
from her because the truth was out of bounds. And there
was another problem she had been worrying over since the
priest's visit.

'I think he was trying to warn us that someone is making trouble for you,' she said. 'Someone is feeding rumours about the valley that you and I are a sham—which is, I presume, their way of making sure we will never gain the people's respect. The other rumour is that you have more or less bought me from my father. Now, who but you and I know anything about that?'

'You think I have been telling tales?'

It was such a ridiculous suggestion that she laughed. 'You mean it *is* possible to get blood from a stone?' she mocked—then released another sigh. 'What's worrying me, Luiz,' she explained, 'is that someone has to have been spying on us. And it sends creepy feelings down my spine just to think of it.' She even shuddered.

A hand came to her naked back and soothed the shudders. 'The spy in this case we already know, *querida*,' he informed her quietly. 'And because we also know he has some right to be bitter enough about the situation to spread rumours which may place us in a poor light, we will allow him a small—indiscretion. It is, after all, all he believes he has left to survive on right now...'

He was talking about Felipe. The name didn't need saying. 'Okay,' she agreed, and curled herself back around him, needing to say more but afraid to say more in case too much came pouring out.

'Okay?' he repeated quizzically. 'Just like that?'

'Mmm.' She snuggled herself into his warm, muscled strength. 'This is too nice to spoil by talking about nasty things. And anyway, I've got far more pressing concerns on my mind right now.'

His eyes began to gleam, the humour she could see running through them heating her blood.

'Shopping!' she announced in mock censure. 'I'm talking about my need to go shopping for some fresh clothes, since you abducted me with only enough clothes to last me three days! *And* I want to buy a really expensive bridal dress with all the trimmings,' she tagged on, right out of the blue. 'Because if I *have* to marry you then I insist that you let me do it in style!'

In the startled silence that followed his eyes narrowed slightly, as if he was reading a return to the old bitterness in what she'd said.

It wasn't there. And a moment later she was being loved again—which she much preferred to talking.

They stayed in that hot, dark, old-fashioned hotel room all night, and made love and ate paella cooked specially by the hotel proprietor's very eager wife, and slept in each other's arms and awoke there. It was the first time Caroline had woken up to find him still there beside her. It made an oddly painful impression on her to realise that.

The next day Luiz had them flown to Cordoba, where Caroline played the future bride to a wealthy man to the hilt and shopped until she dropped. She was bright, she was flirtatious, and she was enchanting to be with. And if Luiz looked at her strangely now and then, as if he was trying to work out what was making her behave this way, Caroline just smiled at him, or kissed him, or demanded more money from him, diverting the risk of any questions.

Because how did you explain to someone like him that while reading his father's diaries she had come face to face with the real Luiz Vazquez? She understood him now, and hurt for him, and loved him more deeply than she dared let herself dwell upon.

Even if Luiz could never come to love her in the same way that she loved him, then she could live with that— just. Because the other thing she had learned while reading those diaries was that love was not automatically given back by right.

CHAPTER TEN

THEY arrived back at the valley to find yet another wave of changes had been wrought while they had been away. The garden had been decorated with fairylights, the castle itself cleaned and polished to within an inch of its life, and the construction of a long banqueting table was in the process of being completed in the main hall as they walked in the door.

'You are pulling out all the stops, I see.' Felipe's lazy drawl emerged before he did, from a dark corner of the hall.

He had a habit of doing that, Caroline thought as she took a small step closer to Luiz. His hand closed round her hand.

'If one has to marry then let no detail be overlooked,' he mocked. 'No festive trick be ignored.'

His derision was acute. Caroline wanted to hit him for being so mean-mouthed. But Luiz took the criticism in his stride. 'It must be the hotelier in me.' He smiled. 'If there is one thing I have learned to do well, then it is to put on a good party.'

'With the relatives obediently gathered around you to help you celebrate.' Felipe nodded. 'It is quite extraordinary what healthy quarterly allowances can make people do that they normally would not deign to tolerate.'

'Is that why you decided to hang around, Felipe?' Luiz countered curiously. 'Because you see the need to secure your quarterly allowance?'

'I have money of my own,' he declared, but Luiz had

147

hit a raw nerve. 'My father did not leave me quite destitute.'

'No, he left you a *finca* in the Sierra Nevada and the means to make a success of it, if you could be bothered to try.'

'While you get all of—this…' Felipe's smile was rancid. 'Tell me…' Suddenly he turned his attention on Caroline. She stiffened instantly, sensing it was her turn to receive the whip of his nasty tongue. 'How did the poker game between your father and Luiz end? There are a lot of people who must be dying to know…'

He must have been there, in the casino, when Luiz had issued the challenge to her father, Caroline realised as she felt her cheeks grow pale. Her hand twitched in Luiz's, in a silent plea for him to answer that question.

He tightened his grip a little, but surprised her by saying absolutely nothing. Instead he lifted his free hand and gave a sharp click of his fingers. Without warning, Vito Martinez materialised in front of them. Big and broad and built to smash rocks against, he stood waiting for Luiz to speak.

'Escort Caroline to her room, Vito,' he instructed, without removing his gaze from Felipe. 'And remain there until I come…'

Caroline's skin was prickling, and the shivery sense that he was issuing some kind of dire warning to Felipe with his security guard's daunting presence was enough to keep her silent when Luiz let go of her hand and instructed quietly, 'Go with Vito. Felipe and I have a few—things we need to discuss in private…'

She went, but she felt sick. She didn't look back, but she could almost feel the two men sizing each other up as if for battle. 'What's going to happen?' she whispered to Vito.

'They will talk,' he answered simply. 'As Luiz said.'

'I don't like him,' she confessed, finding herself moving that little bit closer to this big tower of a man Luiz had made her escort.

'Few people do,' Vito replied. That was all, but it seemed to say more than enough. Both Luiz and Vito had Felipe's measure. And that meant that if Felipe had been checking up on them then Luiz had certainly been checking up on him—using this man she was walking beside to do the checking, she suspected.

Vito didn't leave her even when she slipped away to use her bathroom; he was still standing by the door when she got back.

'You've known Luiz a long time, haven't you?' she questioned curiously.

'Since we were both nine years old,' Vito replied.

Which placed them, by her reckoning, in an orphanage together. 'So you are friends,' she concluded, smiling wryly to herself because she was remembering her own thoughts from the other day, when she'd been sitting in the back of Luiz's car while Vito drove her.

'He saved my life once,' Vito answered, but didn't elaborate, even though Caroline stared at him in disbelief because she couldn't imagine anyone having to save this man's life for him. He was just too big, too *everything* surely, to be put into that kind of danger.

The purchases she'd made while they'd been away began to arrive then, diverting her attention. And a few more minutes after that Luiz arrived. With a quiet word in Vito's ear he dismissed the other man, who left with a grim nod of his head that made Caroline shiver.

'Why the need of a bodyguard?' she demanded, the moment they were alone again. 'Am I in some kind of danger I should know about?'

'No,' Luiz denied. 'Not while I'm still breathing at any rate.'

'So *you're* the one who's in danger,' she therefore concluded.

'Nobody is in danger!' he denied.

'Then why the bodyguard?' she repeated stubbornly.

'Escort,' he corrected. 'He was sent to escort you up here simply to make a point, okay? '

No, it wasn't okay. And her face told Luiz that. 'All right,' he sighed out heavily. 'Felipe would like to stop the wedding from taking place,' he said. 'That much is patently obvious. But how far he would go to stop it I am not entirely sure. So I am protecting my weak spots.'

'And I am a weak spot.'

Suddenly his laziest grin appeared. 'Oh, a very weak spot,' he murmured seductively, and began to pace suggestively towards her.

'Don't you dare!' she protested, putting out a hand to ward him off. 'Not here in this house! Not until we are married!' she added, chin up, amethyst eyes challenging. 'I *will* have your respect *el conde!*' she insisted when he took another step towards her.

He stopped. She had to fight to keep her disappointment from showing. Luiz grinned again, because he saw it anyway. 'If I touched you now, you would go up in smoke,' he challenged softly.

'If you touched me now, I probably would,' she ruefully agreed.

'Then I won't,' he assured her.

'Oh,' she said, and didn't even try to hide her disappointment this time.

'Protocol,' he explained. 'Thanks for reminding me that in this house I must respect all bridal traditions.'

If Caroline was aware that she had changed a lot in the last twenty-four hours, then she was also aware that Luiz had changed too. Gone was a lot of the stiff tension he had brought with them into the valley, and what she saw now was a wonderfully charming, lazily relaxed and very sensually motivated man—in private anyway.

It was that recognition that sent her walking into his arms. 'Just one chaste kiss, then,' she offered invitingly, and snaked even closer to him when his arms slid caressingly about her.

'Chaste?' he mocked.

'Mmm,' she said. But there was nothing chaste in the way they stood there amongst a sea of unopened packages for long, very unsatisfying minutes.

'I have to go,' Luiz groaned out reluctantly.

Go? 'Go where?' she demanded.

'Work,' he said, glancing at his watch. And suddenly he was the frustratingly brisk and businesslike Luiz. 'I have things to do before our wedding. And I need to get out of the valley before it grows too dark to fly…'

'But we've only just arrived!'

'Don't blame me!' he countered at her look of dismay. 'You're the one who has put my schedule back twenty-four hours! A deliciously welcome twenty-four hours, I will admit,' he added ruefully. 'But now I have to play catch-up. So you won't see me again until we meet at the church.'

'Luiz!' she cried out as he walked off to the door. 'W-what about your weak spot?' she reminded him anxiously.

'Vito is staying.' It seemed to say it all. 'Anything you want or are worried about, you go to him.'

'Because he owes you his life and therefore will do anything for you?'

That stopped him. He turned to stare at her in surprise. 'You managed to get him to tell you that?' He sounded truly shocked. 'Well, that's a first,' he drawled.

'What did you do?' she asked. 'Haul him out of the razor fight that put all those marks on his face?'

'No,' he denied, and suddenly he wasn't smiling. 'I

hauled him out of prison and gave him a life. And that wasn't kind, Caroline,' he told her grimly.

He was right; it wasn't. 'I'm sorry,' she mumbled contritely.

He nodded. 'See you Wednesday.'

He was going to go, and she didn't want him to go with bad words between them. 'I like him, actually,' she confessed. 'Mainly because he's so loyal to you, I think. You didn't know Felipe was even staying at your hotel, did you?' she then asked, on a complete change of subject.

'He booked in under a different name,' Luiz explained.

'And proceeded to shadow both me and my father,' she mused frowningly. 'He knew who I was—knew who my father was. Which tells you you have a mole in your midst somewhere, Luiz.'

He nodded. 'I'm aware of that—and dealing with it.'

'Does all of this make my father another weak spot?' she asked.

For some reason the question had him turning to study her curiously. 'Yes,' he replied quietly.

She released a sigh and began to look fretful again. 'Are you protecting him too?'

'Undoubtedly,' he assured her, in a strange tone that matched the strange expression he was wearing on his face. 'He will be here, safe and sound, to give your hand to me on our wedding day. Have no fear about that, *querida.*'

Then he was gone, leaving Caroline to stand there staring at the last spot he had been standing on, wondering why she was feeling so very chilled again when surely what he had just said should have been reassuring?

A tap at the door broke her free from whatever it was that was holding her, and she opened it to find Abril, the little maid standing there. 'Don Luiz send me to help you unpack your purchases,' she explained.

Caroline was glad of the diversion. It seemed nothing here in this valley could stay happy for long. Together she and Abril unpacked box after box bearing the names of designers Caroline would never have normally been able to afford to buy.

When it came to the dress she had chosen to marry Luiz in, the two of them unpacked it together, with a kind of hushed air of expectancy that increased to a breathless delight when the dress was finally hanging on its satin-covered hanger from the tall wardrobe door.

'This is beautiful, *señorita*,' Abril sighed out wistfully.

Yes, it was, Caroline agreed, smiling softly to herself when she remembered the way she had sent Luiz off to get himself some coffee somewhere while she'd chosen the dress on her own. He'd been all lazy mockery as he strode away. But she suspected that secretly he'd rather liked the idea of her choosing a dress aimed exclusively to please him.

'You have a sweetheart of your own?' Caroline asked curiously.

The young maid blushed. 'No,' she denied. 'But when I do, I would wish to marry him in something as lovely as this…'

She was lightly fingering the delicate lace when the idea came to Caroline. She hadn't given a thought to it before, but it suddenly struck her now, when it was almost too late to do anything about it, that she was going to have no friends of her own here to help her dress, or share her excitement, or even one to stand as her witness.

Luiz Vazquez, the fine-detail man, seemed to have overlooked that small but important point.

'Abril…' she murmured slowly, forming the request even as she spoke it out loud. 'Would you do something very—special for me?'

'Of course, *señorita*,' the maid instantly replied.

'If I can get a dress here in time—a pretty dress for you to wear—would you be my bridesmaid?'

For a terrible moment she thought she'd actually horrified the poor girl, she was so still and silent. Then, 'Oh, *señorita,*' she breathed. 'Do you really mean it?'

The doe eyes were suddenly shining with pleasure. 'Yes, I mean it.' Caroline found herself smiling too. 'You must have noticed that I am here on my own,' she pointed out sagely. 'My family and friends are all in England, and though my father is coming I will have no one else. It would be nice, don't you think, to have someone from the valley to stand beside me?'

'It would be an honour,' the young girl answered gravely. 'But, I will have to ask permission of Doña Consuela before I may say absolutely that I will do this,' she added anxiously.

'Of course,' Caroline said instantly, not bothering to point out that it was really Luiz's permission the maid should be seeking. And since she knew what his answer would be without having to ask him, Caroline didn't think that was a problem.

'I'll ask her,' she decided. Abril looked relieved. 'In fact I'll go and do it now, while you finish up here, okay?'

Nothing like striking while the iron is hot, she told herself bracingly as she went in search of Luiz's aunt. But she was beginning to half wish she hadn't started this, being a coward deep down inside.

She found Doña Consuela in the main drawing room. She was just standing there, staring out of the window, watching the construction taking place on the lawn outside. And there was a sad, lonely, isolated look to her stance that touched Caroline's heart a little, even though she now knew exactly how effective this woman had been in ruining Luiz's *mamá*'s life.

'Consuela…' she prompted.

She hadn't even heard Caroline come in the room, she was so lost inside her own bleak thoughts. But she turned at the sound of her name, her expression as smoothly composed as it always was.

Sometimes her relationship to Luiz is all too clear, Caroline mused ruefully.

'I wondered if you would mind if I asked your advice about something,' she ventured carefully—though why she had changed from making it a polite request to the more gentle quest for advice she was not entirely sure—unless it was because Consuela had looked a little like Luiz then.

Luiz when he was hiding hurt, she extended sadly.

'Of course,' the older woman agreed. 'If you think my advice will be of use.'

Taking a deep breath, Caroline explained what she wanted to do and why she wanted to do it. Consuela listened to her without expression, and it was therefore a surprise when the other woman smiled a brief, rather bleak smile and said, 'You are a nice person, *señorita*. It will be comforting to know that I will be leaving the valley in the charge of someone so sensitive.'

'Luiz cares too, you know,' Caroline declared, instantly on the defensive, because she hadn't expected approval from this particular source and was therefore searching for hidden criticism.

The Condesa's smile grew wry. 'I know that,' she said. 'And, yes, it would be a perfect touch for you to have Abril as your maid of honour. The people of the valley will love you for doing it. Give the child my blessing and tell her she is relieved of all her normal duties so she can devote her time to her new exciting role.'

While you do what? Caroline wanted to ask. Keep fading ever more into the shadows of this place that has been your home for so many years?

'What will you do?' she asked impulsively. 'When you leave here?'

The smile was wry again. 'So, Luiz intends to have me banished,' the other woman said. 'I did wonder.'

Caroline felt absolutely horrified that she had inadvertently stepped into something she should not. 'I don't know,' she answered awkwardly. 'Luiz doesn't discuss his family with me.'

'No, I don't suppose he does,' the Condesa murmured, and turned back to the window. It was a dismissal in anyone's books. Feeling like some kind of heel, Caroline took herself out of the room without daring to utter another word.

Next she went to search out Vito. She found him in the garden, overlooking the setting out of what looked as if it was going to be a wooden dance floor beneath a red and white striped awning.

'Vito—' She touched his arm to gain his attention then instantly withdrew her fingers again when they tingled as if they'd just touched solid rock. 'Do you think Luiz would mind if I put his helicopter to use?' she said.

He swung around so lightly for a man of his size that Caroline was startled. 'Why?' he demanded sharply. 'What do you want the helicopter for? What's wrong?'

'Nothing,' she assured him, but even as she spoke his eyes were flicking in all directions, and he seemed to grow another few inches, like a bear getting ready to enfold its prey. Or, in her case, to protect its cub, she amended ruefully.

'I need the helicopter to run an errand for me,' she said. 'A special errand.' Then she went on to explain…

She was just finishing some breakfast on the morning of her wedding day when her father arrived in Luiz's helicopter. The moment she saw it was him climbing out she was up and running, out of the hall and out into the sunshine, to meet him halfway across the lawn.

'Oh, Daddy,' she sobbed, and launched herself at him. 'How could you just walk away from me like that?'

'Don't fuss, Caro. I'm fine!' he censured irritably as she began a detailed check for any physical signs of poor health.

'You don't look fine,' she told him, seeing the changes in him even if he didn't think they were there. He looked older and thinner and— She sighed unhappily.

'Some place—this,' he ventured, deliberately changing the subject, Caroline suspected. 'Never seen anything quite like it. Coming in over the top of that mountain actually took my breath away. Did you know seven years ago that Luiz was heir to all of this?'

'No.' She was trying to catch his eye, but he wouldn't let her, and his hands were grimly keeping her at arm's length. 'It wouldn't have made any difference to the way I felt about him if I had,' she added absently. 'Will you please look at me?' she said impatiently.

He flicked his eyes to hers. She saw the guilt, the shame and the misery, and her own eyes filled with tears. 'I love you so much,' she choked. 'And I've been worried about you!'

His defences collapsed. On a ragged sigh he tugged her to him and wrapped his arms around her tight. 'And him?' he questioned gruffly. 'Do you love him?'

'Like a second skin,' she replied. 'But then I always have done, you already knew that.'

'Yes, I always knew it,' he confirmed heavily. 'But I'm still sorry for getting you into this dreadful mess.'

'No mess,' she denied, then repeated it when she saw his disbelieving look. 'No mess, Daddy. Luiz is what I want. He's what I've always wanted.'

He grimaced. 'But not handed to him on a plate like a damned sacrifice.'

'I'm no sacrifice either!' she informed him crossly. 'Or are you trying to imply that Luiz feels nothing for me in return? Because if you are,' she continued angrily, 'then maybe you should just turn around and go away again.'

'I'm not implying anything.' He sighed again. 'Good grief,' he added. 'The man has twice gone to big enough lengths in his attempts to get you to this day…'

Twice? Caroline felt that chill hit her spine again. 'What do you mean twice?' she demanded.

'Nothing,' he grunted, going all shifty-eyed. 'Well, would you look at that?' he then exclaimed in surprise, diverting her attention to the spot he was looking at near the castle entrance. 'What's he doing here? He never told me he knew Luiz!'

He never told me… Caroline repeated to herself as she too turned to stare at Felipe. And so many, many things began to slide into place. Her own father was Luiz's mole, though unwittingly.

Oh, Daddy, she thought sighingly. And when he went to go and speak to Felipe she stopped him. 'Watch him, Pops,' she warned, and just the quiet use of her childhood name for him was enough to alert Sir Edward to trouble. 'Watch every single word you say to him and watch your back.'

'Why?' he frowned. 'Who is he?'

'He's Luiz's half-brother—the man who thinks he should have inherited all of this…'

Enlightenment came to him as quickly as it had come to his daughter. His soft curse confirmed it.

The helicopter lifted off then, rendering words useless as the sounds of its rotors filled the air. Her father seemed to use the time the helicopter took to sweep off down the valley to come to some kind of decision.

'Let's go somewhere where we can talk in private,' he said flatly. 'I have something I want to say to you...'

Caroline wanted to talk to Luiz. She *needed* to talk to Luiz. But the juggernaut called her wedding was now rolling ahead at full speed, and Luiz, she assumed, was already waiting for her at the tiny church in the centre of the village where, since her father had arrived, so had gathered the full Vazquez family, to witness the event taking place.

'You look beautiful, *señorita,*' Abril's gentle voice brought Caroline's anxious eyes into focus on the mirror she was standing in front of.

The ankle-length ivory crêpe gown was quite simply sensational, even if she did think so herself. The corset-like bodice skimmed her slender ribcage and scooped low over the creamy slopes of her breasts, and the little off-the-shoulder sleeves added just the right touch of vulnerable charm to a bride who was about to walk down a church aisle towards her bridegroom.

To add a final touch, her full-length veil was secured to her head by a delicate diamond tiara. The overall effect was simplicity itself—her style, her way of doing things.

Her wedding.

Luiz, she told her amethyst eyes via the mirror. You are about to marry Luiz.

But how could Luiz want to marry her, knowing how badly she misjudged him seven years ago?

Luiz never said he *wanted* to marry you, only that he *needed* to marry someone, she reminded those anxious amethyst eyes. And all you've been doing these last few days is pretending that this is a marriage made in heaven. For all you know, Luiz could be planning to cast you aside once he's fulfilled the legal requirements of his father's will.

The perfect formula for revenge? He walks away from you the way you walked away from him seven years ago?

Her stomach wanted to perform somersaults. She wanted to run to the bathroom to be sick in the nearest receptacle. She knew Luiz; she knew what he was capable of. And she suddenly remembered his scorpion. It was sitting there right in front of her now, crawling down the mirror as if ready to strike.

'*Señorita?*' Abril's voice sounded concerned. Could she see that Caroline was about to lose every ounce of courage she possessed in one huge wave of guilt?

'*Señorita…*' A gentle hand covered her forearm, the fingers small and brown against her own pale skin. 'You are shivering,' the little maid murmured worriedly. 'Are you frightened, *señorita?* Please don't be frightened,' she urged her comfortingly. '*El conde* is a good man. Everyone in the valley says so. He reminds them of his grandpa, Don Angeles. He was a good man also. A strong man.'

'I'm okay.' Caroline managed to push out the whisper. 'I just…' She shivered again, as if something scaly had walked over her flesh.

With a blink she attempted to pull herself together, shifting her gaze to her little maid of honour, who was standing beside her in a simple gown of virginal white. She looked enchanting. The perfect foil for a fair-skinned bride, with her black hair and black doe-like eyes and her beautiful olive skin.

'I'm fine,' she assured her for a second time, and even managed a smile.

Reassured, Abril handed Caroline her small bouquet of ivory roses, picked only an hour ago from the garden and woven together by Abril herself.

Her father was pacing restlessly in the great hall when he first saw her. He stopped dead and watched as she came down the stairs towards him. 'Goodness, Caro,' he murmured thickly, and that was all. The rest was written in his eyes.

She was surprised to find that it wasn't Vito who was going to drive her to the village, since Vito rarely left her side. But this time it was a stranger who drove Luiz's black BMW. She discovered why Vito had forsaken her only when she entered the church on her father's arm.

For Vito was standing next to Luiz. A Luiz who filled her heart with tears of relief when she saw him standing there in his black tuxedo, his dark head lowered and with a waiting tension clamped across his broad shoulders that made her want to sob with relief—because surely that tension meant this moment was important to him—that *she* was important?

There was a stir as people began glancing round at her; the stir brought up his head. He turned, looked at her—and that was the last thing she remembered for most of the long service. For no man could look at a woman like that unless he was seeing the only person he wanted to spend the rest of his life with. And his hand when it accepted hers from her father was even trembling slightly.

They made their vows in a hushed atmosphere where no one present seemed to breathe. But when Luiz slid not one but two rings onto her wedding finger she blinked, focused for the first time in ages, and saw a simple but exquisite diamond ring resting next to a finely sculptured gold band. She felt her eyes fill with tears.

For this was no ordinary betrothal ring, it was, in fact, her mother's ring. She glanced up into intensely black eyes. Luiz saw the tears and bent to whisper hoarsely. 'Don't…'

It was almost her complete undoing. Then Padre Domingo spoke. 'If you would place the ring on Don Luiz's finger, we can continue…'

Outside in the sunshine the villagers had gathered to

applaud them. Caroline clung to Luiz as if she had been joined to him in more ways than marriage just now. She blushed and smiled and was aware of Vito standing like a mountain beside the tiny Abril, of her father looking rather sombre and drawn. She was even aware of Tía Consuela, standing cool and erect—seeing the whole thing through to its bleak finish like a martyr to her chosen fate.

But Felipe was nowhere. Neither did he turn up when they sat down at the banquet table, now decked out with white linen and the kind of china and silverware that belonged in a museum.

Her hand had not been allowed to leave Luiz's once since he had formally claimed it. Even now, while they sat at the table, they were having to eat one-handed while their entwined fingers lay on the table between them.

'Thank you for this,' she said, catching sight of her mother's ring shining like a prism on her finger. 'What made you think of it?'

'It should have been *my* mother's ring,' he murmured quietly, looking down at the ring also. 'But she never had one so I went for the next best thing and asked your father for your mother's ring. He brought it back to Marbella with him, ready cleaned and altered to fit your finger...'

'Well, thank you,' she repeated huskily. 'It made everything just perfect.'

'No.' Looking up, Luiz caught her eyes with a look that set her head spinning. 'You are what makes everything perfect,' he said, and kissed her gently.

The gathered assembly began clapping, halting something else that felt absolutely perfect.

By the time they retired outside the sun had set and the garden was ablaze with twinkling lights. Luiz drew her into his arms on the makeshift dance floor as a small set of musicians began playing a waltz. It was the closest they had been except for the clasped hands since they had married, and the knowledge of that sparked between them. Electric, tantalising, utterly mesmerising.

His mouth brushed her cheek, then stayed there. 'You look so beautiful today. Walking towards me in the church, you made my heart ache,' he murmured huskily.

When she tilted her head back so she could look at him, her eyes had stars in them. But she paled a little when she remembered how she had been feeling earlier, and—more importantly—why she had felt like that. 'I've been talking to my father,' she murmured huskily. 'He told me what really happened seven years ago. I—'

The man holding her suddenly changed into an entirely different person. Seeing it happen stopped her words, and she watched his hardened eyes flick around the garden in angry search.

'Luiz—'

'No,' he cut in. 'I am angry with him for breaking his word to me and telling you all of this. I am angry with you for bringing it up tonight of all nights!'

'But you didn't take a single penny from him!' It had to be said! 'You left me asleep in bed each night and went down to play cards with him to stop him gambling with anyone else. You knew how I worried about him—so you took it upon yourself to keep him out of danger! I *owe* so much to you for that, Luiz!'

His face was white, his lips thin, his teeth clenched behind them. 'You owe me nothing,' he rasped.

'I owe you an apology,' she said thickly, beginning to tremble in his arms as the full cup of her guilt came pouring out. 'I was in love with you. I should have known you wouldn't do something so crass as to fleece my own father! But I believed him instead of you—when I *knew* what a liar he was! I don't blame you if you *never* forgive me for that!'

'Drop it, Caroline, before I get angry,' he warned.

But he was already angry. 'You let him win thousands from you—the same thousands of pounds he then told me you had won from him! It's no wonder he was so eager to play you again last week,' she said bitterly. 'He truly believed he was in for another easy killing!'

He flinched as if she'd struck him hard. 'I didn't mean it like that!' she groaned, lifting her hand to lay it in apology against his taut cheek. 'Luiz—'

'No,' he said. 'We will not discuss this. Not now, not ever. Do you understand?' And he took hold of her hand to remove it, then stepped right back, turned and walked away!

It was fortunate that the music had come to a stop just then. Luiz's knack for perfect timing, she supposed.

His uncle Fidel took his place. And after that Caroline didn't see him as she was whirled around in the arms of one relative or another. When she did eventually escape the dance floor to go and look for him it was pitch dark beyond the fairylights, while the castle itself was pooled in lamplight.

She couldn't find him amongst the people in the garden, so she went looking for him inside. She was just crossing the great hall when a waiter came up to her. 'Excuse me, *la condesa.*' He bowed politely. 'But *el conde* send me with a message.'

Oh, the relief. 'Where is he?' she asked urgently.

'He say to meet him at the car, just beyond the boundary wall, if you please.'

At the car? What now? she wondered as she moved out of the house again and down the driveway to where all the cars had been left parked outside the castle's boundary. Was she about to be hijacked again and hauled off somewhere else?

Well, if Luiz thought that was going to be a punishment, then he was in for a surprise, she thought, with a smile that took the anxiety from her lips as excitement for the game began to curl through her.

The car was just a dark bulk among many cars, but she picked it out soon enough because it was the only one with its engine running, and she caught a glimpse of Luiz's dark shape behind the wheel just before she opened the passenger door and slipped inside.

'This is all excitingly clandestine, Luiz,' she teased, busily tucking her dress and veil inside before she could close the door. 'But not really necessary any more.' The door closed, the engine gunned, then shot them forwards. 'See,' she said, turning to wave her ringed hand at him. 'I am…'

Words died, and so did her heart, just before it dropped with a sickening thump to her stomach. As she made a lurch for the door handle the central locking system clicked smoothly into place and Felipe turned a lazy grin on her.

'Droit du seigneur,' he drawled. 'It is tradition…'

CHAPTER ELEVEN

HER first instinct was to begin looking wildly about her, to see if anyone had seen them speed away. But there was no one else on this side of the wall to witness their departure, and as Felipe accelerated up the road towards the village her mind was already hearing the smooth, quiet run of the car's powerful engine.

'This is stupid, Felipe,' she said, trying to keep the need to panic under control. 'I don't see what you aim to gain by it.'

'Satisfaction,' he replied, and turned an abrupt right. Instead of taking the road through the village he began driving at speed between the narrow rows of fruit trees. It was a hair-raising experience, one that had Caroline clinging to the door handle, her body flinching each time a tree branch scraped across the car.

Another abrupt turn and they were skirting the side of the valley on a dusty track she hadn't even known was there. Within what seemed like only seconds they had skirted round the village and were climbing through the terraces. With her heart pumping so fast with adrenaline that her hands were trembling, Caroline reached for the seat belt and fastened it around her.

'You're mad,' she breathed.

Felipe just shrugged, spun the car round one of the acute bends in the narrow road and for a few brief moments brought the whole valley into view. She could see the castle, pooled in light and standing out against its dramatic black backdrop. She could even see the people dancing on the makeshift dance floor, or just standing around in groups, talking. Her heart began to throb, her throat to thicken as she tried to pick out Luiz's distinctive figure—before Felipe was swinging them sharply in the other direction.

By the next abrupt turn the castle was far below them, and it was a shock to realise how high they had already climbed. Another couple of these sharp bends and they would reach the cut, the place where the road became a treacherous pass through the mountains.

She didn't want to go there with Felipe. She didn't want this madman driving her at this mad speed on that awful part of the road where the edge dropped sheer down hundreds of feet into the ravines below.

'Stop the car, Felipe,' she commanded shakily. 'A joke is a joke, and if it makes you feel better, I'll admit it—I'm frightened. But now I would like you to stop so I can get out.'

'And walk back?' he mocked. 'In that dress and in those spindly heels?'

'Yes, if necessary.' She didn't care so long as he let her out of here.

They suddenly swung around yet another sharp bend. Tyres screamed and spun. Caroline hung on for dear life and almost cried out when all she could see in front of her was what looked like a wall of pitch black.

Her heart leapt into her throat and remained there until she realised they weren't about to drive off the end of the mountain but were in actual fact heading straight for it.

'I will have been missed by now.' In sheer desperation she tried another tack. 'Luiz's car will have been missed. He will be coming after us as we speak. Do you think he won't have noticed the car lights as we've climbed? Drop me off now, Felipe and you will have a chance to get away! Keep going and he will catch up to us and kill you, I swear it!'

'Starting to panic a bit, aren't you?' He grinned—and swung them round yet another acute turn in the road.

He did it so carelessly that it actually threw her hard against his shoulder. By the time she had righted herself again she was looking at stars glinting between two towering black walls, and realised in horror that they had now reached the mountain pass.

'*Felipe!*' she cried out shrilly. 'Stop this—stop it!'

But he wasn't going to stop anything. Not the car, not his wild and reckless driving, not the stupidity that was making him behave like this.

'It might be an interesting form of revenge to see Luiz's face when he finds you way down there in the ravine amongst the tangled wreckage of his very own car,' he murmured tauntingly.

Then he laughed as Caroline's face went white.

'But I am not quite that hungry,' he said. 'My original plan suits my idea of revenge a lot better.'

'I don't know w-what you're talking about,' she stammered, through tense teeth that were beginning to chatter.

'Yes, you do,' he argued. 'You are from the right stock to know all about ancient tribal rites. If you just think of me as the rightful owner of what we have just left behind, then the whole experience could be quite exciting—a bride on her wedding night who finds herself sleeping with the lord of the castle, rather than the peasant she married herself to.'

'Luiz is not the peasant around here,' Caroline tossed back. 'And if you think I would let any other man but Luiz touch me, you are sadly mistaken.'

'So you are pretending to be in love with the bastard,' he drawled, eyeing her curiously. 'Why? Does it make it easier to let him touch you when you can close your eyes and see *el conde* instead of a New York thug?'

'I don't need to pretend. I *do* love Luiz,' she declared.

'And will you keep your eyes on the road?' she choked out when he took them swerving round a deep curve in the road with scant regard for what might be on the other side of it.

'Stop worrying,' he said. 'I've been driving this road since I was a teenager. I know every twist and rut in it from here to Cordoba.'

Caroline could only hope and pray that was true! One of her hands had fixed itself to the car door handle; the other was clutching the strap of her seat belt. Felipe took in her taut posture—and recklessly swung the car round yet another curve.

She closed her eyes, unable to watch any more.

'You married him because he offered to pay off your father's debts if you did.' He calmly returned to the other subject. 'It had nothing to do with love.'

'I married Luiz because I can't bear to be without him,' Caroline countered through tightly gritted teeth.

'Liar,' he jeered. 'You were bought! Bought with his money. Bought with his name. Bought by the bastard of Don Carlos Vazquez,' he spat out scathingly. 'And you are prepared to lie in his bed and close your sweet English eyes to his low beginnings, his prostitute *mamá* and the questionable way he earned his millions. Because it is better to close your eyes and pretend he is Don Luiz Vazquez *el conde* rather than the crook that stole from his own family!'

'Luiz didn't steal from you.'

'He stole my title!' he rasped. 'He stole my money and my home! He stole what was my God-given right from birth!'

His fist hit the steering wheel in sheer anger. Caroline flinched, and began praying fervently that they made it round the next bend.

'But I will steal one thing back from him before I leave

here for ever,' Felipe continued thinly. 'I will steal his wedding night,' he vowed. 'And my reward will be in knowing that *he* will know every time he looks at you that it was me who had his beautiful wife first!'

'Luiz and I have been lovers for years!' She laughed at the sheer idiocy of what he was saying. 'You can't steal what he has already had!'

'His wedding night, I can,' he insisted grimly.

This was crazy. *He* was crazy! 'You stole from *him*, Felipe!' Caroline contended shrilly. 'It was not the other way around! You aren't even his half-brother! Your mother is a cheat and a liar, and she tricked her own sister out of Don Carlos's life so that she could take her place! She set up a situation and used it ruthlessly to her own ends. She twisted everything around so that it appeared that Luiz's mother had been sleeping with *her* married lover! Then your mother stepped neatly into the breach left by her sister—having first made sure that Serena had safely disappeared to America with her unborn child!'

'That is a lie!' he barked. The car swerved precariously. Caroline's heart leapt to her throat and stayed there while she clung on for dear life.

Don't argue with him! she told herself frantically. Ignore him and just let him get you down this wretched mountain in one whole piece!

But she couldn't seem to stop the words from coming. They burst forth from the cold dark place she had been keeping them hidden ever since she had read the full horrible truth about the Vazquez family.

'A few months later your mother married Don Carlos— with *her* lover's child already spawned in her belly. That child was you, Felipe,' she persisted, quoting almost verbatim Luiz's father's own wretched words. 'Your real father was Don Carlos's best friend. His *married* friend!' she declared. 'And the moment you opened your eyes on the morning you were born he saw his best friend looking back at him and knew—*knew* he had been tricked and used and betrayed by your mother to secure her own future at the expense of her sister's! Since that same day Luiz has always been his father's heir and you have never been led to think otherwise!'

'How the hell do you know all of this?' Felipe rasped, beginning, for the first time, to sound choked by his own wretched lies.

'From Don Carlos himself,' she said. 'He kept detailed diaries of everything that happened, including the years he spent looking for Serena and his true son *and* the fact that he never kept any of this secret from you.'

'I hated the bastard,' Felipe gritted. 'He spent thirty-four years of my life mourning a son he never knew while I was right there, waiting to be loved if he could only see it!'

'He was wrong to treat you like that,' Caroline acknowledged. 'But two wrongs don't make a right, Felipe! And what you are doing here now is wrong—can't you see that?'

She hoped she was getting through to him. She hoped that she could make him see sense, maybe even turn them around and take her back again!

But he suddenly growled out the kind of curse that said a monster had taken over his soul right now, and with a lurch he threw them round another corner, sending the headlamps scanning out across a terrible nothingness that locked a silent scream into Caroline's throat.

They hit a deep rut in the road. The scream found full voice as Felipe began to struggle with the wheel. He was cursing and cursing, and she was screaming, and the car was careering all over the place.

They were going to die; she was sure of it! They were going to tumble off the edge of the cliff and never be found! Sheer terror made her grab hold of the handbrake. Sheer terror made her yank it on hard. On a squeal of hot rubber the car gave a lurch, then began skidding sideways while she sat there and watched in open-eyed horror as they slid closer and closer to the edge of the ravine.

Then they hit something solid—a rock on the edge? She didn't know, but they began lurching back the way they had come. Then, just when she thought the car was going to stop safely, it hit something else, made a terrible groan and toppled very gently onto its side.

Shocked and dizzyingly disorientated, Caroline sat for a few moments, not actually remembering where she was. Then her head began to hurt, and it all came flooding sickeningly back as she lifted her fingers to gently touch the sore area by her temple, realising that she must have hit her head and been knocked out for a while.

Most definitely frightened of what she might find, she turned to look at Felipe. He was at the very least unconscious, sitting hunched over the steering wheel and slightly below her because of the drunken angle of the car.

Carefully, fearfully almost, she reached out and touched her fingers to his neck. She could feel living warmth there and a shimmer of a pulse. 'Oh, thank God,' she breathed out shakily. She closed her eyes and said it again. 'Thank God.'

What now? Where are we? How badly placed are we regarding the ravine? What do I do?

It was then she realised that the car headlights were still burning. With the greatest of care she tried edging herself forward so she could peer out of the car windscreen. It was a miracle it hadn't shattered, she supposed. Beyond it she could just make out in the lights good solid road and the ravine edge, way over to her right.

They must have keeled over into a ditch near the mountain, she realised. And it was such a relief to know it that she relaxed back in the seat with a sigh and took a few moments to let her heart-rate steady before she attempted to get out.

Felipe had locked the doors, she remembered. But surely there was something somewhere she could pull or push to make them unlock again? With shaky fingers scrambling over pitch black metal and leather, she managed to find something on the door that felt as if it would pull up, tugged it and heard the lock spring free.

Next she had to release the seat belt. Then came the tricky bit, opening the car door and keeping it open while she attempted to scramble out. Her dress snagged on something; she heard it rip and lost her shoes in the struggle. But eventually she landed in a heap on the hard road, then just sat slumped there while she got her breath back.

It was all so quiet, so eerie. She shivered, then suddenly couldn't stop shivering—though she didn't think it was because it was that cold up here.

Shock, she presumed. I'm probably shocked. And who wouldn't be after the ordeal I've just had?

The last thought brought a smile to her lips. The smile made her feel better, and she scrambled up on her bare feet and began to take careful stock of the situation.

Felipe obviously needed help; that was her first consideration. But help was either ten miles or so down the mountain or five miles or so back the way they had come. Not much of a choice, really, she mused helplessly. Staying put seemed to make better sense. Someone should have missed her by now, surely?

Never mind merely *someone*, she then scolded herself. Luiz should have missed her!

It was then that she heard it. It was nothing more at the moment than a very distant growl. But it was a car engine, she recognised, fading in and out as it wound round the mountain.

In sheer relief she simply sank to the ground by the drunken car, folded her now aching head onto her knees and wrapped them in her trembling arms.

It had to be Luiz coming to find her. She didn't even let herself think that it might be anyone else. In fact, that was the most stupid part of Felipe's plan of abduction— to actually believe he could just drive away with her without having Luiz hard on his tail. Had he truly believed he would get as far as seduction? The crazy idiot. If she knew Luiz, the road off the mountain towards Los Aminos was probably blocked by now anyway. Felipe would have been stopped before he'd even got started.

The car was coming closer; she could hear the smooth, neat way it was being driven into the bends and corners— could even pick out the gear changes, the braking, the steady increase in speed then the smooth throttling back.

Yet he arrived round the final bend without warning. Odd that, she thought, as she lifted her head and just watched as he brought the strange car to a standstill perhaps ten feet away.

He didn't get out of the car immediately, either. He just sat there with the headlights trained on her and, she presumed, looked at her looking at him.

Then his door came open. His feet scraped on gravel. And, finally, the full lean length of his body appeared. She couldn't see his face—well, she could have done if she'd looked at it, but for some unaccountable reason she just didn't want to.

He walked towards her. Stopped about two feet away and took a look around their remote surroundings. It was so quiet up here you could hear an ant move a leaf. The sky was a navy blue star-studded cloth and the mountains soared like giants standing on guard.

'Where is he?' was the first question he asked her, and he did it softly, with no inflexion whatsoever.

'Unconscious,' she replied. 'In the car.'

Luiz nodded. That was all, no further questions. He didn't even take a look at Felipe. With a flick of his fingers all the other doors flew open on the car he had been driving. Three men got out; one of them was Vito. They came towards them.

'Deal with him,' he said.

Caroline felt her blood turn cold. 'No, Luiz,' she protested, having visions of poor Felipe being thrown off the edge of the mountain. 'He's hurt. He needs help. I…'

Swooping down, he gathered her into his arms and straightened. He began striding back to the car he had arrived in, and Caroline had a ludicrous vision of herself in all her bridal finery, now ripped and soiled, with her pretty lace veil trailing on the dusty ground behind them.

It was only when they reached the open passenger door that she let herself dare look into Luiz's face. What she saw there brought the first tears to her eyes since the whole ordeal had begun.

'Don't,' she whispered unsteadily. 'Don't shut me out.'

He didn't respond, just placed her in the car then walked round to climb in beside her. The engine fired and then they were moving, continuing down the mountain, because even she could see that it was too narrow here to turn the car around.

As they passed the drunken BMW she saw Vito heaving Felipe out of the car by using sheer brute strength. But he was gentle when he laid him out on the road to check him over. It was faintly reassuring to see that gentleness. Surely men like Vito would not be gentle with a man they were intending to tip over the edge of a mountain, she consoled herself.

A half-mile further on Luiz stopped the car where the road was a little wider and turned them back the way they had come. As they passed by the BMW again, she noticed that another car had pulled up behind it and that Felipe was on his own two feet, leaning weakly against it with his head in his hands, while the rest of the men were wrestling the BMW out of harm's way.

'They won't hurt him, will they?' she asked Luiz anxiously.

'No,' was all he said.

It was reassuring, short though it was. On a small sigh she began to shiver. Luiz instantly flicked the car heater on, but the shivering continued. She knew it was shock, not cold—Luiz probably knew it too.

'Tell me what happened after that fool of a waiter let Felipe convince him he was me so he could lure you out to my car.'

'When you start shouting and swearing, I might tell you,' Caroline countered dully. 'But not before.'

'All right.' His fingers tensed around the steering wheel. 'Let's just deal with your problem with my self-control first,' he clipped. 'You want to see the man dead?' he gritted. 'You want to see his head hanging from the castle wall? You want to see me drive you up this mountain the same way he brought you down it?'

'No.' She answered all of his questions at the same time.

'Then tell me what happened after he got you into my car,' he repeated flatly.

So, quietly and as flatly as him, she told him everything, even the way it had been her fault that the car had ended up where it had. The only bit she missed out was the hellish row she and Felipe had had about Luiz's father.

By then they were driving through the village and everyone was out. It was like a replay of the first time they had come through here. Only then it had been daylight and the expressions had been curious. Now they looked pale and worried and anxious. So she waved and smiled and hoped to goodness they couldn't tell that she was just about ready to cry her eyes out.

It was the same when they got back to the castle. Everyone was huddled around Neptune, waiting with anxious eyes as Luiz brought the car to a stop then grimly told her to stay exactly where she was.

He got out, ignored everyone, and came around the car to lift her out of her seat. Some gasped when they saw the state of her lovely dress and her pale face.

Her father stepped up and took hold of her hand. He looked dreadful. 'I'm fine,' she told him, and another one of those reassuring smiles appeared.

'You don't look it,' he rasped.

'Well, I am—I am,' she repeated firmly.

'Nevertheless, I will come with you…'

It was Luiz's uncle Fidel. He fell into step beside Luiz as they walked into the great hall with her father still clinging to one of her hands. The first person she saw inside was Consuela. She was just standing there by the huge banqueting table, her face so white it could have been marble.

'Put me down, Luiz,' Caroline insisted.

He paused in his step but didn't immediately comply.

'Please,' she pleaded.

Without a word, and with his dark face still that tightly closed book, he set her feet onto the cool stone floor and made sure she was steady before letting go of her. Caroline walked up to Consuela and simply—sadly—just put her arms around the older woman.

Instantly Consuela stiffened so violently that Caroline thought it was with rejection. Then she realised, as that stiff body began to tremble, that Consuela just wasn't used to being held in any way. For all she had deserved punishment for what she had done to her own sister, she had paid for it—with thirty-five years of a barren marriage living in a barren atmosphere where love and affection had been non-existent.

'It's all right,' she whispered, for the other woman's ears only. 'He's fine. Luiz's men are looking after him.'

'He should not have done it,' Consuela said, but some of the tension eased out of her.

'He's bitter,' Caroline explained. 'And he has a right to be bitter, Tía Consuela,' she added gently.

The older woman looked into Caroline's face and sighed knowingly. 'The *padre* gave you the diaries,' she said.

At Caroline's nod, she nodded also. That was all. They understood each other. If Caroline had read the diaries then she knew that if Luiz thought his life had been hard, growing up in the slums of New York, then Felipe's life had been no easier, living here with a father who had despised him and a mother who had locked herself away in an emotional prison of her own making.

Then Consuela said. 'We will leave here tonight.' It was a decision that made Caroline glance at her anxiously.

'You don't have to do that, Consuela,' she told her. 'This is your home. It's Felipe's home. Can't we at least try to live here together?'

'No.' Consuela shook her head. 'In truth, I will be glad to go. It is time. Perhaps…' She heaved out a heavy sigh. 'Perhaps more than time that we began making a life for ourselves.'

In a lot of ways Caroline could only agree with her. Felipe, at least, needed to get away from here. It was the only way he would learn to put aside his bitterness.

The sound of another car arriving alerted Caroline to the return of the others, and her immediate concern turned to getting Luiz away from the hall before his men brought Felipe into it.

Releasing Consuela, she turned back to Luiz. He looked so big and grim that she felt the threat of tears tighten her chest muscles as she walked back to him. She turned impulsively to Luiz's uncle. 'Felipe will need you more than I do, Tío,' she told him.

There was a moment when he looked as if he might argue with her, then with a glance at Luiz he changed his mind and nodded. To her father she gave a hug and a kiss. 'I'll see you tomorrow,' she said quietly.

He too understood. He was being dismissed. Standing back, he watched her slip her hand into Luiz's hand, saw the larger fingers tighten possessively around her more slender ones, and together the two of them moved up the stairs.

Behind them, not a single word was spoken.

Instead of to her old room Luiz took her directly to his. It was the master suite of the castle. Huge. Grand. All heavy baroque furniture and ancient artefacts. The moment the door shut behind them Caroline felt reaction begin to set in.

Her legs felt suddenly weak, sending her over to the nearest chair to drop shakily down into it. Still without a word, Luiz walked across the room and into his bathroom. Ten seconds later she could hear the sound of running water.

Coming back into the room, Luiz found her sitting there, with her face hidden in her hands. A muscle along his jaw clenched, but that was the only reaction he showed as he came to stand over her, then bent to gently remove the tiara and veil from her hair before scooping her into his arms again.

'Oh, very macho,' she said, trying to lighten the leaden atmosphere.

He didn't respond to it. Grim-eyed, tight-lipped, he carried her into the bathroom, then set her down on her feet and turned her back to him so he could begin untying the silk lacing that was holding the bodice of her wedding dress together.

'If you don't start talking to me, I'll throw a tantrum,' she informed him quite casually. The lacing gave, the bodice slipped, sending her hand up to catch it before it revealed her breasts.

'Luiz!' she snapped, spinning round to face him.

His eyes caught fire. The fury he had been keeping severely banked down now came bursting out through those hot, bright, burning black eyes to completely envelop her at the very moment his arms did the same. And he was lifting her off her feet, so he could bring her startled mouth on a level with his own mouth.

It was a kiss like no other. It didn't just burn, it consumed. Her arms went up, slender forearms using his wide shoulders as a brace to keep that fierce mouth-to-mouth contact. She didn't care now that the dress was slipping, that her breasts were bursting free to press against him. She didn't care that the knock on her head hurt or that her bare feet were stinging or that he was holding her so tightly that he was in danger of crushing her ribs.

But she cared that she could feel him trembling, that even his mouth, where it fused with hers, was struggling to maintain some control over what was finally pouring out of him.

'I love you,' she murmured through a fevered grab at air. 'I love you so much, and I hate it when you hide away from me!'

'It's either hide or devour you,' he muttered. And he meant it, fantastic though the statement might seem. He meant every harsh, rasping word of it.

He claimed her mouth again, putting a stop to any more talking, because at this moment *doing* was more important. Caroline wound her thighs around his hips, long skirts rustling as she locked her bare feet together at his back. Her fingers were in his hair, her thumbs urgently caressing the tension along his rigid jaw.

On a driven groan he turned back to the bedroom.

'The bath,' she reminded him.

He issued a hoarse curse against her lips and changed direction without breaking the heated contact of their mouths until he absolutely had to. But he refused to let go of her as he bent to turn off the taps. And when he straightened again she was waiting for him, flushed-cheeked, misty-eyed, the two creamy slopes of her breasts heaving against the boned bodice now resting beneath them.

His dark lashes floated downward as he looked her over. She looked delectably pagan, uninhibitedly wanton. A bride ready for the taking by her passionate Spanish husband.

Looking upwards again, he studied her soft, full, inviting mouth, pressed another claiming kiss to it, then let his eyes clash with hers. He was moving again. Back into the bedroom, across the priceless Indian carpet covering its solid oak floor, to the bed, which looked like an island you could quite easily live upon without needing to leave for a long, long time.

Caroline certainly didn't want to leave it. She wanted to take off her clothes and crawl beneath its snowy white linen topped by the really decadent blood-red and dark gold brocade coverlet, to survive on hot kisses and rich dark flesh and the passions of a man who was incomparable.

Allowing her feet to slide to the floor, Luiz took a step back, then began undressing. She didn't move, didn't attempt to take her own dress off. That was for him to do. It was his duty to unwrap his bride himself.

But her breasts pouted provocatively at him all the while he was undressing, and the moist pink tip of her tongue kept snaking slowly around her kiss-swollen lips in needy anticipation.

'You,' he murmured when he eventually reached for her, 'ought to be locked up.'

She just smiled a very wicked smile and lifted up her arms to receive him. The dress slipped lower. On a growl, Luiz helped it the rest of the way, and had seen off everything else she was wearing before he straightened up again.

Outside, beyond the four-foot thick walls, the party went on without them. Somewhere else, in another wing of the castle, two people were packing.

'Luiz...' Caroline murmured tentatively a long time later, when they lay curled up against each other. 'Can we talk?' she begged. 'About Felipe?'

It ruined the moment. His body went taut, his jawline clenched. 'Only if we have to do,' he said tightly—which didn't offer much encouragement.

Caroline pushed on anyway. 'I know you have every right to hate him and his mother,' she allowed. 'And I know he behaved appallingly tonight. But...' Leaning up a little, she looked anxiously into his ice-cold eyes. 'It isn't his fault his mother told wicked lies about your mother, or that she tricked and deceived your father! Just as it isn't Felipe's fault that you had the childhood you did. He *is* your cousin—and it's been tough for him too, you know!' she insisted at Luiz's lowering frown. 'Growing up in your shadow, with a mother who could barely live with herself for what she'd done to her own sister and a so-called father who rejected him at birth and hated his mother for putting him in your place. It's all so very tragic and sad,' she said. 'And I know your father had a right to feel bitter as he wrote it. He broke his own heart by believing your aunt instead of your mother, and spent the rest of his life pun-

ishing himself for it. But Felipe should not have been made
to pay. It—'

'What do you mean—how my father *wrote* it?' Luiz put
in.

'Oh!' she gasped in horror when she realised what she'd
said. Then a long sigh whispered from her, and with a
twisted smile that acknowledged it was probably for the
best she lifted sombre eyes to his darkly glowering ones.
'How he wrote it in his diaries,' she said gently.

Softly and quietly she began telling him everything she
had learned.

When eventually Luiz asked her where the diaries were,
she told him, and without another word he got out of bed,
pulled on a robe and went to get them.

A long time later, on his way back from Caroline's bedroom, he saw Felipe and his mother just about to leave the
castle. Standing there on the upper gallery, he viewed their
sober features and felt something pick at the stone it was
reputed he had for a heart.

'Felipe,' he said. The other man's dark head came up
and he spun on his heel to glance upwards. 'We need to
talk,' he murmured quietly.

Instantly Luiz could see the battle taking place behind
the defensive aggression pasted onto his handsome features. Then, on a sigh, Felipe gave a curt nod of his head.
'One day,' he replied. Maybe he, like Luiz, had had
enough of the lies and bitterness and betrayal. 'One day…'
he repeated, and turned away again.

Luiz watched gravely as his aunt lifted her pale face up
to him. 'I'm sorry,' was all she said, but Luiz understood.
After all, what else could she add that could take away
what had gone before?

When he went back into his bedroom, he found his bride
no longer there. Tossing the diaries onto the tumbled bed,
he went looking for her and found her soaking in a bath

of steaming bubbles. It took him ten seconds to join her, uncaringly sloshing water over the rim onto the tiled floor as he climbed in behind her then sat down and drew her back against him.

'I've just seen Felipe and my aunt leaving,' he told her levelly.

Caroline nodded. 'She told me they would leave tonight.'

'I didn't want them to do that.' He sighed. 'I never meant to actually throw them out of here. Family is family…'

'Warts and all?' She nodded, 'I know,' she said referring to her own feckless father. Picking up one of his hands, she began kissing his fingers. 'Did you read the diaries?' she asked.

'Mmm.' His other hand slid up her slippery flesh until it found and closed around one of her breasts. 'I knew some of it,' he confessed. 'First from my mother and then from my father, when we did eventually attempt to communicate.'

'Seven years ago,' Catherine sighed out bleakly, thinking of all those years they'd lost.

'Seven years ago,' he agreed. 'When I made the trip to Spain to arrogantly lay claim to my roots and met the woman who claimed me instead.'

'I'm sorry,' she said, thinking about how ruthlessly her father had used one of them against the other.

'I told your father that I was in love with you and wanted to marry you,' he informed her heavily. 'He politely informed me where I could go. I wasn't good enough for his daughter, he said. At the time I agreed with him.' He grimaced. 'Still do, actually.'

'But you'll have me anyway,' Caroline added smilingly. 'There really isn't much to pick between you, my father and poor Felipe,' she said. 'You're all too self-motivated to be true.'

'Felipe was right when he compared my father's life with the life of the ancestor who built this castle,' Luiz remarked gruffly. 'It was history repeating itself.'

Twisting in the water until she was facing him, Caroline murmured softly, 'Not this time, though. This time the Conde got his woman. That makes for a happy ending.'

Eyes like dark chasms filled with satisfaction. 'A very happy ending,' Luiz agreed huskily, and began to kiss her...

New York Times bestselling author **Anne Mather** has written since she was seven, but it was only when her first child was born that she fulfilled her dream of becoming a writer. Her first book, CAROLINE, appeared in 1966. It met with immediate success and, since then, Anne has written more than 140 novels, reaching a readership which spans the world. Born and raised in the north of England, Anne still makes her home there with her husband, two children and, now, grandchildren. Asked if she finds writing a lonely occupation, she replies that her characters always keep her company. In fact, she is so busy sorting out their lives that she often doesn't have time for her own! An avid reader herself, she devours everything from sagas and romances to mainstream fiction and suspense. Anne has also written a number of mainstream novels, most recently DANGEROUS TEMPTATION, published by MIRA® Books.

**Look out for Anne Mather's latest sexy
and compelling title:
IN THE ITALIAN'S BED
Coming in July 2004, in Modern Romance™!**

THE MILLIONAIRE'S VIRGIN

by

Anne Mather

CHAPTER ONE

THE man sitting at the table wasn't Martin Price.

Paige's stomach hollowed and she glanced blankly at the waiter who was escorting her across the restaurant. There'd been some mistake. Martin's shoulders weren't as broad, his skin wasn't as dark, and his fair curls bore no resemblance to the thick black hair that erupted in rough splendour over the rim of white collar that was visible above his charcoal tailoring.

She was about to make her protest when the man rose to his feet and turned to face her. 'Ah, Paige,' he said, as her legs threatened to slip out from under her. 'How good of you to come.'

Paige didn't know what to do; what to say. There had been a mistake. She saw that now. And she'd made it. She'd believed she was coming here to meet her ex-fiancé, but it was obvious that that had only been a ploy on someone's part to get her here. She turned frantically to the waiter but he was already walking away, and although she badly wanted to follow him people were watching them and she was too much of a coward to make a scene.

'Won't you sit down?' he said, indicating the chair opposite. His lips parted in a thin smile. 'It's good to see you again.'

Paige hesitated. 'I don't understand.'

'You will.' His dark eyes narrowed between lashes that had always been absurdly long for a man. 'If you'll give me a few minutes of your time.'

'Why should I?' Paige was panicking now, but she couldn't help it.

'Oh, I think you owe me considerably more than that,'

5

he remarked, his expression hardening. 'Please—' It was hardly a request. 'Sit down.'

Paige drew in a breath but unless she wanted to embarrass herself she didn't have a lot of choice. Still, it was with evident reluctance that she subsided into the chair across the table, wrapping her hands about the purse in her lap as if it provided a lifeline.

'Good.' Having succeeded in his objective, he resumed his seat just as the wine waiter arrived at his elbow. 'Now, what will you have to drink?'

He was drinking wine, she noticed. Red wine that reflected the light from the chandeliers above their heads and gave off a ruby brilliance. She was tempted to join him; she loved wine and he knew it, but she had no intention of giving him any advantage and in her present condition it would probably go straight to her head.

'Um—just mineral water, please,' she murmured, after a moment, addressing herself to the waiter, and he gave her a polite little bow before going to attend to her order.

'Mineral water?' His tone was mocking now but Paige refused to be intimidated.

'What do you want, Nikolas?' she asked, avoiding his sardonic gaze. She didn't want to look into his eyes again, didn't want to feel the sudden rush of sexual awareness she'd felt when she'd first realised who he was. 'Where's Martin?'

'He's not coming.' He said the words without apology. 'Ah, here's your—water.'

Paige gazed at him now, ignoring the waiter completely. 'What do you mean, he's not coming?' she demanded. 'I think you'd better tell me what's going on.'

'Do you?' His tone was ironic. 'I gather he didn't explain the situation when he spoke to you.'

'No.'

Paige swallowed. She refused to admit that it was Martin's secretary who had contacted her and arranged this meeting. She'd been so relieved to hear from him again, she hadn't questioned why, after breaking their engagement, he'd suddenly decided to invite her to lunch at one of London's most exclusive restaurants. The fact that it used to be their favourite restaurant had persuaded her that Martin had had second thoughts and wanted to start seeing her again.

What a fool she'd been.

'So you have no idea why I invited you here?'

'Haven't I just said so?' Paige was abrupt, but she couldn't help it. This was just another occasion when nothing turned out as she'd expected.

'Tell me,' murmured Nikolas after a moment, his low, attractive voice barely exhibiting any trace of an accent, 'how long were you and Price—what shall I say?—' he frowned '—together?'

Paige stiffened. 'What business is that of yours?'

'Humour me.'

'Why should I?'

'Well…' He paused. 'If we are to have any kind of a working relationship—'

'A *what*!'

She interrupted him then, getting half out of her chair before his hand on her forearm pressed her down again into her seat. He did it so effortlessly, she thought, rubbing her arm when he released her, glaring at him with resentful eyes. All trace of sexual awareness was swamped now by the very real feelings of outrage that were gripping her.

'Calm down,' he said mildly. 'You are looking for a job, aren't you?' He regarded her dispassionately. 'I may have one to offer.'

'No, thanks.'

Paige looked away from his dark-skinned face, wondering how Martin could have done this to her. She'd thought he'd loved her. But she'd been wrong about that, too. Wrong about everything.

'Don't be too hasty,' Nikolas murmured now. He pushed the glass of water towards her. 'Drink. You'll feel better after some refreshment.'

'I don't want anything.' Paige realised she was behaving like a petulant child, but events were moving too fast for her to keep any kind of control over her emotions. She straightened her spine. 'I'd just like to know how Martin knew that you—that you and I—had—had—'

'Been lovers?' Nikolas suggested softly, and despite herself her face suffused with colour.

'Known one another,' she amended tersely. 'We were never lovers.'

'No.' He conceded the point with a certain amount of regret. 'Or you would not have done what you did, *ohi*?'

'I did nothing,' she insisted. 'Nothing wrong, that is.' Then, realising she was getting into deep waters, she added, 'How did Martin know we knew one another?'

'He didn't.' Nikolas was careless. 'As far as your—fiancé is concerned, we had never met before today.'

'He's not my fiancé.' Paige could feel her jaw quivering and hurriedly pressed her lips together to control it. 'I suppose you thought it was amusing, deceiving him like that?'

'I deceived no one.' His harsh features mirrored a momentary displeasure. 'Your Martin is not the most perceptive of men.'

'He's not my Martin.'

'No.' An air of satisfaction surrounded him at this admission. 'He told me that also.'

'He told you—' Paige's lips parted in dismay. 'He discussed our relationship with you.'

'Let us say that when your name entered the conversation I—persuaded him to confide in me,' declared Nikolas smugly. 'I can be very persuasive, as I'm sure you remember.'

Paige shook her head, refusing to explore that particular time bomb. 'What did he tell you? How do you know him?'

'Ah.' Nikolas relaxed back in his chair and Paige was reminded of a sleek predator that, having successfully subdued its prey, was now prepared to play with it. 'I happened to be looking for a new financial advisor and the firm of Seton Ross appeared to have an excellent reputation.'

'So you met quite by chance?'

'How else?'

She shook her head. 'I don't believe you.'

'Why not?' He adopted an air of injured innocence.

'Because if Nikolas Petronides approached a firm like Seton Ross he wouldn't be put off with one of the minor associates. Either Neville Ross or Andrew Dawes would have dealt with you personally.'

'Indeed.' Nikolas smiled. 'It pleases me that you would think I warrant a more expert evaluation than your—friend was able to offer. It proves that you have not been entirely deceived by his rather obvious charms. Be thankful he broke the engagement, *aghapita*. You can do much better, I am sure.'

Paige fumed. 'Don't patronise me.'

'Was I doing that?' Nikolas moved his silk-clad shoulders in a dismissive gesture. 'I am sorry.'

She was sure he was nothing of the kind, but she waited impatiently for him to go on. When he didn't, she said shortly, 'I'd still like to know how you came to discuss my—situation.'

'Yes…' He was evidently in no hurry to satisfy her curiosity. 'Well, let me see, how did the conversation go? I think we were discussing the recent fall in the stock market and how even recognised firms of stockbrokers were not immune from collapse. Naturally, Tennants was mentioned—'

'Naturally!'

'It was, after all, one of the most disastrous falls of the decade, was it not? And your father's untimely death was a real tragedy.' There was nothing but compassion in his face as he continued, 'Please: I cannot tell you how sorry I am; how much sympathy I feel for you and your sister.'

'We don't need your sympathy,' retorted Paige tightly, but even though it was months since her father had suffered the massive stroke that had ended his life she still felt totally bereft.

'*Etsi ki alios*, it is sincere,' Nikolas assured her. 'Although I had no love for the man, I would not wish what happened to him on my worst enemy.'

Paige regarded him coldly. 'So you decided to offer me a job,' she said scornfully. 'How kind!'

'Do not be bitter, Paige.' Nikolas sighed. 'It does not become you. Just because your fiancé has deserted you, do not—'

'How dare you?'

Once again, Paige attempted to push her chair away from the table, but this time the waiter thwarted her. Misunderstanding, he assumed she was trying to pull her chair closer to the table, and he assisted her in doing just that before presenting her with the menu.

'I'll be back in a few minutes to take your order,' he said politely, and Paige was obliged to stay where she was, at least until he had returned to his station.

But as soon as he'd moved away she fixed Nikolas with a furious stare. 'How dare you?' she demanded again. 'How dare you discuss my private life with—with—?'

'With the man you'd hoped to share your life with?' suggested her companion drily. 'Perhaps you should be asking him why he's telling all and sundry that the Tennant sisters are virtually penniless.'

'Oh, I intend to.'

'What?' Nikolas's brows rose sardonically. 'And give him the satisfaction of knowing how much he's hurt you? Think again, Paige. As I said before, he's not worth it.'

'And you are?' She was contemptuous.

'Let us say, I have reason to enjoy your humiliation. He does not.'

Paige glanced about her. 'And that's what this is all about? Humiliation?'

'No.'

'Oh, please…' She gazed at him disbelievingly. 'At least have the decency to tell me the truth.'

'I will. If you'll let me.' He shrugged. 'Have lunch with me. That is why you came, after all.'

'To have lunch with Martin,' she corrected him tersely, and then, remembering what her ex-fiancé had done, she realised how pathetic that sounded. She hesitated. 'Why should I?'

'Because you're here; because you're curious.' His thin lips twitched. 'Let me tell you why I let Price arrange this meeting.'

Paige took a considering breath but once again the waiter made the decision for her. Returning to take their order, he regarded them both with polite, enquiring eyes, and Nikolas turned somewhat impatiently to his own menu.

'Shall I order for us both?' he enquired, and because Paige was too bemused to argue with him she gave an unwilling nod. 'We'll have the avocado mousse and the grilled salmon,' he told the waiter smoothly. 'It is fresh salmon, not farmed?' After gaining the waiter's reassurance, he said, 'Thank you.'

Paige had forgotten how efficient Nikolas was in any situation. How easily he could make a decision and act on it without resorting to discussion. He could decide what he was going to eat in less time than it had taken Martin to open a menu, and he had an effortless air of command that would persuade even the hardiest *maître d'* to do his bidding.

The waiter collected the menus and went away and they were alone again. But not for long. The wine waiter returned with his list, but this time Nikolas was ready for him. 'A bottle of the '97 Chardonnay,' he said, waving the list away. 'That's all.'

Paige breathed deeply, trying desperately to achieve even a little of his composure, but it was almost impossible. Despite her frustration at being put in such a position, she couldn't deny a certain exhilaration at this unexpected turn of events. It was a long time since anything had inspired her to the kind of emotional upheaval Nikolas had so effortlessly created. And, while she still resented the way both he and Martin had treated her, her eyes were continually drawn to the lean brown fingers that played with the stem of his glass and the coarse black hair that dusted his wrists below the pristine cuffs of his shirt.

Nikolas was such a masculine animal, she thought, a sense of suffocation at his nearness almost overwhelming her. The only man she'd ever known who could reduce her to trembling supplication with just a single look. Or, at least, he had when she was younger, she corrected herself fiercely. She was much older—much wiser—now.

'So,' he said, startling her out of her reverie, 'you would like to know about the job, *ne*?'

'If I must,' she answered tautly. 'If there really is a job.'

'You think I would be here otherwise?'

Paige realised that to admit that that was what she had been thinking was conceited, and amended her response. 'Perhaps.'

'First of all, am I right in assuming that you are looking for employment?' he asked softly, and two red flags of colour burned in her pale cheeks.

'If Martin said it, then it must be true,' she replied frostily, resenting the question. 'I suppose he also told you I have no qualifications to speak of.'

'You have discussed your problems with him?' Nikolas frowned.

'No.' Paige was indignant. 'Sophie did. She's desperate for me to get a job so we can find somewhere else to live.'

'Ah, Sophie.' He nodded. 'Your sister. Regrettably, we were never introduced.'

Paige shrugged. 'She was at school when—when—'

'When your father was attempting to blind me with his elder daughter's beauty?' suggested Nikolas ironically. 'Yes, I know. How old is she now?'

'Sixteen.' Paige pursed her lips. And then, because she couldn't let him get away with defaming her father's memory, she added, 'And Daddy only introduced us. It wasn't his fault that we—that you betrayed his trust.'

Nikolas's lips twisted. 'You do not really believe that.'

'Why not? And the Murchison deal appeared to be an attractive proposition. He was trying to do you a favour by offering you the chance to invest…'

'In something that folded only a few months later,' remarked her companion bleakly. 'At which time, I'd have lost a considerable amount of money.'

You could afford it, thought Paige defiantly, but she kept that opinion to herself. 'It might have succeeded if you'd been prepared to back it,' she said instead, only to meet a blank wall of contempt.

'Be honest,' said Nikolas harshly. '*Theos*, the shipping line was already losing money and all your father really wanted was someone else to share the burden of his mistake. Why else do you think he destroyed our relationship? As soon as he realised he was wasting his time with me, he moved on to the next—what is that word you use?—sucker? Yes, sucker.'

'That's not true.'

'Of course it's true.'

'No—'

'Yes—'

'Avocado mousse, madam.'

The arrival of the meal put an end to any further argument, and although Paige had the feeling she was betraying her father's memory by even being here now she refused to let Nikolas Petronides have the last word. All the same, meeting his dark eyes across the table, eyes that could turn from black velvet to burnished agate in a twinkling, she suspected she was playing a dangerous game.

'Perhaps we should discuss why I had Price invite you here,' he declared, after the waiter had departed again. 'I'm sure you understand why I prevailed upon him to offer the invitation. I was fairly sure that were I to contact you you would not submit.'

'Submit?' Paige pushed the delicate mousse around her plate. 'That's a typically Petronides word to use, isn't it? But you're right. I wouldn't have come.'

'I thought not.' He paused. 'That was why I suggested that as Price was a friend of yours he should arrange this meeting.'

Paige absorbed this as the wine waiter poured some of the deliciously flavoured Chardonnay into her glass. But when they were alone again she exclaimed, 'And Martin had no idea that—that we knew one another?'

'I'm afraid not.' Nikolas looked at her over the rim of his own glass. 'Poor Paige. The men in your life do seem perfectly willing to throw you to the—wolves, do they not?'

Paige refused to let him provoke her. 'Is that a warning, Kirie Petronides?' she asked mockingly, and had the satisfaction of seeing his eyes darken accordingly.

But, 'Maybe,' was all he said, and it was Paige who felt every nerve in her body tingle at the veiled menace in his voice.

They didn't speak again until the grilled salmon had been served and then it was Paige who felt compelled to break the uneasy silence that had fallen. 'I—I would have expected Yanis to handle any employee recruitment,' she murmured, aware that she had barely touched the mousse and was only making a paltry effort with the salmon. A morsel caught in her dry throat and she was forced to cough and resort to her wine before continuing, 'He is still with you, I assume?'

Nikolas was not deceived by her attempt at casual conversation. 'Yanis is still my assistant, *ne*,' he conceded evenly. 'But this is a rather—delicate affair.'

'Why?' Despite herself, Paige was puzzled. She couldn't believe it was anything to do with her.

'Because it is a personal matter,' he replied, taking another mouthful of his wine. Then, because she was still looking at him enquiringly, he went on, 'The job I have in mind concerns my ward. In such circumstances, it is not—suitable—to leave the decision in Yanis's hands.'

Paige gasped. 'Your ward?' She looked stunned. 'I didn't know you had a ward.'

'That is because I did not have a ward when we—knew one another,' he told her. 'Ariadne's father was a close friend, and when he and his wife were killed three years ago I discovered they had appointed me their daughter's guardian. She has no other close relatives, you understand? *Oriste*, I have a ward.'

'I see.' Paige moved her shoulders uncertainly. 'That's quite a responsibility. How old is she?'

'Ariadne is seventeen years of age. Not too much of a responsibility, as you can see.'

'Oh.' Paige was surprised. 'Then why—?'

'I am looking for a young woman of good family to—how shall I put it?—keep her company for the summer. And to share with her all those womanly confidences she can no longer share with her mother.'

'And you thought that I—?'

'In the absence of any other offers, yes,' he essayed mildly. 'Why not?'

Paige gasped. 'I couldn't work for you.'

'Do not be too hasty, *aghapita*.' He speared her with a penetrating look. 'The position carries a generous salary with all expenses found, and the hours would not be too arduous.'

'I'm not for sale, Nikolas.'

'No, but you are short of funds, are you not? And you said yourself that your sister is eager for you to find alternative accommodation, *ne*?'

Paige put down her fork. 'This is a pointless conversation. I don't speak Greek.'

'Ariadne understands English. She is still at school, of course. But she has been educated to a very high standard.'

'Then she's probably perfectly capable of taking care of herself,' said Paige, thinking of her own sister. Sophie would die if anyone suggested she needed a chaperon. 'Besides, as you've just mentioned, I have a sister, who— who—' *Had been quite a handful since Paige had had to remove her from the expensive boarding school she'd been attending.* 'Who I couldn't possibly leave on her own.'

Or with Aunt Ingrid, she appended ruefully. Ever since their father died, they'd been staying with their mother's sister in her 'bijou' cottage, as she described it, in Islington. And it was only because Paige was there to keep the peace between them that Sophie and her aunt remained on speaking terms...

'Then bring her with you,' said Nikolas carelessly. 'She will be on holiday, too, will she not? And I would prefer Ariadne to stay at my house on Skiapolis for the summer.' He shrugged. 'There is plenty of room, as you know, and your sister may befriend Ariadne. They are of a similar age.'

They were, but Paige could imagine Sophie's reaction were she to drop this particular bombshell in her lap. Although her sister resented the circumstances in which they were now being forced to live, blaming their father for not making adequate provision for them during his lifetime, she would find the idea of leaving London for some unsophisticated island in the Aegean even more unacceptable. Besides, she'd just settled down at the local comprehensive; she'd made friends; and although Paige wasn't altogether enthusiastic about the crowd Sophie was mixing with she had no desire to uproot her again.

'I don't think so,' she said now, bestowing a slightly warmer smile on the waiter when he came to remove her barely touched plate. 'No, it was fine,' she assured him when he expressed his concern. Then, looking at Nikolas again, she said, 'I'm afraid you've wasted your time.'

'No time is ever wasted,' he responded, his brooding expression giving the lie to his words. 'At least think about it, Paige. I shall be in London for a few more days and you can always contact me via this number.' He drew out a card and scrawled some figures on the back before pushing it across the table towards her. 'Take it.'

Somewhat against her better judgement, Paige reached for the card, but as she did so Nikolas covered her hand with his, successfully imprisoning her fingers within his cool grasp. And, although she made a futile attempt to free herself, she knew she had no real chance of competing with his strength.

'Think about it. Please,' he begged softly, and Paige was overwhelmed by the sensual appeal in his voice.

Dear God, she thought, dragging her eyes away from his to gaze unsteadily at the powerful fist encasing hers. A fiery warmth was spreading up her arm and invading every quivering pore of her slender frame, and no matter how she tried to rationalise her reaction she knew her body hadn't forgotten anything about this man. It remembered; her *skin* remembered; and that was something she had never expected.

Eventually, he was obliged to let her draw her hand away and she cradled it in her lap, as if it had been abused. That was what it felt like, she thought shakily, the vibration his touch had evoked still rippling through her veins. She just prayed he wasn't aware of her upheaval.

Somehow she got through the next few minutes. Although she didn't want it, she agreed to coffee in lieu of a pudding, and endeavoured to come to terms with the fact that she had more than one reason for refusing his offer. Even if it was the only offer that came her way, she couldn't work for him. Apart from anything else, she didn't want to be hurt again, and Nikolas Petronides would have no qualms about recovering what he saw as his pound of flesh...

CHAPTER TWO

PAIGE caught the Underground back to Islington. At this time of the afternoon, the trains weren't busy, and after finding herself a seat she reflected how quickly she'd adapted to using the Tube instead of taking taxis everywhere.

All the same, it had been raining when she'd left the restaurant, and she'd had to resist Nikolas's offer to get a taxi for her. Although it was June, the weather was still unseasonably cold, and the pretty cream Chanel suit she'd worn to impress Martin was now dotted with damp patches.

She just hoped it didn't pick up any dirt on the way home. She and Sophie were having to conserve what clothes they had, and it had been quite a drain on their meagre resources outfitting her sister with clothes for her new school.

She sighed. If only their father were still alive, she thought wistfully, but Parker Tennant had died as he'd lived: without making any provision for the future. He'd left his daughters with a mountain of debt besides, and the unhappy task of having to salvage what little they could from his possessions. Not that there had been much. The beautiful home they'd had in Surrey had been mortgaged twice over, and even their mother's jewels had had to be sold to satisfy their creditors.

Paige thought it was just as well their mother hadn't lived to see it. Annabel Tennant had died of an obscure form of cancer when Paige was seventeen and Sophie only ten, and she'd sometimes wondered whether that was when her father had started taking such enormous risks with his clients' money. It was as if his wife's death had persuaded him that there was no point in planning for a future that might never happen, and there was no doubt that losing her mother had affected him badly.

It was why Paige had left school without finishing her education; why she'd appointed herself his protector. She'd been there when he needed her, taking care of him when he didn't, and somehow getting him through those first awful months after Annabel died.

It had taken a toll on her, too, but she'd never considered herself. She'd been happy making him happy, and until she'd been introduced to Nikolas Petronides she'd cared little for the fact that the only men she'd dated had been men her father had had dealings with.

Of course, he'd approved of Nikolas, too—at least to begin with. It was only when he'd discovered that the Greek had had no intention of investing money with him that he'd turned against him. And Paige had had no doubts where her loyalties lay…

Which was why there was no way she could accept Nikolas's offer now. Apart from the fact that they had once known one another too well, she wanted nothing from him. In his own way, he was like Martin: he was using her situation to humiliate her, and however attractive the prospect of a summer in Greece might be—not to mention the generous salary he'd tried to bribe her with—she needed a real job with someone who wasn't out for revenge.

But she didn't want to think about that now. It was four years since her relationship with Nikolas had foundered and since then she'd insisted on taking charge of her own life. She sighed. Not that she'd been any more successful, she conceded wryly. Her association with Martin Price had hardly been a success. But then, she hadn't been aware that the handsome young accountant had been more interested in furthering his own career, and in paying court to Parker Tennant's daughter he had envisaged a partnership in her father's investment brokerage firm as his reward. Of course, when Parker Tennant died in such inauspicious circumstances, he'd quickly amended his plans. In a very short time, Paige had found her engagement had only been as secure as her father's bank balance, and although Martin had made some excuse about finding someone else she'd known exactly what he really meant.

She stared dully out of the window. That was why she'd felt so mortified when she'd learned that Martin had arranged for her to see Nikolas Petronides. It was galling to think that his prime concern was to put some distance between them, and she half wished she could tell him exactly what she and Nikolas had once been to one another. Would he be jealous? She doubted it. Of Nikolas's wealth, perhaps, but nothing else.

The train pulled into her station and, leaving her seat, she discovered to her relief that it had stopped raining. Which was just as well, as she had a ten-minute walk to Claremont Avenue, and no umbrella.

Aunt Ingrid's cottage was about halfway down the avenue, and Paige approached the house with some relief. It had been quite a day, one way and another, and she was looking forward to changing into shorts and a T-shirt and spending some time weeding her aunt's pocket-sized garden. It was what she needed, she thought: mindless physical exercise, with nothing more momentous to think about than what the soil was doing to her nails.

She heard her aunt's and her sister's voices before she'd even opened the front gate. The windows of the cottage were open and their raised tones rang with unpleasantly familiar resonance on the still air. Several of her aunt's neighbours were taking advantage of the break in the weather to catch up on outdoor jobs, and they could hear them, too, and Paige offered the elderly couple next door an apologetic smile as she hurried up the path.

What now? she wondered wearily. She glanced at her

watch. It was barely three o'clock. Sophie shouldn't even be home from school yet. For heaven's sake, didn't she have enough to worry about as it was?

'You're a selfish, stupid girl,' Aunt Ingrid was saying angrily as Paige let herself into the house.

'And you're a harried old bag,' retorted Sophie, before there was the ominous sound of flesh meeting flesh. There was a howl from her sister before she apparently responded in kind, and Paige slammed the door and charged across the tiny hall and into the over-furnished parlour just as her aunt was collapsing into a Regency-striped love-seat, her hand pressed disbelievingly to her cheek.

'For goodness' sake!' Paige stared at them incredulously. 'What on earth is going on? I could hear you when I turned into the avenue.'

That was an exaggeration, but they were not to know that, and it had the effect of bringing a groan of anguish from her aunt. The thought that someone else might have been a party to her disgrace was too much, and Paige, who had been hoping to shame her sister, gave a resigned sigh.

Of course, Sophie was unlikely to care what anyone else thought, and as if to prove this she would have pushed past her sister and left the room if Paige hadn't grabbed her arm. 'Where do you think you're going?' she demanded. 'I asked what was going on here. You might as well tell me. I'm going to find out anyway. Have you been excluded from school? What?'

'Ask her.' Sophie's face was mutinous. She gave her aunt a baleful look. 'She's the one who's been poking around in my things.'

Paige didn't make the mistake of letting go of her arm. 'I asked you,' she reminded her shortly, although her heart sank at the thought that Sophie might have some justification for her complaint. Casting a silent appeal in the older woman's direction, she added, 'This is Aunt Ingrid's house, not yours.'

'Ask her what she's got hidden in her underwear drawer.'

Aunt Ingrid's voice was frail and unsteady, and for a moment Paige wanted to smile. Dear God, what had Sophie been hiding? See-through bras; sexy knickers; what? Then, the reluctant admission that Ingrid shouldn't have been looking through Sophie's belongings anyway wiped the embryo grin of amusement off her face.

'Yeah, how about that?' Sophie broke in before she could respond. 'The old bat's been prying into my drawers, in more ways than one. Nosy old bitch! I told you that we had no privacy here—'

'She's a drug addict, Paige.' The older woman's voice trembled now. 'An addict, in my house. I never thought I'd live to see the day that my own sister's child—'

'What is Aunt Ingrid talking about?' Despite the fact that the old lady had been known to exaggerate at times, her words had struck a chill into Paige's bones. 'Why should she say you're a drug addict?'

'She's lying—'

'No, I'm not.'

'She is,' insisted Sophie scornfully. 'She doesn't know what she's talking about.' She gave a short laugh. 'I'm not an addict. For God's sake, I doubt if she'd know one if she saw one.'

'I know what marijuana smells like,' retorted her aunt tremulously. 'You're not the first generation to discover illegal substances, you know.'

'So?' Sophie sneered. 'You're no better than me.'

'I didn't use heroin!' exclaimed Aunt Ingrid, with evident disgust, and Paige's jaw dropped.

'Heroin?' she echoed weakly, turning to stare at her sister. 'Oh, Sophie, is this true? Have you been using heroin?'

'No—'

'Then what was it doing in your drawer?' demanded her aunt, and Paige endorsed her question.

'Oh, I should have known that you'd take her side,' muttered Sophie sulkily, without answering. 'Whatever I say now, you're not going to believe me.'

'Try me.'

'You don't have to take my word for it,' persisted the old lady. 'Go into your bedroom, Paige. You can smell it for yourself. Marijuana has a most distinctive scent: sweet and very heady. That was why I looked though Sophie's belongings. I was expecting to find a pack of joints.'

Paige shook her head. 'I wouldn't recognise marijuana, Aunt Ingrid. It may sound stupid, but I've never smoked a joint in my life.' She frowned. 'But I thought you said you found heroin in the drawer?'

'I did.'

Sophie snorted. 'She has no right to criticise me. She's obviously familiar with drugs or she wouldn't be accusing me.'

Paige caught her breath. 'You admit that you've been smoking marijuana?' she exclaimed, horrified, and Sophie gave her a pitying look.

'Where have you been living for the past ten years, Paige?' she exhorted. 'Not on this planet!'

'Don't you dare try and justify it,' cried her aunt, but Sophie wasn't listening to her.

'Everyone uses these days,' she said, and Paige stared at her with disbelieving eyes.

'I don't,' she said, but somehow that wasn't enough.

A sense of panic gripped her. What was she going to do now? When she'd accepted responsibility for Sophie, she'd never expected anything like this.

Her aunt shifted in her chair. 'Aren't you forgetting something, Paige?' she asked. Then, after fumbling in the pocket of her trousers, she declared, 'This.'

'This' was a tiny plastic packet of white powder and Paige could only guess at what it was. 'Oh, Sophie,' she exclaimed, feeling sick to her stomach. 'Where did you get it? What is it doing in your drawer?'

Sophie hunched her shoulders. 'That's my business.'

'Not as long as you're living in my house, young lady,' retorted her aunt sharply, and Paige wanted to groan aloud when her sister answered back.

'We won't be living in your house much longer,' she announced triumphantly. 'Paige is going to find us a decent place of our own, aren't you, Paige? Somewhere better than this shoebox, without any crazy old woman telling us how to live our lives.'

'Sophie—'

Paige's protest was useless. There was only so much their aunt would take, she knew that, and Sophie had tried her patience for the last time. Struggling to her feet, she pointed a trembling finger at the younger girl. 'That's it,' she said. 'I've had enough of you and your insolence. I don't care what Paige does, but I want you out of here tonight!'

Two weeks later, Paige stood at the window of their room in the small bed-and-breakfast, watching somewhat anxiously for the taxi that was going to take them to the airport. It was already fifteen minutes late and her palms were damp with the realisation that if they missed the flight they would also miss the ferry that would take them to Skiapolis.

Behind her, Sophie lounged sulkily on her bed, making no attempt to gather her belongings together. She had left her sister to do all their packing, and Paige had had to bite her tongue against the urge to tell Sophie that this was all her fault. But it was. And Paige could have done with some reassurance that she wasn't making yet another mistake.

Glancing round, she met the younger girl's defiant gaze with some impatience. If only Sophie were older: if only she could have been relied upon to pull her weight, they might have got through this. Aunt Ingrid wasn't a monster. With a little persuasion on Sophie's part, the older woman would have come round.

As it was, with no other job in prospect and bills to pay, Paige had been compelled to call the number Nikolas Petronides had given her. At least working for him would give her a breathing space, she'd consoled herself, and if she saved every penny he paid her there might be enough to put the deposit down on a small apartment by the time they came back to England.

It had been a relief to find that someone other than Nikolas had answered when she'd rung. A man, who had introduced himself as Donald Jamieson, and who was apparently Nikolas's solicitor, had been left to handle the details. He'd explained that Mr Petronides had had to return to Greece, but he'd issued instructions to the effect that if Paige should decide to take the job Jamieson should make the necessary arrangements for their journey.

Although she'd been reassured by Jamieson's involvement Paige had wondered briefly if she was being entirely wise in accepting the position. It was useless telling herself that Nikolas couldn't possibly have known she'd change her mind. That the instructions he'd left had been a logical attempt to cover all eventualities. But the fact was, Nikolas was an arrogant devil, and had it not been for Sophie's problems she'd have done almost anything rather than accept his help.

Still, she consoled herself, it was only for the summer, and a lot of things could change in three months. Aunt Ingrid had been horrified when she'd explained what they were planning to do. As far as she was concerned, Paige was jeopardising her own future for the sake of a girl who had no appreciation of the fact. And, because the Petronides name meant nothing more to her than the logo on the side of an oil tanker, she'd considered Paige's decision reckless in the extreme.

Which hadn't improved her relationship with Sophie one iota. The younger girl continued to assert that despite the presence of the heroin in her drawer she'd never actually touched hard drugs, but Paige had known she couldn't trust her not to use them in the future. She'd been horrified to learn that Sophie's introduction to marijuana wasn't a recent thing either. According to her, it had been in common use at her boarding-school, but if she'd thought that might reassure her sister she couldn't have been more wrong. Paige had been appalled, and more convinced than ever that she was doing the right thing by getting Sophie out of London.

She scanned the street again for the mini-cab that had promised to pick them up twenty minutes ago. She hoped it came soon. In spite of everything, she didn't want to admit that she was getting cold feet.

'Come on, come on,' she muttered impatiently, and Sophie, who had been viewing her sister's agitation with a certain amount of satisfaction, now sat up. Pushing back the crinkled shoulder-length perm that was several shades lighter than Paige's toffee-streaked blonde hair, she looked more optimistic than she'd done since Paige had first told her that she was going to accept the job in Greece.

'Does this mean we're going to miss the plane?' she asked smugly, and Paige knew exactly how her aunt must have felt when she'd confronted Sophie's insolent stare.

'No,' she retorted at once, although she wasn't absolutely sure what she'd do if they did miss the flight. After all, it was the holiday season. Flights were booked well in advance. 'We'll just take a later plane,' she added shortly, 'so you might as well resign yourself to the fact that we're going to Skiapolis.'

'Skiapolis!' Sophie spoke disparagingly. 'It wouldn't be so bad if it was Athens, or Rhodes, even. Somewhere I'd heard of. But Skiapolis! I don't know how you can even justify what you're doing to me. If Daddy was alive, he'd—'

She broke off, and Paige seized her chance. 'Yes?' she prompted. 'If Daddy was alive—what? What would he do?

Do you think he'd be proud to learn that his younger daughter was a—a junkie?'

Sophie sniffed. 'I'm not a junkie.'

'So you say.' Paige was scornful now. 'And what about what you did to Aunt Ingrid? Daddy was very fond of Aunt Ingrid. Do you think he'd applaud you for beating her up?'

'I didn't beat her up.' Sophie was indignant. 'She slapped me first.'

'There are other ways of beating up old people than by hitting them,' retorted Paige without hesitation. 'What if she'd had a seizure? How would you have felt then?'

Sophie's shoulders hunched. 'She'd been nosing about in my things. She had no right to do that.'

'And you had no right to sneak out of school before your last period,' Paige reminded her sharply. 'If you'd had nothing to hide, we wouldn't even be having this conversation.'

'I wish we weren't.'

'I dare say you do. But we are, and that's all there is to it.' Paige heard the unmistakable sound of a car in the cul-de-sac outside and breathed a sigh of relief. 'Here's the taxi. Grab your things. We're leaving.'

Sophie flounced off the bed. 'I'll never forgive you for this, Paige. Never! Forcing me to go and live on some grotty old Greek island with some grotty old business acquaintance of Daddy's. I'm going to be bored out of my mind.'

'Better bored than stoned,' replied Paige tersely, wishing she felt more positive. And at least Sophie knew nothing about Nikolas, other than the story she'd invented about how she'd got the job. In fact, she'd left Sophie with the impression that if she hadn't gone crying to Martin about their problems Paige might never have been offered the position at all.

It was late afternoon when they arrived in Athens and the heat was palpable. Even Sophie breathed a little sigh of wonder as they walked down the steps off the plane. With the sun striking on the airport buildings, reflecting back off the glass, and heat rising up from the tarmac, the unaccustomed brilliance was dazzling. For a few minutes, even Sophie forgot her complaints as they walked the short distance to the arrivals hall.

The formalities were soon dealt with. The Greek officials were not immune to the attractions of two young women travelling alone, and in a very short time their luggage was stowed in the boot of an ancient cab, and they were on their way to Piraeus. The ferry was due to depart at seven o'clock that evening, and Paige was hoping they might have time to grab a bite to eat before they boarded the ship. She had no idea what facilities might be provided on the vessel. Her own trips to Greece with her father had never entailed travelling between the mainland and the many islands that dotted the area. Of course, they had visited Skiapolis—but that had been as guests aboard Nikolas's yacht. This was an entirely different situation, and she had no illusions about the position she now occupied in his life.

Piraeus was the largest and busiest port in Greece. Ferries ran from its harbour to most of the larger islands in the Greek archipelago, some of the bigger ones looking as luxurious as cruise ships.

Paige doubted that the ferry to Skiapolis would fall into that category. Her memory was that it had been one of the smaller islands in the group. Nikolas owned most, if not all, of the island, and he hadn't wanted to encourage tourists, at least in those days. A small ferry had brought mail and essential supplies, she remembered, but she doubted it possessed tourist accommodation. She was grateful the trip wasn't a long one. They might have been obliged to sleep on deck.

The instructions they'd been given obliged them to collect their tickets from an agent at the Plateia Karaiskaki, and after the car had dropped them off they carried their

bags across the busy concourse. Sophie was briefly stunned
by the heat and the smells and the alien language, but although she exclaimed at the brilliance of the sea she was
beginning to find the late afternoon sun more of a burden
than a blessing. She grumbled every time someone jostled
her, or the strap of her rucksack dug into her shoulder.

They eventually found the office they were looking for.
Paige went to see about their tickets and was given the
number of the quay where the ferry was supposed to leave
from. But she was also informed that a seven o'clock departure schedule meant very little. If the ferry was late arriving at the port, they could be looking at nine o'clock or
later.

Sophie understood little of the conversation Paige was
having with the agent. The office was hot and stuffy, and
she was quite happy to spend her time guarding their luggage beside the open door. And exchanging provocative
glances with a curly-headed youth in jeans and trainers,
whose brown, sun-bronzed arms were seen to advantage in
his sleeveless T-shirt.

Their silent flirtation had not gone unnoticed, however.
Paige, trying to concentrate on what the agent was saying,
made furious gestures at her sister, but without much success. Hot and frustrated, Paige was beginning to wish
they'd never left London. At least in England she could
understand what was going on.

With the tickets in her hand, she eventually escaped the
counter and pushed her way across to where Sophie was
waiting. The youth was chatting her up now and, judging
by the becoming flush in Sophie's cheeks, she was having
no trouble understanding him. Indeed, she hardly noticed
Paige's arrival, her husky laugh attracting the attention of
more than one pair of eyes.

'Sophie!' Paige dug her in the ribs with her elbow, bending to pick up her own bags before confronting her sister

with a baleful look. 'Come on,' she said, ignoring the boy. 'Let's go and find a café. I'm dying for a cool drink.'

'Wait a minute.' Sophie grabbed her arm, and although Paige prepared herself for an argument it didn't come. 'This is Paris,' she said, as if that was of some interest to them. 'Mr Petronides has sent him to meet us. Isn't that great?'

Paige blinked. 'What?'

'Kirie Petronides,' ventured the young man helpfully. 'You are Kiria Tennant, *ohi*? And Thespinis Tennant,' he added, smiling at Sophie. '*Kalostone, kiria.* Welcome to Greece.'

Paige dropped her bags again. 'Kirie Petronides asked you to meet us?' she asked disbelievingly, even as the boy's distinction between greeting an older woman and a younger one caused her to grit her teeth. Still, she probably looked a lot older, she conceded, right at this moment. She was hot and tired, and she wasn't in the mood for precocious youths.

'*Ne,*' he said, looping the strap of Sophie's rucksack over his shoulder and picking up her suitcase without obvious effort. 'If you will come with me…'

'Wait.' Paige hesitated. 'How do I know—?' she began, only to have Sophie override her protests.

'Come on, Paige,' she muttered in a low voice. 'How else did he know our names?'

'Perhaps he heard me speaking to the ticket agent,' replied Paige uneasily. And then, realising she hadn't mentioned Nikolas's name, she muttered, 'Oh—all right.'

But she wasn't about to stagger across the quay again with both her bags. If the boy could carry one suitcase so easily, he could carry two. Tapping him on the arm, she gestured towards the other bag, and although his smile slipped a little he nodded and picked it up.

'Isn't he a babe?' Sophie whispered as they followed his sinuous saunter away from the busy ferry terminal and along a narrow quay where private yachts and motor vessels bobbed on the rising swell. 'Great buns!'

'Sophie!' Paige realised she sounded like an old maid, but her sister's language was too liberally peppered with comments of that kind. 'You watch too much television.'

'Well, I won't be watching it from now on, will I?' Sophie retorted, and Paige didn't know if that was a blessing or not. When she'd insisted on them coming out here, she hadn't considered that there might be other distractions, and Paris—if that was his name—might be far too available.

Still, she couldn't worry about that now. This was their first real introduction to the blue waters of the Aegean, and the breeze blowing off the water was refreshingly cool against Paige's hot cheeks.

By the time they reached their transport, a steady trickle of perspiration was dampening the skin between her breasts and the hair on the back of her neck was wet. Although she'd warned Sophie against wearing anything skimpy to travel in, she was wishing she hadn't taken her own advice now. The denim skirt and matching waistcoat, worn over a simple round-necked navy blue T-shirt, had seemed perfectly suitable when they'd boarded the plane in London. Now, however, the shirt was sticking to her, and she wished she'd taken the time to go into the restroom at the airport and remove the white tights that were cutting into her legs.

Sophie looked hot, too, but she'd pulled her shirt out of her cropped jeans and tied it beneath her breasts. Paige hadn't had the heart to stop her, even though she knew no Greek girl would dress that way. Well, no Greek girl of Nikolas's family, she amended, thinking of Ariadne. But if Nikolas didn't like it he had only himself to blame.

The vessel that awaited them was not a yacht. Paige, who had briefly entertained the thought that Nikolas himself might have come to meet them, quickly revised her opinion. The sleek motor launch was much smaller than the other vessel and it was deserted, its fringed canopy flapping in the breeze. But at least it would provide some protection, she thought gratefully. She couldn't wait to get out of the sun.

Paris threw their bags onto the deck and then jumped aboard. Paige felt a momentary twinge of irritation at his treatment of their luggage and then decided it was probably no worse than the handling they'd suffered on the plane. He held out his hand to Sophie, and she quickly followed after him. Then he did the same for Paige, taking a good look at her white-clad thighs as her skirt lifted in the breeze.

He grinned then, aware of her indignation, and although she wanted to be cross with him she found herself smiling, too. He was only a boy, she told herself as he took her suitcase from her and stowed it with the rest of the luggage in the steering cabin. He probably lived and worked on the island, and they were unlikely to see him again.

CHAPTER THREE

PAIGE regarded her reflection in the long mirrored doors of
the closet and wondered why she was taking so much trouble over her appearance tonight. It wasn't as if she wanted
to impress anyone; not with her looks anyway. But she was
nervous about meeting Ariadne for the first time and finding
out if they were likely to get along.

She had wondered if the girl would be curious to meet
them but evidently Ariadne did not regard paid companions
as honoured guests. Instead, it had been left to a black-
garbed housekeeper to greet the new arrivals, and although
Paige thought she was vaguely familiar Kiria Papandreiu
had given no indication that they had met before.

The journey to the island had not been unpleasant,
though it had taken rather longer than Paige remembered.
Still, once they were out of the busy harbour, Paris had
provided light refreshments, and because she'd eaten little
of the lunch on the plane Paige was grateful for his consideration.

So much so that she hadn't objected when Sophie had
asked if she could go up front with Paris. Of course she
hadn't anticipated that Sophie would spend most of the
journey seated beside him at the controls. But having given
her permission there was little she could do about it and at
least it had kept her sister occupied throughout the two-
hour trip.

Arriving at the small port of Agios Petros had been rather
nerve-racking. It had been dark, and although Paige hadn't
expected anyone to meet them at the quay she had anticipated that Nikolas would be waiting at the house. But she'd
been wrong. When they'd emerged from the car that had

34

brought them up from the harbour, Kiria Papandreiu had explained, albeit in barely comprehensible English, that Kirie Petronides was away. Where he was, she didn't say; nor when he'd be back. But, once again, Paige got the impression that as employees they didn't warrant that kind of information.

It was all a far cry from the last time she was here, she reflected wistfully, and then chided herself for allowing thoughts of that kind to colour her mood. She'd been a guest then, not a servant, and Nikolas had done his best to make both her and her father welcome.

But Parker Tennant hadn't known what was really going on…

She stiffened now, smoothing down the calf-length skirt of her turquoise taffeta sheath. She'd hesitated some time before choosing the fairly formal outfit, but until she knew what was expected of her, she'd rather not take any chances. However, the clothes she'd bought for the trip, both for her and Sophie, had been off the peg. Sophie, who had grown in the last year, had needed a selection of summer clothes, but Paige herself had had to make do with a couple of dresses.

Fortunately her hair was easy to handle. Unlike Sophie's, she wore it fairly short and straight, the simple bob curling under at her chin. When she'd known Nikolas before, her hair had been long and she'd worn it in a French braid, but that was in the days when a visit to the hairdressers' was a weekly event.

She sighed, touching her hot cheeks with nervous fingers. She wasn't beautiful, not like Sophie anyway, who seemed set to rival their mother's looks when she'd been young. Paige had expressive green eyes and a generous mouth, but her features were not particularly memorable, which was why she'd never really believed that any of the men she'd dated had wanted her for herself.

A knock at the door aroused her apprehension. What

now? she wondered anxiously, but it was only Sophie, who came into the room without waiting for a response. She'd changed, too, but the yellow slip dress she was wearing barely covered her bottom, and her clunky wedges clomped across the rug.

'Are you ready?' she asked, viewing Paige's appearance with critical eyes. 'Is that new? I don't remember seeing it before.'

'It's not new,' said Paige, wondering if she dared broach the subject of Sophie's appearance, but her sister just pulled a face and sauntered over to the balcony doors.

'I wonder what the view's like from here?' she mused, drawing back as a particularly large moth came and fluttered against the glass. 'You did say you'd stayed here before, didn't you? I couldn't see much of the island as we drove up from the harbour, but the house seemed huge.'

'It is.' Paige chose her words with care. 'Is that what you're wearing for dinner?'

'Well, I'm not going to get changed again,' retorted Sophie, swinging round. She looked down at her dress. 'What's wrong with it?'

Paige hesitated. 'Nothing, I suppose—'

'Just because you like to wear frumpy clothes doesn't mean I have to.' Sophie's jaw jutted belligerently. 'I bet Paris would approve.'

Paige shrugged. 'I dare say he would, if he could see you,' she declared evenly. 'But until we know what our position is here—'

'I thought we did know,' countered Sophie, frowning. 'We're going to keep some old man's ward company. But don't expect me to dress like a nanny. You can, but I've got better things to do.'

Paige shook her head, deciding not to pursue it right now, and changed the subject. 'So,' she said pleasantly, 'have you unpacked your things and put them away?'

'I've unpacked some,' said Sophie carelessly. 'I'll do the

rest in the morning.' She scowled suddenly, turning on her high heels that added inches to her five-feet-six-inch height. 'Hey, your room is bigger than mine. That's not fair.'

Paige glanced about her. In all honesty, she'd paid little attention to the spacious apartment she'd been given. She'd noticed the bed was square, with a solid wooden frame, and that the quilt that covered it was made of hand-woven silk. But she'd scarcely admired the carved oak furniture or heeded the high arching ceiling above her head. There were rose chiffon curtains at the windows, she saw now, and richly patterned rugs dotted about the polished floor. In other circumstances, she wouldn't have failed to be charmed by its simple elegance, and she could understand why Sophie was so impressed.

'Do you want to swap?' she asked.

'No.' Sophie had the grace to look slightly shamefaced now. 'I was just admiring it, that's all.' She went to take a look into the adjoining bathroom. 'I think my bathroom's bigger than yours.'

'Good.'

Paige decided it was time they were leaving. It was no use putting it off any longer, however apprehensive she felt. She took another look at herself in the mirror, and tucked a loose strand of brown-gold hair behind her ear. Then, after checking that the gold hoops she was wearing in her ears were secure, she picked up her purse and turned towards the door.

'Shall we—?'

'This guy—'

They both spoke together, and although Paige wasn't sure she wanted to hear what her sister had been going to say she knew they couldn't leave until she did.

'Nikolas Petronides,' went on Sophie, after receiving a silent go-ahead, 'he must be filthy rich, mustn't he? I mean, according to Paris, he owns a fleet of oil tankers and you have to admit, this house is something else.'

Paige suppressed a groan. The last thing she needed was for Sophie to start getting ideas about Nikolas. And she hadn't even seen him yet! Her sister thought he was old, but Nikolas was only about forty. And he was still a disturbingly attractive man.

'I don't think that's of any interest to us,' she declared reprovingly, as if talking about Nikolas didn't bother her in the least. Didn't remind her of the first time she been introduced to him by her father, or of the hot dark eyes that had seduced her on the spot...

'Get real, Paige. I wouldn't mind marrying someone with pots of money,' retorted Sophie, with a grimace. 'I wonder how he'd feel about taking a child-bride?' She giggled, and Paige knew an almost irresistible impulse to slap her. 'Or perhaps he has a son. What do you think?'

'I think you're being very silly,' said Paige, aware that she was overreacting. But right now she couldn't think about Nikolas without remembering the past they'd shared. It was this house, she thought. It had so many connotations—even though he'd never made love to her here...

'What's silly about wanting to marry a millionaire?' exclaimed Sophie at once. 'Or wanting to know if he has a son?'

'He doesn't.'

Paige was abrupt, and Sophie's eyes widened. 'Of course,' she blurted excitedly. 'You've met him. I'd forgotten about that. Go on: tell me what he's like.'

'Not now.' Paige was determined not to get into that discussion. 'Come on, we're going to be late for dinner.'

'So what? Petronides isn't here. You heard what that old witch said when we arrived. I'm not worried about keeping some Greek schoolkid waiting.'

Paige forbore to mention that the Greek schoolkid in question was a year older than she was. And, looking at Sophie as they left the bedroom and started along the upper gallery, she was reluctantly aware that the younger girl was probably years older when it came to experience of life. Ariadne might have lost both her parents, but she hadn't been left alone. She'd been protected and cared for all the time she was grieving, and she had the comfort of knowing that her future was secure.

But now was not the time to be having negative thoughts about the girl she'd come here to chaperon. Instead, Paige concentrated on her surroundings, finding that her memory hadn't deserted her when they reached the top of the stairs. Marble treads led down to an Italian marble foyer, a black iron balustrade following their sweeping curve.

'Wow!' Sophie was impressed, and she paused on the first stair to admire the cut-glass chandelier that illuminated the hall below. 'What a pity we don't have an audience,' she taunted. 'We could make quite an entrance from here.'

'Thank goodness we don't—' Paige was beginning, when a tall figure moved out of the shadows and into the light.

'*Parakalo,*' said Nikolas, a black silk shirt and black trousers accentuating his darkly tanned appearance. 'Please—Sophie, is it not?—feel free to descend the stairs any way you choose.'

Even Sophie was taken aback and Paige wished she could just fade into the woodwork behind her. Evidently Nikolas had returned and it was him they'd been keeping waiting. Always supposing he intended to eat with the hired help this evening, of course. Until she knew what their position in the household was going to be, she couldn't be sure of anything.

'Is that *him*?'

Sophie's stage whisper must have reached Nikolas and Paige gave her sister an exasperated look. 'Go on,' she urged, pushing the girl forward without answering her, and Sophie returned her look with interest before obediently starting down.

'I only asked,' she muttered, but Paige wasn't in the

mood to be placated. She was already wondering how she'd ever thought that bringing Sophie here would be a good idea.

Nikolas had stepped back as they came down the stairs but now he approached them, greeting them in his own language as if to reassure them that he hadn't heard what Sophie had said. '*Kalispera,*' he said, his deep voice scraping across Paige's already frayed nerves. '*Kalos orissate sto Skiapolis.*'

Sophie blinked, clearly not understanding his words, and he took her hand and said easily, 'Welcome to Skiapolis. Did you have a good journey?'

'Oh—yes. Thank you.' Paige was amazed to see that her sister had actually turned fiery red. 'I'm sorry about—you know—saying what I did. But this house is, like—way cool.'

'I am glad you like it,' he responded smoothly, but Paige closed her eyes for a moment, praying for deliverance. She dreaded to think what Sophie was going to say next and she started violently when Nikolas murmured, 'Paige?' in a concerned voice. 'Are you all right?'

He was standing in front of her now and she had no choice but to allow him to shake her hand, too. But her fingers tingled within the strong grasp of his, her damp palm sliding revealingly against his firm flesh.

'I—I'm fine,' she managed, extracting her hand again as soon as she possibly could. He was so close, much closer than he'd been across the table at the restaurant in London, and she was instantly conscious of his height and the broadness of his shoulders, and the intimidating awareness that this might not have been such a good idea on her part either. 'I'm sorry if we've kept you waiting. Your housekeeper said you were away.'

'I was. But now I'm back.' Nikolas continued to regard her with considering eyes, and Paige, whose eyes were on a level with the opened collar of his shirt, concentrated on

the V of dark hair that was visible above the placket.
'You're flushed, *aghapita*. Are you not feeling well?'

'I've told you, I'm fine—' Paige started protestingly,
only to be overridden by her sister's voice.

'She didn't eat any lunch on the plane,' Sophie told him
smugly, not to be outdone, and as if realising they had an
audience Nikolas took an automatic step away.

'That was unwise,' he said softly, his eyes lingering on
her embarrassed face. 'Was it so stressful? The journey, I
mean.'

'No. No, of course not.'

Paige wished he would leave her alone. Sophie wasn't a
fool and if he continued to behave as if her well-being was
of some importance to him her sister would begin to suspect she had something to hide.

But perhaps that was his intention, she mused uneasily.
She'd never truly believed he'd offered her this job out of
the goodness of his heart. Men like Nikolas Petronides
didn't forgive—or forget. And, although she had no illusions that she'd ever meant a great deal to him, she had
walked out on him, which in his eyes was probably unforgivable.

'*Kala*,' he murmured now, inclining his head towards a
room on his left. 'Ariadne is waiting for us. We will go
and introduce you, *ne*?'

Paige nodded, glancing at Sophie before accompanying
him across the vast expanse of marble that lay between
them and what she seemed to recall from her previous visit
was an elegant drawing room. Around them, the plain walls
of the reception hall were hung with literally dozens of
paintings, large and small, that added vivid colour to what
was essentially a neutral area. But there were flowers, too:
huge bouquets of magnolia and oleander and lily in
sculpted vases, whose distinctive fragrance hung sweetly in
the cool conditioned air. It was all very beautiful and very

civilised, and Paige wished she could relax and stop thinking that she'd made a terrible mistake.

The lamplit salon they entered was as she remembered: high ceilings above striped silk walls; long undraped windows at either side of an enormous stone fireplace, above which hung an impressive portrait of a woman she knew to be Nikolas's mother; several upholstered sofas in green and gold; and rich, subtly woven rugs scattered over a polished floor. The many display cabinets were the repository for delicate china and ceramics, a collection Nikolas's grandfather had begun in his lifetime and which his late father had continued. And, although there were other paintings here, too, there were also a handful of jewelled icons to draw the eye. It was a beautiful room, casually luxurious, yet revealing a lived-in comfort and informality in the sprinkling of cushions on the sofas, in the sprawl of magazines decorating a low granite table, and the squat vase of wild flowers residing on the mantel.

But it was the girl who was standing on the hearth who took Paige's eye. Ariadne—Stephanopoulous, as Donald Jamieson had advised her—was nothing like the schoolgirl she had been expecting. Tall and slender, with a long coil of night-dark hair hanging over her shoulder, she looked years older than the seventeen she admitted to. She was wearing black: an ankle-length gown that moulded her figure, and would not have looked out of place on a woman twice her age. She looked more like Nikolas's wife than his ward, thought Paige in some dismay, wondering how on earth she was supposed to deal with her.

And, indeed, Ariadne reacted to their appearance with the kind of studied arrogance that seemed to confirm Paige's assessment of her. 'Nikolas!' she exclaimed, ignoring the two women with him and going towards him, her hands held out in front of her so that he was obliged to take them in his own. *'Ola entaksi?'*

'Speak English, Ariadne,' Nikolas chided her mildly.

'Our guests are not familiar with our language. And, after all, that is one of the reasons I have invited Miss Tennant here: to help you improve your accent.'

'My accent doesn't need improving,' retorted Ariadne at once, with a little less maturity. But Paige had to admit she was right. The Greek girl appeared to speak English very well indeed. A lot better than the schoolgirl Greek she could manage.

'Whatever...' Nikolas's tone had hardened now. He turned to Paige. 'My ward,' he said simply. 'I hope you'll become good friends.'

'I hope so, too,' said Paige firmly, taking the limp hand Ariadne offered her. 'It's very nice to meet you, Miss Stephanopoulous.'

'Miss Stephanopoulous!' Nikolas was impatient. 'Her name is Ariadne.' He glanced at the girl beside her. 'And this is Sophie. Miss Tennant's sister.'

'Hi.' Sophie greeted the other girl without enthusiasm, and Paige hoped she wouldn't say anything too outrageous. 'I guess we're the same age, right?'

'Are we?' Ariadne sounded bored, and she immediately turned back to her guardian, wrapping her hands around his forearm and gazing up at him with wide, appealing eyes. '*Isos*—maybe we can have dinner now?'

'After I have offered Miss Tennant and her sister an aper-itif,' Nikolas answered evenly, removing her hands from his wrist. 'Paige?' He indicated that she should follow him across to an ebony drinks cabinet. 'What will you have?'

Paige hesitated; then, after exchanging a warning look with Sophie, she crossed the room. She wasn't happy about leaving the two girls alone, and she kept glancing back over her shoulder as if she expected something awful to happen.

'Ouzo? Retsina? Or something more familiar?' asked Nikolas at her approach. 'And relax. It will do Ariadne good to spend time with someone of her own age for a change.'

Paige expelled a breath. 'I thought you said she still attended school.'

'I did.' Nikolas lifted a bottle of white wine from the refrigerated cabinet and arched an enquiring brow. Then, after she'd nodded her approval, he went on, 'But Ariadne has been too much with older people this past year. She's had a series of minor infections which have kept her away from school, and I had to hire a tutor to give her extra lessons.'

'I see.' Paige watched him pour her wine. 'She seems very—attached to you.'

'You noticed.'

'It would have been hard not to.' Paige took the glass he offered, carefully avoiding his fingers, and then looked up to find him watching her with a whimsical expression. 'What?' she exclaimed. Then, glancing over her shoulder again, she said, 'Well—she's hardly discreet.'

'Unlike you,' he remarked drily, pouring a generous measure of Scotch into a cut-glass tumbler. 'I must admit I was surprised when I heard that you'd been in touch with Jamieson. If I'd thought for a minute that you'd change your mind, I'd have hung on for a few more days. Why did you?'

'Why did I what?'

He pulled a wry face. 'Don't pretend you don't know what I'm talking about.'

'Oh—' Paige knew she should have been prepared for the question, but she wasn't. 'I—I decided it was too good an opportunity to miss.'

'Did you?'

His eyes were lazily intent and she hurried to explain herself. 'Financially, I mean,' she assured him. 'And although it meant taking Sophie out of school a couple of weeks early all her exams are over.'

'Ah, yes, Sophie.' His eyes moved past her to where her

sister was waiting, a look of resentment on her face now. 'She's not at all like you, is she?'

Paige shrugged. 'If you say so.'

'I do.' His mouth took on a sensual curve. 'And before I ask your sister what she would like to drink, let me say that you have many advantages that she has not.'

'I'm older, you mean?'

Paige refused to let him disconcert her, and Nikolas's eyes narrowed on her tense face. 'Older, of course. But age has its compensations. You know what I am saying,' he added softly, and then broke off as an argument erupted across the room.

'Who the f—? I mean, who the hell do you think you are?' Sophie's voice rose in outrage. 'You can't speak to me like that. You're not the mistress here!'

'*Arketa! Arketa!* That is enough!'

As Ariadne opened her mouth to respond, Nikolas slammed down his drink and strode across the room. For a moment, he seemed to have forgotten his command that they should speak English, and his initial remonstrance was issued in the language of his youth.

Then, as if realising that Sophie couldn't understand him, he gathered himself, and when he spoke again his manner was more controlled. 'Ariadne,' he snapped. 'Do you want to tell me what is going on? What have you been saying to upset our guest?'

Ariadne looked indignant at first. And then, as if realising her guardian was not going to respond to that kind of attitude, she mumbled, 'It was nothing, Nikolas. Really. I was merely saying that Kiria Papandreiu does not like to keep dinner waiting.'

'That's not true.' Sophie didn't mince her words. 'What she actually said was that we weren't welcome here; that she saw no reason why she had to put herself out for people she didn't even like.'

Paige, who was behind Nikolas now, had the feeling that

her sister had edited the exchange for their benefit. Or perhaps she hadn't understood everything the Greek girl had said. Whatever, judging from Ariadne's smug expression, she had said something to cause offence, and there was an awkward silence as Nikolas assessed the situation.

'Is this true, Ariadne?' he asked at last, and the smugness disappeared to be replaced with wounded indignation.

'Of course not!' she exclaimed, ignoring Sophie's cry of protest. 'I'm afraid she misunderstood what I was saying.'

Nikolas breathed deeply. 'Is that so?' he said heavily, and Sophie immediately jumped to her own defence.

'No, it's not,' she argued hotly. 'I wouldn't make up something like that. Tell him, Paige. I'm not a liar. She's just a jealous cow who seems to think that wearing granny clothes gives her the right to—'

'Shut up, Sophie.'

Paige broke in now, aware that she didn't really know who to believe. Until recently, she'd have believed Sophie without hesitation, but after the incident with the heroin she couldn't be sure.

'Oh, right.' Her sister was glaring mutinously at her now, and Paige realised she'd switched the blame. 'Thanks a bunch. She bad-mouths both of us and I'm the one who gets dumped on.'

'Nobody is being—what was the expression you used?—dumped on,' declared Nikolas bleakly. 'As far as I am concerned, the matter is closed. Whatever was said—' he looked at each of them in turn '—you *will* get on with one another. Whatever happens, I do not intend to make any other arrangement. That is my decision. *Katalavenete?*'

Paige was fully prepared for Sophie to turn on him as she'd turned on her more times than she cared to remember in the past six months. But she didn't. With a careless shrug of her shoulders, she appeared to accept what he'd said, and it was left to Ariadne to express her resentment.

'But I said nothing, Nikolas,' his ward murmured plain-

tively, her look of pained distress not fooling Paige for a
minute. She had the uneasy feeling that Sophie had been
telling the truth all along, while she had no real idea what
was going on behind Ariadne's innocent mask.

'As I told you, we will say no more about it,' said her
guardian flatly. 'And now I suggest you offer Sophie a soda
before we go into dinner.'

CHAPTER FOUR

PAIGE did not sleep well.

She should have done so. After all, she was very tired, her bed was superbly comfortable, and there were none of the outside disturbances that had disrupted her nights at the bed-and-breakfast.

But it didn't work out that way. She tossed and turned for hours, continually replaying the events of the evening in her mind until she was hot and sweaty and too over-wrought to relax. Her brain buzzed with the realisation that this was not going to be the escape from Sophie's problems she'd consoled herself it would be. Ariadne was not the placid schoolgirl she'd imagined; she didn't want them here, and her relationship with Nikolas was not the simple one Paige had expected. Sophie had been right; Ariadne was jealous—probably of anyone who distracted her guardian's attention from herself—and Paige suspected she was going to do everything in her power to make their stay on Skiapolis as unpleasant as possible.

Which didn't make for an easy night. Paige eventually fell into a shallow slumber towards dawn, but she was up again as soon as it was light, taking a shower, tidying her room, writing a few lines to Aunt Ingrid at the bureau in her bedroom. It wasn't easy finding the right words to describe their arrival to her aunt either, and she contented herself by sticking to the facts and not attempting to touch on any more personal matters.

It was still only seven o'clock when she stepped out onto her balcony and took her first real look at the view from her window. It was as spectacular as she'd expected, a sweeping panorama that encompassed the tiny port of

Agios Petros on the western side of the island, and the wooded slopes below the villa that fell away to a private beach. Paige knew that below the cliffs that hid the shoreline there was a wooden jetty where she and her father had landed from Nikolas's yacht four years ago. A dinghy had ferried them the short distance from the yacht itself, which had been anchored out in the bay, and she remembered gazing up at the villa as they sped across the water and thinking she had never seen a more beautiful house in her life.

But such memories were not welcome now, and Paige turned her gaze to the small town. Flat-roofed, white-washed dwellings clustered around the harbour, their steep, cobble-stoned streets something she did remember with affection from the evening before. She could see the tall cupola of a church and the sails of a windmill, turning in the warm breeze that blew off the ocean, and the simple beauty of it all was impossible to deny. She determined there and then that, whatever happened, she was not going to let anyone intimidate her. Neither Ariadne nor Nikolas. She was here to do a job and she was going to do it, however difficult it might prove to be.

Turning back into the bedroom, she decided she might as well act upon it right away. If she stayed up here any longer, she was likely to lose what little confidence she'd found, and after running a brush through her hair she opened her door and went out onto the gallery.

She'd hesitated over what she should wear for her first morning as Ariadne's companion and had finally decided to choose the kind of outfit she'd have worn if she'd been a regular visitor to the island. A butter-yellow T-shirt and matching shorts might not meet with Ariadne's approval but she'd determined to start as she meant to go on. If Nikolas did not approve of such leniency in her dress, he would have to tell her. Until then, she intended to please herself.

Her feet, in white canvas deck shoes, made little sound on the polished floor and she reached the head of the stairs without incident. She felt a bit mean passing Sophie's door without telling her where she was going, but her sister was unlikely to be awake yet and she was looking forward to having a few minutes on her own.

One of the maids who had been on duty in the dining room the night before was dusting the elegant pillars that supported the balustrade. She gave Paige a polite smile as she passed, but apart from a mumbled, *'Kalimera, kiria,'* she didn't attempt to detain her. Paige returned the greeting, the Greek words rolling instinctively off her tongue. Perhaps she should try to improve her knowledge of the language while she was here, she thought consideringly. It was possible it might be of some value in the future.

She couldn't help wondering what the maid had thought of the dinner party she'd served in the family dining room the night before. Nikolas had described the room as intimate, and she supposed it was compared to the formal rooms she'd seen before. Easily thirty feet square, with an oblong maple table and six matching chairs upholstered in gold silk brocade, it was hardly homey, but it did give some indication of the size of the rest of the house.

Still, it wasn't the room Paige was thinking about right now. She was remembering the meal, and the uncomfortable silence that had reigned after Nikolas had been called away. Until then, he'd done his best to entertain them, delighting Sophie with anecdotes about the famous people who'd stayed on Skiapolis, and she'd been disappointed when one of the menservants had come to tell him he had an urgent call.

Paige had wondered, rather uncharitably, she was sure, if Nikolas had arranged it that way; if he'd left the three women alone together in the hope that they'd settle their differences. If so, he couldn't have been more wrong. Despite all her efforts, Ariadne had given monosyllabic answers to everything Paige had said. She only came to life when she was giving the servants orders—just as if she considered herself the mistress of the house, Paige reflected. Exactly as Sophie had said.

It hadn't been easy for Paige, being treated as if she were no older than her sister, as if her opinion were of no consequence. But it had been their first day, she'd been tired, and she hadn't had the energy to assert herself. Besides, she hadn't wanted to get into an argument with Ariadne, not over anything so trivial.

The huge reception hall was empty, she saw now, glancing about her. She smiled, enchanted anew by the beauty of her surroundings, by the paintings, and the flowers, and the exquisite pieces of sculpture that she saw now were half hidden in niches in the walls. The scent of the beeswax the maid had been using mingled with the perfumes of the flowers, drawing her towards the open doorway where they'd entered the night before.

Outside, a cool verandah stretched in either direction, while ahead of her shallow steps led down to the formal gardens that surrounded the villa. The sun was gaining strength and as she walked to the top of the steps its heat was warm on her bare arms. It was a perfect morning, the sky a bowl of china blue overhead. Despite her thoughts, she found her spirits lifting. Surely in a place like this nothing could be all that bad?

The sun-baked walls of the villa curved away for quite a distance, blending into other buildings that she guessed housed some of the servants she'd met the night before. There would obviously be garages, too, and perhaps some stables. She knew Nikolas enjoyed riding. She'd ridden with him when she was here before.

When she was here before...

Resting her hands on the pillared walls that edged the verandah, she felt the warmth of the sun beneath her fingers. She took a deep breath, trying to regain her earlier optimism, and then started in surprise when a low, amused voice remarked, 'How did I know you would be up?'

She'd been so absorbed in her thoughts, so intent on the unhappy memories of the past, that she hadn't heard his approach. He was standing in the doorway behind her, his shoulder propped idly against the pillar. In a black T-shirt and loose white cotton trousers, his dark hair tumbling over his forehead, he looked big and broad, and undeniably sexy, and years younger than she knew him to be. But then, she had never thought of Nikolas as being that much older than herself.

'Nikolas,' she acknowledged him now, straightening, not knowing what to do with her hands for a moment and then stuffing them into the pockets of her shorts. 'I— Good morning.'

'Good morning.' He left the doorway to come towards her. 'Did you sleep well?' he asked, and then shocked her into immobility when he brushed his fingers across the hollows beneath her eyes. 'Ah, no.' He answered his own question. 'I see you did not. Poor Paige. Coming here has been stressful for you, has it not?'

'What did you expect?'

Paige was stung into an involuntary response by the sensuous touch of his knuckles against her cheeks. He was playing with her, she thought unsteadily. He was enjoying having her at a disadvantage.

'What did I expect?' he echoed now as she flinched away from his hand. 'I don't know. That you might have realised I was trying to help you? That we might be able to forget the past?'

'As I've told you before, don't patronise me, Nikolas.'

His brows arched. '*Me sinhorite.* I'm sorry,' he corrected himself quickly. 'I didn't realise. Obviously, I shall have to be careful what I say in future.'

'That's not necessary.' Paige sighed impatiently. 'I'm

here, aren't I? I wouldn't have accepted the job if I hadn't thought that we—that *I*—could make it work.'

'No.'

But Nikolas's expression was unreadable, and when he came to rest his broad, long-fingered hands on the wall beside her she knew a sudden urge to get away from him. She didn't want them to become familiar with one another again; she didn't want to feel this unwelcome softening towards him. She wanted to remember he'd been using her just as much as he thought she'd been using him, and his only regret had been that she had ended their affair before he'd had the chance to do so.

'I—I think I'll go for a walk,' she said now, moving towards the steps that led down to the gardens. It was getting hot and she had no protection for her skin, but she didn't intend to stay out long.

'If you'll permit me, I'll join you,' he said at once, and she realised there was no escape.

But she had to try. 'Oh, please,' she murmured. 'I'm sure you have better things to do.' Her eyes challenged his. 'And your ward might wonder where you are.'

'She might,' he conceded carelessly. He followed her down the steps, his trousers billowing against his muscled thighs. 'But it will give us an opportunity to discuss your— what shall we call them?—your duties, *ne*? As you pointed out so charmingly, you are here to do a job of work.'

Paige shrugged as he joined her on the paved path below the verandah. 'If you say so, Nikolas,' she replied tightly. 'Or would you rather I called you Kirie Petronides instead?'

'Nikolas will do,' he answered shortly, his nostrils flaring with sudden impatience. He gestured for her to precede him. 'We will go this way.'

Paige decided not to argue in the circumstances. She accompanied him along a vine-shaded pathway that led along the side of the house. A pergola-like arch, overhung with roses, brought them around a corner and onto a sprawling terrace, where the shell of a swimming pool glistened in the sun. Beyond the terrace, the lush greenery sloped away towards the rocky grandeur of the cliffs.

They walked that way, down through orchards of peach and citrus trees, buzzing with insects and heady with the scent of the fruit. Underfoot, dwarf orchids and other plants grew in wild profusion, the grass still cool from the dampness of the dew.

But it was hot. Paige could feel herself sweating, beads of perspiration causing honey-gold strands of hair to cling to the back of her neck. Her forehead, too, was drenched with moisture, and she surreptitiously wiped her wrist across it as they walked.

She was thirsty, which was probably responsible for the slight ache that was developing in her temples. She wasn't used to such intense heat so early in the day. The only relief to be had was by walking in Nikolas's shadow, but that wasn't always easy when she didn't want him to notice what she was doing.

They stopped at the top of the steps that led down to the private beach. There was a seat there, etched into the limestone of the cliffs, that provided a small oasis of shade. Trying not to look too eager, Paige moved gratefully into the overhang, raising her arms without thinking to lift the hair from her neck.

'You're tired,' said Nikolas, putting one foot on the bench beside her, and she was immediately conscious of how provocative her action had been. Lifting her arms had caused her breasts to press against the thin fabric of her T-shirt, and although she was sure her bra was adequate she could feel their arousal for herself.

But it was difficult to read his expression. With eyes dazzled from the sun, all that was evident was the concern in his voice. 'Just—hot,' she contradicted him, not wanting him to think she might not be capable of doing the job he'd hired her for. She licked her dry lips and concentrated on the ocean. 'Um—I thought your yacht would be anchored out in the bay.'

Nikolas dropped his foot and turned to look where she was looking. 'Why would you think that?' he asked. 'I keep it in Piraeus, as you know.'

'I just thought—' Paige gave an awkward shrug. 'I wondered about your arrival.'

'Ah.' He nodded. 'You didn't hear the helicopter, then?'

'No.'

Paige shook her head, but with hindsight she did recall hearing a noise the evening before. It had been while she was taking her shower and she'd assumed it was just a low-flying aircraft. It was obvious now that it had been a helicopter instead.

'It is a much more efficient means of getting here from the mainland,' he told her. 'And, before you ask, I did not know if I would be able to get away last night, or naturally I would have arranged for you and Sophie to join me.'

Paige sank down onto the bench. 'I wasn't implying—'

'Did I say you were?' Her eyes had adjusted now and she could see the faint flare of irritation he was controlling. 'So—' He came down on the bench beside her. 'Tell me why you really changed your mind.'

Paige took a deep breath, and then wished she hadn't. She was far too conscious of him as it was, and smelling the distinctive scent of his cologne mixing with the slightly musky odour of his body was disturbing to say the least. All she could think about was his nearness, and the urge she had to touch his flesh.

'I told you,' she said, tension bringing a betraying sharpness to her tone, and he regarded her with dark, disbelieving eyes.

'You also told me you wouldn't work for me,' he reminded her softly. 'You knew your circumstances were desperate before you left the restaurant, yet you were painfully insistent that you were not—how did you put it? Oh, yes. You were not *for sale*.'

Paige blew out a breath. Dear God, what could she tell him? If he refused to accept her explanation, such as it was, what could she say? If she told him they'd left England because she'd found out that Sophie was getting involved with the drug scene, what would he think of her then? He might even decide that it was too high a price to pay for his revenge.

'Does it matter?' she muttered now, the headache that had plagued her ever since they'd left the villa becoming more insistent. She'd been foolish to allow her pride to overrule her head. But she'd been afraid that if she'd said she was going to have breakfast he'd have joined her. As it had turned out, she hadn't gained any advantage.

'I think so,' he declared now, turning to look at her, and although her face was turned away something in her manner must have betrayed her weakness. 'You are not well,' he added, cool fingers on her nape discovering her racing pulse. 'The sun is an unforgiving enemy. I will take you back to the villa.'

'There's no need—'

'There's every need,' he interrupted her harshly, and his fingers on her neck tightened for a moment to turn her face to his. 'We will continue this conversation at some other time,' he told her, allowing his hand to slide away across her shoulder and down her arm. She shivered then, and his mouth curved with sudden irony. 'Do not lie to me, *aghapita*. We know one another far too well for that.'

It seemed an incredibly long walk back to the house, but Nikolas kept a restraining hand on her arm, not allowing her to go too fast. Perhaps he'd guessed that, left to herself, she'd have raced back; that, despite her throbbing head, she just wanted to get away from him.

As it was, she couldn't ignore the possession in the strong fingers that detained her, or deny the dark power that both attracted and repelled in equal measures. She mustn't allow him to know he had any kind of control over her emotions, she told herself, and then expelled a sigh of resignation when they emerged from the trees to find Ariadne breakfasting on the terrace.

It was an enviable spot. The round white-clothed table was protected by a striped umbrella. It was set outside open French doors, one level up from the curving swimming pool, the reflection of the water dancing on the swaying canopy.

Ariadne was wearing white this morning: a loose, long-sleeved white tunic over white leggings that hugged her slender form. She evidently didn't feel the heat or, if she did, she managed not to show it. Whereas Paige, in only shorts and a T-shirt, couldn't wait to strip them off.

Nikolas's hand fell away from her arm as they stepped up onto the terrace, though he kept pace with her as they crossed the patio. Still, his attention was diverted as Ariadne rose to her feet and came to meet them, and Paige wondered if she could escape into the house without any-one noticing.

'*Kalimera*, Nikolas,' Ariadne greeted her guardian warmly, reaching up to bestow an eager kiss on his lean, tanned cheek. Then, because she had learned her lesson, she added, 'Good morning, Miss Tennant. You look very hot. I do not think our climate agrees with you.'

Paige gave her a thin smile, giving up any hope of mak-ing a hasty exit. 'I'll get used to it,' she said, not prepared to be patronised again.

'It's my fault,' put in Nikolas gallantly. 'I invited Miss Tennant to join me in a walk.' His eyes narrowed as he turned back to Paige, as if daring her to contradict him. 'Do you have some cream to put on your arms and legs? I fear the sun has already staked a claim.'

'I'll be fine,' Paige assured him, but before she could

excuse herself his hand in the small of her back urged her towards the table.

'Come,' he said. 'We will join Ariadne. I will ask Kiria Papandreiu if she has some aspirin for your headache.'

'Oh, really, I—'

Paige wanted to refuse, but Nikolas had already approached the table, picking up a glass and filling it from the jug of freshly squeezed orange juice beside Ariadne's plate. 'There,' he said as she hesitated, and Paige subsided onto one of the wrought-iron chairs. 'Drink this,' he added, handing the glass to her. 'It will make you feel better. It's full of Vitamin C.'

Paige doubted if anything could make her feel better, short of lying down in a darkened room, but in fact the orange juice did help. Even with Ariadne glaring at her from across the table when Nikolas wasn't looking, she found the drink cool and refreshing, so much so that she could view the basket of sweet rolls and honeyed pastries without revulsion.

Kiria Papandreiu appeared to serve them herself. After ordering fresh coffee for himself and his guest, Paige heard Nikolas ask if she had any *aspirini* for Kiria Tennant. The housekeeper answered in the affirmative, and Paige resigned herself to staying where she was. Besides, there was a breeze here that had not been evident out in the open, and its coolness was helping her to relax.

'Miss Tennant has a headache, too?' Ariadne only just managed to keep the satisfaction out of her voice. 'Oughtn't she to go and lie down?'

'It's just a slight headache,' Paige found herself replying, and then raised defensive eyes to Nikolas's face. 'It is,' she insisted. 'I'm feeling much better already.' She deliberately leaned back in her chair. 'The heat has never bothered me before.'

Ariadne looked sceptical. 'You're used to the heat, Miss Tennant?' Her mockery was evident. 'You're used to spending your—what is it?—two weeks' holiday in the sun?'

'Actually, we used to spend several months in the South of France in summer,' Paige corrected her, biting back the urge to tell her about Nikolas. She could imagine the girl's chagrin if she reminisced about their relationship or mentioned that she and her father had spent a few days on Nikolas's yacht.

But that was petty, and she had no desire to start a feud with the girl. Or continue one, she added wryly, aware that Ariadne was already looking for trouble. In any case, it seemed fairly obvious that Nikolas hadn't told his ward that they'd known one another before she'd taken up this appointment, and it wasn't up to her to bring it up.

But Ariadne wouldn't leave it alone. She waited impatiently while the housekeeper served them with fresh coffee, fresh orange juice, and another basket of warm pastries, and then returned to the subject again.

Watching Paige take two of the aspirin from the bottle Kiria Papandreiu had brought for her, she asked, 'What did you do in the South of France, Miss Tennant? Were you working at one of the hotels?'

Paige almost choked on one of the tablets, but somehow she managed to get it down. 'No,' she said, beating Nikolas to it. 'I wasn't working at that time. I was still at school.'

'So this is a long time ago,' suggested Ariadne innocently, and Nikolas fixed her with a warning look.

'It's not your concern,' he said. 'Miss Tennant's private life is her own. And what she did before she came here is of no importance to you.'

'Oh, but Nikolas…' Ariadne adopted the wounded air she'd assumed the evening before. 'I was interested, that is all, *aghapitos*. If we are to be friends, there should be no secrets between us.'

'Friends do not ask personal questions,' retorted her guardian, reaching for the coffee pot and pouring some into

Paige's cup. 'Come…' He picked up the basket of rolls and offered it to her. 'We have still not discussed what your duties here are going to be.'

'I do not need a nursemaid, Nikolas,' put in Ariadne sulkily before Paige could answer him, and she heard his indrawn breath as he controlled his temper.

'No,' he conceded, with the utmost patience, 'but you do need a companion. Someone who can keep you company when I return to Athens.'

'But I want to return to Athens, too,' protested Ariadne, and Paige guessed that this was the crux of the problem. Nikolas was responsible for the girl but he was finding it difficult to look after her and maintain the workload he'd inherited from his father when he retired. It was a relief to feel that she was needed; that the job he'd offered her was genuine, after all.

'It is—better for your health if you stay here on the island,' said Nikolas now, helping himself to coffee. Paige noticed he didn't eat anything, but she guessed he'd had breakfast earlier. 'You've become far too susceptible to infection, Ariadne. You know that. Staying here will give you time to regain your strength; to relax.'

Ariadne was not to be placated. 'What you mean is, you do not want me with you,' she accused him, and Nikolas breathed through his nose as he endeavoured to be polite.

'What I want is not part of this equation,' he told her. He sighed. 'Athens is not the place to be in the height of summer. It is hot, and much too busy. In any case, you are safer here.'

'But I want to be with you—'

'That is not possible, Ariadne.'

Nikolas swallowed half his coffee in one gulp, but when he would have turned to Paige the girl spoke again. 'Why not?' she pleaded. 'I will not be a nuisance to you. And you know I am only ill when you are not around.'

'*Ftani pya!*'

In his urgency to bring the discussion to an end, Nikolas resorted to his own language, and Paige realised it was a measure of his frustration that he didn't even notice.

But Ariadne did. 'Why are you speaking Greek, Nikolas?' she demanded. 'Do you not wish Miss Tennant to know that we have become such—close friends?'

'I warn you, Ariadne—'

Paige got abruptly to her feet. She had no wish to witness any more of this humiliating display. It was embarrassing listening to Ariadne demean herself, and although she had little sympathy for the girl she couldn't help the suspicion that Nikolas had brought this upon himself. He had obviously allowed Ariadne to have her own way for far too long, and now he was paying the price.

'If you don't mind, I'd like to go and take a shower,' she murmured as she pushed back from the table. 'Perhaps we could discuss what you want me to do at some other time.'

Nikolas rose to face her. 'But you've hardly eaten anything.'

'I'd really rather get a shower,' Paige insisted, not wanting another altercation. 'If you'll excuse me...'

He let her go without further argument and Paige hurried across the patio towards the house. Only to come face to face with Sophie who was just coming out.

'Hey, Paige.'

Her sister sounded cheerful for once and Paige refused to show the dismay she felt when she saw what Sophie was wearing. In a pink spandex top and frayed denim shorts, her sister was obviously making a statement. But Paige was too eager to get away to care about that now.

'I'll see you later,' she said, letting Sophie make what she liked of that, but she couldn't prevent a smile from tugging at her lips at the thought of Nikolas's reaction as she went into the house.

CHAPTER FIVE

WHEN Paige emerged from the bathroom some twenty minutes later, she found that someone had left a tray containing coffee, rolls and fresh fruit on the table in her bedroom. She didn't want to believe it was Nikolas who had been so thoughtful, but who else could it be? And she was grateful. Now that she was clean and cool again, she was starving, and she crunched on a crisp apple as she dried her hair.

Then, after eating one of the rolls and drinking a cup of coffee, she dressed in a simple linen shift that exposed her knees. She refused to cover herself up, as Ariadne had done, but she wanted no comparisons to be drawn between her and Sophie either.

Besides, the apricot linen was flattering to her pale cream colouring. And, with her hair newly washed, and curling against her nape, she looked decidedly less harassed than she'd done earlier. A touch of brown eye-shadow and a bronze gloss for her lips completed her toilette, and, content that she could hold her own with a schoolgirl, Paige left the room.

Downstairs again, she followed an arching passage that led to the back of the house. Long windows with black shutters gave tantalising glimpses of the view, the sails of a yacht on the horizon looking like a painting on a blue, blue canvas. She could see the pool, too, and its rippling surface revealed that someone was swimming laps. But it was impossible to see who it was, and, reaching the sun-drenched garden room that opened out onto the patio, she decided she would soon find out.

It was Sophie. As Paige crossed the patio and descended

to the tiled apron that surrounded the pool, her sister saw her and swam to the side. Her curly blonde hair was dark with moisture, which was why Paige hadn't recognised her, and she was wearing a string bikini that Paige hadn't seen before.

'Coming in?' she asked, resting her elbows on the rim.

Paige shook her head. 'Where is everyone?' she asked, looking around. There was no sign of Nikolas or his ward. The table where they had sat at breakfast was deserted, and she was uneasily aware that she really knew next to nothing about their relationship.

'Your boss said he had some work to do,' answered Sophie carelessly, her fingers playing with the three gold circles that defined the shape of her ear. 'I don't know where the black widow is.'

'Sophie!' Paige sighed. 'In any case, you can hardly call her that this morning. She's all in white.'

'She's still a pain,' muttered Sophie unrepentantly. 'Anyway, she disappeared soon after Petronides did. She's probably keeping out of the way, hoping we'll go away.'

Paige didn't say anything, but she suspected that Sophie had a point. Ariadne wasn't going to make things easy for them, and she dreaded what the girl would be like once Nikolas wasn't here to chastise her.

'So—why don't you come for a swim?' asked Sophie practically.

'Because I've just had a shower,' replied Paige, looking uncertainly about her again. 'I wonder if the housekeeper knows where she is?'

'Who cares?' Sophie pushed herself away from the wall and turned a backward somersault. She came up streaming with water, and wiped her eyes with the back of her hand before going on, 'We might as well enjoy it while we can. It's sort of like a holiday. And something tells me that Madame Ariadne isn't going to let us enjoy it for long.'

Although Paige had been thinking the same thing herself,

she refused to believe it. 'She can't stop us,' she said, and Sophie groped for the side and looked up at her with suspicious eyes.

'You sound very sure,' she remarked. 'What do you know that you're not telling me?'

'Look, Ariadne didn't employ me; her guardian did,' replied Paige shortly. 'I'll leave here when he tells me to and not before.'

Sophie's eyes narrowed. 'You like him, don't you?'

'What I know of him.' Paige refused to be diverted. 'As employers go, he's all right, I suppose.'

'I don't mean that, and you know it,' retorted Sophie, watching her closely. She gave a short laugh. 'I don't believe it. After what you said to me, you're stuck on him yourself!'

'That's not true—'

'Oh, right. And I'm Madonna's uncle! Come off it, Paige, you think you've got a chance.'

'I don't.' Paige was horrified. 'Just because he wasn't what you expected, don't shift your fantasies onto me.'

Sophie shrugged. 'He is sexy.'

'And you're not the first female to think so.'

'Well, you can't deny it.' Sophie's tongue circled her lips. 'I wonder what he's like in bed?'

'For God's sake!' Paige was half afraid someone might hear them. Voices carried over water, and the last thing she needed was for Nikolas to hear them talking about him. 'I'm going to sit on one of those loungers. You can join me when you've finished.'

'Wait.' Sophie pulled herself up onto the rim of the swimming pool. 'What had you been doing? Earlier on, I mean. Why did you suddenly need another shower? I assume you had one as soon as you got up.'

'I did.' Paige was uncomfortable with the explanation. 'I'd been for a walk, that's all. But it was very hot and I wanted to get out of my shirt and shorts. They were sweaty.'

'A walk?' Sophie looked up at her enquiringly. 'Where did you walk to? Were you on your own?'

'No, I was with Mr Petronides,' answered Paige shortly, realising there was no point in lying about it when Nikolas could just as easily tell her himself. 'We walked as far as the cliffs, but unfortunately I got a headache. As I said, it was very hot so we came back.'

'I see.'

But Sophie's expression was provocative now and Paige lost her patience. 'Don't look at me like that,' she said. 'I was going alone but he saw me and decided to take the opportunity to talk to me about the job. Don't imagine that if you embarrass me enough I'll change my mind about staying here. I've accepted this position, and I'm going to do it to the best of my ability.'

'Big deal.' Sophie looked a little less pleased with herself now. 'And what am I supposed to do while you're doing your job?'

'You seemed to be having a good time when I came down,' Paige reminded her drily. 'Look, it's too hot to argue. Why don't you finish your swim?'

Paige was just beginning to wish she'd brought some sunscreen cream when she heard the unmistakable sound of footsteps behind her. For a moment, she thought it might be Nikolas, but when she turned her head she saw Ariadne trudging with evident reluctance towards her.

'Oh—hi,' she called, deciding it was up to her to try and get the girl to talk to her. 'Are you coming to join us?'

Ariadne looked as if she would have liked to turn around and go back into the house but she didn't. Despite her unwillingness to accept Paige as a friend, she had apparently been directed to make the best of it, and, after trailing down the steps, she positioned herself on another of the sunbeds, and opened the book she'd brought with her.

Paige compressed her lips. So much for a change of heart, she thought. Then, determined to make some headway, she asked, 'What are you reading?'

Ariadne turned the spine of the book up so that Paige could see it for herself, her eyes moving past her as she caught sight of Sophie in the pool. Her indignation was evident, and it didn't help that Sophie chose that moment to climb out onto the side. Wearing only the scanty bikini, she was clearly a source of irritation to the Greek girl, and Paige wondered if her sister was aware of how difficult she was making it for her.

Of course, she was. Sophie stood beside the pool, drying herself on one of the towels she'd taken from the stack on a table nearby. Then, as if she knew she was being watched, she bent and picked up her equally skimpy shorts, drawing them up over her damp legs with deliberate provocation.

Paige had to distract Ariadne, and, leaning forward, she said, 'Oh—you're reading *Jane Eyre*.' She'd recognised the author's name, not the title, but it was a fair guess that that was what it was. 'Are you enjoying it? I love the Brontë books.' She paused, seeking inspiration. 'Mr Rochester is such an attractive hero, don't you think?'

Ariadne pulled her hostile gaze back to her companion. 'Not as attractive as Nikolas,' she declared dispassionately. 'Don't you think Nikolas is attractive, Miss Tennant? So big, and dark, and powerful!'

Paige didn't know what to say. To deny it wasn't really an option, but, equally, to concede that she found him attractive would lay her open to all kinds of derision. Ariadne had already shown her contempt for the Englishwoman, and Paige had no desire to give her more ammunition for her arsenal.

'I'm not sure your guardian would approve of us discussing him,' she said at last. 'Um—have you read anything else by the Brontës? *Wuthering Heights*—that's by

Emily, of course—is very good, and Anne's novel, *The Tenant of Wildfell Hall*—'

'Don't you have a—how do you say?—a boyfriend, Miss Tennant?' Ariadne seemed determined to disconcert her. 'I am wondering how he feels about you spending several weeks away from home.'

Paige sighed, speculating on how far a companion was expected to go to satisfy the demands of her charge. 'Whether I have a boyfriend or not is no concern of yours, Ariadne,' she replied, keeping her tone pleasant with an effort. 'Now, perhaps we can talk about what you usually do when you're staying here. Do you swim? Go snorkelling? Ride?'

'Why are you so unwilling to talk about yourself, Miss Tennant?' countered Ariadne, without answering her. 'I shall begin to think you have something to hide.'

Paige expelled a weary breath. 'Why are you so determined to talk about me?' she retorted. 'I can't believe my history is of any interest to you whatsoever.'

'Oh, but you are wrong.' Ariadne laid her book aside and regarded her with bright, malicious eyes. 'I am curious as to why Nikolas would agree to bring both you and your sister to Skiapolis, when I clearly have no need of one companion, let alone two.'

Paige shrugged. 'Perhaps you should ask him,' she declared, looking up with some apprehension when a shadow fell across her. But it was only her sister.

'Ask who what?' asked Sophie irrepressibly, towelling the blonde tangle of her hair as she spoke. 'Let me guess: it has to be Nikolas. What's wrong? Is Ariadne showing her claws again?' She gave a derisive laugh. 'God, she's such a cliché!'

Ariadne's face darkened with anger. 'What? What are you saying? What did you call me?'

'I said you were a cliché,' replied Sophie carelessly, before Paige could stop her. 'You are. You're a sad case. Why don't you grow up?'

Ariadne gasped. 'I am—grown-up.'

'Yeah, right.' Sophie flopped down onto the nearest lounger and began drying her legs. 'I mean…' She stifled another giggle. 'Where did you get those clothes? Puhleeze!'

'There is nothing wrong with *my* clothes,' began Ariadne furiously, but Sophie wasn't even listening to her.

'Leggings!' she scoffed. 'Like they're still in style!' She looked at the other girl disparagingly. 'Come off it, Ari. Get a life!'

'Sophie!'

Paige was afraid she'd gone too far, but Ariadne was too agitated to notice. 'If—if you think *I* would wear what—what you are wearing—'

Her lips curled in disgust but Sophie wasn't offended. In the past six months she'd had to cope with much worse, and she was ready for her. 'You couldn't,' she retorted airily, lifting one leg and examining it with evident satisfaction. 'You don't have the figure for it.'

'There is nothing wrong with my figure.'

'What figure?' Sophie smirked. 'You say that enough times, you may just start believing it.'

Ariadne seethed. 'You—you are—insolent!'

'Yeah. Fun, isn't it?' Sophie stretched out on the lounger and crossed one ankle over the other. 'You know,' she added, glancing at Paige, 'I could get used to this.'

'You—you—'

Ariadne sprang to her feet, searching for a word to describe what she thought about the other girl at that moment, and then gave it up, and berated both of them in her own language. Her face was red and her hands trembled as she gesticulated her feelings, and for a moment Paige had visions of her attacking Sophie and both girls rolling about on the ground.

'Ariadne...' she protested, realising she had to say something to calm the situation, but it was too late. With a final imprecation, Ariadne charged away, her high-heeled sandals clattering noisily across the patio as she fled into the house.

The silence after she'd gone was almost deafening. And ominous, thought Paige gloomily. God knew what Ariadne was going to tell her guardian about this. It was all very well assuring herself that she couldn't be held responsible for her sister's behaviour, but the truth was she'd let her get away with it and she wasn't proud of herself for doing nothing to stop her.

Sophie had no such inhibitions. 'That's better,' she said. 'This place is half decent when she's not around. God, she's so boring! She acts more like seventy than seventeen.'

'All the same, you had no right to speak to her like that,' said Paige heavily. 'What she wears is nothing to do with you.'

'So what?' Sophie sniffed. 'It's time someone burst her bubble. She thinks she can say what she likes and no one's going to complain. Asking you whether you had a boyfriend, and why her old man invited both of us here. I mean—like that's anything to do with her.'

'He's not her old man.' Paige made the correction automatically. Then she realised what else Sophie had said. 'How do you know what we were talking about?'

'I've got ears.' Sophie was unrepentant. 'Sound carries around a pool, Paige; you know that. Anyway, you should be grateful I spoke up for you. You're too naïve. Being polite gets you nowhere with bitches like her. I know. I deal with them every day.'

Paige made an incredulous sound. 'I don't believe this. Sophie, we're not guests here. We're employees—or I am, anyway. And employees don't start throwing their weight around with their employers. I may be naïve, but I know that.'

'You also said that Ariadne wasn't your employer,' her sister reminded her shortly. 'Chill out, Paige. She's not likely to say anything, more's the pity.'

'What do you mean by that?'

'I mean, we're going to be stuck here no matter what,' muttered Sophie, brushing a fly away from her bare midriff. She grimaced. 'Still, I suppose it has its compensations. I'm looking forward to seeing what the ward-from-hell does when she realises she's got some competition.'

Paige gasped. 'That's ridiculous!'

'No, it's not. I've seen the way he looks at you.'

Paige couldn't help it; her face flamed with hot colour, and Sophie pointed at her triumphantly. 'You see!'

Paige got to her feet. 'I'm going to find Ariadne.'

'Why? Because you can't stand the heat?' Sophie arched a mocking brow.

'No, because I don't intend to sit here and listen to your nonsense any longer.'

'Okay.' Sophie shrugged. 'Have it your own way.' She glanced round. 'Would you mind moving that umbrella closer? I don't want to get burnt.'

Paige pursed her lips, but before she could tell the younger girl to do it herself Sophie spoke again.

'Hey, look who's here! Did I prick a nerve or what?'

Paige swung round, quite sure that this time it was Nikolas, coming to discipline Sophie, or, worse, to give them both notice, and caught her breath. Ariadne was walking back across the patio, the demure white outfit replaced by a cropped halter top in stripes of blue and yellow and a denim miniskirt that exposed the slender length of her legs. With her feet pushed into heel-less wedges, she looked young and pretty, and far different from the girl who had fled into the villa fifteen minutes before.

But her attitude didn't appear to have changed. Ignoring the two English girls, she subsided back onto the lounger she had occupied earlier, picking up her book and settling back against the cushions. Whether she was actually reading it or just using it as a means to avoid conversation, Paige couldn't be sure, but either way her own presence seemed superfluous.

'I'll see you later,' she said flatly, speaking mainly to Sophie. 'If you see Mr Petronides, tell him I've gone to finish my unpacking.'

Sophie propped herself up on her elbows. 'And what am I supposed to do with her?' She jerked a thumb in Ariadne's direction.

'Just—be civil,' said Paige wearily, realising that was probably impossible for her. 'I shan't be long.'

CHAPTER SIX

PAIGE didn't see Nikolas again that day.

He didn't appear for lunch, which she and the two girl
shared at the table on the patio, and afterwards Ariadn
declared that she was going to take a rest. Paige guesse
the girl was still recovering from the series of infection
that had kept her away from school during the past term
and in all honesty she was tempted to do the same. Sh
was tired, too, after the restless night she'd had, but sh
reminded herself again that she was not a guest here, an
employees did not take time off when it suited them.

In consequence, she and Sophie spent the afternoon be
side the pool. She even took a swim in the late afternoon
when the shadows were lengthening and the water in th
pool was deliciously warm from the heat of the sun
Pleasantly tired, she took a shower before getting ready fo
dinner, quelling the unwanted sense of excitement she fel
at the prospect of seeing their host again.

She needn't have worried. Nikolas didn't join them fo
dinner either. Kiria Papandreiu conveyed the news tha
Kirie Petronides was dining elsewhere this evening. Paig
had great difficulty understanding her, but the phrase 'The
ineh etho!' or 'He's out!' was familiar to her. Evidently
Nikolas did not consider it necessary to entertain them thi
evening. He'd apparently left that to Ariadne, who arrivec
rather later than was polite wearing the same resentful ex
pression she had worn earlier.

But this evening Paige had no intention of allowing th
younger girl to get the upper hand. Whatever Nikolas ha
had in mind when he'd brought her here, she couldn't be
lieve he expected her to put up with Ariadne's insolence

But she did wish her position had been more thoroughly defined.

'You have caught the sun, Miss Tennant,' Ariadne remarked somewhat smugly as she took her seat. 'It was very unwise to spend all afternoon beside the pool.'

'It was very pleasant,' replied Paige, helping herself to stuffed olives, endeavouring not to be aggravated by the girl's mocking tone. 'Are you feeling better?' she added, playing her at her own game. 'You looked rather pale when you went to take your rest.'

Ariadne's lips tightened. 'I'm perfectly all right.'

'Are you?' Paige regarded her without conviction. 'But your guardian told me you'd been ill. That's why he wants you to spend the summer here on the island.'

'That's not the reason,' said Ariadne crossly, and Paige was reminded of the argument the young girl had had with her guardian that morning. She could almost find it in her heart to feel sorry for Nikolas. It couldn't be easy for him dealing with someone of Ariadne's fiery temperament.

'Whatever,' she murmured now, and Sophie chose to intervene.

'Well, I think Ariadne would have much more fun in Athens,' she observed, following her own agenda. 'The island's okay, but it's dull. There's nothing going on.'

'What would you know?' enquired Ariadne sharply, and Paige could see another confrontation in the offing. It was apparently all right for the Greek girl to object to staying here, but, like any territorial animal, she defended her own.

'More than you, evidently,' began Sophie, always ready with an answer, but once again Paige cut her off.

'It doesn't really matter, does it?' she declared. 'We're all staying here for the summer. I suggest we try and make the best of it. It is a beautiful place.'

'Like the Garden of Eden,' said Sophie provokingly. 'And, like all earthly paradises, there has to be a serpent.'

'Are you implying—?'

'Where did you live before your parents died?' Paige broke in swiftly, not entirely sure that it was a suitable topic, but desperate to distract the girl from what Sophie had said.

'In Athens, of course.' To her relief, Ariadne chose to boast about it. 'My father had a huge villa not far from Nikolas's house there. That's how I know him so well.'

Paige inclined her head, acknowledging the explanation. 'And you went to school there, too?'

'Does it matter?' Ariadne was impatient now. 'I shall be leaving school very shortly. I'm almost eighteen, you know.'

Paige did know, and it was difficult to make conversation with someone who was so determined to be objectionable. Everything the Greek girl said was designed to provoke her and it was very hard not to let her succeed.

However, when Ariadne turned her frustration on one of the young maids, Paige felt obliged to say something in the young woman's defence. 'If you don't want any meat, Ariadne, don't have any,' she advised her shortly. 'Don't take your grievances out on innocent people, just because you've got a grudge against the world.'

Ariadne's jaw dropped. 'I don't know what you're talking about.'

'Yes, you do.' Paige was succinct. 'You've worn a sulky expression ever since we arrived. Well, I'm tired of sustaining this one-sided relationship. Where I come from, people treat each other with respect. I suggest you learn to do the same.'

Ariadne gasped. 'You can't speak to me like that.'

'I just did.'

'I'll tell Nikolas.'

'Go ahead. I doubt if he'd approve of your attitude either.'

Ariadne's nostrils flared. 'You know nothing about

Nikolas!' she exclaimed, and for once Paige was too angry to be discreet.

'More than you might imagine,' she declared crisply, realising belatedly that Sophie was listening to their exchange, too. 'Now, let's get on with dinner, shall we?' She glanced warningly at her sister. 'Without any more sly remarks.'

Ariadne stared at her disbelievingly for a few seconds, and then she got abruptly to her feet. 'I don't have to listen to this. I'll ask Kiria Papandreiu to serve my meal in my room.'

'No, you won't.' Now that she'd committed herself Paige had no choice but to go on. 'If you leave this table, you won't have any dinner. Do you understand? Now, stop behaving like a child and sit down.'

It didn't work. Not that she'd really thought it would. With a gesture of indignation, Ariadne threw down her napkin and, pushing past the startled maid, she left the room.

'Hey, way to go, Paige!'

Sophie was delighted, but Paige found no relief in her sister's approval. With slumped shoulders, she was forced to acknowledge that the direct approach hadn't worked, and she wondered if it would be any easier after Nikolas left for Athens. She wasn't hopeful. The girl had a severe case of bad attitude, and Paige suspected it would take more than her guardian's departure to alter her mood.

By the next morning, Paige had managed to shelve her own feelings of depression. This had to work. Somehow, some way, she had to gain Ariadne's confidence, and, deciding that the first thing she had to do was talk to Nikolas, she went down to the patio, hoping he and Ariadne might be having breakfast together.

But, although the table was laid for four, there was no one about. Paige propped her hands on her hips and stared somewhat uncertainly about her, wondering if Nikolas was up yet. It was typical that the previous day, when she hadn't been looking for him, he'd been there, whereas now…

'Tha thelateh pro-ino, kiria?'

Paige had to applaud the housekeeper's assiduity. She hadn't been aware that anyone had noticed her arrival, but they obviously had and now Kiria Papandreiu was asking her if she would like breakfast. 'Um—*kati elafro, efharisto,*' she murmured, dredging up the words from her small knowledge of the language. 'Just something light, thank you.'

'Ne, kiria.'

The old woman nodded and went away again, and Paige was relieved to find that she'd understood her. Deciding she might as well sit down while she waited, she seated herself at the table and gazed out towards the hazy line of the horizon. It was another beautiful day, and, she hoped, a more successful one.

A maid brought her warm rolls and orange juice and a steaming pot of coffee. And, because she'd eaten little after Ariadne had stormed out on them the night before, she ate three rolls, spread with some of the rich sweet conserve she found in the bread basket. Then, fortified with two cups of strong black coffee, she asked the maid to tell Kirie Petronides—if he asked—that she had gone for a walk.

She had intended just to go as far as the cliffs, but the beach looked so inviting, she couldn't resist it. She had no headache this morning, and although she wanted to speak to Nikolas she'd found she couldn't just sit meekly waiting for him to put in an appearance on the patio. Besides, it was still only just eight o'clock, and she had no idea what time he'd got home the night before.

Or where he'd been, she conceded as she descended the cliff steps. Not that it was any concern of hers. But she had thought he would stick around until Ariadne had learned to accept the situation. He knew what a sulky little madam she could be, and that was what Paige wanted to talk to him about. She wanted to know how much authority—or how little—she was expected to exert.

It was cooler on the beach. Kicking off her shoes, she curled her toes into the sand, enjoying the sensation of the grains sliding between her toes. She found if she walked in the shadow of the cliffs she could pretend she was back in England, walking along the sands at Bournemouth. When she was a little girl, her father had used to take his family to Bournemouth for two weeks every August, and she and Sophie, who had been little more than a toddler, had spent hours digging sandcastles and trying unsuccessfully to make a moat.

Of course, her mother had been alive then, and her father hadn't been so stressed about making a success of Tennants. He'd enjoyed his life in those days; they all had. It was only after her mother died that he'd turned all his energies into more and more reckless schemes to make money.

For the first couple of years, she'd been happy to support him. She'd been glad he'd had something to distract him from her mother's loss. She'd done whatever he'd asked of her, even to the extent of making herself pleasant to those of his business colleagues who needed the encouragement of being seen with a young and moderately attractive young woman to persuade them to part with their money.

And then he'd introduced her to Nikolas Petronides...

They'd been at a party in Monte Carlo at the time. Her father had been attending a seminar being run by a consortium of European financiers, and the Greek shipping magnate had posed a challenge he couldn't resist.

For some time, Parker Tennant had been trying to offload shares in a merchant shipping line that she'd later discovered had been in financial difficulties. Her father had invested his clients' money rather heavily in the enterprise, and he was looking for someone who might be willing to spend some of their own money to turn the company around.

Or, at least, that was what he'd told his daughter.

And she'd believed him.

Paige's lips twisted ruefully. She knew now it had all been a lie. Even before Nikolas had accused her of being a party to her father's scheme, she'd learned exactly how hollow Parker Tennant's promises were. In the years that followed, she'd lost count of the number of times he'd assured her that this time he was going to make a killing, only to find himself at the end of the day even deeper in debt. By the time he'd died, he'd owed a small fortune, and Paige had been left to salvage what she could from the wreckage.

Which was why Sophie was so bitter; why Paige couldn't altogether blame her sister when she did something outrageous. She was only following in the family tradition, after all. Goodness knew, Paige had made enough mistakes in her life.

But she'd never agreed to take part in any business negotiations after the affair with Nikolas. Whatever the truth was, he'd hurt her badly, and she'd had no intention of putting her heart on the line again.

Which was how she'd become involved with Martin Price.

She couldn't honestly say that she'd fallen in love with him as she had with Nikolas. Their relationship had been based on a mutual liking for one another, and she'd had no idea that Martin had a hidden agenda. She'd been so delighted to find someone who had no apparent connection to her father that she'd taken everything he said at face value, only learning the truth when the rest of her world was falling apart. In his own way, Martin had been just as ambitious as her father, and just as ruthless when things didn't go his way.

She sighed. That was all in the past now, and there was

no doubt that since meeting Nikolas again she'd realised how shallow her relationship with Martin had been. The affection she'd felt towards him had barely brushed the surface of the passion she'd shared with Nikolas, and a lump came into her throat at the thought of what she'd lost.

Feeling chilled, as much by her emotions as by the shadows cast by the cliffs, she walked out into the sunlight, going down the beach to the wooden jetty that jutted out into the water. Climbing onto it, she walked along, peering down into water that was so clear, she could see the many colourful fish swimming beneath its surface.

She didn't know what caused her to look back, but when she did she saw Nikolas strolling across the sands towards her. Either Kiria Papandreiu had given him her message and he'd come looking for her, or he'd had the same thought; she couldn't be sure. But as he got closer she saw the snorkelling mask dangling from his hand.

'Good morning,' he said as she reached the end of the jetty. 'I thought I might find you here.'

Paige forced a polite smile. 'You got my message, then,' she murmured, looking away from the searching warmth of his dark gaze. In an open-necked green shirt and black shorts, he was far too familiar. After the thoughts she'd been having, it would have been safer if they'd met up at the house.

'I saw Kiria Papandreiu, *ne*,' he agreed as she pretended to be looking at the fish. He paused. 'I see you find our wildlife fascinating. Perhaps you'd like to join me?'

'Join you?'

She looked up then, and he held up the masks so that she could now see he'd brought two. 'Why not?' he asked. 'I'm sure you'd enjoy it. It's early yet. I doubt if the girls are even up.'

Paige shook her head as if to clear it. 'I—as a matter of fact, I'd like to talk to you about Ariadne,' she said, glad of the opening he'd given her. 'I had hoped to speak to you yesterday, but, as I didn't, perhaps we could discuss my duties now.'

Nikolas's expression sobered. 'Your duties?' he queried. 'Or perhaps how I expect you to deal with Ariadne's attitude?' He frowned. 'She has told me you have been—what would you say?—short with her, *ohi*? I know it is not easy for you to believe, but she is a very insecure little girl.'

'But that's the point—she's not a little girl,' retorted Paige at once, stung at the thought of the two of them discussing her behaviour behind her back. 'And it's going to be useless if you countermand every instruction I give her. Last night, at dinner, she was especially—awkward. You said she needed a companion. In my opinion, she needs something more than that.'

Nikolas's mouth compressed. 'Did I say I had countermanded your instructions?' His eyes darkened, and she was intensely conscious of the fact that it was only because he was still standing on the sand that she was on a level with him. 'All I am saying is that appearances can be deceptive. She may seem very confident to you, but underneath she is crying out for—affection.'

Paige's lips tightened. 'Well, you'd know that better than me.'

Nikolas stepped up onto the jetty. 'What is that supposed to mean?'

His tone was harsher than before, and she was suddenly aware of her own insecurities. 'Just that affection is the last thing she'd ever want from me.'

'You think so?'

'Don't you?'

'Perhaps I am not the best person to judge,' he responded coolly. 'In your eyes, at least, my opinion does not count for very much.'

Paige had the feeling that they were getting off the subject. And, what was more, into deeper waters, figuratively speaking, than she wanted to go. It was difficult to keep her mind focussed on what she'd wanted to talk to him about when he persisted in turning the argument against her. She was also aware that she was sweating, and that she wasn't wearing a bra.

'Look, perhaps we can talk about this later,' she said, wondering if she could get past him without touching his lean frame. He was far more disturbing in casual clothes than he'd been in the more formal clothes he'd worn the day before, and defining her position as far as Ariadne was concerned did not seem half as important as getting away from him.

'You're nervous,' he said, disconcerting her still further. 'Surely I do not intimidate you?'

'Whether you intimidate me or not is hardly relevant,' retorted Paige tightly. 'As far as Ariadne is concerned, we must agree to differ. I'll keep what you say in mind, but I can't promise that she'll cooperate.'

Nikolas sighed. 'For what it's worth, I'll trust your judgement,' he said. 'Now—what's your decision?'

'My decision?' Paige's mind was blank. 'My decision about what?'

'About joining me for a swim,' he prompted, successfully blocking the end of the jetty. He unbuttoned his shirt as he spoke, exposing the V of coarse hair that arrowed down below the waistband of his shorts. 'Come on. You'll enjoy it.'

Paige found that she was embarrassed by his suggestion. 'I don't think so,' she said stiffly. And then, remembering their changed relationship, she added, 'Thank you.'

'Why not?'

'Why not?' She swallowed. 'I think you know the answer to that as well as me. If you'll excuse me, I'll just go and see what Sophie is—'

'You're concerned because you don't have a swimsuit,' he remarked drily. 'So? I have seen you naked before.'

He would bring that up! Paige felt the blush of heat all

over her body. But she had to stop this, and stop it now, before he made a complete fool of her.

'I don't want to go swimming,' she said, refusing to submit to his blackmail. 'It's getting very hot. I'd rather go back to the house.'

'It's cooler in the water,' remarked Nikolas softly, and she was irresistibly reminded of how soft the water would feel against her hot skin. Her hot, *bare* skin, she recalled, avoiding the dark sensuality of his muscled flesh. 'Have you become a prude, *aghapita*? Surely you know that no one but I can see you here?'

Paige breathed shallowly. 'That's not the point.'

'So what is the point, *pirazi*?'

Inspiration came to her. 'I'm your employee. Not your guest.'

Nikolas lifted his shoulders. 'I do not believe that bothers you.'

'It should bother you.'

'And if it does not?'

'It would bother Ariadne,' said Paige childishly, and it was only when his eyes narrowed that she realised she had said the wrong thing.

'So?' He moved towards her and, because there was nowhere to go but off the end of the jetty, she was forced to stay where she was. 'You are jealous, Paige.' His hand cupped her nape, and she steeled herself against his mocking appraisal. 'You would like to go swimming with me, but you're afraid of upsetting that stubborn little streak you call a conscience, *ohi*?'

'No!' She was horrified at his perception. 'I just see no point in raking up the past. And besides, you're only having fun at my expense. What do you really want, Nikolas? Flesh? Or blood?'

'I want…' His thumb brushed the corner of her mouth, and she bit her lip to prevent its sensual invasion. 'Oh, there are many things I want, Paige.' He looked down at her breasts, which were taut and swollen against the thin cotton of her shirt. His lips twisted. 'And you naked is not on my agenda.'

Paige held up her head. 'I'm—I'm pleased to hear it.'

'Are you? Are you really?' He moved even closer and his powerful thigh brushed against her own. His breath fanned her temple. 'So I'm not disturbing you? Not even a little? Knowing that we're here and completely alone doesn't bother you at all?'

Paige moved her neck against his fingers. 'Should it?' she managed at last, striving for indifference, and at last she succeeded in provoking him.

'*Hristo*, it bothers me,' he bit out savagely, his fingers tight on her shoulders now. And then his mouth was on hers, and his tongue allowed no resistance as it thrust between her lips.

If it had been a game on his part, it had backfired. When he kissed her, she knew instantly that what he was doing was beyond his control. But then, it was beyond hers, too, and she clutched dizzily for his arm to prevent herself from tumbling backwards into the water. For a few mindless minutes, she was too bemused to think of anything but him, anything but the searing heat of his mouth.

Then she was in his arms, close against the urgent demands of his body, aware of the violent reaction he was having towards her that he wasn't even trying to disguise. Not that he could, she thought unsteadily, imagining how she would feel if he pulled her down onto the sun-warmed slats beneath them. How hot and heavy *he'd* feel, pressing her to the jetty, how hot and heavy and hard his arousal would feel sliding into her wet sheath…

She opened her legs almost instinctively, wanting him to touch her, wanting him to know how aroused she was. But instead of slipping his hand beneath her hem he thrust her away from him, a superhuman effort that left him swaying and red in the face.

'*Exipnos*, Paige,' he muttered. '*Poli exipnos*. Clever. Very clever.'

And, without giving her a chance to defend herself, he tore off his shirt and dived cleanly into the water.

CHAPTER SEVEN

PAIGE heard the helicopter as she was having her shower that evening. Now that she knew what it was, she had no difficulty in identifying the throbbing blades, and her nerves tightened at the realisation that Nikolas must have sent for it. Which probably meant he was leaving. But when? Tonight? Tomorrow? She expelled a painful breath. Soon.

She wasn't surprised. After what had happened that morning, he was unlikely to want to prolong his stay on the island. The wonder of it was that she hadn't been given her marching orders, too. She'd certainly expected it. She'd shamed him and she'd shamed herself and he was unlikely to forgive her for that.

Luckily Ariadne hadn't been about when she'd returned to the villa from the beach. She'd had time to go up to her room and compose herself before she'd been obliged to go down and face her responsibilities. And, although she was sure the girl must have wondered why she hadn't wanted anything but coffee, it apparently hadn't occurred to her that Paige might have been up earlier.

Besides, she'd been intent on convincing Paige that she was sorry for the way she'd behaved the night before. She'd made some excuse about letting Sophie upset her, and Paige had had to concede, to herself at least, that her job might have been easier without her sister's particular brand of provocation.

Whatever, by the time Nikolas had appeared, dark and unsmiling in a navy blue shirt and matching cotton trousers, his damp hair slicked back behind his ears, they'd been chatting together in comparative harmony. If the conversation had been slightly one-sided and Ariadne had chosen to use the time to talk about her guardian and the things they'd done together, Paige hadn't complained. She'd been too relieved to find they could have a civil conversation, and if the girl's words had sometimes scraped a nerve she'd managed not to show it.

Nikolas's arrival, however, had disturbed Paige more than she'd cared to admit. His brusque, *'Kalimera,'* issued for Ariadne's benefit, she had no doubt, had done nothing to reassure her, and his invitation to his ward to accompany him on a trip he intended to make to the other side of the island had left her feeling chilled and superfluous.

There had been no question of her going with them, and after the exchange she'd had with Nikolas earlier she'd been half prepared for him to issue her dismissal. He hadn't then, but she'd spent the whole day in a state of extreme agitation, and, of course, Sophie had assumed that Ariadne had arranged the whole thing.

'Hey, don't let them get to you!' she'd exclaimed, while they were having lunch together. Nikolas and his ward hadn't returned, and Sophie thought Paige was worrying that Ariadne might take the opportunity to complain about her behaviour the night before. 'So what if she slags you off to her old man?' she'd added carelessly. 'He's not going to listen to anything she has to say. You've got to have some authority. I thought you did good, myself.'

Paige had denied it, of course, consoling herself with the thought that Nikolas was unlikely to discuss his real reasons for firing her with either of the girls. If he did decide to fire her. Whatever happened, she had only herself to blame.

But nothing had happened. Even though she'd been sitting on the patio when they'd arrived home, no one had disturbed her. She'd heard the scrape of the car's tyres as they'd swept across the gravel, listened to the sound of footsteps crossing the entrance hall, felt her skin prickle with the awareness that Nikolas was back, but that was all. Eventually, she'd had to come upstairs to change for dinner without any idea of where Nikolas was or what he planned to do.

Standing in front of her mirror now, fastening her bra, she endeavoured to think positively about the evening ahead. If Nikolas could treat her with indifference, she should be able to do the same. If only...

She sighed. Perhaps it would be easier if she took the initiative and told him she was leaving. Simpler, certainly, she reflected bitterly, viewing her mini-brief-clad hips without liking. It would obviously remove all the uncertainty from her position, but then she'd be forced to go back to London and face all the problems she'd left there.

She groaned. When had her life become so complicated? When her father had died? When Martin had arranged for her to meet Nikolas again? Or four years ago, when she'd walked into a cocktail party and fallen in love with a man whose only interest in her had been sexual?

She started when the door behind her opened suddenly. Sophie sauntered carelessly into the room, but although she was relieved Paige was in no mood to treat her sister with her usual tact.

'Can't you knock?' she exclaimed, snatching up the long-sleeved black knit she was planning to wear for dinner and holding it to her chest. 'I'd prefer a little privacy, if you don't mind.'

'Tough!' Sophie dismissed her feelings as if they were of no account. 'Don't take it out on me because you can't cut it. I've told you. You've got nothing to worry about.'

Paige wished she could be as confident. Changing tack, she said, 'You're not planning on going down to dinner in that outfit, are you?'

'Why? What's wrong with it?' Sophie regarded her thin cropped vest and lacy miniskirt with obvious satisfaction. 'Chill out, can't you? I look okay.'

'You look—tarty,' said Paige, deciding she was running

the risk of creasing her own dress and wriggling into it. 'I'd have thought you'd want to look your age, at least.'

Sophie pulled a face. 'That's not going to work, Paige.' She admired the stud she'd put into her nose this evening and scowled at her reflection. 'Think again.'

Paige shook her head. The piercing of Sophie's nostril had been a bone of contention between them weeks before the marijuana incident, and she had hoped she'd persuaded her not to wear the stud again. But evidently this evening her sister was looking for trouble, and Paige was too weary to start another argument.

'So what do you want?' she asked, picking up her brush and tugging it through her honey-gold bob.

'Some excitement. Somebody interesting to talk to. A *joint*!' Sophie emphasised the final demand with defiance. 'Do I have to have a reason for coming into your room? I thought you might be glad of my support.'

Her support? Paige couldn't believe she'd said that. Shaking her head, she said ruefully, 'Not dressed like that.'

'Then stuff you!' said Sophie rudely, striding back to the door. She jerked it open and then turned to regard her sister with a mocking gaze. 'You can tell your precious employer that I'm not hungry.' Her lips twisted. 'Oh, and by the way, your bum does look big in that!'

With a grimace of satisfaction, she slammed the door behind her. Paige was tempted to go after her, but she knew it wouldn't do any good. In this mood, Sophie was unlikely to listen to anything she had to say, and it was a bit late to wish she hadn't been so negative about her clothes. That dig about wanting a 'joint' was worrying, and it was only the fact that she knew she couldn't get into any trouble here that persuaded her to abandon the problem.

She sighed. It was time she was going downstairs. She wasn't looking forward to it, but she didn't have a choice. Besides, if it was at all possible, she had to try and repair the damage she'd done that morning. If Nikolas was leaving, he might have decided to give her a second chance. She could only hope so.

Despite her best efforts, her nose had caught the sun, and she used a blocking cream to disguise its redness. Then, after darkening her lids with eyeshadow and smoothing a beige lip gloss over her generous mouth, she was ready. Or as ready as she'd ever be, she thought ruefully. She just hoped Ariadne was still in a good mood.

Her heeled sandals announced her progress as she went downstairs, and as no one came to meet her she walked purposefully towards the room where they'd gathered for drinks the night Nikolas had dined at home.

She paused uncertainly in the doorway at the sight of a strange man helping himself to a drink from the cabinet. He wasn't as tall as Nikolas, but he was equally dark, with a stocky build and hair that appeared to be receding from a high forehead. There was no sign of Ariadne or her guardian, however, and Paige allowed a small sigh to escape her. What now?

'*Kalispera*, Miss Tennant.'

She'd turned to look back towards the stairs when the man spoke, and she swung round again in some confusion. 'I'm sorry. Do I know—? Yanis!' She realised suddenly who he was. 'Yanis Stouros. I didn't recognise you.'

'*Then pirazi.*' Yanis smiled. 'It doesn't matter, *kiria*. We are all getting older. I've put on a little weight, and my hair—' He ran a rueful hand over his scalp, before coming towards her to grasp her outstretched fingers. 'It's good to see you again. Are you well?'

'I—I'm fine.' Paige let him enclose her hands with his. 'I didn't realise you were here. Where have you been hiding yourself?'

'I only arrived a short time ago,' he explained warmly, and she remembered the helicopter she had heard earlier. 'But I hear you are now working for Nikolas. We are both—what is that expression you use?—in the same boat, *ohi*?'

Paige managed a thin smile. 'Is that what he told you?'

'No.' Yanis shrugged. 'He told me you are here to make a friend of Ariadne. That is good. She needs female companionship. The little one is too much on her own.'

'Is she?' Paige reserved judgement. She was fairly sure that Ariadne wouldn't agree with him, despite their conversation that morning. And as for calling Ariadne 'the little one'—Paige felt a rueful disbelief. The girl had evidently wrapped both men round her little finger. 'Well, we'll see,' she added determinedly. 'I'm not sure how it's going to work out.'

Yanis's smile gentled. 'Do not let her—give you the hard time,' he urged softly. 'Ariadne can be wilful, I know, but she means well. And you have Nikolas's confidence. Remember that.'

Do I?

This time Paige kept the comment to herself, but she suspected from his expression that Yanis knew exactly what she was thinking. 'So,' she murmured, changing the subject, 'how are you?' She looked down at his blunt-fingered hands still clasping hers. 'You're not married?'

'Who would have me?'

Yanis pulled a wry face, but his eyes were intent on hers and she remembered how kind he'd been to her when her relationship with Nikolas had ended. But she didn't want his admiration. Particularly as any mistakes she'd made now were peculiarly her own.

'I'm sure that isn't a problem,' she said hurriedly, aware that somehow their conversation had become too personal. Her fault, probably. She should never have made that reference about him not being married. What he did or didn't do was nothing to do with her. She took another breath. 'Um—where's Nikolas?'

'I'm here.'

Paige was startled. As always, Nikolas had found a way to disconcert her, and the realisation that he was standing right behind her now caused an uneasy fluttering in her stomach. She couldn't help wondering how long he'd been there and what interpretation he'd put on her exchange with Yanis. The two men were much of an age and she hoped he didn't imagine she'd been flirting with his assistant.

'Let me get you a drink, *kiria*.' Yanis found a way to ease her misgivings and Paige was glad of his intervention. She stepped further into the room, allowing Nikolas to move past her, and the two men approached the drinks cabinet together.

'Miss Tennant prefers wine,' Nikolas remarked as he joined his assistant, and Paige thought how elegant he looked this evening. In a cream shirt and black trousers, a tissue-thin black leather jacket accentuating the width of his shoulders, he was more formally dressed than usual, and Paige wondered tensely if he was leaving tonight. It was possible he had a dinner engagement in Athens, and her pulse quickened at the thought that he might be meeting some other woman. She was struggling to come to terms with how she felt about this possibility when he added, 'Am I not right?'

'What?' She couldn't think what he was talking about and, although she'd been avoiding his eyes, now she was caught and held by his sardonic gaze. 'Oh—the wine. Y-yes,' she stammered as a latent comprehension dawned. 'Thank you.'

'*Efharistisi mou,*' he replied politely, turning back to Yanis, and Paige's hand sought the gold chain that circled her throat almost protectively.

Obviously he'd had time to put what had happened that morning into perspective, she decided bleakly. The cold detachment he'd exhibited earlier had disappeared, or perhaps the presence of Yanis had mellowed his mood. Either way, the fears she'd been stressing over all day seemed to have been unfounded. Unless he intended to wait until after dinner to deliver his ultimatum.

Whatever, she determined not to feel threatened by his ability to act like a chameleon. If her past experience had taught her anything it was that men rarely put their true feelings on display. No matter how uncertain she might feel, she had to behave as if nothing had happened, as if being in the same room as Nikolas didn't shred what little composure she had left.

She turned deliberately to Yanis. 'Did you fly in from Athens?' she asked, and he stepped forward to hand her a glass of white wine.

'*Sosta,*' he agreed. 'That's right.' He lifted his own glass of retsina in a silent salute to her. 'Regrettably, it is to be a short visit. We have to return to the office tomorrow.'

'Tomorrow?' Paige knew she sounded dismayed, but she couldn't help it. 'So soon.'

'But it is the reason you are here, is it not?' enquired Nikolas, moving to stand between them. 'It is the reason I employed you. You are not having second thoughts, are you, Paige?'

Paige took a deep breath. 'Are you?'

It was a gamble, asking him outright, and Nikolas's eyes darkened with sudden emotion. 'My feelings are not in question here,' he declared. 'I offered you the job. However...' he paused, and her nerves stretched endlessly '...if the situation is not to your liking, I can always look for someone else.'

Paige felt a tremor deep inside her. 'If you have confidence in my abilities, I'm prepared to continue,' she said, aware that Yanis was watching their exchange with sudden interest. 'You're happy with the way Ariadne responds to me? You have no complaints about her treatment at my hands?'

'You make yourself sound like a—how do you put it?

A termagant, *ohi*?' Nikolas mocked her. 'You are not so tough.'

She wasn't. But she resented him commenting on the fact. 'Don't be fooled,' she said tersely. 'I can be quite tough when I want to be. Appearances can be deceptive, you know.'

'I do know,' he said harshly, and then, as if remembering they were not alone, he turned abruptly away. 'Where is Ariadne? And your sister? Surely they know what time dinner is served?'

'Um—Sophie won't be joining us,' said Paige awkwardly. Conversely now, she wished she was, miniskirt and all. 'She—er—she says she's not hungry.'

'That's a shame.' It was Yanis who spoke. 'I would have liked to meet her. She is younger than you, I think.' His eyes twinkled. 'But not so beautiful, *isos*?'

'She is skin and bone,' retorted Nikolas, before Paige could say anything in Sophie's defence. He scowled. 'At least Paige does not appear to be starving herself to death.'

'In other words, I could lose some weight,' said Paige tersely. 'Thank you, Nikolas. That's just what a woman wants to hear.'

'That was not what I meant,' he snapped, his temper dangerously close to erupting. 'Oh—' He swore in his own language. 'Here is Ariadne; at last.'

It was just as well. Paige had the feeling that he no longer cared what Yanis thought. But she did. She had no desire for Nikolas's assistant to guess what had been going on. He would think she was a fool. And she was. But where Nikolas was concerned it was hard to be detached.

Ariadne had evidently decided to get dressed up this evening. Her short-skirted coral-pink dress was obviously new, its low neckline drawing attention to the smooth skin of her throat. She'd plaited her hair and wound it into a coronet, and pearl earrings dangled from her ears. She looked older, and more sophisticated, and Paige saw Nikolas's eyes widen with obvious pride and admiration.

'*Theos!*' he exclaimed, going to meet her. 'You look—' He paused, and then added softly, 'Very beautiful.'

'Do you think so?' Ariadne preened herself, her dark eyes caressing his lean figure. 'So do you.'

Nikolas's mouth thinned. 'Men do not look beautiful, *pethi*,' he corrected her a little curtly, and Paige stiffened when his gaze drifted briefly in her direction. 'But your parents would have been proud of you. As I am. You look so much like Leni did at the same age.'

Ariadne's lips tightened. 'You treat me like a child, Nikolas.' She looked round as if seeking a scapegoat, and then frowned. 'Where is Miss Tennant's sister?'

'Sophie is not joining us this evening,' replied her guardian smoothly. 'Miss Tennant says she is not hungry. Perhaps she has had too much sun.'

'Oh.' Ariadne wasn't pleased. Paige could tell that. She'd obviously hoped to impress the younger girl, however offhand she'd been towards her.

'I think she's tired,' Paige murmured placatingly, glancing ruefully at Yanis. Then she turned once more towards the girl. 'I—er—I like your dress. It's very pretty.'

'Pretty!' Ariadne was clearly not impressed by her compliment. 'Versace does not make pretty dresses, Miss Tennant. They are works of art. Original creations of style and design—'

'That is a Versace original?' Nikolas interrupted her. His brows drew together in a way Paige knew well. 'When did you—?'

'*Entaxi, entaxi!*' Ariadne's face had flushed with unbecoming colour. 'All right, all right. It belonged to my mother, okay? There, are you satisfied now?'

'No, I am not satisfied, *thespinis*.' Nikolas's face was bleak. 'Who gave you permission to riffle through your mother's belongings? Who said you could wear Leni's clothes?'

'I don't need anyone's permission.' But Ariadne was looking less sure of herself now. 'They were just hanging there, in the closet in the house in Athens. They looked so beautiful, and so neglected. I thought you wouldn't mind if I brought some of them with me.'

Nikolas was breathing deeply. 'Do you not have anything suitable of your own to wear?'

'Of course I do.' Ariadne looked resentfully at Paige, as if she blamed her for this debacle. 'Oh, don't be cross with me, please, *aghapitos*. I wanted to look beautiful for you.'

'And you could not accomplish this without wearing your mother's dresses?' Nikolas was obviously controlling his temper, but his tone was hardly less remote. 'What nonsense is this when your closet is stuffed with—' He broke off and stifled an oath before continuing. 'We will speak of this later, Ariadne. You have embarrassed me in front of our guests.'

'You've embarrassed me—' protested Ariadne defensively, but then seemed to think better of it. Going up to her guardian, she laid her hand on his sleeve. 'I am sorry, Nikolas. Will you forgive me?'

Paige saw Nikolas hesitating, and she had to steel herself not to remind him of how rude the girl had been earlier. 'I will think about it,' he said, but it was obvious he was softening. 'Enough. Do you want a Coke? Or would you rather have some wine?'

'May I?'

Ariadne followed him across the room as he went to attend to her needs, but not before casting a rather malevolent look in Paige's direction. It was obvious she blamed her for bringing the matter up in the first place, and Paige's spirits drooped at the thought that this morning's progress might never have occurred.

Dinner was served on the terrace this evening. A table

had been laid beneath an awning and the delicious smell of barbecued meats greeted them as they stepped outside. It was already dark, but the terrace was illuminated by dozens of candles, their mellow light more subtle than the oil lamps that hung from the balcony.

The meal was served, buffet-style, from long tables which had been set up beside the pool. Paige guessed their situation was deliberate. It meant the waiters couldn't eavesdrop on their conversation.

Paige couldn't help but be impressed by the organisation that had gone into preparing the meal. As well as the lamb and pork that was roasting on the grills, the tables were spread with cold meats and salads, savoury eggs and stuffed tomatoes. There was swordfish, served with a Greek salad, and aubergines filled with a ragout of vegetables and herbs. And, to finish, a selection of rich puddings, served with ice cream or some of the delicious thick yoghurt that tasted nothing like the supermarket variety they got back home.

Paige decided it was lucky that she wasn't particularly hungry. With so many fattening things to choose from, she could easily add several inches to her hips. It was a pity Sophie wasn't here. Even she might have been tempted by the deep-fried doughnuts, dipped in honey syrup and sprinkled with cinnamon. Though, knowing her sister, it was unlikely she'd eat anything she couldn't count the calories of first.

Still, she would have liked her to meet Yanis. She had a soft spot in her heart for the man. He hadn't judged her as Nikolas had done. He'd realised her father had used her, too. It was he who'd arranged her flight back to London four years ago; who'd understood her need to get away.

'By the way, I am leaving in the morning, Ariadne,' Nikolas remarked casually as they were enjoying some of Kiria Papandreiu's strong black coffee after the meal. Until then, conversation had been light and impersonal, and Paige had been glad to concentrate on the food. 'Yanis and I have a morning meeting in Athens, and we'll be flying to Paris at the end of the week. But I should be able to spend the following weekend with you. So long as there are no un-expected problems, of course.'

'But that's almost two weeks!' Ariadne was horrified. 'And I have to stay here? On my own?'

'You are not staying here on your own. You have the company of Miss Tennant and her sister,' Nikolas reminded her crisply. 'I suggest you use the time to get to know one another.'

Ariadne hunched her shoulders. 'That's easy for you to say,' she muttered. 'When you're not here, I get bored.'

'Bored?' Yanis intervened. 'You must be joking. I wish I could stay here. Who wouldn't want to exchange the noise and pollution of the city for the peace and beauty of the island?'

'I would,' retorted Ariadne sulkily. 'I miss the city, Nikolas. I miss my friends.'

'You will have friends here,' said Nikolas, once again having to control his patience. 'Ariadne, I want you to build your strength up. I want you to play squash and tennis and to swim—'

'I am not an athlete,' declared Ariadne coldly. 'I like going shopping, going to the movies, eating out.'

'We have had this discussion before,' her guardian warned her curtly. 'I grow tired of it, and so, I would as-sume, does Miss Tennant. I suggest you make the best of it. Otherwise I may make other arrangements in the fall.'

Ariadne gazed at him. 'What do you mean? What other arrangements?'

'Another tutor, perhaps,' said Nikolas quellingly. 'If you are not completely well. It might even be an idea for you to be tutored here, on the island. As Yanis says, it is prob-ably healthier for a growing girl.'

Ariadne caught her breath. 'You wouldn't do that.'

'If you push me far enough, I can be a formidable foe,'

replied her guardian, sipping the brandy he'd been served after the meal. 'What do you say?'

'I don't have a lot of choice, do I?' Ariadne blew out a breath and then got to her feet. 'May I be excused?' she asked, and Nikolas inclined his head in agreement.

'Goodnight, little one,' he said, his voice gentler, and Ariadne rounded the table to bestow a kiss on each of his dark cheeks. Whatever hostility there had been between them was evidently forgotten. Ariadne looked as smugly confident as ever when she left the room.

Conversely Paige felt awkward after the girl had gone. After all, she was only here to keep Ariadne company, not to socialise with her employer and his guests. Lifting her cup, she swallowed the remains of her coffee, but before she could make her escape Yanis spoke again.

'Young people,' he said, looking sympathetically at her. 'They always want to grow up too soon.'

Paige forced a smile. 'I think all teenagers are the same,' she murmured, grateful for his understanding. 'I know Sophie was just as awkward when she heard we were coming here.'

'Was she?' To her dismay, it was Nikolas who took her up on her words. 'You didn't tell me that.'

'Well…' Paige tried to be offhand. 'It wasn't relevant. I only mentioned it now to show that Ariadne isn't the only one to think that island life can be—can be boring.'

'Perhaps you think it is boring, also.' Nikolas's eyes had narrowed, and Paige gave an indignant sigh.

'Of course I don't,' she said. 'I was talking about Ariadne. And Sophie. In any case, my feelings are not in question here, are they?' she added, turning the words he had used to her back on him. 'Don't be so sensitive, Nikolas.'

Nikolas shrugged. 'Do you think I am too lenient with Ariadne?'

Paige shook her head. 'That's not for me to say.'

'So you do?'

'I didn't say that.'

'You didn't have to.' His tone was disparaging. 'I could see it in your expression when we were talking about the dress.'

She would have to be more careful, Paige thought as he helped himself to more brandy. He was far too perceptive where she was concerned. 'I wouldn't dream of questioning your behaviour,' she said at last, finishing her coffee. 'And now, if you'll excuse me also—'

'You're not going to bed?' Yanis was on the point of rising to go and get himself more coffee from the buffet table, but now he paused, his empty cup in his hand.

'I'm afraid so.' Paige was sorry to disappoint him, but she suspected Nikolas was taking his frustration with his ward out on her. 'It's been nice seeing you again, Yanis. I hope we'll meet again before too long.'

Yanis nodded. 'Sleep well,' he said. 'I shall look forward to seeing you again when I return. And meeting your sister, too. Give her my regards, won't you?'

'I will.'

As if sensing he was in the way now, Yanis went to get his coffee, but when Paige would have left her seat also Nikolas intervened. 'What do you think you are doing to me?' he demanded, his voice low and impassioned, his anger so unexpected that Paige sank back into her chair.

'I beg your pardon—?'

'You are baiting me,' he said harshly, leaning across the table towards her. 'Not content with making a fool of me this morning, you seek to humiliate me again tonight.'

'To humiliate you?' Paige's gaze was uncomprehending. 'I don't know what you're talking about,' she whispered, afraid that Yanis might overhear them. 'I wanted to apologise, as a matter of fact. What happened this morning—'

'*Nothing* happened this morning,' Nikolas broke in

grimly. 'Do not imagine for one moment that it meant anything to me.'

'I don't.' But she was paralysed by his fury. 'I hoped you'd forgotten it, actually. I—I've been trying to do the same.'

'I just bet you have.' Nikolas scowled, in no way appeased by her admission. 'Tell me, Paige: do you think this is a game we're playing?'

'A game?' Paige was confused. 'I don't understand. You're not making any sense.'

'Because I should warn you,' he added, 'there can only be one winner. Do you think you've got what it takes?'

CHAPTER EIGHT

IT WAS after ten o'clock before Ariadne appeared the following morning.

Paige had been up before the helicopter took off, and although it flew out over the ocean she didn't know how anyone could sleep through it. But evidently Ariadne had, and Sophie, and she decided it must be because she was burdened with a conscience that she found it so difficult to rest. She seemed to have been in a state of turmoil ever since her father's death and nothing she did seemed to turn out the way she expected.

But today was a new day, she told herself firmly. Nikolas was gone and wouldn't be back for over a week, which was surely time enough for her to get some organisation into her life. By the time he returned, she wanted to be able to tell him that she had established a routine, and if that meant going head-to-head with his ward, then so be it.

Nevertheless, it was daunting when her charge chose not to put in an appearance until a quarter-past ten. Half the morning was over, and even Sophie had turned up to drink three cups of coffee and nibble on a slice of toast before taking up her position beside the pool. Their breakfast table had been cleared, and Paige hoped Ariadne didn't think she was going to spend another hour choosing what she wanted to eat.

In consequence, she was pacing the patio when the Greek girl sauntered out of the house. In a cropped vest and white shorts, her hair hanging in a long braid over one shoulder, she looked absurdly young and vulnerable, and Paige tempered her impatience with the thought that this couldn't be easy for Ariadne, having strangers living in the house.

'Good morning,' she said, pushing her own hands into the pockets of her navy skirt. 'Did you oversleep?'

Ariadne's eyes sparkled with momentary hostility, but then she said carelessly, 'I never get up early unless there's something I want to do.'

'Okay.' Paige weathered the barb without expression. 'So, you don't think there's anything to do.' She gestured towards the table. 'Do you want anything to eat, or is that something you don't consider important either?'

'Oh, I have had breakfast.' Ariadne cupped her hands around her eyes and gazed towards the pool. 'And, unlike your sister and yourself, I do not have to fry my flesh to give my skin some colour.'

Paige controlled her temper with difficulty. 'Do you ever say anything pleasant about anybody?' she asked, refusing to be provoked, and Ariadne shrugged.

'Of course,' she said, her hands falling to her sides. 'When it's warranted.' She heaved a sigh. 'I think I'll go and get my book—'

'No.' Paige broke in before she could finish the sentence, and Ariadne gazed at her in some surprise.

'No?' she echoed. 'I beg your pardon?'

'It's a simple word.' Paige regarded her steadily. 'I said, no. You will not go and get your book.'

Ariadne gasped. 'I will if I want to.'

'No, you won't.' Paige was getting into her stride. 'So long as your guardian's not here, I am responsible for your well-being, and despite what you told Nikolas I think some exercise will do you good.'

'If you think I'm going to waste time on those machines in the gym—'

'Who said anything about going to the gym?' Paige blew out a breath. 'I think a walk will suffice for this morning. But you can show me the gym later. I may wish to use it myself.'

Ariadne put her hands on her hips. 'Well, some of us

need exercise more than others,' she declared rudely, and Paige had to restrain the impulse to walk away.

'As you say,' she managed, apparently without taking umbrage. 'But as I'm in charge that's what we're going to do.'

Ariadne's jaw jutted. 'You can't make me.'

'D'you want to bet on it?' Paige's height and more statuesque build gave her some advantage, after all, and Ariadne glowered at her.

'I'm going to ring Nikolas tonight and tell him what you've said,' she muttered, but Paige wasn't alarmed. She'd been threatened by better people than Ariadne, she thought wryly. Nothing the girl said could hurt her as much as Nikolas's bitterness had done.

'Ring him, with pleasure,' she said carelessly. 'But be prepared for a less than favourable response. He employed me, remember? Your guardian has a great—respect—for my good judgement.'

And that was as far as she was prepared to go in defending herself, Paige decided firmly. She was still unconvinced about the reasons Nikolas had brought her here, and she couldn't entirely dismiss the notion that he was seeking some revenge.

Ariadne sniffed. 'I thought you got a headache when you went out in the sun.'

You wish, thought Paige drily, but she held her tongue. 'I'll survive,' she said instead. 'Shall we go?'

'What about—your sister?'

'Well, I'll ask her if she wants to join us, but don't hold your breath.' Paige pulled a wry face. 'Let's go.'

As she'd expected, Sophie insisted that she was going to swim laps as soon as her breakfast had been digested. And, although Paige was tempted to point out that coffee and dry toast needed little digesting, she didn't press her. She was determined to get Ariadne to talk to her, and she was unlikely to do that with Sophie picking on her at every opportunity.

'Where are we going?' asked Ariadne sulkily as Paige led the way through the gardens and into the shade of the fruit orchard. 'Not down to the beach!'

'Why not?'

Despite what had happened the day before, Paige did intend to go down to the beach. It would be cool beneath the cliffs, and she was hoping it would exorcise the images that had stuck in her mind.

'I hate the beach,' said Ariadne sullenly. 'I never go down there.'

Paige cast a disbelieving glance over her shoulder. 'You must do when you go swimming.'

'I swim in the pool,' declared Ariadne shortly. 'I hate the sand. It gets everywhere. In your hair, in your shoes—'

'Not if you take your shoes off,' replied Paige practically. 'I love the beach. I love the feeling of sand sliding between my toes.'

'You would.' Ariadne was disparaging.

'Yes, well—so will you if you stop behaving like a temperamental prima donna.' Paige shook her head. 'I can't believe you spend months of the year in a place like this without swimming in the sea. A pool is so—tame.' She frowned as another thought occurred to her. 'You can swim, I suppose?'

'Of course I can swim.' Ariadne was indignant. 'I'm not stupid, you know.'

'I never thought you were.' Paige gave a shrug. 'That's not your problem.'

'I do not have a problem.' Ariadne scowled. 'Did you tell Nikolas that I did?'

'How could I tell Nikolas anything?' countered Paige reasonably. 'I expect he knows you better than I ever could.'

'Yes, he does.'

Ariadne sounded smug, but Paige was feeling a little more optimistic. Although she might not be saying anything very much, at least Ariadne was talking to her again. In time, she was sure she could get her to open up to her. She hid a smile. Athens, like Rome, had not been built in a day.

They went down the zigzagging steps to the beach and Paige immediately stepped out of her shoes. She had hoped the girl might follow her example, but she didn't. Instead, she picked her way delicately across to the firmer sand that had been left damp and unblemished by the receding tide.

'So.' Paige determined not to be downhearted. 'You attend school in Athens?'

'Usually.' Ariadne regarded her suspiciously. 'Why do you want to know that?'

'No reason.' Paige sighed. 'I suppose you live with your guardian during term time.'

'With Nikolas, yes.' Ariadne's voice grew soft and dreamy. 'He has a beautiful house near the Plaka. Next year, I will be its mistress.'

For an awful moment, Paige thought she'd said *his* mistress, and her pulse had quickened unsteadily at the thought. 'But surely you'll be going to university next year?' she said, regaining her composure. 'I'm sure—Nikolas—has great plans for your future.'

Ariadne laughed then, the shrill sound jarring on Paige's nerves. 'Nikolas knows what I want,' she said confidently. 'And it is not to go to the university, Miss Tennant.'

Paige didn't push it—but whether that was because she didn't believe what Ariadne was saying or because she did she couldn't say. In any event, it was nothing to do with her, she assured herself. She was only here for the summer...

'Did you go to the university, Miss Tennant?'

Ariadne was asking her a question now, and Paige had to shake herself to remember why she was here. 'Um—no,' she said, after a moment, marshalling her scattered thoughts. 'No, I didn't.' She turned to look at the sea. 'Oh, look! Is that a windsurfer, do you think?'

Ariadne gave the distant sails only a cursory glance. 'It looks like a dinghy,' she said, without interest. 'Why didn't you go to the university, Miss Tennant?'

Paige shrugged, realising she was going to have to give an explanation, even if it did bring back memories she would sooner forget. 'My mother died when I was seventeen,' she said. 'My father took her death rather badly. It didn't seem appropriate to leave him at that time.'

'But he had your sister, did he not?'

'Yes, but she was only a child. He needed someone older. Someone who could—act as his hostess, when he needed one.'

'As I do with Nikolas,' agreed Ariadne triumphantly. ' I am glad you realise that at seventeen I am no longer a child, Miss Tennant. Nikolas forgets it sometimes, I think.' She gave a slow, secretive smile that made Paige feel rather uneasy. 'But only sometimes, *ohi*?'

Paige decided belatedly that she'd asked for that. Ariadne took every opportunity to emphasise the close relationship she had with her guardian. But it was hard enough for Paige to keep her own memories at bay, without encouraging Ariadne to think she'd found a confidante.

'I suppose you have lots of friends of your own age in Athens,' she said positively. 'What do you do in your free time?'

'That depends on what Nikolas is doing,' replied Ariadne at once. 'What do you do, Miss Tennant? Are you sad because there is no man in your life?'

'There are men in my life,' said Paige, determining again not to let the girl irritate her. 'And there are more important things in life than having a boyfriend, Ariadne.' She spread her arms. 'Isn't this a beautiful place? You're so lucky. And what a view. You can see for miles and miles—'

'You do not have to pretend with me, Miss Tennant,' Ariadne declared, and Paige's nerves tightened resignedly. 'I think Nikolas was right. I think you did take this job because your—your *aravoniastikos*—your fiancé—let you down.'

Paige's mouth dropped and her arms fell to her sides. 'What did you say?'

'You were going to be married, were you not?' Ariadne enquired innocently. 'I am sure that is what Nikolas said. But something happened. Your engagement was severed. That is why you were so eager to get away from London. To put some distance between you and this man who hurt you so much.'

Paige was finding it incredibly difficult to breathe normally. 'Nikolas,' she choked, trying not to reveal her anguish. 'Nikolas told you that?'

'But of course.' Ariadne was complacent. 'Nikolas tells me everything, Miss Tennant.' She tilted her head to one side. 'You are upset, but you must forgive him.' Her smile was almost triumphant now. 'He has betrayed your confidence, but do not worry. I will not reveal your unhappiness to anyone else.'

Paige dragged air into her lungs. Was the girl lying? Had Nikolas discussed the circumstances behind her acceptance of the position with his ward? It seemed unlikely. He'd even stopped Ariadne asking her personal questions. Why had he done that if he'd intended to tell her himself?

So how had she found out?

Whatever the truth of the matter, Paige had no intention of feeding the girl's ego. 'Well,' she murmured, with admirable composure, 'he must have misunderstood.'

'What do you mean?'

Ariadne was wary, and Paige knew she mustn't overplay her hand. 'Well, I wasn't sure if he'd believed Martin,' she admitted ruefully. 'But—obviously he did.'

'Martin?' Ariadne looked puzzled now. 'Who is this…this Martin?'

'But I thought you knew,' said Paige, and was half relieved when Ariadne showed she did not. 'Martin is the man I'd agreed to marry. My father introduced us, and for a time I thought it was going to work. But we really had nothing in common. He's really rather immature. It was quite a relief when we broke up.'

Ariadne brooded on this for a few moments, and then she said, 'So what has this Martin to do with your accepting this position?'

'Ah.' Paige realised that if Nikolas had told his ward anything he hadn't been totally indiscreet. 'Well, Martin knows your guardian, and when he heard he was looking for someone to spend the summer here with you on Skiapolis he suggested I should apply for the job.'

Ariadne hunched her shoulders. 'But I thought—'

'It doesn't really matter what you thought.' Paige managed not to show her own frustration. 'If Nikolas chose to tell you he rescued me from a desperate situation, that's only his interpretation of the facts. I'm sorry if you feel I'm ungrateful, but I can't have you thinking some man has broken my heart.'

Well, not that man, anyway, Paige conceded bitterly, still resentful that Nikolas had chosen to share any part of her history with his ward. Martin had let her down, it was true, and she had been hurt by his betrayal. But compared to the pain Nikolas had inflicted it barely counted at all.

Ariadne had to content herself with this explanation. She wasn't happy about it, obviously, but in the absence of any proof to the contrary she had no choice. Paige, meanwhile, was glad to get it out of the way, but she determined to be very careful about what she had to say to Nikolas in future. She'd never dreamed he'd betray her confidence to someone else.

It was almost lunchtime by the time they returned to the

house, and after another alfresco meal Paige was grateful to relax by the pool for a while. Ariadne wasn't exactly a friendly companion, but at least she wasn't sniping at her all the time. In fact, they had quite an interesting discussion about the kind of music they both enjoyed, and Paige decided the girl simply wasn't used to making conversation. She certainly seemed more amenable than before.

But perhaps that was because she didn't consider Paige any competition. Sophie had disappeared into the house after her meal and it was easier when she wasn't making provocative remarks. She emerged some time later, red-faced and sweating from her exertions. She'd found the gym, she explained, and she'd been using the equipment. Anything to work off the handful of calories she'd consumed at lunch, Paige reflected drily.

'They've got everything!' Sophie exclaimed, flinging herself down on the lounger beside her sister. 'There's a step-machine and a treadmill, and all that stuff for strengthening your arms and legs. You ought to try it, Paige. You might enjoy it. You're always saying you'd like to knock a few pounds off your butt.'

Paige couldn't remember ever saying that, and she cast a resigned glance in Ariadne's direction. This was just the sort of ammunition she could use, if she chose to. She was annoyed with her sister for bringing it up.

'Does everything have to come down to weight with you?' she demanded shortly. 'At least I'm not just—just skin and bone!'

'Nor am I.' If there was one thing Sophie didn't like it was being told she was skinny. 'God, you're so touchy! What's the matter? Is Ariadne getting you down?'

'No—'

'Why don't you go and take a shower?' broke in the Greek girl disdainfully. 'It isn't very feminine to—to smell.'

'How would you know?' Sophie rounded on her as the

easier target. 'I doubt if you've ever done anything energetic in your life.'

'You are so—so—'

Ariadne couldn't find the words, and Sophie snorted disparagingly. 'All you ever do is sit around criticising other people,' she said contemptuously. 'When you're not mooning after Petronides, of course.' She put two fingers into her mouth in a deliberate gesture. 'No wonder you've got no friends of your own age. Get a life!'

Paige gave an inward groan. Sophie had just undone all the progress she'd made. It didn't matter that she'd been thinking the same thing earlier. Sophie had no right to make fun of the other girl because she'd noticed she had a crush on Nikolas. As Ariadne's parents were dead, it was natural that all her love and affection were focussed on her guardian.

'Sophie—' she protested, but Ariadne was ahead of her.

'I do not—what was that you said? Moon? Yes, moon about Nikolas,' she cried sharply.

'Sure you do.' Sophie was unrepentant. 'I've seen the way you look at him. If it wasn't so laughable, it'd be pathetic!'

'That's not true.' Ariadne was incensed now, and Paige didn't know how to defuse the situation. 'You don't know anything about my relationship with Nikolas. I am his friend; his confidante. Your sister will tell you that. You could not begin to understand what we share, what we have been through together. You are a child! What would you know about a man like him?'

'About as much as you, I'd say,' replied Sophie scornfully, ignoring Paige's attempt to silence her. 'Get real, Ari. He's not interested in you. For God's sake, he's old enough to be your father. If you're hoping he sees you as anything more than a surrogate daughter, you're going to bomb, big time.'

'You do not know what you are talking about.' Ariadne

was flushed now, her hands moving agitatedly as she spoke. 'I am not a child like you; I am a young woman. I will be eighteen soon, and when I am we will be together. Together, do you understand? He has told me so. He loves me. He is only waiting until I am old enough to announce it to the world. Next year, he is going to make me his wife!'

CHAPTER NINE

IT WAS a beautiful evening. But then, most evenings were beautiful in the islands, and Paige thought she'd never grow tired of watching the sun sink, bronzed and magnificent, into the horizon.

She smiled at the poetic turn of phrase. There were plenty of young men on Skiapolis who fitted that description, too. Not least, her employer, she conceded drily, though she'd managed to avoid thinking of him for several days. She'd confined her waking hours to doing the job she was being paid for, and despite its shaky beginnings she still believed she was making some progress.

Her bare toes curled into the sand, and the skirt of the voile shift she was wearing blew softly about her legs. It was unusual for her to be on the beach so late, but Ariadne had a headache this evening, and Paige had decided to take a stroll before having dinner in her room.

Sophie was making do with fruit, as usual. She seldom joined her sister and the Greek girl for the evening meal. But there had been no more violent confrontations like that one that had taken place a week ago, and Paige had decided not to play the heavy at night.

There was no doubt it was easier to deal with Ariadne when her sister wasn't there. Despite the uneasy truce that had prevailed since the afternoon after Nikolas's departure, both girls seemed to feel the need to compete with one another whenever they could. Paige was tired of acting as a mediator, and it was so pleasant to have this time to herself.

Still, the week had passed fairly uneventfully on the whole, and although Ariadne could still be a pain sometimes Paige did feel some sympathy for her. It was obvious she was a lonely girl and she evidently adored Nikolas. Which wasn't so surprising. Paige knew to her own cost that he was fatally easy to love.

As far as the things Ariadne had claimed were concerned, Paige was inclined to take them with a pinch of salt. She was fairly sure Nikolas had no idea how the girl felt about him, and the idea that he might be considering marrying his ward was too ludicrous to be true. Or was it? Just occasionally, Paige had felt a twinge of unease. But it was really nothing to do with her, she'd told herself. And there was no doubt that Ariadne would make an ideal wife.

But not for him…

Paige sighed. If only the girl acted more like Sophie. Oh, not rebelliously, she didn't mean that, but more lightheartedly; more her own age. When they'd gone into Agios Petros, as they'd done a couple of times in the past week, Sophie had flirted outrageously with the waiters in the café, where they went for morning coffee, or with the young men who whistled as they walked along the quay. Conversely, Ariadne had remained rigidly indifferent, ignoring any friendly overtures that had come her way.

Which was probably just as well, Paige conceded now, digging her toes into the damp sand as she walked towards the water. She doubted Nikolas would approve if his ward became too friendly with the locals. He might encourage her to make friends, but with the sons or daughters of people he knew, people he socialised with.

Just as her own father had done, when she was younger. Though Parker Tennant had seldom introduced her to *young* men. In the main, the men he'd had dealings with had been older. The younger ones hadn't been influential enough for him.

Was business always conducted that way? she wondered. Did people really attend dinner or cocktail parties without networking the room? Not in her experience, she brooded ruefully. From the time she'd accompanied her father to her first reception, she'd been aware of what he'd expected of her, of the role he'd intended her to play.

By the time she'd met Nikolas, Paige remembered, she'd already begun to balk at the restrictions her father had placed on her. Yet, because he'd seemed happier than he'd done since her mother's death, she'd struggled to hide her feelings from him.

They'd met at a cocktail party. It was May, and, as well as the European delegation, Monte Carlo had been busy with the film festival that was taking place along the coast. Many famous faces flocked to Monte Carlo to take advantage of the casinos, and Paige had been people-watching for hours.

She had been feeling particularly good about herself that evening. She'd spent part of the day sunbathing beside the hotel pool and her skin had acquired an appealing blush of peach. The taupe embroidered silk gown she'd worn had complemented her colouring, and her hair, which in those days had been quite long, had swung in a soft beige curtain about her shoulders.

She supposed she had looked different from many of the women at the reception. She'd worn little make-up for one thing, and although her clothes were fashionable her father had always made sure they were not too sophisticated. He'd wanted her to project an image of youth and innocence, which he'd known would be especially noticeable in such surroundings.

Nikolas had arrived at the party with his cousin, Anna. Paige hadn't known she was his cousin when she was first introduced. But she'd thought they were two of the most attractive people she'd ever seen, and she'd envied them their sophistication.

Of course, her father had encouraged her to talk to them, and because Nikolas had been so approachable it had been easier than she'd thought. She'd hardly noticed when her father had excused himself to speak to someone else. She'd been too bemused, too absurdly flattered, that Nikolas should have wanted to speak to her.

He'd told her that he wasn't staying in Monte Carlo itself. That he had a yacht, the *Athena*, that was anchored out in the bay. She'd learned later that he'd already hosted a couple of glittering gatherings aboard the yacht earlier in the week. It hadn't surprised her that he'd known a lot of famous people—or that her father had been so eager to be accepted into his circle.

The evening had been magical. For the first time, she'd actually enjoyed herself, talking more about her life and her ambitions than she'd ever done before. Nikolas had seemed really interested in her opinions about everything, and it wasn't until much later that she'd suspected he'd been using her just as much as her father had intended to use him.

The following day a huge bouquet of spring flowers had been delivered to their hotel, with a note from Nikolas inviting Paige and her father to have dinner with him that evening on his yacht. Her father had been delighted, congratulating Paige for effecting the opportunity to talk with him in private, but for once Paige had been reluctant to see the invitation in that light.

Still, to begin with, it had seemed as if Parker Tennant had been right. Nikolas hadn't seemed surprised when the topic of their conversation had turned to business matters soon after their arrival. He'd listened to what her father had to say with bland attention, and if Paige had had doubts that he was as interested in her father's business as he'd seemed she'd kept them to herself. The alternative was too incredible, and she'd never believed for one moment that Nikolas might actually be attracted to her.

But then her father had been called back to London.

A fax had arrived one morning informing him that a client he'd been dealing with for many years had died, and there was some controversy about the terms of his will. Sufficiently so to warrant Parker Tennant's involvement in the distribution of his assets, and Paige had prepared herself for the disappointment of never seeing Nikolas again.

She'd told herself it was for the best. Whatever his intentions were, she'd begun to like him too much, and common sense had warned her that she was courting disaster. A man like Petronides was unlikely to get seriously involved with someone like her. She was too young for him, for one thing, and she shouldn't mistake his kindness for anything else.

But it hadn't turned out as she'd expected.

When her father had phoned the yacht to explain that he was having to cut his visit short, Nikolas had suggested that Paige might like to stay on and spend a few days cruising the Mediterranean. 'Anna will be with us, of course,' he'd added, though Paige had known his assurances were unnecessary. From the moment he'd made the offer, there'd been no question that her father would allow her to refuse.

And so, later that same day, Paige had found herself installed in a luxurious stateroom aboard the *Athena*. As Nikolas had promised, Anna did accompany them—but so did Anna's fiancé, Lukos Panagia—a fact that Nikolas had conveniently forgotten to tell the older man.

Paige shivered now. She remembered that first evening very well. How could she not, when it had been the start of something so momentous in her life? With a warm breeze stirring the smooth surface of the water and the lights of the principality disappearing into the distance, it had seemed like a dream—or perhaps the beginnings of a nightmare, she acknowledged. Whatever, she'd been incredibly excited, and determined to enjoy herself no matter what.

When she'd arrived on deck, she'd discovered that a table had been set beneath an awning. Four places had been laid, but only Nikolas had been standing against the rail, drinking from a tumbler that she had guessed contained whisky. His powerful legs had been braced against the movement of the vessel, his collarless shirt and black mole-skin trousers less formal than she'd been used to...

He turned at her approach, his eyes darkening at the sight of her hovering at the top of the steps that led up from the lower deck. 'You look nervous,' he remarked, viewing her black strappy top and loose chiffon trousers with narrow-eyed intensity. 'Would you rather have returned to London with your father?'

Paige took a breath. 'No,' she admitted honestly. 'I'm—very grateful you invited me to spend a few days on the yacht.'

'Are you?' Nikolas's eyes sparked with sudden impatience. 'Well, perhaps I don't want your gratitude,' he said flatly. 'I invited you to stay because I want us to get to know one another better.' He grimaced. 'Without your father running interference.'

Paige felt a catch in her throat. 'I'm sure you don't mean that,' she murmured, half turning to rest a hand on the rail. 'It's a beautiful evening, isn't it?' Then, forcing a casual tone, she asked, 'Where are Anna and Lukos?'

He didn't answer her. Not immediately anyway. 'Why don't you think I mean it when I say I want to get to know you?' he asked instead, and she shifted from one sandal-clad foot to the other.

'You—you don't have to pretend, Mr Petronides,' she told him steadily, unable to use his given name. While her father was there she'd got away without using either of the alternatives, and he scowled now at her deliberate formality.

'I am not pretending, Paige,' he assured her, with studied patience. 'And I would prefer it if you use my Christian name when you speak to me.' He paused. 'Why should you assume I didn't want you here?'

'I didn't say that, precisely.' Paige chose her words with care. 'I suppose it could have been awkward for you with your cousin *and* her fiancé on board.'

'You think I invited you to join me to—how is it you say it?—to even the score?'

'The numbers,' murmured Paige automatically. 'To even the numbers.' She licked her dry lips. 'I'm sure you understand what I mean. But anyway, I do appreciate it.'

'You know nothing about it.' Nikolas left the rail and crossed the deck towards her. 'You really think I'd do that to you? Make you a—a convenience, *ne*?' He stopped beside her, dark and disturbing in the lights that hung between the bulkhead and the bridge. 'I am not your father, Paige.'

She stiffened. 'What is that supposed to mean?'

But she knew; she knew what he was implying. And, although she was indignant, she couldn't altogether blame him for his interpretation of events.

Nevertheless, she was startled when he put out his hand and stroked the soft curtain of her hair. 'I am sorry,' he said. 'I do not wish for us to be—*ti*—at odds. *Na pari i oryi*, Paige, let us not talk about your father. Please believe me when I say I invited you because I want to spend some time—alone—with you.'

Paige was stunned. 'But Anna and Lukos—'

'—Are here to chaperon you,' declared Nikolas, stroking her hair again. 'Do you think your father would have allowed you to stay on the yacht if—?' He broke off then and when he spoke again he was rueful. 'Well, perhaps he would,' he conceded drily. 'But I would not.'

'You're doing it again.' Paige stepped away from him, her back coming up against the rail. 'I'm sure you told my father that your cousin would be accompanying us.' Her face burned suddenly. 'He's—he's not my—pimp, you know.'

'Now why would you make such a declaration?' Nikolas's mouth twisted sensually, and although he wasn't touching her Paige could feel his heat penetrating the thin fabric of her clothes. 'You do know what your father is like, do you not, *aghapita*? Perhaps you have had some reason to suspect that what I say is true.'

Paige caught her breath. 'How dare you?'

'How dare I what?' To her dismay, Nikolas had moved towards her and now she had nowhere to go. 'Paige, I don't care what his motives were. I don't care if you've done this before. I'm grateful that you're here now. With me.'

Paige stared up at him, aghast. 'You think I make a habit of this?'

'Of what, *aghapita*?' He placed one hand on the rail at either side of her, successfully trapping her within his arms.

'Of—of appearing to be left alone? Of needing someone's protection?' She gazed up at him with horrified eyes. 'Do you think my father arranged the whole thing?'

'If he did, I'm grateful for it.' His eyes on her mouth were an almost palpable caress. 'Relax, Paige. I won't hurt you. I am enchanted by your sweetness and your joy of life.'

Paige shook her head. 'But not by my innocence?' she said bitterly, and he lifted a hand to cup her hot cheek.

'That, too,' he said, hearing the tremor in her voice as she accused him. 'Sweet Paige. Do you have any idea how adorable you are?'

Paige jerked back. 'You're making fun of me.'

'No, I'm not.' His expression sobered, and his hand slid down to caress her neck. He studied her face with a searching gaze and then added softly, 'If you continue to look at me with such soulful eyes, I shall begin to think I frighten you.'

'You don't frighten me.'

But he did, and he knew it. Or rather he knew she was afraid of the emotions he aroused inside. She wanted to remain wary of him, to distrust him because of the things he'd said about her father. But the truth was, he excited her in a way she'd never experienced before.

'So…' His thumb moved sensuously against the fine bones that defined her throat. 'Will you forgive me for what I said?'

Paige could feel her pulse pounding in her ears. 'Do I have a choice?' she asked, finding it difficult to breathe.

'We all have a choice,' replied Nikolas softly. 'You do wish to stay with me, do you not?'

To stay with him!

The connotations behind that simple statement were breathtaking. He hadn't asked if she wanted to stay on the yacht; he'd asked her if she wanted to stay with *him*.

'And—and if I don't?' she said, and caught her breath when he bent his head and his tongue brushed her ear.

'Then I should have no choice but to obey your wishes,' he whispered softly. 'But I'm hoping that won't happen.'

Paige's hands came up against his chest. 'You—you had no right to accuse my father of double dealing.'

'I know.'

'He really did get a fax, you know. He didn't want to go back to London and leave me here.'

'I believe you.'

Paige blew out a breath. 'Then why did you say what you did? Why did you let me think you were suspicious of him?' She sighed. 'If Daddy really knew how you felt, he'd never have let me accept your invitation.'

'Wouldn't he?' Once again, there was that note of disbelief in his voice, but before she could remark upon it he spoke again. 'Well…my opinion of your father isn't of any importance,' he declared, tracing a line with his finger from her shoulder to her elbow and beyond. 'I'm far more interested in what you think of me.'

'What I think— Please don't do that.' Paige wrapped her arms about her waist now. 'I'm not a fool, Mr Petronides. You don't have to humour me.' But then, because whatever she said she knew her father wouldn't be very pleased if she offended him, she told him, 'Until this evening, I'd always thought you were a—a very pleasant man.'

'A very pleasant man?' he echoed. '*Theus*, I think that is what you call being damned with faint praise, *ohi*?' His eyes caressed her face and she prayed he couldn't see what she was really thinking. '*Kala*, I do not feel very pleasant at this moment. You have made me feel very cynical and very old.'

'You're not old.'

She said the words automatically, and his eyes narrowed as they focussed on her mouth. 'I'm thirty-five,' he said. 'Almost twice your age. And regrettably far more experienced in the ways of the world.'

Paige moved her shoulders in a nervous gesture. 'More jaded, you mean?' she said, hoping she sounded more confident than she felt. She had the feeling this conversation was becoming far too dangerous for someone of her limited experience and she didn't honestly know where it was going. 'Appearances can be deceptive, you know.'

'Oh, I know.' Nikolas regarded her humorously. 'Who would have thought that such a timid little cat would have such sharp claws?'

Paige looked warily up at him. 'You're making fun of me.'

'Only a little.' He smiled. 'You're so delightful, it's hard to resist.' His hand shaped her cheek. 'Perhaps if you remembered to call me Nikolas I'd stop teasing you. I can't make love to a woman who insists on addressing me as Mr Petronides.'

Paige's jaw dropped. She had no idea what to say. She supposed someone like Anna would have a ready response, but she didn't. The very idea of making love with him was too incredible to consider, and the thought that he might be making fun of her again caused her to turn abruptly towards the rail.

'I—' She sought wildly for some neutral topic and when her eyes discovered lights on the horizon she said stupidly, 'Is—is that a ship?'

'As we are at sea and there are no doubt many ships in our vicinity, it seems likely,' Nikolas remarked, behind her. He moved in closer and once again she was trapped within the circle of his arms. 'Do not be afraid of me, Paige,' he added, his shower-damp hair brushing her cheek as his teeth nibbled her shoulder. 'I promise I will do nothing to hurt you. But I want you and I think that, despite your fears, you want me.'

He wanted her!

Paige's knees turned to water, and she was glad she was gripping the rail for support. Not teasing now, she could feel the muscles of his pelvis close behind her and the realisation that he was becoming aroused caused the blood to thunder in her ears.

When she said nothing, he caught the skin of her neck between his teeth and sucked, very gently. 'You do understand what I am saying, don't you, Paige?' he asked huskily. 'You knew how I felt about you before you accepted my invitation.'

She hadn't, but to admit it would sound immature and naïve. Instead, she simply lifted one shoulder, as if in silent acknowledgement, and his mouth slid the strap of her satin vest aside and again nuzzled her flesh.

She had to say something then to still the panicky feelings inside her. 'Will—will Anna and Lukos be joining us?' she murmured, when she was sure she could speak the words without betraying how she felt. At least he couldn't see her face in the shadows cast by the awning. Here, against the rail, they had a small measure of privacy from the rest of the ship.

'Not yet.' Nikolas's voice had harshened slightly, she noticed. 'Not until much later,' he added, taking a deep breath. 'Forget about my cousin and her fiancé. I imagine they have better things to do than to think about us.'

Oh, God!

Paige realised then that he really did think she was used to this. When his hand caressed her waist and then shifted upwards so that his thumb was brushing the underside of her breast, she had to stifle the moan that rose into her throat. Yet, despite her inexperience, she knew he was right: that she wanted to give in to him. However ignorant of sex she was, she had no trouble in understanding her own body's needs.

He turned her then, both hands at her midriff now, reminding her of how alone she was. And he knew all the moves; all the ways to make her want him. And, dangerous as it was, she couldn't stop herself from looking up into his dark face.

He was so attractive. Her pulse quickened uncontrollably as his dark gaze moved over her upturned face. Her lips parted, unknowingly provocative, inviting his tongue's invasion. Her breasts puckered delicately, tightening the satin across their swollen peaks.

He bent towards her, his lips seeking hers, feathering light butterfly kisses across her mouth. He was in no hurry, whereas Paige was eager for him to kiss her properly, the hunger he was arousing in her making her a stranger to herself.

Her hands came up without her volition, gripping his neck and bringing his mouth to hers. 'Tell me what you want,' he urged, when he heard the frantic sounds she was making, but Paige could only press herself closer, her breasts cushioned by the muscled hardness of his chest.

He groaned then, his hands sliding down her back to bring her fully against him, and his kiss grew more urgent, his tongue sliding hungrily into her mouth. Paige had thought she would be frightened of the power he had over her, but the need he was creating inside her demanded to be met.

Her senses swam. A kind of mindless delight had taken over her body, making any kind of resistance futile. She was suddenly so close to him that she could feel every bone and sinew, and the throbbing heat of his erection pressed hard against her stomach.

Excitement pulsed along her veins, making her nerves tingle, turning her blood to fire. His hands slid beneath the hem of the satin top and discovered she was not wearing a bra and she trembled with anticipation. No man had ever been this intimate with her before and the fears she'd had earlier fled before the sensual pleasure of his touch.

He murmured to her in his own language, telling her she was beautiful, urging her to believe him when he said he'd wanted her from the moment he'd first seen her. When he lowered his head to suckle her nipples, she realised he'd exposed her breasts to his possessive gaze. At once, an unfamiliar slickness was palpable between her legs, a pool of heat that dampened the bikini briefs she was wearing.

'Come,' he said at last. Taking her hand, he drew her across the deck and down a short companionway to his stateroom. 'Much as I would like to make love to you on deck, we cannot scandalise Captain Stavros. Besides,' he added huskily, 'I want to look at you. I want to see your face when I finally make you mine.'

Paige reflected now that he had given her an opportunity to stop him. She hadn't been unaware of what she was doing when she'd accompanied him to his cabin. She hadn't even had the excuse of having drunk too much and he had taken advantage of her. In fact, in many ways, she had taken advantage of him.

She sighed. She supposed she'd been carried away by her first real experience of sexual passion. Men had kissed her before; some of them had even wanted to make love to her. But none of them had affected her as Nikolas had done. Neither before nor since, she added painfully. She'd been lucky nothing more had come of it. Thankfully, it had been the wrong time of the month for her to conceive.

Of course, Nikolas had had no idea how inexperienced she was. She must have been a better actress than she'd thought, she mused, half amazed at the self-possession she'd shown when he'd undressed her. Perhaps it had been the subtle ambience of the cabin: the stateroom had been lamplit and romantic, bronzed shades casting a golden light over the dais where the bed was set. Silk sheets, cool against her back; the fragrance of soap and shaving lotions; and the musky scent of Nikolas's body as it crushed hers to the mattress.

Whatever, she'd been too bemused to do anything but watch the master at work. Her only moment of trepidation had been when she'd seen the rearing power of his arousal, but when he'd drawn her hand to him she'd touched him eagerly, revelling in the pulsing life she could feel within the clasp of her fingers.

The need that throbbed in his loins had seduced her. With a sensuality she hadn't known she possessed until that night, she'd surrendered eagerly to his demands. Everything he'd done, every breath he'd taken from her, every scorching touch that had drawn her even further into his sensuous web, had been given freely, and she'd ached for the knowledge she knew only he could impart.

But Nikolas had been in no hurry, she remembered. Despite his own obvious needs, he'd indulged himself in a long and languid exploration of her body first. He'd even kissed each one of her toes before tracing a line of kisses up her calf to the sensitive hollow at the back of her knee. Then on to the quivering flesh of her inner thigh.

By the time he'd buried his face in the moist curls at the junction of her legs and tasted her with his tongue, Paige had been unable to stop shaking. Nikolas had been trembling, too, she recalled, the control he'd been exerting up until then slowly slipping away. It was probably that evidence of his own vulnerability that had robbed her of any inhibitions, she thought tremulously. Looking back now, she had to admire the courage she'd shown in not betraying how innocent she was.

Nikolas had soon found out, however. But by then it had been much too late for him to do anything about it. She'd shown such passion, such unknowing skill, he'd been totally convinced of her experience, but she hadn't been able to stifle her cry of pain when he'd thrust into muscles that had never known a man's invasion before.

The memory could still disturb her, she discovered. Had she really been so naïve as to believe that Nikolas wanted anything more from her than sex? She acknowledged now that it had been the only time in her life when she'd truly trusted a man. Since then, she'd had good reason to regret her gullibility.

Yet, at the time, she'd had no reason to doubt him. In fact, Nikolas had been tenderly solicitous of her needs. Although his lovemaking couldn't have turned out as he'd expected, the only anger he'd shown had been towards himself.

He had made love to her again. But only because she'd begged him to do it. Perhaps, also, he'd wanted to leave her with a happier memory than the pain his first attempt had achieved. Whatever the reason, that second time had been magical. She remembered she'd steeled herself for it, dreading the moment when the sensitive muscles would rebel. But instead there'd been no pain, only an expanding sensitivity, and ultimately a satisfaction so intense, she'd cried for the beauty of their love…

CHAPTER TEN

THE realisation that waves were curling about her ankles now brought Paige to her senses. She'd been so wrapped up in her thoughts, she hadn't noticed the rising tide, and she sighed in frustration when she saw the stains of seawater on the hem of her dress. It flapped against her legs, cooling her emotions, reminding her of where she was and why she'd been so absorbed.

No wonder she'd been so unsure about coming here, she thought ruefully. Seeing Nikolas again had stirred up more than just memories of the past. But if she wanted to keep this job she had to put their previous relationship behind her. She was only tormenting herself by remembering how sweet it had been.

Sweet, but brief, she sighed regretfully. The day after he'd made love to her in his cabin, Nikolas had begged her forgiveness for taking advantage of her, and insisted it would never happen again. Despite her unwillingness to forget it, he'd spent the remainder of the cruise trying to make it up to her, and her confusion had been expunged by the tenderness he'd shown towards her.

Paige remembered she'd thought it was because he really cared about her. She wouldn't have believed he could treat her with such care and consideration unless he'd had some genuine feelings for her. As for herself, she'd fallen madly in love with him, and she was sure both Anna and Lukos thought Nikolas felt the same.

When her father had returned, unexpectedly, some five days later, she couldn't wait to tell him how she felt. Nikolas had had a call from Parker Tennant asking him if he could arrange to put his daughter ashore at some point convenient to them both. Nikolas's answer had been to propose that her father meet the yacht at Piraeus. He had gone on to suggest that Tennant might like to come aboard and sail with them to Skiapolis. He'd issued an invitation to them both to spend a few days at his villa there, and Paige had been thrilled at what she'd seen as this evidence of his intent.

From the moment her father had come on board the *Athena* however, she'd known that something was wrong. He'd confessed to having a headache, but, although he'd tried to hide it, it had been obvious to her that it was more than that. She'd also noticed that when Nikolas wasn't looking the glances her father had cast in his direction had been strangely malevolent. She'd hardly been able to contain herself until she could speak to him alone.

But, in the event, it had been the following afternoon before she'd had a chance to share his confidence. Although it had still been light when they'd arrived at the small harbour of Agios Petros, her father was clearly not well. He'd been subject to migraines for years, and he'd been obliged to retire to his suite of rooms immediately. In consequence, Paige had spent a rather anxious evening wondering what was going on.

The following day, she and Nikolas—and Yanis, who had been staying on the island in his employer's absence— had spent the morning touring the island. Her father had been invited to join them, but although he'd been looking much better Parker Tennant had decided to stay at the house. A wise precaution, Nikolas had said, but Paige had had her own ideas about why her father hadn't come. She'd consoled herself with the thought that if he'd had any reason not to trust Nikolas he wouldn't have encouraged her to go with him. And as it was it had been difficult not to enjoy herself with the two men when Nikolas had made it so obvious that he considered her special.

After lunch, Nikolas and his assistant had excused themelves to attend to business. Several matters, which had arisen while Nikolas was away, had required his attention, and Paige and her father had sought a sheltered spot beside the pool. Paige had been relieved to see that some of the tension had left her father's face and he was actually looking quite cheerful. He'd even smiled when she'd curled up on the lounger beside him.

She should have been warned, she supposed now. Whenever her father had smiled at her like that, it had usually meant she was doing something he wanted. Since his death, she'd been forced to accept that Parker Tennant had seldom considered her feelings at all.

He'd begun by telling her how pleased he was that she and Nikolas were getting along together so well. He'd confessed that their host had told him what a pleasure it had been to entertain his daughter, and that he was obviously interested in her. Which was just as well, he'd added, confusing her a little, because he'd had no success in getting him to invest in the Murchison deal.

He was depending on her to persuade him, he'd said confidently, accompanying this assertion with a conspiratorial smile. It was obvious Nikolas would do anything for her if she asked him to, he'd insisted, and if he did prove reluctant she should sweeten the request in any way he chose.

Paige had been appalled. The idea that her father should virtually suggest that she go to bed with Nikolas to gain some kind of advantage over him had horrified her. Too late she'd remembered the comments Nikolas had made about her father and her reaction to them. Suddenly, they'd seemed all too valid, and even Nikolas's seduction had been tainted by the suspicion that he'd known what her father had intended all along.

At first, she'd pretended not to understand him. She'd tried to be sympathetic, even though her heart had been heavy with dread. But there'd been no mistake: her father

expected her to use any influence she had to gain what he
wanted. And when, albeit reluctantly, she'd confessed what
had happened, he'd called her a fool and a traitor, which
had destroyed any lingering doubts she might have had.

The horror of that day still had the strength to depress
her. What she had treasured as a gift had turned into a
burden. She'd had nowhere to turn. No one she could turn
to. She'd only known she had to get away without seeing
Nikolas again.

That was when Yanis had come to her rescue. He'd
found her in a corner of the garden, desperately trying to
come to terms with what she'd learned. He hadn't asked
any questions, but, seeing her ravaged face, he'd probably
assumed Nikolas was to blame. In any event, he'd arranged
for a boat to take her to the nearby island of Mykonos, and
from there she'd been able to get a flight back to England.

Her father had come after her. He'd obviously realised
how abominably he'd behaved, and he'd spent the rest of
that summer trying to make it up to her. He'd blamed
Nikolas for his behaviour, of course, accusing the other
man of stringing him along with empty promises, of only
using him as a way to get to her. He'd never had any
intention of investing with Tennants, Parker had insisted,
and when weeks passed and Nikolas hadn't even tried to
contact her Paige had come to the painful conclusion that
her father had been right all along.

Her only consolation had been the fact that she hadn't
waited for Nikolas to ask her to leave. She was sure that
that must have annoyed him a lot. He wasn't used to
women using him, and her walking out as she had must
have irritated him enormously. Perhaps that was why he'd
jumped at the chance to get his own back by making her
his employee.

If so, it would explain why he'd been so angry that morning when he'd kissed her. Despite himself, there must still
remain some shred of sexual attraction towards her, after

all. Not that it was of any advantage to her, feeling as she did about him. Until she'd seen him again, she hadn't realised how deep and vulnerable her wounds still were.

But she didn't want to think about that now. Treading into deeper water, which was now threaded with moonlight, she allowed the waves to surge about her thighs. Her dress was ruined anyway. Salt water did terrible things to fine fabrics. And besides, there was a certain appeal to destroying something beautiful in her present mood.

Was that how Nikolas had felt when he'd seduced her? Had he enjoyed thwarting a man for whom he'd obviously had no respect? What had he thought when he'd discovered her innocence? she wondered. Had he felt any remorse for what he'd done? Or had he considered that her father's behaviour had warranted no remission? That the victory had been sweeter than he could have hoped?

Her body was hot now and over-stimulated by the unwilling feelings she had instigated, and, choking back a sob, she waded further into the sea. Her dress was soaked, clinging sensuously to her body, and when she looked down she saw her nipples outlined in sharp relief.

The sight was absurdly provocative somehow, and, although her hands went to pull the cloth away, when her fingers touched her breasts they didn't obey her commands. Memories of the way Nikolas had caressed them had created an overwhelming need inside her, and she touched them almost reverently, afraid of the dark emotions spiralling in her head.

Oh, God, she thought, horror overtaking her, and she raised her arms above her head in an agony of self-disgust. Was this what she was reduced to? Living a life in her imagination? How amused Nikolas would be if he could see her now.

'*Perimeno!* Paige! In God's name, come back!'

The hoarse cry that arrested her came from the shore. Turning, all she could see was a dark figure waving at her, and for a heart-stopping moment she thought it was her father's ghost. But Parker Tennant had never been so tall or so broad, nor moved with such arrogance. As he splashed into the shallows and the moonlight fell on his dark face, she saw it was the man she least wanted to see.

She trembled then, and for the first time she realised how cold the water was. Or perhaps it was the fact that her dress was wet and clinging clammily to her. Whatever the reason, she had no choice but to turn back.

'Go back,' she cried, when he came further into the water, and, tucking her tumbled hair behind her ears, she started towards the shore. What was he doing here? she wondered. Kiria Papandreiu had said he wasn't expected back for another three days. She'd never have taken such liberties if she'd had any suspicion that he might find her.

He didn't do as she asked. When she came within reach, he grabbed her wrist and tugged her ruthlessly back onto the beach. 'Are you mad?' he demanded, when she was standing, shivering, in front of him. 'What were you trying to do? Kill yourself?'

Paige drew a steadying breath. 'Of course not.'

'Of course not?' He mimicked her denial with harsh disbelief. 'Paige, I saw you. You were about to dive into the water. No one goes swimming fully clothed.'

'I wasn't going swimming,' protested Paige, wishing she'd brought a towel with her. 'I—I was paddling, and I got out of my depth.'

Nikolas scowled, his dark face with its unfamiliar shadow of beard strangely tense. 'Paddling,' he muttered incredulously. 'Paige, this is me you're talking to. No one goes paddling at this time of the evening. Besides, you're not the type.'

Paige held up her head. 'So what type am I?'

Nikolas shook his head. 'That's not the point.'

'What is the point, then?' she asked. 'And why should you think you have the right to tell me what to do? If I want to go swimming after dark, that's my business, not yours.'

'Not so long as you are here,' he retorted frustratedly. He noticed she was shivering, and, stripping off his suit jacket, he swung it about her shoulders without another word. 'As long as you are living on Skiapolis, you are my responsibility. For pity's sake, Paige, tell me this was a mistake.'

She wanted to shrug his jacket off. There would have been some satisfaction in having it fall on the sand at her feet. But it was warm and comforting and it smelled of him, of the heated strength of his body. It reminded her of where it had been until a few seconds ago.

'I'm wet,' she said instead, and his expression softened.

'I know,' he said, looking down at her, and she was intensely conscious that she was no longer feeling so cold.

'Your jacket will be ruined,' she murmured, trying to instil some shred of practicality into the moment, and his dark lashes dipped to shade his glittering eyes.

'Do you think I care?' he demanded, and she knew he was aware of the sudden intimacy that had flowered between them. '*Theus*, Paige, I was at the top of the cliff when I saw you. I've never come down those steps so fast.'

'But—you could have fallen,' she protested, almost anxiously, and his lips twisted at her sudden concern.

'Yes, I could,' he agreed. 'Does it matter?'

'Of course it matters. You could have been killed!'

Paige was frustrated by his indifference, but she broke off abruptly when Nikolas's hand trailed softly across her throat. 'Would you have cared?' he asked. 'Or would you have said I deserved it? Perhaps it would give you some pleasure to be chief mourner at my funeral.'

'Don't joke about such things.' Paige dashed his hand away and struggled to take a steadying breath. 'In any case, what are you doing here? I thought you weren't supposed to be back until the end of the week.'

'I changed my mind.'

Nikolas loosened his tie and pulled it free of his collar, and she realised he must have come straight down to the beach before doing anything else. He was still wearing the suit in which he'd flown from Athens. She hadn't heard the helicopter, but as it flew in over the other side of the island that wasn't so surprising. Besides, her ears had been filled with the thunderous roar of the sea.

'It was as well I did,' he added now, and the shadows couldn't hide the impatience that still showed in his face. 'If I'd not been here—'

'I'd have had to do without this gallant gesture?' Paige interrupted him, and despite her reluctance to remove it she swung his jacket from her shoulders and thrust it back into his hands. 'I'm sorry it's so wet, but I did warn you.'

Nikolas scowled. 'Keep it,' he said shortly. 'I don't need it.'

'Nor do I,' lied Paige, deciding this conversation had gone on long enough. She began to edge round him, saying politely, 'I'm grateful for your concern, but I'm perfectly capable of looking after myself.'

'Are you?' Nikolas swore then. 'But you haven't forgiven me, have you? You haven't forgotten what I said before I went away.'

Paige stiffened. 'Before you went away?' She shook her head. 'Oh, you mean when you accused me of provoking you?' she declared, with what she thought was admirable inconsequence. She held up her head. 'Well, I haven't been fretting about it, if that's what you think.'

She had paused to deliver this denunciation, but she realised her mistake when his fingers circled the chilled skin of her upper arm. The memory of what she'd been thinking about before he'd interrupted her was still too vivid, and she felt appalled and excited, all at the same time.

'I shouldn't have said what I did,' he muttered, his thumb moving almost abrasively against her damp flesh. '*Theus*,

Paige, sometimes I think you are intent on destroying my peace of mind.'

'Your peace of mind?' Somehow she got the words past her frozen lips. 'So this is all to do with you, not me.' She looked pointedly at his restraining fingers. 'I think you should let me go.'

'I think so, too.'

But he didn't do it. Instead, Paige felt the warmth spreading from his hand along the whole length of her arm. His eyes drifted over her, causing an almost palpable heat to invade her breasts, to surge into her throat and fill her face with fiery colour.

Which, thankfully, he couldn't see. But that didn't stop her from tingling all over in anticipation of his touch. Or prevent the needs he was arousing and the pulse deep inside that demanded to be stilled.

But she couldn't allow that to happen.

With a feeling of desperation, she knew she had to stop this before she totally lost her mind. She was allowing emotions, feelings she should have more sense than to nurture, to blind her to the realities of the situation. She didn't know what he was thinking, what unwilling impulse was driving him on. She only knew what he chose to tell her, and did she really want the humiliation of being at his mercy again?

'Let me go, Nikolas,' she said, without any real hope of his obeying her. And then she realised she had the perfect way to achieve her ends. 'It would be difficult to justify your behaviour to Ariadne,' she added, her confidence hardening at the memory. She was so stupid. She'd almost forgotten what the younger girl had said.

'To Ariadne?' Nikolas had bent his head to bestow a lingering kiss on her bare shoulder, but now he lifted his head and looked at her with narrowing eyes. 'Why would I feel the need to justify what I do to her?'

'Well, you tell her everything, don't you?' Paige taunted, gaining strength from his obvious confusion. 'You even told her why I took this position. Why I was foolish enough to believe every word you said.'

'I think not—'

'Oh, I think so.' Paige was determined not to let him get the upper hand. 'How was it Ariadne put it? Oh, yes. She said that you'd told her you'd only offered me the job because you felt sorry for me.'

'Iseh trelos!'

Nikolas spoke harshly and, although she didn't understand his words, she understood his anger very well. 'You can't deny it. She told me everything,' she insisted steadily. 'Apparently, I was desperate to put some distance between me and the man who had—who had let me down.'

'Then ineh alithia! That's not true!' Nikolas exclaimed furiously, and Paige despised herself for the sense of loss she felt when his hand fell away from her arm.

'But it is true, isn't it?' Paige demanded painfully. 'To all intents and purposes, she wasn't telling a lie.'

'She did not get any information from me,' said Nikolas grimly. 'In God's name, Paige, what do you think I am?'

Paige shook her head. 'So—are you calling her a liar?'

'I—no.' He raked back his hair with an impatient hand. 'You must have misunderstood.'

'What was there to misunderstand?' countered Paige coldly, all warmth draining out of her. She took a deep breath. 'I suppose you thought Ariadne was too polite to betray your confidence, but you were wrong. It gave her a great deal of pleasure to humiliate me.'

'You're exaggerating.'

'Am I?' Paige gave him a pitying look before starting towards the cliff. 'Well, once again we'll have to agree to disagree, won't we? And now, if you'll excuse me, I would like to get out of these wet clothes.'

CHAPTER ELEVEN

PAIGE half expected to wake up the next morning with a chill or a streaming cold at least. Indeed, she'd half hoped she would. Anything to give her an excuse to avoid seeing Nikolas again in the immediate future. But either the warmth of the evening air had protected her, or she was hardier than she'd thought, because she found she had no unpleasant symptoms at all.

Not unless you could call an uneasy feeling in the pit of your stomach an unpleasant symptom, she thought ruefully. And a tendency for her palms to become uncomfortably damp. But there was no doubt that, psychologically, she was suffering. Much more than any outward signs could betray.

However, in the event, she needn't have worried. It appeared that Nikolas was as reluctant to spend any time with her as she was with him. Apart from occasional glimpses of him walking in the gardens with Yanis, or crossing the hall of the villa, he spent most of his time closeted in his study, taking all his meals with his assistant and no one else.

Paige assumed he spent some time with Ariadne. The girl was occasionally absent for no apparent reason and when she returned from wherever she'd been she looked as smug as a bee in clover. If Nikolas had chided her for her indiscretion, she'd got over it, and on the whole the household functioned much as it had while its master was away.

For her part, she was persevering with her relationship with Ariadne. Although there was still something about the girl she didn't like, there was no doubt that they'd achieved a level of communication that made Paige's job easier.

Ariadne was still unwilling to spend time on the beach, but she did now, occasionally, join Paige and her sister in the pool. And, before her guardian had returned, Paige had encouraged her to play tennis in the mornings. Ariadne didn't put much effort into her game, but that, combined with a minor programme of aerobics that Paige had devised, had helped to put some much needed colour into her face.

All in all, Paige considered she was being reasonably successful at her task, and were it not for Nikolas's presence and her continuing awareness of it she believed she'd be moderately content. Sophie seemed happy, which in itself was a minor miracle. She was away from the undesirable influences she had had in London, and although she was still avoiding dinner most evenings she didn't appear to be losing any weight.

And then one evening, about a week after Nikolas's return to Skiapolis, Paige discovered her sister's secret.

Despite her reluctance to run into Nikolas, Paige had continued to dine downstairs. She and Ariadne—and occasionally Yanis—often shared a table on the patio, and, although there were obviously pitfalls to avoid, generally speaking they were quite pleasant occasions. To begin with, Ariadne had been stand-offish with Yanis, and Paige guessed she considered that dining with an employee was hardly the done thing. But Paige had pointed out that she was an employee, too, and Yanis deserved just as much respect as anyone else.

Whether Ariadne had accepted that was questionable. But as he worked with her guardian and was obviously in his confidence she'd evidently decided not to rock the boat. Besides, Yanis was fun. He had a wealth of stories compiled during the almost thirty years he'd worked for the Petronides family. Paige always found it fascinating listening to him reminisce about Nikolas's father and grandfather, the latter having founded the shipping line that Nikolas now controlled.

In consequence, she rarely went up to her room before ten o'clock. And, because Sophie usually retired so much earlier, she'd never disturbed her sister when she went up to bed. Sometimes, she'd wished Sophie was awake, so that she could share some particular anecdote with her. But she'd always decided it would wait until the next day. They had plenty of time to talk during the long afternoons when Ariadne went to rest.

On the evening she found out what Sophie was doing, Paige had had dinner alone. Neither Yanis nor Ariadne had joined her at the table on the patio, and she'd assumed they were having dinner together. It was possible they'd gone out, of course. She knew from past experience that Nikolas had friends on the island. Nevertheless, she didn't enjoy eating alone, and as it was only a quarter to nine when she went upstairs she decided to see if Sophie was still awake.

She wouldn't admit it, but she was desperate for company. Despite her determination not to let Nikolas's attitude bother her, this past week had been something of a strain on her nerves. It was all right when she was busy or when there was someone else around to distract her. But she wasn't sleeping particularly well and she had no desire to spend the rest of the evening alone in her room.

She knocked at Sophie's door, and when there was no response she opened it. She'd guessed her sister was sitting on the balcony and hadn't heard her. But when she switched on a lamp she found the room was empty. The balcony, too, was deserted. Wherever Sophie was it wasn't here.

Refusing to allow herself to panic, Paige went out of the room again and looked up and down the shadowy corridor. The lamps were lit, and their illumination glinted softly on sculptured alcoves and jewel-toned vases, elegant paintings and long draperies that moved in the air-conditioned draught. But there was no sight or sound of her sister. The corridor was deserted. She could almost believe she was alone in the house.

Taking a steadying breath, she closed Sophie's door again and went back to her own room. Then, twisting her hands together, she paced anxiously across the floor. She had to think, she thought. There was a logical explanation for this, if she could think of it. Could it possibly have anything to do with the fact that she'd had dinner alone?

But that was clutching at straws, and she knew it. She couldn't believe that Sophie and Ariadne were likely to have gone out together. Yet it was possible, she supposed, and the fact that Yanis hadn't joined her tonight probably meant that he had dined with Nikolas. But surely Sophie would have told her if she and Ariadne had planned to spend the evening elsewhere?

She shook her head. No. She had to think of another explanation. Sophie must be in the house somewhere. She couldn't be anywhere else. Unless she'd gone for a walk. After all, it was what she herself had done on another occasion. But she didn't want to think about that now. Or about the fact that Sophie wasn't likely to walk alone.

Paige's mouth went dry as an alternative explanation occurred to her. What if Sophie made a habit of going out in the evening? What if that was why she never joined them for dinner? What if somewhere on this island she'd found a supplier? Someone who could provide her with drugs.

Paris!

The youth's name sprang instantly into her mind. As far as she was aware, Sophie hadn't seen the young Greek since he'd piloted the motor cruiser that had brought them to the island, but what if she had? What had he said to her while Paige had been recovering from the journey? What arrangements had they made to see one another again?

If they had.

Paige sighed. Was she overreacting? Just because Sophie wasn't in her room, that was no reason to think she'd left the house. For heaven's sake, it could be that she'd gone to the kitchen because she was hungry. It might be something as simple as foraging for a snack.

Or it might not.

Paige wrapped her arms about her waist and walked over to the windows. Beyond, the lights of Agios Petros glittered in the distance. How far was it to the small town? Two or three kilometres, at least. Too far for Sophie to walk. And, despite the island's idyllic reputation, too dangerous.

She couldn't have gone there, Paige reassured herself firmly. Sophie might enjoy working out, but she wasn't the type to walk anywhere she didn't have to. She couldn't drive so there was no way she could have borrowed one of Nikolas's vehicles. No, she had to be in the house. But where?

She'd wait, she determined, glad to have come to a decision. Sooner or later, Sophie was bound to come back. When she did, Paige intended to give her a piece of her mind for frightening her like this. If she'd intended to leave her room, why couldn't she have told Paige where she was going?

But that aroused more trepidation than it pacified. Paige realised she was beginning to face the possibility that her sister might have left the house. And if she had, if she'd gone into town by some means Paige could only guess at, what was she doing there? And, more importantly, who was she with?

Deciding to wait in Sophie's room instead of her own, just in case she came back without her knowledge, Paige left her room again and walked towards her sister's door. As she did so, she heard voices—both male and female— echoing from the landing at the top of the stairs.

She'd run back along the corridor before she realised they were speaking in Greek, and she was brought up short at the sight of Nikolas and Ariadne, sharing what appeared to be an intimate embrace. The girl was in his arms, her face pressed confidingly into the open V of his jacket, and Nikolas was comforting her, his hand moving soothingly over her slim shoulders.

Paige was glad she was wearing rubber-soled shoes. She'd taken to wearing casual clothes in the evening, trousers or shorts teamed with a pretty blouse or a sleeveless top. This evening she was dressed in a violet silk vest, matching shorts and deck shoes. Not exactly the outfit to impress anyone, but Sophie had told her that these days anything you liked to wear was 'cool'.

Sophie...

Paige shrank back against the wall, hoping they hadn't seen her. Obviously now was not the moment to ask Nikolas if he knew where her sister was. Never mind the fact that seeing him with Ariadne had been a shock, and had reminded her of the outrageous things Ariadne had claimed about her guardian, she had no right to interrupt them. God knew, maybe what Ariadne had said hadn't been so outrageous, after all. Maybe Nikolas was grooming his ward to be his wife.

It was too much. Paige felt as if she was in danger of throwing up. First Sophie; now this. How many more surprises was she supposed to stand before her system rebelled in the most fundamental way?

Shaking her head to clear the slight dizziness that had gripped her, she prepared to make a discreet retreat. But before she could move Nikolas saw her. 'Paige!' he exclaimed, putting Ariadne away from him. He stared at her across the width of the landing. 'Is something wrong?'

'I— No.' Paige straightened away from the wall. She couldn't confide her worries to him now.

'Then why are you so pale?' Leaving Ariadne's side, he crossed the landing to stand in front of her. His brows drew together and his voice softened with unbearable kindness. 'You can tell me. Are you not feeling well?'

'Oh—'

Ridiculously, Paige wanted to cry suddenly. She'd been so anxious and now Nikolas was offering to share the burden with her. But she couldn't ask him for help, not when it would entail too many explanations she didn't want to give.

'Nikolas!' Ariadne's petulant tone drew his attention. 'What is the matter? I thought you were going to bed.'

'You go to bed, Ariadne.' Whatever he'd planned to do, Nikolas was not prepared to be disobeyed.

'But Nikolas—'

'I said, go to bed,' he retorted, his words inflexible. 'I will speak to you in the morning, *pethi*. *Kalinihta sas*.'

Paige wanted to leave them to it, but Nikolas had braced a hand against the wall and it would have meant ducking under it to go back the way she'd come. But she had no desire for Ariadne to think she was afraid to speak to her guardian, or that Nikolas should think she had some reason for running away.

Ariadne left them with obvious reluctance. Apart from anything else, Paige was sure she was curious to know what was going on. Which was another reason not to confide in Nikolas. She wouldn't give Ariadne any more ammunition to use against them.

'Now?' Nikolas looked interrogatively at her. 'We are alone, so perhaps you will tell me why you came rushing along the corridor as you did? Were you looking for me? Had you heard my voice as I was comforting Ariadne? It is the anniversary of her parents' deaths today. She was upset, so I took her out for dinner.' His lips compressed briefly. 'There: that is my explanation. Will you satisfy my curiosity now?'

Paige squared her shoulders. 'I didn't want to speak to you,' she said, despising herself for not being honest about it. 'I—I was looking—looking for my room.'

'I am sure you know where your room is perfectly well,'

replied Nikolas flatly. 'You will have to do better than that if you expect me to believe you.'

'I don't care whether you believe me or not.' Paige didn't have the will to argue with him. 'I'm tired. If you don't mind, I'd like to go back to my room.'

'Ah, but you don't know where that is,' he reminded her, mocking her confusion. 'Come along. I'll take you there. It's this way.'

He indicated the corridor that Ariadne had followed moments earlier, but when he stood back for her to precede him she refused to go. 'My room is this way,' she said wearily, gesturing behind her. 'All right. I wasn't looking for my room. Can I go to bed now?'

Nikolas's nostrils flared. 'If you were not looking for your room, what were you looking for? Let me guess: Sophie. Am I correct?'

'How do you—?' she began, and then stopped when she realised she'd betrayed herself. 'Very well. Sophie's not in her room. I think she must have gone downstairs.'

'Downstairs?'

Nikolas was unconvinced, and Paige sighed in frustration. 'I don't know where she is,' she admitted honestly. 'Perhaps she wanted a drink.'

'And have you asked Kiria Papandreiu?'

'Of course I haven't asked Kiria Papandreiu.'

'Then let's do it.' Nikolas slipped his hand around her wrist. 'Come along. I'm sure she will still be about.'

'This isn't necessary,' muttered Paige as they descended the stairs together. And then, because he'd ignored her, she added provokingly, 'Aren't you afraid Ariadne will wonder what's going on?'

'I will treat that remark with the contempt it deserves,' he said, and she knew a ridiculous lightening of her spirits. 'Ariadne is my ward, Paige. Not my keeper.'

'If you say so.' Paige tried to hide her relief.

'I do.' Nikolas glanced back at her briefly and then released her wrist as they reached the hall. 'Come: we will see if my housekeeper has seen or heard from your sister. If not…' His mouth compressed. 'I suppose we will have to think again.'

Kiria Papandreiu's apartments adjoined the kitchens. An enclosed walkway gave access to a pretty, creeper-hung building that was completely self-contained. Whitewashed walls, in the Greek style, thick and receptive to the temperature, gave access to a small parlour, and the old woman came to see what they wanted, wrapping a flannel dressing gown about her angular form.

As Paige had half expected, she insisted she knew nothing of Sophie's whereabouts. Nikolas spoke to her in their own language to save time, so Paige could only understand a word here and there. Then, as they were leaving, she came after them, whispering something that was inaudible to Paige in her employer's ear, causing Nikolas to scowl consideringly as they walked back into the villa.

As soon as they reached the kitchen, Paige turned to him. 'What is it?' she demanded. 'What did she say? I know she said something about Sophie. I can see it in your face.'

Nikolas was silent until they'd entered the reception hall. Once they were there, he stopped and looked down at Paige with guarded eyes. 'Kiria Papandreiu thinks your sister may have gone to Petros. If she has, I will find her. Go to bed, *aghapita*. I will see that she tells you all about it in the morning.'

Paige took a step back. 'Petros?' she echoed. 'She's gone into Agios Petros?'

All her worst fears were compounded when Nikolas inclined his head. 'It's possible,' he said, but she knew he was only playing down the situation to reassure her. He glanced towards the salon. 'Would you like a drink first to help you sleep?'

'A drink?' Paige gasped. 'Do you think I can go to bed not knowing where she is or what she's doing? Sophie doesn't know her way around Agios Petros. Anything could have happened.'

'I think not.' Nikolas considered his words before continuing. 'It is possible that this is not the first time she has—how would you put it?—absconded, *ohi*?'

'What do you mean?' She frowned. 'What else did Kiria Papandreiu say?'

Nikolas sighed. 'Perhaps I am wrong,' he said, lifting his shoulders, but she was sure he knew something he wasn't telling her. He paused. '*Poli kala*, if you will not go to bed, I suggest you stay here. I will be as quick as I can—'

'I'm coming with you,' said Paige emphatically. 'I have no intention of letting you go alone.'

Nikolas's brows arched. 'Even though I do not wish it?' He shook his head. 'I have a mobile phone in the car, Paige. Wouldn't it be more sensible if one of us stayed here in case she returns?'

Paige expelled a frustrated breath. He had a point. But the idea of hanging about here while Nikolas went into town was not appealing.

'Do—do you have any idea where she might be?' she asked at last, without answering him, and he shrugged.

'At one of the tavernas near the quay, maybe.' He was thoughtful. 'There is music there, and alcohol. I assume that is what you are concerned about? The fact that Sophie might be drinking and she's under age?'

Paige felt the heat rising up her throat and prayed he wouldn't notice. 'Well—yes,' she murmured, consoling herself with the thought that it wasn't a lie. It just wasn't the whole truth, that was all. 'I just wish I knew how she's got to town, if indeed that's where she is.'

'Ah.' Nikolas looked slightly discomfited now. 'Well, I may have the answer to that as well.'

'You do?' Paige was confused, and he nodded.

'Um—Kiria Papandreiu said something about a *motosik-*

leta, a motorbike?' he replied ruefully. 'Does Sophie know someone who rides a—motorbike?'

'Only Paris, perhaps,' said Paige at once, and saw Nikolas's expression darken with sudden impatience.

'Paris Gavril?' he demanded, and Paige felt as if she'd betrayed a confidence of sorts.

'I don't know his surname,' she confessed awkwardly. 'He's the young man you sent to meet us at Piraeus.'

'I sent no young man to meet you at Piraeus,' retorted Nikolas, obviously annoyed now. 'I asked Michaelis Gavril to meet you. Paris is his younger son.'

CHAPTER TWELVE

'OH.' PAIGE caught her lip between her teeth. 'Well…' She
didn't want to get anybody into trouble unnecessarily. 'It
was only a thought. He may not be involved.'

'Even though he does drive a Japanese Suzuki?' suggested Nikolas drily. He balled his fists in frustration. 'And
you think Sophie may be with him?'

'Well, she might. They seemed to get on awfully well
on—on the boat.' She felt guilty for not having foreseen
this complication. 'I'm sorry…'

'It is not your fault.' Nikolas gave her an impatient look.
'You weren't to know that your sister might be flattered by
Paris's—I have to say rather practised—attentions.' He
frowned. 'I wonder if his father knows what's going on?
Somehow, I doubt it.'

Paige felt awful. 'Sophie's not an innocent, you know,'
she murmured, and then could have cut her tongue out at
her particular choice of words. 'That is—she's fairly—
streetwise, you know.'

'Unlike her sister,' observed Nikolas flatly. 'Thank you,
Paige, but I didn't need to be reminded of that. I hadn't
forgotten our experiences, I assure you. But perhaps it ex-
plains why she liked Paris, *ne*?'

Paige groaned. 'I didn't mean—'

'Of course you didn't.' But he was practical. 'Ah, well,
let us return to the matter in hand.' He hesitated. 'Tell me,
has Sophie ever done anything like this before?'

'Like what?' she asked warily. Then, 'She's a teenager,
Nikolas. Teenagers do this kind of thing. Or they do if they
feel they have a grudge against life.'

148

'A grudge against life?' She should have known he'd take her up on that, and she didn't have a glib explanation.

'Oh—you know,' she murmured helplessly. 'The fact that Daddy died without making—adequate provision for her future.'

'Or for yours,' Nikolas appended gently, and to her dismay his hand came beneath her chin and tilted her face up to his. 'Was it really worth it?'

'Worth what?' Paige was confused. 'I don't know what you—'

'Denying that we had any future together,' he said astonishingly. 'I know your father was angry with me for thwarting his plans, but I had thought you were different from him.' His lips twisted regretfully. 'Was I wrong? Had you been in his confidence all along?'

'You're mad!' Paige jerked her chin out of his hand and crossed her arms tightly about her waist. 'I don't know why you're bringing that up. Sophie's missing and I'm going out of my mind!'

'As am I,' said Nikolas harshly. 'And you're right. Now is not the time to indulge in old grievances from the past. But that time will come, Paige; depend on it. I have no intention of letting you leave here without telling you exactly what your father said.'

Paige's nerves tightened, but although he looked as if he would have liked to say more he moved instead towards the door. 'The number of the car phone is beside the phone in the library,' he said, stepping out into the jasmine-scented evening. 'If she comes back before I do, let me know.'

'I will.' Paige followed him onto the verandah. Then, because this was Nikolas and, whatever he said, she still had feelings for him, she added, 'Take care.'

His lips twitched. 'I will,' he said drily, coiling his length behind the wheel of the four-by-four that was parked outside. He put the car into gear. 'Try not to worry.'

The car began to roll forward, but before he'd gone more than a few yards Paige heard the unmistakable whine of a motorcycle accelerating up from the road. Nikolas must have heard it, too, because he braked, the red bulbs glowing briefly before he cut his engine and his lights.

Paige pulled the door closed behind her, to prevent the hall lights from betraying her presence, but she needn't have worried. Long before the motorbike reached the forecourt, it veered away into the trees, its headlight arcing briefly across the walls of the villa before being engulfed by the lush vegetation.

Nikolas vaulted out of the car. 'They've gone round to the back,' he said, starting after them. 'Wait here.'

There were a nerve-racking few moments. Paige waited until he had been swallowed up by the darkness of the rose pergola before turning and going back into the house. Closing the door behind her, she hurried across the hall and along the corridor that led to the back of the villa. Concealed lighting along the tops of the walls meant she didn't have to switch on any lights as she went, but that didn't stop her from letting out a little cry of surprise when a black-clad figure burst out of the shadows and into her involuntary embrace.

'Let go of— Paige!'

Sophie's shocked exclamation was reassuring, but Paige's relief was short-lived. The realisation that her fears about her sister had been justified overcame any momentary satisfaction at finding she was unharmed, and when she could get hold of her properly she gave her an angry shake.

'Where the hell have you been?' she demanded, not even noticing that Sophie was wearing her black shirt and black jeans—clothes her sister would have normally shunned like the plague, but which were obviously more suitable than a miniskirt for riding a motorbike. 'How long has this been going on?'

'Not now, Paige.' Sophie was agitated, trying to free

herself, glancing back apprehensively over her shoulder. 'Let's talk about this in the morning, right? Not now.'

'Why not now?' Paige wouldn't release her. 'So you can have the time to think up a convenient excuse as to why you weren't in your room? The game's up, Sophie. I saw the motorbike. Paris's motorbike. So don't try to deny it.'

If she'd had any doubts about Nikolas's interpretation of events, they were stifled by the look of shocked discovery in her sister's face. 'How did you—?' she began, and then evidently decided she didn't have time to discuss it now. 'Look, all right. I've been out with Paris, yeah? But I think someone else saw us.' She glanced over her shoulder again. 'Why don't we get out of here before whoever it is puts two and two together and comes after us?'

'After us?' said Paige coldly. 'There is no *us*, Sophie.'

'Okay.' Sophie's face hardened. 'Have it your own way. But how long do you think your job with Petronides will last if he finds out I've been sneaking out every night to meet one of his own employees?'

'He knows,' remarked Nikolas, appearing from the same direction as Sophie. Dark and disturbing, he moved into the light, and Paige saw her sister give her a wary look. 'I have just had a very interesting conversation with your—what shall I say?—your accomplice, *ne*?'

Sophie wrenched herself out of Paige's grasp. 'Oh, I get it,' she said, looking from her sister to Nikolas and back again with resentful eyes. 'The gang of two. Or should I say the gang of three? I knew I couldn't trust that—that little bitch not to say anything.'

Paige's eyes had widened in disbelief, but it was Nikolas who spoke. 'You are claiming that Ariadne knew of this?' he demanded. 'No. That cannot be.'

'Don't you think so?' Sophie was defiant now, propping her hands on her hips, and regarding them both with equal contempt. 'Well, she did. Her room overlooks the olive grove where we—where Paris usually drops me off. She was waiting for me one night when I let myself into the villa.'

Paige was horrified. 'What did she say?'

'What do you think?' Sophie gave a careless shrug. 'I'd have said she was jealous only she's got something going on with him, hasn't she?' She jerked a thumb towards Nikolas. 'She told me all about it.' Her mouth curled. 'They're lovers. Or that's what she said.'

Paige caught her breath. 'Sophie—'

'It's true, Paige. Why d'you think she agreed not to tell you what I was doing? She said as long as I stopped making cracks about their relationship she'd keep her mouth shut. But now—'

'Ariadne told us nothing,' said Paige, through parched lips. She turned disbelieving eyes in Nikolas's direction. 'Is this true?' she added faintly, and even Sophie looked staggered at the presumption of the question.

She was even more shocked when Nikolas said flatly, 'Do you believe it is?' and Paige didn't immediately reply.

'For God's sake, Paige!' she exclaimed impatiently then. 'Of course it's true. She gave me all the sordid details. It's been going on for ages. Don't let him make a fool of you just because you're afraid to lose this job.'

'I'm not afraid of losing my job,' said Paige steadily, still looking at Nikolas. 'I think you should go to bed, Sophie. We'll talk about this in the morning.'

'No.' Nikolas spoke again. 'No, Paige, I want her to hear what you really think. Now. Not in the morning. Do you really believe I am having a relationship with my ward?'

Paige took a deep breath. 'I—I wouldn't have thought so,' she said weakly, and Sophie gave an angry exclamation.

'You're crazy,' she said. 'You should have heard what she has to say. All about what they do in bed, stuff like that.'

Paige sighed. 'Sophie, anyone can make up stories of

that kind. You only need to buy a video; read a book. These days nothing is left to the imagination.'

'All right, then.' Sophie was desperate to find a way to convince her. 'Why don't you ask Ariadne? I'll go and wake her up, shall I? That is, if she is asleep yet.' Sophie eyes swept Nikolas with a scornful look. 'But you'd know that better than me.'

'Sophie!'

Paige was tired of her sister's constant provocation, but it was Nikolas who chose to speak again. 'I intend to ask Ariadne myself,' he said. 'But not tonight. In the morning. Contrary to your beliefs, Sophie, I know nothing of my ward's sleeping habits.'

Sophie grunted. 'You would say that.'

'Yes, I would.' Nikolas's patience was thinning, and even Sophie shrank before the grim determination in his face. 'I intend to get to the bottom of this. And speaking to Ariadne is the very least I intend to do.'

Sophie hunched her shoulders. 'I'd like to be present at that interview,' she muttered sulkily, and to Paige's surprise Nikolas nodded again.

'You will be,' he promised her. 'Both of you. You can depend on it.'

'Yeah, right.' Sophie shifted uneasily. 'When you've had a chance to prime her about what to say.'

'I have no intention of priming her,' retorted Nikolas shortly. 'As I hope your sister knows, I am an honourable man. When Ariadne's parents were killed and I was appointed her guardian, I was well aware that as she grew older certain arrangements would have to be made. That is one of the reasons why I asked Paige to become her companion, even though I realise chaperons are considered passé in this day and age.' His lips twisted. 'Or perhaps not.'

Paige shook her head. 'There's no need for this, Nikolas,' she murmured unhappily. 'You don't have to justify the situation to me.' She turned to her sister. 'I believe him, Sophie. I know he's not lying. So let this be an end of it. I don't want to hear any more accusations from you.'

Sophie's expression was sardonic now. 'You know?' she countered sarcastically. 'How do you know?'

Paige expelled a weary breath. 'I just do.'

Sophie blinked. And then comprehension seemed to dawn. 'You mean—oh, God! That's what all this is about. You're having an affair with him, too.'

'Don't be ridiculous—'

'As a matter of fact, your sister and I did have an affair four years ago,' Nikolas interrupted Paige steadily. 'She and your father were my guests here and on board my yacht. I'm not sure she would wish you to know this, but there it is. I think you could say that she knows me—intimately.'

Sophie's jaw dropped. 'I don't believe this.'

'What don't you believe?' Nikolas enquired.

'This. All of it. Paige never said anything about an affair to me.'

'Why would she?' Nikolas's tone was mild. 'Your father did not approve of our relationship. Paige was obviously unable—or unwilling—to ignore his wishes.'

'You're saying Daddy knew about it?' Sophie stared at him.

'He learned about it afterwards,' Nikolas amended. 'I can tell you on good authority, he was not pleased. Unfortunately, Paige and I had had little time to get to know one another before she left the island. I did try to reach her after she returned to London but she never returned my calls.'

Returned his calls?

It was Paige's turn to look startled now. What calls? she wanted to say. There had never been any calls from him.

'I expect, like her father, she blamed me for what had

happened,' Nikolas continued ruefully. 'I admit my behaviour was not inclined to win her trust.'

Sophie shook her head. 'So that's why you gave her this job?'

'No.' Nikolas denied that, much to Paige's surprise. 'I offered her the job to help out a friend.'

'A friend!'

Sophie snorted, but Nikolas was implacable. 'Yes, a friend,' he agreed. 'I knew she would never ask for my help, no matter how difficult things had become since your father's death.'

'You know about that?'

'It was hardly a secret,' he said levelly, glancing at Paige, and she realised he had no idea how confused she felt. 'In my country, in times of stress, we try to help one another. Offering Paige the job was my way of atoning for the past.'

Atoning!

Paige just wanted this conversation to be over. She wanted to go to her room and think about what Nikolas had said. But, whatever he'd meant, nothing could alter the fact that he'd regretted what had happened. Though not as much as she had, she thought wryly.

Sophie lifted her shoulders now, turning to her sister with resentment as well as resignation in her eyes. 'So that's why you were so keen to come here,' she said accusingly. 'It wasn't because of me at all.'

Paige didn't ever remember telling Sophie that she was keen to come here. But she knew better than to call her on it right at this moment. Sophie was like a loose cannon, and in her present mood there was no telling what she might say next.

But she'd forgotten that Nikolas was there, too, and his brows drew together at Sophie's words. 'Because of you?' he asked, evidently curious, and Sophie seemed to realise she had a means of turning the tables on Paige.

'Yeah, me,' she said airily, daring Paige to contradict

her. 'She wasn't too keen on the gang I was running round with back home. Didn't she tell you why she was so keen to get me out of London? She was afraid I was in danger of becoming an addict. Just because our dotty old aunt found a gram of heroin in my knicker drawer.'

CHAPTER THIRTEEN

PAIGE had already been served her breakfast when Sophie appeared. The young girl looked heavy-eyed and apprehensive, and Paige guessed she must have disturbed her when she'd opened her door.

She'd looked into her sister's room before coming downstairs. But Sophie had appeared to be sound asleep, and although she felt no sympathy for her this morning Paige had decided not to awaken her. Besides, it had crossed her mind that Nikolas might ask her to leave at the earliest opportunity, and she'd decided she'd prefer her humiliation to be a private, rather than a public, thing.

Which was why she'd been glad Ariadne wasn't around either. Right now, she didn't think she could look at the Greek girl without her resentment showing. Ariadne might not be totally to blame for what had happened the night before, but without her fabrications Sophie would never have dared confront Nikolas as she had.

Or provoke such a damning evocation of their shared past, Paige conceded painfully. She had no idea why Nikolas had felt the need to acquaint her sister with the truth about their relationship, but he had. Yet even that had paled beside Sophie's malicious revelations. She couldn't believe Nikolas would want her to continue as Ariadne's companion after what he'd learnt last night.

The sad thing was, she'd thought she was making such good progress. She and Ariadne had had their differences, goodness knew, but on the whole she'd believed they'd all adapted amazingly well in the circumstances. How foolish she'd been! Ariadne had been feeding her sister lies about

Nikolas and Sophie had been spending most evenings with Paris, and laughing at her behind her back.

Of course, Sophie had denied it. The laughing-behind-her-back bit, at least. When they'd eventually reached her room the night before, she'd sworn she'd never intended to hurt Paige. But spending every evening at the villa had been a dead bore, she'd protested. Agios Petros was fun. All she and Paris had done was visit a few tavernas. There'd been disco music and dancing, but no drugs, she'd insisted. And she'd never drunk more than a couple of beers.

A couple of beers! Paige had had a hard time getting her head around the fact that Sophie had been drinking alcohol. She was under age, after all. Apart from the fact that she knew it was wrong, she could have faced conviction or worse. But Sophie's face had taken on its wooden expression at that point, and she'd known that her protests were going over the girl's head. Besides, Sophie had been agitating to go back to London for as long as they'd been on the island. Whatever happened, she had nothing to lose.

But Paige had.

She'd refused to discuss her association with Nikolas. Despite Sophie's exhortations that she was no better than she was, she hadn't been drawn. But it would come, she thought ruefully, looking at Sophie's mutinous expression. And sooner rather than later if Sophie had her way.

'Sleep well?' she asked now, sheltering behind a cup of coffee, and Sophie sniffed before helping herself to a glass of freshly squeezed orange juice.

'You don't have to make small talk,' she said. 'I know I'm in the doghouse. But I'm not to blame if you told lies about why you decided to take this job.'

Paige shrugged. 'I'd rather not discuss it.'

'I bet you wouldn't.' Sophie glowered at her across the table. Then she shook her head. 'I don't believe it, you know. You and Petronides getting it on.'

'Don't use that expression.'

Paige's tone was sharp, but Sophie seemed indifferent to any sensitivities her sister might have. 'Okay,' she said. 'It's hard to believe he'd want to—have sex with someone like you.'

'Why?' Paige had to ask. She found her self-respect was not totally shredded after all.

'Well, like—he's a millionaire, right?' said Sophie, grimacing. 'I mean, okay, you're not bad-looking, but he could have any woman he wanted.'

'And does, probably,' said Paige tightly, wanting to change the subject now. 'Anyway, you'd better start packing after you've had breakfast.'

'Start packing?' Sophie looked stunned. 'Oh, no. We're not leaving!'

'Well, what did you expect after you practically bragged about possessing drugs last night?'

'But it's not true.' Sophie groaned. 'The only thing I've tried is grass. The heroin wasn't mine. It was Justine's.' She heaved a sigh. 'She asked me to keep it for her the last time she came to the house.'

'Justine's?' Paige stared at her. 'Justine Lowery?' The girl was one of Sophie's friends from boarding-school. She was Judge Lowery's daughter. 'Heavens, I can imagine her father's reaction if he finds out.'

'But he won't find out, will he?' Sophie was dismissive. 'You emptied it into the loo. She was pretty miffed when I phoned her and told her. I doubt if she'll ever trust me again.'

'Thank heavens for small mercies,' said Paige drily, though she was dreading what might happen when they got back to England. To begin with, she was going to have to ask Aunt Ingrid if they could stay with her for a few days until Paige could find them an alternative. But even if Nikolas paid her for the three weeks she'd been here it wasn't going to be easy to find a flat.

'Anyway, Petronides hasn't asked you to leave, has he?' Sophie persisted, but before Paige could give an answer Ariadne appeared. In cropped trousers and a T-shirt she looked particularly complacent this morning, and Paige sought refuge in her coffee cup again as she sat down.

'Good morning,' she said, including both of them in her greeting. 'I am sorry if I am late. I must have overslept.'

'Didn't Nikolas disturb you when he got up?' enquired Paige drily, drawing a startled look from her sister. 'Kiria Papandreiu said he had something to eat earlier on.'

'How am I supposed to know where Nikolas is?' Ariadne glanced at her warily. 'I have no idea what time he got up.'

'You do surprise me.' Paige wasn't inclined to be charitable this morning, and she was pleased that Sophie was keeping her mouth shut. She guessed her sister was stunned by her uncharacteristic bravado. 'I thought you told Sophie that you and your guardian were having an affair.'

Ariadne went scarlet. If Paige had nurtured any doubts about Nikolas's sincerity, they were dispelled by the guilty look on the other girl's face. 'She—she told you that?' she stammered, her throat muscles moving convulsively as she swallowed. Then she seemed to decide she had no choice but to bluff it out. 'What happened? Did you find out she's been going into Agios Petros every night?'

'She told me about that, yes.' But Paige was not about to explain how she had found out. 'And about the little bargain you supposedly made. Does your guardian know you're spreading these stories about him?'

'They're not stories.' Ariadne tossed her head. 'I'm glad she's told you what I said, but I really don't think it's anything to do with you.'

Paige caught her lower lip between her teeth. 'But it's not true, is it?' she persisted softly. 'You made it up because Sophie was teasing you about not having any friends.'

'No!' Ariadne looked at Sophie's smug face, and Paige

realised she'd never admit anything in the younger girl's presence. 'It's true. I expect you'll find it hard to believe, but Nikolas and I have been lovers for months.'

'You lie!'

Paige didn't know which of the three of them was most surprised by Nikolas's sudden interjection. She'd thought they were alone on the patio but now she saw that Nikolas had been sitting on one of the loungers beside the pool all along. He rose from his chair, which had been concealed by one of the striped umbrellas, and she saw he was still wearing the formal clothes he'd had on the night before. He'd removed his tie and his dress shirt was open at the neck and judging by the stubble of beard that shadowed his jawline, she guessed he'd been there all night.

'You are lying,' he repeated, climbing the steps from the pool deck and crossing the patio towards them. 'Sophie told me what you had said, but I still hoped that she might have misunderstood you. But there was no misunderstanding, was there, Ariadne? You disgust me. You have sullied our relationship by making claims that are an embarrassment at best and at worst a crude attempt to destroy my reputation.'

'No...' Ariadne scrambled to her feet. 'No, that's not true.' She wrung her hands in anguish. 'Nikolas, do not be angry with me, please. You do not know what it has been like for me.' She cast Paige's sister an agonised look. 'She—she made me do it. Sophie is always making fun of me. I had to say something to—to make her stop.'

Nikolas was unmoved. 'So you chose to slander me.'

'No.' Ariadne gazed up at him with frantic eyes. 'She said she didn't know why I put up with you telling me what to do, so I let her think that—that we were—more than friends.'

'You let her think we were lovers,' Nikolas corrected her contemptuously. He folded his arms and regarded her with such a look of distaste on his dark face that Paige almost found it in her heart to feel sorry for the girl herself.

'Well—perhaps.' Ariadne took a deep breath and then added imploringly, 'It is not so incredible, is it? I will be old enough to get married next year.'

'Not to me,' said Nikolas heavily, and the girl stepped back at the bitterness in his voice. 'In fact, I think it would be more convenient if you became a boarder at the convent from now on. I am sure I could arrange for them to accommodate you for the rest of the summer and school will begin again in September, as you know.'

Ariadne was horrified. 'You don't mean that, Nikolas—'

'I do.'

'But—but you said I could stay here until school starts again.'

'That was before you revealed this rather unpleasant side to your nature,' he retorted coldly. 'How do you think I feel knowing you have been entertaining such thoughts?'

Ariadne's mouth was open. She was breathing noisily and Paige guessed that at any minute she was going to burst into tears. It made her feel uncomfortable being a party to the girl's humiliation. Even Sophie wasn't gloating over it, though her sister guessed she'd say that Ariadne had brought it all upon herself.

Coming to a decision, Paige put her hands on the table. 'I think, if you'll excuse us…' she began, but that was as far as she got.

'Stay.' Nikolas's tone was sharp, but he tempered it with, 'Please.' And, although she was sure Ariadne wouldn't thank her for it, she sank back into her chair.

Sophie felt no such obligation, however. With a roll of her eyes at her sister, she sidled off into the house. 'I'll start packing,' she said, and Paige wondered if she realised how provocative her words sounded. Apparently, as far as Sophie was concerned, Ariadne was on her way back to school.

'You said you'd always take care of me,' Ariadne cried now, seeming incapable of understanding that by defaming his name she'd done something totally unforgivable in Nikolas's eyes. 'When Mama and Papa died, you said I could always depend on your support for—for everything. You told me you considered it a privilege that Papa had made you my—my—'

'Guardian,' said Nikolas bleakly. 'I was proud that your father considered me a suitable substitute for him. I have tried to behave as a parent would, Ariadne. I loved you as a father. Nothing else.'

Tears began streaming down Ariadne's cheeks. 'But you said I was beautiful.' She sniffed. 'That night—that night I wore Mama's dress, you said I looked a lot like her.'

'And so you did.' Nikolas spoke wearily now. 'You do. You are her daughter, Ariadne. But please don't confuse admiration for—for love.'

The girl gasped. 'You don't love me?'

'I have never loved you as a man loves the woman he wants to marry.'

'And—and you're sending me away—'

'I'm sending you back to school.' Nikolas's lean face was etched with tiredness. 'Do not think to change my mind, Ariadne. I suggest you spend the time between now and September deciding which courses you would like to take next year when you enrol in college.'

'In college!'

Ariadne's sobs grew louder, and casting a pain-filled look at Paige, she turned and rushed through the French windows into the house. Her shoulders were hunched and she looked so young suddenly that Paige was moved by her plight, and despite Nikolas's expression she got determinedly to her feet.

'I'll go after her,' she said, even though she was not at all convinced that Ariadne would want any sympathy from her. But she had to do something. The girl had looked so desperate when she'd rushed away.

'Paige.' As she'd half expected, Nikolas's voice detained her. 'I want to speak to you,' he said. He rubbed a rueful hand over the rough stubble on his jaw. 'After I've cleaned up.'

'Very well.' Paige could guess what he wanted to talk about. If he was sending Ariadne back to school, there was no job for her here. If indeed there had been after last night, she conceded flatly. 'I'll be in my room,' she said, moving her shoulders in a uncertain gesture. 'Or Ariadne's. Although I doubt if she'll welcome any help from me.'

In fact she caught up with the girl as she was climbing the stairs. Her steps had slowed considerably, and, judging by the hopeful expression she turned on Paige, she must have expected her guardian would come after her. Her mouth pursed when she realised her mistake, but for once she had no ready retort to make. Instead, she looked at the other girl rather warily, as if she suspected Paige was here to gloat.

'Are you all right?'

Paige knew it was a silly question in the circumstances, but it was difficult to think of anything else to say. At least Ariadne had stopped crying. She confined herself to an occasional hiccough as they reached the landing on the first floor.

'As if you care,' she muttered at last, but there was no heat in the words now. Paige realised this must have been a salutary lesson for her. She had obviously believed she could say and do anything she liked and Nikolas would never turn against her.

'We all make mistakes,' said Paige with deliberate optimism, thinking that she'd made more than most. 'Look, don't quote me on this but I'm sure in time Nikolas will forgive you. He's angry right now, but he'll get over it. If you keep out of his way, he'll probably allow you to stay here until school starts again.'

Ariadne's eyes widened. 'Do you really think so?'

'Well, it's a possibility,' said Paige, unwilling to say any more than that. 'Why don't you go and wash your face and brush your hair and then get some breakfast? You'll feel heaps better after you've had something to eat.'

'All right.' Ariadne hesitated. Then, pressing her palms together, she said, 'Thank you.'

Paige shrugged. 'No problem.'

'No, I mean it.' Ariadne clearly wanted to say something more and, although Paige wasn't sure it was justified, she added, 'I think you understand Nikolas better than I do.'

Paige gave a wry smile. 'I wouldn't say that.'

'I would.' Ariadne took a deep breath. 'He always listens to you.'

'Does he?' Paige doubted that, and she chided herself for the little germ of suspicion that flowered at Ariadne's professed confidence in her. 'Well, don't speak too soon. I don't have any influence on his decisions.'

'But you could have,' urged Ariadne, encouraging Paige to accompany her to her room. 'If—if you told him how sorry I am; how much I wish this had never happened. That it was all a mistake. That I never intended him to find out.'

'Look, Ariadne…' Paige halted, not prepared to be drawn into an alliance with her. 'Quit while you're ahead. I've told you what I think, but I can't fight your battles for you. It's up to you to prove to your guardian that you're sorry. And telling him that you never intended him to find out about what you were saying is not going to do it.'

'Then what?'

Ariadne looked as if she would have liked to continue their conversation, but Paige had had enough. Giving the younger girl's hand a comforting squeeze, she started back the way they'd come. She just hoped Sophie was in her room, doing what she'd promised. The last thing she needed right now was another confrontation with her.

Sophie was in her room, but she wasn't packing. She was sitting out on the balcony, and she tilted her head un-quiringly when Paige came in. 'Well?' she said carelessly. 'Did you sort it out? Hey, I thought Petronides was going to hit her, didn't you? Poor Ariadne! She must have wanted to die when she realised he'd been listening to her all along.'

'Yes—well, it's nothing to do with us,' said Paige shortly, reminded of how the whole sorry mess had come to light. 'And I thought you said you were going to do your packing.'

'We're not really leaving, are we?' Sophie gazed up at her with disbelieving eyes.

'What else did you expect? You heard Nikolas say he was sending Ariadne back to the convent.'

'Well, yes, but that was in the heat of the moment.' Sophie sighed. 'He'll listen to you,' she added wheedlingly. 'Couldn't you talk him round?'

'No, I couldn't.' Paige found she resented the fact that both girls thought they could use her to get what they wanted. 'In any case, I thought you were keen to get back to London.'

'I was.' Sophie was sulky. 'But that was before—be-fore—'

'Before you started going into Agios Petros every night?' Paige was caustic. 'Honestly, Sophie, you really are the limit. You don't think of anyone but yourself.'

'I was just having fun,' protested Sophie, scuffing the toe of her training shoe against the balcony railings. 'I bet you had plenty of fun when you were my age.'

'When I was your age, Mummy was ill and Daddy was going frantic worrying about her,' retorted Paige flatly. 'It was another three years before I met Nikolas, if that's what this is all about.'

Sophie frowned. 'Did you know him for a long time?'

'No.' Paige would have preferred not to talk about him at all. 'Daddy introduced us, and I suppose we knew one another for about two weeks.'

'Two weeks!' Sophie was impressed now. 'Way to go, Paige. You snagged yourself a millionaire in less than fourteen days!' She grinned. 'So—tell me all about it. Was he your first lover? What was he like?'

'You have to be joking!' Paige cringed at the thought of what her sister would think if she told her how gullible she'd been. She headed for the door before Sophie noticed her embarrassment. 'I'm going to start my own packing. I— Nikolas has asked to see me, and I don't need a crystal ball to wonder why.'

CHAPTER FOURTEEN

SHE decided to give Nikolas an hour to send for her before going to look for him herself. Whatever happened, before she left here she needed to know what he'd meant last night when he'd told Sophie he'd tried to get in touch with her after she and her father had returned to England. He'd probably said it to spare her feelings, but, just in case Sophie asked, she wanted to know the truth.

Or that was what she told herself...

As she took her suitcase out of the closet and set it on the rack, she couldn't help the troubling thought that her father could have intercepted Nikolas's calls. But what if he had? she asked herself defensively. He could only have been protecting her. After the way Nikolas had behaved, her father had had every right to distrust the man.

Or had he...?

She shook the disloyal thought aside and went to get her shoes from the bottom of the tallboy. Her father might not always have been scrupulous in his dealings, but he'd always been entirely honest with her. She was his daughter, for heaven's sake. He'd loved her. Look at the way he'd behaved when he'd found out what Nikolas had done!

She refused to remember the way he'd urged her to treat Nikolas before he'd discovered what had happened. In retrospect, she was sure she must have misunderstood what he'd said. After all, it wasn't the first time he'd asked her to charm one of his clients. He'd been angry with Nikolas and she'd caught the backlash, that was all.

She was putting her underwear into the suitcase when someone knocked at the bedroom door. Guessing it was one of the maids, come to tell her that Nikolas was waiting in his study, she called, *'Beno mesa,'* and continued with her task. But some sixth sense told her it wasn't the maid almost before the door opened, and she wasn't entirely surprised when Nikolas entered the room.

She was surprised when he closed the door behind him, however, and she straightened to face him with wary eyes. It was so totally out of character for him to invade a woman's bedroom uninvited, and she was aware of an anxious tingling in her belly as he leaned back against the panels.

'What are you doing?'

His question was not unexpected even though he must have been able to see perfectly well what she was about. 'I don't know what time the flights leave from Athens,' she said, pushing her thumbs into the waistband of her shorts at the back, and then pulling them out again when she realised it caused her breasts to bead against the thin cotton of her shirt. 'I—I—' She struggled to hide her nervousness. 'Perhaps you could ask Yanis to find out for us.'

'Why would I do that?' Nikolas regarded her with narrowed eyes. He had showered recently, and drops of water sparkled on his dark hair. In a black T-shirt and black cotton trousers, he looked lean and masculine, even if there were lines of weariness etched on his grim face. 'You are not going anywhere.'

Paige blinked. 'But I thought—'

'Yes? What did you think?' Nikolas pushed away from the door. 'That I would allow you to run out on me again as you did before?'

Paige's breath rushed out on a gasp. 'I'd have thought you'd have been glad that I've made it so easy for you,' she said, swallowing her astonishment. 'Is that what you wanted to talk to me about?'

'Partly.' Nikolas was terse. 'But first I wanted to apologise for Ariadne's behaviour. I am afraid I have spoiled her badly. I had no idea that she thought there was more to my affection for her than—well, affection.'

Paige shook her head. 'Young girls often conceive crushes on older men,' she said. Then, seeing his lack of comprehension, she explained, 'I mean puppy love, of course. Infatuation.' She made a helpless gesture. 'She'll get over it.'

'As you did?' asked Nikolas roughly. 'Yes, I suppose you would understand her feelings better than most.'

Paige's jaw dropped. 'I hope you're not implying that what I—what I shared with you was a childish infatuation!' she exclaimed, and he moved his shoulders in a dismissing gesture.

'What else?' he demanded. 'Though I have to say you soon got over it.'

'You don't know anything about my—my feelings,' cried Paige indignantly. And then, because she had to say something in her own defence, she went on, 'I hope you're not going to pretend it meant anything to you. Even if you did tell Sophie that you'd tried to reach me after I went home. What was all that about, by the way? Was it to save my feelings or your own?'

Nikolas's mouth thinned at her deliberate provocation. 'And why would I wish to save your feelings?' he enquired bitterly, and Paige pressed her quivering lips together.

'Indeed,' she said, when she had herself in control again. 'Your own, then. I should have known. I hope you realise that for a few moments you had me actually doubting my father's word.'

'And so you should.' Nikolas spoke hoarsely now. 'I did not wish him dead, Paige, but that man has a lot to answer for.'

'How dare you?' Paige found strength in indignation. 'How dare you defile my father's name? My God, he said you were an unscrupulous bastard, and he was right!'

'Is that what he told you?' Nikolas pulled a wry face. 'Well, what is it the English say? It takes one to know one.'

Paige was incensed at his insensitivity. 'You—you have no right to criticise someone who—who can't defend himself—'

'No? Even when that someone did his best to ruin my reputation?' Nikolas moved closer, and as he did so a stunned expression came over his face. '*Hristo*, he really didn't tell you, did he?'

'Tell me?' Paige stared at him suspiciously. 'Tell me what?'

Nikolas shook his head. 'Yanis swore it was possible but I didn't believe him. I thought he was only saying it to save his own sorry skin.'

'Yanis?' Paige was totally confused. 'Why would Yanis need to save—?'

'Because he was the one who arranged for you to leave the island,' Nikolas broke in impatiently. Then, with a groan, he added, 'Didn't you ever question the fact that I had apparently lost all interest in you when you left?'

Paige shook her head. 'I— No.'

'It meant so little to you?'

Paige flushed. 'I didn't say that.'

'What are you saying, then?' Nikolas gazed at her imploringly. '*Theus*, do you have any idea how I felt when Yanis told me you'd gone?'

'Relieved, I should think.' Paige strove for a glib tone and failed, miserably.

'Desperate,' Nikolas corrected her grimly, stepping forward to grasp her shoulders, and although she made a half-hearted attempt to free herself the anguish in his eyes kept her where she was. 'Paige, didn't you realise how I felt about you, about our relationship? Did it not occur to you that if all I had wanted was to take you to bed, then I would not have respected your innocence for the rest of the time you were on the yacht?'

Paige didn't know how to answer him. 'I—I thought—' *That you were bored with me; that as soon as you discovered how inexperienced I was you regretted getting involved with me...* She shivered suddenly. 'I—I didn't know what to think.'

'Then hear this: I did try to get in touch with you after you returned to London. Several times, in fact.' His lips twisted. 'Until your father told me that I was wasting my time, that there was another man in your life, and that in any case you had only been acting on his instructions.'

'No—'

'Yes.' When she would have stepped back from him, he used her momentary imbalance to jerk her closer. 'Why do you think I was so angry with myself when I betrayed my feelings to you that morning down at the jetty?' he demanded, thrusting his face close to hers. '*Theus*, Paige, for four years I thought you had made a fool of me. My only consolation was that Tennant—your father—hadn't got what he wanted, what he'd traded your innocence to achieve—'

'No...'

But it was a pitiful sound she made, and when he gathered her close against the taut strength of his lean body she trembled in his embrace.

'I didn't betray you, Paige,' he said thickly, his hands sliding up to cradle her skull. 'I fell in love with you. I wanted to marry you. But your father couldn't accept defeat, and although it cost him dearly in the end he destroyed the thing I most desired.'

Paige shook her head. 'Daddy's dead—'

'Do you think I don't know that?' Nikolas spoke bitterly. 'You were right, you know. That day when we had lunch together you understood my motives perfectly. It was no coincidence that I had contacted Price's firm. I'd been waiting four years to have my revenge and when I heard that

Tennant—that your father—was dead I thought any chance of retribution had died with him.'

Paige gazed up at him, aghast. 'Why are you telling me this now?'

'Because I want you to know the truth,' said Nikolas grimly. 'There will be no lies, no half-truths between us. If you decide to forgive me, it will be because you are in possession of all the facts. Not just those I would wish you to know.'

Paige's tongue appeared to moisten her lips, and, as if he couldn't stop himself, Nikolas bent his head to allow their tongues to touch; to mate; to seek an intimacy that had Paige's knees shaking and her hands reaching unsteadily for his waist; for some place she could anchor herself while he took possession of her mouth.

Her senses swam, but, as if he realised that seducing her again was not the answer, Nikolas pulled his mouth away and allowed his thumbs to take its place. *'Gliko,'* he said huskily. 'Very sweet. You have a taste like no other, *agape mou*. But I must not be distracted. I want you to know all my sins, and persuading Price to talk about you was only the least of them.'

Paige shook her head. 'I can't take this in.'

'But you want to?'

She wanted to deny it. She wanted to hold onto the fragile belief that her father had always had her best interests at heart, but it was becoming harder and harder to achieve. And, looking up into Nikolas's dark, anxious face, she knew that being honest with him was more important than hanging onto the crumbling reputation of a dead man.

'Yes,' she said softly. 'Yes, I want to.' And had the satisfaction of seeing the heat of emotion flare in his eyes.

'Very well,' he said, and now she detected a slight tremor in his voice, too. 'So—you must know that it was common knowledge that your father died owing a small fortune, and I watched with interest your efforts to rescue something from the wreck he left behind. Oh, yes.' This, as her eyes widened in shocked denial. 'I am not proud of my actions, *aghapita*, but you must remember I had your father's word that you had been a party to your own se-duction.'

Paige shook her head. 'He—he wouldn't say that.'

'Ah, but he did. And more besides.' Nikolas's thumbs caressed her cheeks. 'He wanted me to believe that every-thing that had happened had been for a purpose; that you did whatever he asked of you, and the reason that you'd left was because you were ashamed that you'd failed.'

Paige blinked. 'But how could you believe that?'

'How could I not, when you consistently refused to re-turn my calls?'

'But I didn't—'

'Know about them? Yes, I realise that now. But at the time I am afraid my anger blinded me to the most trans-parent of explanations. If I had not been so childishly ag-grieved at your apparent behaviour, I would have come to London and had the truth from your own lips.'

Paige took a trembling breath. 'If—if you had come to London, it might not have made any difference,' she mur-mured unhappily. She hesitated. 'Daddy had told me that you had laughed when he'd expressed his outrage at—at what you'd done. He said you'd told him it was his fault for being fool enough to trust you in the first place.'

Nikolas swore then in his own language, and although Paige didn't understand the words he used she could un-derstand his frustration at the way her father had deceived them both. It was as if Parker Tennant had had no care for his daughter's happiness at all; as if his own loss had de-stroyed any finer feelings he had once possessed.

After a few moments, Nikolas had himself in control again, but there was a dogged determination in his voice that proved how difficult it was for him to go on. 'So,' he said, his words tight with emotion, 'it is better not to dwell upon the past. Let it be enough to say that we both thought we had our reasons for despising the other, *ohi*?' His eyes searched her pale face. 'But perhaps you can understand now why I was so curious to see how you would handle the situation you found yourself in. Price's behaviour was predictable, of course. I'd known for some time that that young man had an eye to the—to the main chance, *ne*?' His eyes darkened briefly. 'Did you love him?'

Paige gave a rueful sigh. 'You must know I didn't or you wouldn't be asking that question.'

'I hoped,' he said, and, as if unable to resist, he bent his head and brushed a light kiss over the corner of her mouth. 'But I digress. I am nothing if not determined, and if there is something I want I will wait any length of time to get it.'

'But you said—'

'Revenge,' said Nikolas regretfully. 'I wanted revenge, and your vulnerability provided the ideal opportunity.'

'I see.'

'Do you? I wonder.' Nikolas's lips twisted now. 'You have no idea of the torment I went through, wondering if you would prove to be your father's daughter, after all.'

Paige frowned. 'What do you mean?'

'Oh, Paige, surely it must have occurred to you that you could have easily found yourself and Sophie a wealthy protector? You must have met dozens of men in the course of your father's business. I am sure many of them would have been only too glad to—'

'Sell myself, you mean?' Paige stiffened. 'I told you once before, Nikolas—'

'You are not for sale.' He finished the sentence for her. 'I know that now. But at the time…' He sighed. 'I am not proud of the thoughts I had about you, *agape mou*. But when you removed Sophie from her public school and took up residence with your aunt in Islington I knew the time had come for me to act.'

'You knew all that, and yet you still believed that I—'

'No.' Nikolas stopped her there. 'No. Deep down, I suppose I had always known that the creature your father had painted for me bore little resemblance to the beautiful, sensitive woman I had fallen in love with.' He shook his head. 'Yet I still believed that you had betrayed me, that that was the reason you had run away—'

'It wasn't.'

Nikolas grimaced. 'I can believe that now. But I have to admit that at the time I did not have such confidence. I had only your father's word—and the evidence of my own eyes—to convince me that you had no further use for my affections.'

'Oh, Nikolas!'

'You do believe me, don't you?'

'Yes, I believe you.'

'Because I have to tell you that after the lies Ariadne has been spreading about me my ego is sadly dented.'

'I believe you,' Paige said again, and this time when he bent to kiss her she wound her arms around his neck.

Hunger and sweet, sweet desire flowered inside her. Nikolas's lips and the damp heat he was generating filled her heart and her mind with an aching need that only he could assuage. His breath was warm in her mouth, his tongue touching and exploring all those dark and moist places that opened to his sensual caress. Her eyes closed, and she gave herself up to sensory pleasures, an involuntary moan escaping her when he released her mouth to seek the scented hollow of her throat.

Memories enveloped her, but they were good memories now, and only heightened her response to his urgent embrace. His hands spanned her shoulders briefly and then curved down the arching column of her spine, bringing her yielding body even closer to the powerful thrust of his. His hands cupped her bottom, lifting her against him, his fingers

kimming the cleft that tightened almost automatically at
is touch.

She was no innocent girl now, and when he eased one
muscled thigh between her legs her eyes opened wide to
ee the hot passion in his face. His own need, stark and
hrilling, darkened his eyes, burned like a torch in their
depths, drove her to grab fistfuls of his hair and drag his
mouth back to hers.

She wanted him, she thought dizzily. She'd always
wanted him, and it was incredible to believe that that impossible dream was almost within reach...

'Hey, Paige—ooh, whoops!'

Sophie's eruption into the room was as unexpected as it
was unwelcome and Paige felt an almost agonising pang of
egret when Nikolas stifled a groan and slowly, but firmly,
ut her away from him.

There was an awkward moment's silence when Paige
urtured the faint hope that Sophie might show some dis-
retion and walk out again. But she'd known it was an
nlikely possibility. Her sister was far too curious to allow
omething so intriguing to go unchallenged, and when she
ropped her shoulder against the jamb Paige knew she was
oing to demand an explanation she didn't have.

'Does this mean we won't be leaving, after all?' Sophie
sked, with her usual insensitivity, and Paige wanted to die
vith embarrassment.

'*Sophie!*' she exclaimed, hoping her sister would get the
message, but before the younger girl could respond
Nikolas's hand had looped around Paige's wrist.

'I take it you wouldn't have any objections?' he en-
uired, addressing himself to Sophie, but all Paige was
ware of was his thumb rubbing sensuously against her
alm.

Sophie blew out a breath. 'Are you serious?' she ex-
laimed, looking at her sister with a staggered expression.
I mean—I thought—' She broke off in some confusion,

and Paige enjoyed the experience of seeing her sister speechless for once.

'Yes? What did you think, Sophie?' Nikolas, too, appeared to be enjoying the moment, but Paige was not conceited enough to think that anything Sophie said would influence him one way or the other.

'Well, I—' Sophie gulped. 'Like—is this supposed to be some kind of joke or something?' She looked to her sister for support, but Paige was still too bemused by the feelings Nikolas was so effortlessly inspiring to have an answer for her. 'I thought you said Ariadne was going back to school.'

'*Me sinhorite!*' For a moment Nikolas was so disconcerted by this apparent *non sequitur* that he lapsed into his own language, and Sophie sighed in frustration.

'Paige said we were leaving,' she declared resentfully staring at her sister. 'Didn't you, Paige? Well, are we or aren't we? I have a right to know.'

'Ah…' Nikolas recovered his composure before Paige could say anything, but instead of answering her he adopted a rather humorous expression. 'Well, Sophie, I would say that your question is a little—how shall I put it?—premature?'

Premature!

Oh, God!

With a feeling of complete devastation, Paige detached her hand from Nikolas's and put some space between them. She'd been such a fool, she thought painfully, avoiding his curious gaze. Why hadn't she seen what was happening? Why hadn't she realised that he had spoken in the past tense? He'd said he had fallen in love with her; that he'd *wanted* to marry her. Then, not now. Now all he wanted was satisfaction—a chance to prove to himself that she was still as vulnerable to him as she had ever been…

'Premature?' It was Sophie who was speaking again, and Paige wanted desperately to shut her up. 'What do you mean, premature? There didn't seem to be anything premature about the way you two were acting when—'

'Sophie!'

Paige was mortified, but Nikolas seemed to find Sophie's candour amusing. 'You're right,' he said as Paige started across the room to push her sister out of the door. He came after her, and although she attempted to resist he slipped his arm around her waist, successfully halting her in midflight. 'We had just begun to understand one another, hadn't we, *aghapita*?' he whispered. And, to her ignominy and Sophie's amazement, he bestowed a lingering kiss on her nape. 'For the first time in four years, we were being completely honest with one another.'

Paige drew a trembling breath. 'Is that what you call it?' she muttered in an undertone, but she couldn't prevent her automatic response to the heat of his body at her back.

'It will do for now,' he chided her softly. 'Stop fighting me, *mora*, or your sister will think you do not love me, after all.'

'Love you?' The words fell helplessly from Paige's lips, and, ignoring Sophie's stunned face, he turned her in his arms and lowered his mouth to hers.

'As I love you,' he conceded gently.

Paige quivered. 'You said—you said Sophie's question was premature—'

'And it was. I have not yet had the time to tell you how I feel; to ask you to do me the honour of becoming my wife.'

Paige's knees sagged, and now even Sophie found the naked emotion between them just too private to intrude upon.

'I guess we are staying,' she mumbled ruefully, backing out of the room, and wasn't really surprised when no one even noticed that she'd gone…

EPILOGUE

PAIGE awakened to the sound of rain pattering against the deck above her head. The weather had broken at last, she thought ruefully, but she couldn't altogether say it mattered. Despite the fact that they had been cruising through the Ionian Islands and into the Adriatic, she and Nikolas had spent much of the past three weeks closeted in their stateroom, and there was something intensely appealing about the intimacy the rain was creating.

She sighed contentedly. It was early yet and she knew she ought to close her eyes and go back to sleep again. But she couldn't resist turning her head, and the sight of Nikolas's dark head buried in the pillow beside her was an irresistible temptation. Although it was three weeks since they had stood together in the small church in Agios Petros and made their vows to one another, she still found it incredibly hard to believe that he was her husband; that he loved her just as much as she loved him, and that the mistakes of the past were just a painful memory.

She had long since forgiven her father for his part in their separation. It was terrible what the pressures of a failing business could do, she thought. She could only be grateful that he had brought her and Nikolas together in the first place, and she had come to bless her husband's subsequent desire for revenge for making their reunion possible.

Of course, she knew now that Nikolas would never have done anything to hurt her. Where she was concerned he was totally vulnerable, and even their closest relatives had been amazed at the feelings he didn't even try to hide.

After her experiences with Ariadne, Paige had been afraid that Nikolas's parents might object to their only son marrying an Englishwoman, particularly the Englishwoman who had apparently caused him such pain four years ago. But Elena and Constantine Petronides had been so relieved that their son was going to get married at last that their congratulations had been warmly sincere. They wanted a daughter-in-law; they wanted more grandchildren; and if Paige had suspected that they had any doubts about her suitability to be Nikolas's wife Eleni Petronides had quickly disposed of them. Ever since his earlier encounter with Paige, Nikolas had refused to consider the possibility of marrying anyone, and they had been unhappily convinced that their son was never going to achieve the kind of happiness his parents had shared.

His sisters, Oriana and Melina, had been less easy to win over. Although they were both married with children of their own, they loved their brother dearly and had perhaps been more aware than their parents of how Paige's apparent betrayal had affected him. But, gradually, they too had been forced to acknowledge that Nikolas had never been happier, and Melina, who had two little girls, had shown her approval by allowing them to join Sophie and Ariadne as Paige's bridesmaids at the wedding.

Paige allowed a sound of pure delight to escape her. It had been such a beautiful wedding, she thought, remembering how handsome Nikolas had looked with genuine pride. Aunt Ingrid had seemed totally bemused by the occasion, but she had happily agreed to stay on afterwards and keep an eye on both Sophie and Ariadne while Paige and Nikolas were on honeymoon.

Yanis was staying on the island, too, sharing the running of the Petronides corporation with Nikolas's father—who had been persuaded to come out of retirement for the weeks his son would be away. A situation which relieved Paige enormously. Aunt Ingrid was sweet, but Sophie could run rings around her, and Ariadne, who had been so relieved not to be sent back to school before the start of term in

September, had developed a totally unexpected attachment to the younger girl.

It had been agreed that both Sophie and Ariadne would board at school from the start of the autumn term: Ariadne at the convent she had previously attended, and Sophie at an English school in Athens. Both girls would spend weekends with their adoptive guardians, when possible, but Nikolas had no intention of leaving his new wife behind when business took him on trips about Europe and to the United States. Being permanently responsible for two teenagers would have prevented this.

In fact, both the girls had accepted the new arrangement without protest, and although Paige was sure the future wasn't all going to be such plain sailing—pardon the pun, she thought humorously—as long as she and Nikolas were together there was nothing they couldn't face.

But thinking about Nikolas had made her restless and she turned onto her side to gaze at her husband with mischievous eyes. He looked so comfortable, she thought, lying on his back, legs splayed, one arm above his head, the other at his side, an indication that even in sleep he trusted her completely.

Which was a dangerous thing to do, she thought whimsically, drawing the covers back from his waist to expose the whole length of his body to her possessive gaze. He was so appealing; so male, she acknowledged tremulously, not immune to the powerful strength of his torso or the sensual growth of dark hair that sprinkled his chest and arrowed down to the impressive cluster of curls that guarded his sex.

Her breath caught in her throat and, unable to stop herself, she spread her hand on his flat stomach. The muscles flinched beneath her fingers but his breathing didn't falter, and gaining confidence, Paige allowed her exploration to move lower. His sex lay within her reach now, lightly aroused and velvety soft to touch, as she knew, but when she attempted to enclose him within her grasp his sudden erection had her pulling back in surprise.

Yet she shouldn't have been surprised, she thought ruefully. She'd had plenty of experience to know how easy it was for her to bring him to an immediate state of arousal. But she'd thought he was asleep, and it was all the more daunting to find he was awake and watching her with lazily amused eyes.

'A little curiosity?' he asked mockingly. 'I hope I satisfied all your expectations.'

'Don't you always?' demanded Paige, stung into a defensive retaliation. And then, because she knew he was only teasing her, she pulled a face at him before bending her head to circle his navel with her tongue. 'I hope I've satisfied yours.'

'How could you doubt it?' said Nikolas, his voice a little less controlled now. And, as she allowed her tongue to trail lower, he added, 'I hope you realise what you're doing.'

'I think so,' said Paige, lifting her head to give him an impish grin. 'I'm just—waking you up, that's all. Don't they say that even Sleeping Beauty was awakened with a kiss?'

'Not there,' said Nikolas in a strangled voice, and, struggling up on his elbows, he managed to remove part of his anatomy from her caressing tongue. 'Come here,' he muttered, hauling her over him, and then groaned when she parted her legs so that the hot, moist core of her was cradling his sex.

'Let me,' she said, when he would have rolled her over, and, straddling him, she allowed him to invade her tight, wet sheath.

There was a delicious delight in knowing she was giving him pleasure and Paige moved slowly and sensuously over him until her own needs quickened her pace. Their release was almost simultaneous, and Nikolas did roll her over then

and buried his face in the scented hollow between her
breasts.

'Do you have any idea how much I love you?' he asked
huskily, his still shuddering body trembling in her arms,
and Paige felt a surge of love for him thicken in her throat.

'About as much as I love you?' she offered unsteadily,
but he pushed himself up from her and shook his head.

'And more,' he told her softly, a catch in his voice.
'These last two months have been the happiest time of my
life.'

'And mine,' said Paige, lifting a hand to shape his cheek,
allowing him to take her fingers into his mouth. 'We're so
lucky. Some people go through life and never find the one
person who is important to them.'

'And to think I nearly lost you,' agreed Nikolas, bringing
her palm to his lips. 'I was such a fool.'

'We both were,' said Paige, not allowing him to take all
the blame. 'You know, Daddy wasn't always so unscrupulous. I think he and my mother shared something special,
too, and when she died...' She sighed. 'Do you understand?'

'I'm trying to,' said Nikolas, nodding. 'I have to say that
at this moment I can only bless your father for bringing us
together in the first place. I think we can leave the rest. I'm
only sorry he never knew how much I love his daughter...'

'And mine,' said Paige, lifting a hand to shape his cheek, allowing him to take her fingers into his mouth. 'We're so lucky. Some people go through life and never find the one person who is important to them.'

'And to think I almost lost you,' agreed Nicholas, brushing his nose to her lips. 'I was such a fool.'

Jane Porter grew up on a diet of Mills and Boon® romances, reading late at night under the covers so her mother wouldn't see! She wrote her first book at age eight and spent many of her high school and college years living abroad, immersing herself in other cultures and continuing to read voraciously. Now, Jane has settled down in rugged Seattle, Washington, with her gorgeous husband and two sons. Jane loves to hear from her readers. You can write to her at PO Box 524, Bellevue, WA 98009, USA. Or visit her website at www.janeporter.com

Watch out for Jane Porter's latest passionate read:
THE SULTAN'S BOUGHT BRIDE
On sale this month, in Modern Romance™!

THE ITALIAN GROOM
by
Jane Porter

For my grandmother, Elizabeth.
I adore you. Jane

CHAPTER ONE

"Ten years, and you still haven't changed." Niccolo's softly accented voice echoed with disgust, his sensual mouth flattening in anger. "You never would listen to reason—"

"Nic, I'm only asking for the spare set of keys to my parents' house," Meg interrupted, trying to ignore the churning in her stomach. "These are not trade secrets."

One of his black eyebrows lifted. "Is that a joke?"

She fought her fatigue and impatience. It wouldn't help to get into an argument with Nic. Nic would win. He always won.

Struggling to sound reasonable, she reminded him of the long-standing agreement between their families. "It's always been policy to keep a spare key for each other, in case of emergency. It's never been a problem before, and I don't know why you're making a big deal out of it now."

"Because it's not safe for you to stay alone at your parents'. The ranch is isolated. I'm ten minutes away if something should happen."

"Nothing will happen."

His voice fairly crackled with contempt. "Maggie, you attract trouble like pollen attracts bees. I've saved your skin from more scrapes—"

"I never asked for your help!"

"No, but you needed it."

"You don't know what I need, Nic. You just like

5

to think you do.'' She clenched her jaw, furious with herself for coming to the villa in the first place. If she hadn't misplaced the key ring to her parents' house, she wouldn't be having this conversation with Niccolo Dominici, nor would she be receiving another of his famous lectures.

He made a choking sound and muttered something in Italian.

"What was that?'' she demanded, knowing how he loved to resort to Italian when he wanted to say something particularly unflattering.

"I said I should give up on you.''

Meg stiffened indignantly, her shoulders squaring. She'd allowed him to crush her years ago, her tender heart broken by his harsh rejection, but thankfully she wasn't a teenager anymore. "Then do! I don't need your so-called help.''

"So-called?'' He bristled, golden eyes glinting. The rapid pull of muscle in his jaw revealed her barb had hit home. She'd insulted him, bruising his considerable Italian machismo. Nic stared at her through narrowed eyes. "You're fortunate that we have a very old friendship.''

"It's not much of a friendship,'' she retorted grimly. "In fact, you're the last person I'd describe as a friend.''

His jaw tightened again, but he didn't answer her. Instead his eyes searched her face. She kept her expression purposely blank. She wouldn't give him the satisfaction of letting him see how strongly he still affected her. "Give me the key.''

"No.''

"My parents know I'll be staying there. I left a message with the cruise line.''

"You cannot stay there alone."

"I *live* alone."

His mouth pinched tighter, and he crossed his arms, straining his green sport jacket. Yellow light glowed behind him, the villa's French doors open to embrace the warm California night. "Which is quite dangerous in New York. The city is full of strangers who prey on young women."

Inadvertently Mark, her baby's father, came to mind.

What was the expression? A wolf in sheep's clothing?

But she didn't want to think about Mark, didn't want to be reminded that she'd fallen for Mark partly because he'd reminded her so much of Niccolo. The fact that even after ten years Meg still desired men like Nic confounded her. Nic might be sinfully attractive, but he was also insufferably high-handed.

As it turned out, Mark and Nic were really nothing alike. Whereas Nic had scruples, Mark had none.

Mark wasn't just any old wolf, but a married wolf with three kids and a wife tucked in an affluent Connecticut neighborhood. Greenwich, to be precise.

Her stomach heaved at the memory. Mark had insisted she get rid of the baby, going so far as to make an appointment at a clinic, but Meg refused, and used the opportunity to head to California to get a start on her new landscape renovation.

Her stomach gurgled again, a squeamish reminder that it had been a long day and promised to be an equally long night. She was four and a half months into this pregnancy and still quite sick. She'd been prepared for nausea, but this...it felt like a flu that wouldn't end.

"I'm only in town for a few days," she said, bone-weary and beginning to feel a little desperate. "I'm meeting with clients till Thursday and then back to New York on Friday."

"It doesn't matter if you're only staying for a night. It's not safe."

Meg swallowed hard and fast. "I'll lock the door."

"No."

"*Please.*"

"No."

"Nic, you're not my dad. And you're not Jared."

For a moment he said nothing, stunned to silence. Then the small muscle popped again in his jaw, revealing his tightly leashed temper. "Is that so?"

She swallowed her anger, appalled at what she'd said.

Of course he wasn't her brother. Nic had been her brother's best friend. Jared and Nic had been inseparable up until the minute Jared had crashed the car that one horrible Christmas Eve.

It was a terrible thing to say to Nic, and she took a frightened step back, hating herself for her unkindness. Silently she cursed her quick temper and even quicker tongue. There were times she wished she had a little of Niccolo's control.

"I'm sorry." She apologized, completely ashamed.

He nodded, his full lips pressed tight beneath his straight nose. She'd once teased him that he had a face Michelangelo would have loved. Nic had responded that he'd rather have been drawn by da Vinci. Something basic and spare. But there was nothing basic or spare about Niccolo. He was beautiful.

Repentant, she gazed at Nic, still horrified by her thoughtlessness. She'd struck below the belt and she knew it. Bile rose in her throat. She'd broken her cardinal rule. Any discussion of Jared and the accident was absolutely off-limits. "I shouldn't have said that about Jared—"

"It's okay. You're tired. It's late."

Instead of feeling relieved, she felt worse. "I don't want to fight with you. Please just let me have the key."

"There's a rash of robberies in the area lately. Nine local ranches and wineries have been hit. Last time an elderly woman, a very nice woman, was hurt. I can't let you take that risk."

Some of her anger dissipated. Meg's shoulders slumped wearily. So that was it. There'd been trouble in the area, and he was afraid for her. So like Niccolo. Still trying to protect her.

Meg turned and gazed across the villa's flagstone terrace to the magnificent view of the valley. In the moonlight the orderly row of grapes looked like olive green pinstripes against rounded hills.

In the ten years she'd been away, it seemed that nothing—not the grapes nor handsome, proud Niccolo—had changed. Oh, she'd been back a number of times, but she'd made it a point to visit when Nic was away. Somehow Nic and Jared and the past were so tangled together that she found it too painful to return home often.

"Who was hurt?" she asked, still drinking in the moonlit landscape. Unlike so many others, her parents used their fertile land for cattle and crops. Nic had once approached them about buying their acreage for top dollar. Her father had quietly but firmly refused. Nic had never brought the subject up again.

"Mrs. Anderson," he answered.

Her old piano teacher.

"How awful," Meg whispered.

"Which is why I can't let you go to your parents' home." Nic towered above her, exuding authority even in a casual sport coat and khaki trousers. "I've promised to look after your parents' place while they're gone. I know they wouldn't want you there, not after what happened to Mrs. Anderson."

"Of course." But she couldn't help a flash of disappointment. It was so late and she was so incredibly tired. It would have been wonderful to creep into bed in her old room with the nubby white chenille bedspread, the girlish ballet pictures on the wall, the row of Raggedy Anns on a shelf, and just sleep. To momentarily escape the exhaustion and her worry about the future and just be young Maggie again.

But young Maggie was long gone. When she left Healdsburg for college on the East Coast ten years ago, she'd vowed to make a new life for herself with people who didn't know her past or her name.

After finishing her studies Meg took a job with a prominent Manhattan landscape design firm, working her way up from fetching coffees to designing secret jewel-box gardens for Fifth Avenue mansions.

Meg knew she had a talent for design and was willing to work harder than anyone else in the firm. Which is how she'd landed the Hunt account in California. Actually, landed wasn't quite right. She'd fought for the job tooth and nail. The Hunts' garden renovation would take years and yet it would be the jewel in her crown. With the Hunt renovation on her résumé, she could open her own design firm, work from home, be independent.

Thus she'd squashed her apprehension about returning to Napa, resolving to give the Hunts the very best of her time and ability.

She'd be her own woman. She'd be her own boss. And she'd be a great mother, too.

Her convictions were undermined by moisture beading her brow, her nausea growing worse. "That's fine," she said, striving to sound casual. "I'll stay at a hotel tonight."

"That's absurd. I won't have you staying in a hotel. If you need a place to stay, you'll stay here."

The moisture on her skin felt cool and clammy. It was no longer a question of *if* she'd be sick, it was a question of *when*. "I don't want to put you out. There's a good hotel not far from here."

Quickly, she moved down the front steps toward her car, concentrating on every blue colored flagstone. *Just walk,* she told herself, *one foot and then the other. Don't let yourself get sick here. Don't do it. Don't do it.*

Niccolo's footsteps sounded behind her. She tried to hurry, practically running the last several feet. Just as she reached her car, he grabbed her arm and spun her around.

"Stop it!" Emotion vibrated in his voice. "Stop running away."

Her stomach heaved. Her forehead felt as if it were made of paste. Her mouth tasted sweet and sour. "This isn't the time for this."

His fingers gouged her arm, his grip tight and punishing. "Will there ever be a good time? We haven't talked in ten years. I haven't seen you since you ran away the last time. Why does it have to be like this?''

"Nic."

"What?"

"I'm going to be sick."

He passed a fresh facecloth to her in the bathroom. Meg gratefully accepted the cool, damp cloth and placed it against her temple. She leaned against the bathroom sink, her legs still weak, her hands shaking. "Thank you."

"You should have told me you weren't well."

His gruffness drew a lopsided smile. This was Niccolo at his most compassionate. She ought to be grateful for small mercies. Fortunately the facecloth hid her smile. It would only infuriate him. "I'm fine," she breathed, her voice still quivering. "Just tired, but nothing that a good night's sleep won't fix."

"You're not one to throw up when you're tired."

Lifting her head slightly, she met his eyes. His expression unnerved her. There was nothing gentle in his cool golden gaze.

She buried her face in the damp cloth again. "It was a long trip," she said. "I haven't eaten much today."

She couldn't tell him that sometimes just the smell of food made her stomach empty and that lately, Mark's relentless pressure had killed what little remained of her appetite. Mark's constant phone calls had changed in tone, becoming increasingly aggressive as she refused to cooperate with his plans. Mark made it sound so simple. Just terminate the pregnancy. That was all there was to it.

Meg trembled inwardly, furious. Terminate the pregnancy, indeed! As if her baby was an appointment or an insurance policy.

She couldn't tell Niccolo any of this. Instead she answered glibly something about not having enough time. His brows drew together. His expression was severe.

"When did you arrive in Napa?" he asked.

"I flew into San Francisco this morning." She lifted her head, her hands resting against the cool porcelain of the sink. The sink was imported from Italy, like nearly everything in the stone villa. "The flight was delayed—fog, I think it was—so I drove straight up to make my appointment on time."

"You couldn't call and let your appointment know you needed a lunch break?"

"I bought a sandwich at the airport."

"Cuisine at its finest." His lovely mouth curled derisively and she sat back, still fascinated by the faint curve of his lips. That one night she'd kissed him years ago burned in her memory. He kissed the way she'd imagined he would. Fiercely. With passion. Not at all the way boys her own age kissed.

"Francesca is in the kitchen putting something together for you," he continued. "She had fresh tomatoes and little shrimp she thought would be perfect."

Fresh shrimp? Meg's stomach churned. She'd never be able to eat shrimp. "Really. That's not necessary."

Nic's expression darkened. "Don't tell that to Francesca. She's got three pots on the stove and is singing in Italian. You'd think we were having a midnight dinner party from the way she's carrying on.'' He turned and leaned against the doorjamb. ''But then, she's always had a soft spot for you. You *are* part of the family.''

''Even if I don't call or write for ten years?'' She'd meant to be flippant, but Nic didn't crack a smile.

''I don't laugh at your bad jokes.''

He could be so stuffy sometimes. She wrinkled her nose and rolled her eyes. ''It's not really a bad joke. I think it's more your mood—''

''You see, *cara*, I did call,'' he interrupted smoothly. ''I wrote, too. I wrote to you at your university. Then later when you had your first apartment. Even during the year you spent in London, as an apprentice for Hills and Drake Design.''

Her legs suddenly felt shaky again, and she sat down rather heavily on the edge of the toilet. ''Yes, you wrote me. You wrote pages and pages in the harshest tone imaginable.'' His censure had hurt, hurt terribly. ''Of course I didn't answer your letters! You were cruel—''

''I've never been cruel to you.''

''Nic, you humiliated me!''

''You humiliated yourself. I still don't understand what you were thinking, climbing on my lap, acting like a—a…''

''Say it.''

He visibly recoiled. ''Never mind.''

She balled up the facecloth in her hands, frustrated with his rigid views. Poor, proper Nic raised to view girls as helpless creatures and boys as inheritors of the earth.

''I won't apologize for that evening,'' she told

him, blood surging to her cheeks. "I'll never apologize. I did nothing wrong."

"*Cara,* you weren't wearing panties."

Her face burned and yet she tilted her head, defiant. She'd been crazy about him, utterly infatuated, and she'd desperately wanted to impress him. "I'd read it was considered sexy."

"You were a schoolgirl."

"I was seventeen."

"Sixteen."

"Almost seventeen."

"And you were wearing a white lace—what do you call it?"

"Garter belt."

"Yes, garter belt beneath your skirt. White lace garter belt and no panties. What was I supposed to think?"

It was beyond his ability to see her as anything but Jared's kid sister. "That I liked you, Nic. That I had a teenage crush and I was trying to impress you." She stood up and tossed the crumpled facecloth at him.

He caught the damp cloth, knuckling it. "It didn't impress me. It made me sick."

This was exactly why she hadn't answered his letters. He didn't understand how harsh he'd been. How harsh he could be. Niccolo had been raised in a wealthy, aristocratic Italian family. His values were old-world, old-school, and despite the fact that he embraced much of the American culture, he still believed a woman's virtue was by far her most precious asset. Instead of being flattered by her attempt at seduction, he'd been appalled. Appalled and disgusted.

Meg stood up, catching a glimpse of herself in the

vanity mirror. Shadows formed blue crescents beneath her eyes. Her dark curls had come loose from their twisted knot, creating inky tendrils around her pale face.

She turned from the mirror, too tired and worn out to make an attempt at smoothing her stray curls. "This won't work, Nic. Let me go to a hotel. Francesca will understand."

He stopped her as she tried to step past him, catching her by the hand, his fingers sliding up to capture her wrist. He held her closely against him, just as he had when she was younger and needing comfort after Jared died.

"But I won't understand," he murmured. "I don't know what's happened to us. I don't know why you're so angry with me. You can't even talk to me without spitting and hissing like a frustrated kitten."

She didn't hear his words, only felt his warmth. She'd forgotten how sensitive he made her feel, as if her limbs were antennae, her skin velvet-covered nerve endings. It was a dizzying sensation to be so close to him, intense and dazzling. He might have been Jared's best friend but he didn't feel like Jared. He didn't feel like a brother at all.

Her heart thumped painfully hard, and for a second she longed to wrap her arms around him, to seek the warmth she'd once found in him.

Before she could speak, Francesca, the housekeeper of the last thirty three years, appeared, wiping her hands on a white apron.

"Dinner's ready," Francesca announced, beaming with pleasure. "Come, Maggie, I've made you a special pasta, very light, very fresh. I think you will like it very much. Please. Come. Sit down."

*   *   *

The kitchen smelled of olive oil and garlic. Francesca had set two places at the rough-hewn pine table near the massive stone fireplace. A fire crackled in the hearth, and the fat beeswax pillar candles on the table glowed with light.

"Smells wonderful," Meg said, surprised that the scent of garlic and onion didn't turn her stomach. She sniffed again, checking for a fishy smell or a hint of shrimp, but nothing rankled her nose. In fact, her stomach growled with hunger. But then, Francesca had always been an incredible cook. She could make the simplest ingredients taste exquisite.

Niccolo held a chair out for her, and Meg took a seat at the table.

"Everything is very fresh," Francesca said again, serving the bowls of pasta and presenting them at the table. "I remember you like olives in your pasta, and these are just perfect. Clean and sweet, not bitter."

Nic opened a bottle of Dominici red from his private reserve. They ate in near silence, making small talk about the weather and the local wines.

Meg was grateful that Nic steered the conversation away from personal topics, and gradually her tension headache began to ease.

The phone rang down the hall. Although it was close to midnight, Francesca answered it. "The papa," she said, returning to the kitchen.

"My father," Nic said, standing. "I must take this call."

"Of course," Meg answered, breaking her crusty roll. She knew that with the time difference between California and Florence, Nic did a lot of business late at night. The Dominici family owned wineries in Italy and northern California. Niccolo was in charge of the California winery. His father and younger brother managed the Italian estates.

Francesca waited until Nic was gone to approach Meg. She didn't waste any time with small talk. Instead she gave Meg a long, considering look. Meg shifted uncomfortably, avoiding the housekeeper's eyes.

Tension mounted. Francesca didn't move.

Finally Meg dropped the crusty roll on her plate and wiped her fingers on her napkin. "Yes, Francesca?"

"You're pregnant, aren't you?"

"No." The denial was so automatic, the response so instinctive, that Meg didn't even consider admitting the truth.

The housekeeper clucked and shook her head. "Do your parents know?"

"They've been on vacation."

"So you are pregnant." Francesca folded her hands across her middle. "You came to the right place. Niccolo will take care of you."

"No! No, Francesca, that's not even an option. Nic and I...no. Absolutely not."

The housekeeper looked offended. "What's wrong with my Niccolo?"

"Nothing's wrong with Nic, but this isn't his problem." More firmly, she said, "I'm doing very well. I don't need help."

"But you're not married."

"I don't have to be married to have a baby."

Francesca's displeasure showed. "You don't know anything about babies. It's not easy being a mother. I know."

"I'll learn." Meg pushed back from the table.

"I've always wanted children. This is a good thing. I'm not ashamed."

"So why won't you tell him?"

"Tell me what?" Nic asked from the doorway. He took his seat at the large pine table and glanced from his housekeeper to Meg. "What should I know?"

Meg raised her chin. "About my new job working with the Hunts."

He shot the housekeeper a quick glance. Francesca shrugged and turned away. Nic looked at Meg. "Your job?" he prompted.

"Yes," Meg answered, sending a wary glance in Francesca's direction. "With the Hunts. They're interested in renovating their gardens."

Pots suddenly banged in the deep cast-iron sink.

Meg raised her voice. "It's a century-old estate." More pots crashed. Meg winced but bravely continued. "I've spent the last year courting them. I really wanted this opportunity—"

"Francesca." Niccolo's reproach silenced the pot banging. The housekeeper shrugged and turned to other tasks. "Please, *cara*," he said to Meg, "finish your story."

"It's not really a story. It's just my job." And the opportunity of a lifetime, she mentally added.

"Your parents mentioned that the Hunts interviewed six landscape designers, but you were the only American."

"Flattering, isn't it?"

"They picked you."

"Yes." She couldn't hide her pride, or her pleasure. The Hunt gardens were among the finest in California. "I'm thrilled. This isn't just work, it's a dream. Ever since I was a little girl I've been fascinated with the Hunt estate. I remember creeping around their hedges, hiding in the old maze. Their gardens were magical, and now I have a chance to work new magic.''

''Is that who you were meeting with today?''

''Yes. I'll be meeting with them for the next several months. I'll commute back and forth from New York. It'll be quite an intensive project.''

Nic raised his wineglass. ''To you, *cara*. I'm proud of you. This is really quite an achievement.''

She raised her glass, and Niccolo clinked goblets with her, the fine crystal tinging. But instead of sipping the wine she set her goblet down and took another bite from her pasta.

''You're not drinking?'' Niccolo set his goblet down.

Of course he'd notice something like that. He was a winegrower. He made some of the finest table wines in California. ''I have to be up early,'' she answered. ''I'll need to be sharp.''

''Of course,'' he murmured, his eyes fixed on her.

Francesca suddenly turned from the sink. ''I'll make a lunch for you tomorrow. A roll, some fruit, meat and cheese. You like yogurt, yes? I shall send a yogurt, too, that way you can nibble whenever your stomach doesn't feel so good.''

Meg remembered the picnic lunches the housekeeper used to pack for them when they were kids. They were the best sack lunches in the world. ''Thank you, Francesca,'' she said, touched by the housekeeper's kindness. ''I'd like that very much, as long as it's no trouble.''

''No trouble at all,'' Francesca answered stoutly. ''You're family. You will always be family.''

It was the same thing Niccolo had said earlier.

This time the words evoked a rush of longing so intense that Meg's eyes nearly filled with tears. She was suddenly reminded of the years come and gone and the pain they'd all shared when Jared died that horrible Christmas and Maggie had taken the blame. For a split second she wished she could go back through time and make it the way it once was, but that was an impossible wish. Jared was gone, and her friendship with Niccolo had never been the same.

"Thank you, Francesca," Meg answered softly. "Have a good night."

"Seeing you again makes it a good night."

Despite her protests, Niccolo walked with her to her car to claim her overnight bag. "You're not worried I'm going to sneak away, are you?"

The corner of Nic's mouth lifted wryly. "No. I have your parents' house key here," he said, patting his sport jacket.

"You don't trust me."

"Should I?"

"I'm wearing panties, I promise."

"These jokes…I don't find them funny at all."

She stood up on tiptoe and patted his cheek. He smelled like oranges and sandalwood, decidedly Roman. He had his fragrance made for him on the Continent. Another little luxury he took for granted. "You never did, Nic. I drove you crazy even when I was eleven."

His golden eyes glinted in the moonlight. She thought he looked troubled, almost sad. He gazed at her, taller by a full head and shoulders. His thick hair hung long enough to brush his collar. He'd always worn his hair long. It was more European, and it suited his features. Niccolo might own a home in northern California, but he was pure Italian. Old-world Italian, at that.

"You look thin," he said, after a moment. "Are you starving yourself?"

"You only date broomsticks, Nic. How can I be too thin?"

His mouth curved, transforming his darkly handsome face into something impossibly beautiful. She suddenly wondered if he knew how devastating his smile was. He had to know.

She tried to picture him practicing his smile at the mirror but failed. Niccolo didn't practice charm. It just happened. He wore his strength and elegance as if it were one of his Armani suits.

"But you're Maggie," he answered, his smile fading. "You're not meant to be a broomstick."

He still didn't understand that she'd grown up. She was certain he only saw the sixteen-year-old hellion when he looked at her. "I'm twenty-eight, Niccolo, and I'm not Maggie anymore. I go by Meg."

"No."

"Yes. Meg or Margaret, take your pick."

His brow furrowed, his upper lip curled. She reached up and pressed two fingers against his lips. "Oh, Nic, don't. That's an awful face."

"But you give me such awful choices, *cara*," he said against her fingertips.

Her fingers tingled, and she pulled them away. "But those are your choices. Meg or Margaret."

"Never Margaret. You're not a Margaret. And Meg? That sounds like a seasoning. I prefer Maggie.

It fits you. Quick, lovely, unpredictable. That's my Maggie.''

A bittersweet emotion filled her. ''Am I lovely?''

He didn't immediately answer, considering her question. Then deliberately he tilted her face up, studying her in the moonlight. The intensity in his gaze stole her breath. ''More lovely than you have the right to be after all the heartache you've caused me.''

''I've caused *you* heartache?'' She felt her mouth tremble. Hope and pain blistered her heart. She hated the complexity of her emotions. It wasn't fair. Her world had changed. She had changed, and yet here she was, still so drawn to Niccolo.

His palm felt rough against her jaw. The pad of his thumb lightly caressed her cheek. ''More than you'll ever know.''

CHAPTER TWO

NICCOLO tramped across a half acre of his vineyard, his Western-style boots crunching the ground. The air felt crisp, exhilarating, and he breathed in the richness of the early fall morning.

Even though it had been years since he helped harvest the grapes, Nic still inspected the crops every morning. An excellent wine required more than sun, rain, good soil; it needed passion. While the Dominici family had numerous business ventures, the Dominici wines and extensive vineyards were Niccolo's passion.

Passion.

The word immediately brought Maggie to mind, and as he thought of her, his mouth curved wryly.

Maggie wasn't easy. She tended to arouse fierce emotions in people. Some admired her, others disliked her, but either way, you had an opinion.

Frankly, like Jared, he'd adored her. Maggie had been an irresistible little girl. A scamp, really. She created more mischief than a dozen children put together. Yet her antics amused him, just as she amused him, her dark curls and expressive eyes arousing his protective instinct as if he really were another big brother.

He'd helped teach her to drive, escorted her to a high school dance, tutored her in calculus. When she'd had a falling out with her parents, she'd asked him to intercede. When she had been kicked out of class for arguing with a teacher, Niccolo was the one to pick her up from school.

Maggie.

Hotheaded, impulsive, passionate Maggie.

His smile faded. If only she hadn't pulled that silly prank and tried to seduce him. Even now he felt uncomfortable when he thought about that evening. She'd shocked him by sliding onto his lap and passionately kissing him. Her openmouthed kiss, the flick of her tongue. Nic's jaw tightened.

He'd tried to push her away, but she'd clung to him. When he attempted to lift her off his lap, he'd encountered a bare thigh and a very naked bottom.

He should have laughed about it. Should have made a joke, teased her or something. But he hadn't been able to. He'd been responding to her kiss and her warmth. His desire had mortified him. Nic had thrown her off his lap and said something far harsher than he intended. She'd looked stunned. She'd stood there clutching the hem of her schoolgirl skirt, trying not to cry.

Then she'd left. He should have gone after her, should have tried to talk to her. But his pride and shame wouldn't let him. He'd told himself she owed him an apology. He'd convinced himself that she just needed time, and truthfully, they both did.

Niccolo headed toward the house, periodically stopping to inspect the new vines he'd planted last spring at the base of a massive trellis. These were his newest additions to his grapes, and he checked for frost damage on the tender shoots, but happily found none.

With Maggie away at college, Niccolo had begun to feel the loss of her company. Healdsburg was a sleepy little town and without Jared and Maggie, California lost its charm. Niccolo returned to Florence for a second business degree and to help his father run the vast Tuscany vineyards.

He'd learned a great deal working with his father and brother. Four years later his father had approached him, asking if Niccolo would be interested in managing the Napa Valley vineyards and overseeing the California businesses. Niccolo had jumped at the opportunity. He wanted to experiment with new grape varieties and dreamed of producing a California Chianti reserve with the family's Tuscany grapes.

Nic neared the house, reaching the corner terrace with the arbor trellis. In mild weather he ate his breakfast on the sunny terrace. Francesca had already laid a light breakfast on the wrought-iron table. He took a seat, opened the paper.

The French doors opened, and Maggie appeared. As their eyes met, he felt an inexplicable spark of awareness. He suddenly remembered how it felt to hold Maggie. Touching her was like grasping a live wire. She was nothing short of electric.

"Good morning, Nic."

Her voice, smooth, soft, quiet, made him feel disturbingly unquiet. He folded his paper, aware of the distance between them. "Good morning, *cara*. How did you sleep?"

She smiled at him, but her smile looked forced. "Surprisingly well. The bed in the guest room is heavenly."

She held her briefcase. Her travel bag hung from her shoulder. She'd packed. "So why leave?"

For a moment Maggie appeared at a loss for

words. Then she wrinkled her nose, a trait left over from her childhood. "It's easier, Nic. Less complicated."

"You're worried you're forming an unhealthy attachment to the bed?"

The corner of her mouth quirked. "You sound like a therapist."

"I dated one once."

"When?"

"Last year. Alas, it did not work. Anna felt competitive with the grapes. She asked me to choose."

"Oh, Nic!"

"I know. How could she ask such a thing?"

"No, Niccolo. How terrible for her. She obviously didn't know you or she wouldn't have posed the question."

"You wouldn't make me choose?" he teased.

"No, I know better. You're in love with your grapes. You always have been." She turned from him to gaze across the golden hills marked by rows of neat green vines. Lifting her face to the rising sun, Maggie closed her eyes. "Nowhere else smells like this. Mornings smell so new."

He couldn't take his eyes off her, awash in ambivalent emotions. On one hand he wanted to protect her, the old big-brother instinct. But there was another instinct, one far more primitive, one colored by a hunger he didn't quite understand. "The mornings are my favorite, too."

Maggie opened her eyes and smiled at him. "I can't believe how much I've missed this place. I've even missed you."

"What a painful admission," he answered dryly.

She made a face at him, shifting her briefcase to

the other hand. "You're lucky, you know. You're lucky you love this land and find so much happiness with the vineyard. Most people don't love what they do."

He crossed the terrace to stand beside her, gazing at the same view. The land rolled and undulated like burnished waves, acres of vines contrasting with the white and gold hills. "Is it just me you've avoided, Maggie, or is it more?"

He felt her tense, and glancing at her profile, he noticed the tears on her black lashes, delicate tears of love and longing and not quite buried pain.

"How can anyone love a place and yet hate it at the same time? How can such a good place be so brutal?" Her voice quivered with passion.

"The land didn't kill your brother."

"No, but it took him anyway."

He didn't contradict her. Even now he couldn't drive the back road where Jared had crashed without feeling anger and loss. And guilt. Guilt that Jared had been the one at the wheel. Guilt that he'd survived and Jared died. Guilt that Maggie had taken the blame for Jared's mistake. He knew better than anyone that the accident had nearly destroyed Maggie's parents.

He glanced down at her bent head. "I still miss him."

She tried to smile through her film of tears. "Thank you."

"Do not thank me. I loved your brother."

She bit her lip, working the flesh between her teeth. He could feel her silent pain, and it tore at him. "Your brother was my closest friend. He was more of a brother to me than my own."

"Mom and Dad don't talk about him anymore. I know it's painful for them, but I miss saying Jared's name. I miss hearing stories about him."

"You can always talk about him to me. I like to remember him, too. I like to remember the good times." Then he lifted the travel bag off her shoulder. "So you will stay tonight. It's decided."

"Nic—"

"We agreed last night that this was the best place for you to stay."

"We didn't agree. You told me to stay. That's different than me agreeing."

He tried to keep a straight face. "Must be a translation problem."

"Your English is perfect. So is your tendency to dominate. Which is why it'd be better if I stayed somewhere else. I don't need to quarrel with you. I have too much on my mind."

He merely smiled. Maggie had never been easy. "Agreed. Now, come sit down and tell me about your work. I'm anxious to learn more about the Hunt gardens."

She wrinkled her nose again, obviously skeptical. "You don't like gardening, Nic. You only care about grapes and wine."

"That's not true. I'm very proud of the Dominici gardens."

"The only reason you have gorgeous gardens is your grandfather and mother labored over them for nearly forty years. You'd plow the whole thing under if you thought you could get away with it."

"But I'd put the soil to good use."

"Pinot noirs, perhaps?"

He chuckled, delighted. She might have grown up,

but she was still feisty, still spirited. "They're certainly easier on the tongue than topiaries."

She laughed, just as he intended, and he felt a rush of tenderness. Jared had once said there were two ways to change Maggie's mood—tease her or kiss her. Either worked to diffuse her notoriously quick temper.

Tease her or kiss her.

Niccolo gazed at Maggie's mouth. She was wearing sheer lipstick, a soft shade that suited her dark hair and fair complexion. Despite the elegant cut of her blue tailored jacket and the thick strand of pearls around her neck, she looked far from cool, definitely not conservative. It was her mouth that betrayed her warmth. Her lips were lush, her upper lip bowed, a mouth made for champagne, dark chocolate and lovemaking.

Niccolo sucked in air, stunned by the thought. Make love to Maggie? Never. She might not be a girl anymore, but she was still young, still inexperienced. He cared for her deeply, but his feelings were platonic. She was the sister he'd never had.

He was resolved that nothing would come between them again. He refused to let their relationship change. She needed him, and he needed her. Period.

Francesca opened the door and emerged balancing a silver tray with pots of hot coffee and warm milk.

He seated Maggie, and Francesca poured her café au lait, heavy on the milk.

"Would you prefer less milk?" he asked Maggie, noticing Francesca's heavy handed pouring.

"She likes milk," Francesca answered firmly, passing a platter of sliced melon and another of warm pastries. "Milk is good for her."

Niccolo didn't comment and Maggie lifted her coffee cup, inhaling the steam and fragrant blend. "I've tried to give this up, but I can't. I love good coffee too much. One cup every morning, that's my limit, yet I do enjoy it."

"If coffee is your only vice, you're doing quite well, *cara*."

"It all depends on your definition of vice, doesn't it?" she answered.

He noticed the delicate pink blush staining her cheeks, her coloring so fine that even a hint of a blush made her vivid, exquisite.

"*Amore*, you've grown up. I don't see how you could possibly have a vice."

She shook her head, biting her lower lip. He stared at the soft lip with fascination and almost envy. There was so much sweetness in her, sweetness and mystery.

"I'm having guests tonight. A dinner party that's been planned for months. I'm introducing my new Chianti. It's one of the first American Chianti ever made with Tuscany grapes. I hope you'll be free to join us."

Meg's second day with the Hunts was again spent in deep discussion. Though the Hunts were committed to renovating their century-old gardens, they found it painful to discuss removing aging trees even though they understood many of the older trees were diseased and dying. Most of the afternoon was spent working through their concerns and acknowledging their sorrow at losing such majestic trees.

Their great devotion to the land was something she understood. Meg sometimes felt trapped in New York, even though she'd chosen for business purposes to make it her home. There were times when all the concrete and asphalt made her head spin. Too much noise, too much smog, too much activity.

Perhaps that's why she'd channeled her love of gardens into a career. People needed places of refuge. Sanctuary from the busy, modern world. Trees, shade, cool green places, these could restore one's soul.

Meg's eyebrows arched at her archaic word. *Soul.* It wasn't a very modern notion, and yet nearly everyone called her a very modern woman. Especially her father. But when her father called her modern, he didn't mean it as a compliment.

Her eyebrows arched even higher as she imagined his reaction to the news of the baby. He'd be upset, angry, disappointed—but not surprised. Certainly not surprised. He'd come to expect the worst from her. He almost expected her to fail him again.

Meg flexed her hands against the steering wheel, miserably aware that her cool relationship with her father was about to get colder.

She pulled into the formal gates leading to the Dominici villa. Valet drivers waved her over. She'd forgotten all about Niccolo's dinner party, and approaching the stucco and stone house, she heard the sweet plaintive notes of a violin. The Dominicis always mixed music and wine.

Meg hesitated outside the massive front door, listening to the string quartet. It was gorgeous music. A piece by Pachelbel. The brighter notes were tempered by an underlying longing. Much like her own emotions.

Jared. Her father. Niccolo. Everything here felt so complicated. Coming home was the hardest thing she knew how to do. There was a reason she avoided Napa Valley, and suddenly she was in the thick of it, caught up in the intensity and the memories and sorrow. If it weren't for the Hunts, she'd grab her suitcase and catch the nearest plane to New York. Right now the noise and glare of Manhattan seemed infinitely more palatable than this muddle of emotion.

The Pachelbel piece ended, and Meg shook off her melancholy mood. She was here to work, not to continuously examine her feelings.

Meg discovered Niccolo in the great room that had been designed as a ballroom. It was Niccolo's favorite room for large parties and winery-related entertaining.

Although Francesca was present, tuxedo-attired waiters served the catered appetizers. Offered a tray of toasted Brie rounds, Meg accepted one and nibbled on it, watching Nic mingle with his guests. He wore a pale green suit and a crisp white shirt. The shirt was open at the neck, revealing a hint of his broad chest, his skin golden from hours in the sun.

He laughed at something one of his guests said, throwing his head back, his dark hair brushing his collar. Supremely male, Meg thought, as he turned to greet another guest. Beautiful, sleek. Powerful.

Suddenly he was looking at her. Their eyes met, and slowly one corner of his mouth lifted in recognition. She felt a bubble of warmth form inside her chest and she smiled back, pleased.

He broke free from the circle of guests and moved through the crowd toward her. Meg balanced the remains of the toasted round on a paper napkin, her appetite gone.

His arms encircled her. His face dipped. Her nose was pressed against the exposed skin at the base of his throat. She felt his pulse and the heat of his chest.

A tremor coursed through her as he lifted her chin, kissing both cheeks. "Maggie, *cara*, when did you arrive?"

He held her loosely, and yet she was aware of the length of him, his taut hips inches from hers, his strong chest brushing her breasts. Her nipples tingled. She tingled. "Just a bit ago," she answered breathlessly, disposing of the appetizer on a server's empty tray.

It was crazy to respond to him like this. She knew how he felt about her, knew he wasn't attracted to her, and yet her body ignored her brain and flooded her limbs with warmth, filling her with a hot, languid need that had nothing to do with reason and everything to do with desire.

"You look tired," he said, brushing a tendril from her cheek.

"Do I?" She reached up to pat her French twist, feeling better than she had in days. She hadn't felt all that tired until now. In fact, she hadn't been queasy once today. "Perhaps I should go upstairs and put on some lipstick."

"Not to worry, you look lovely. Now come, let me introduce you around."

Dinner was delicious, and Niccolo's guests were interesting, but by ten o'clock Meg had slipped away from the festivities to her room.

The guest wing in Niccolo's stone villa offered elegant sanctuary, and after a long soak in the sunken tub, and after lathering lotion on her skin, Meg pulled on her cotton nightshirt and sat at the dressing table.

Mark hated her roomy blue striped nightshirt. She'd taken it with her on their one and only weekend getaway. Later he'd gone out and bought her a satin and feather concoction that made her giggle. She remembered holding the scrap of fabric to the light. "Mark, what on earth is this?"

"You don't like it," Mark had answered flatly, his feelings obviously injured.

"It's not that I don't like it, it's just not *me*."

Mark had told her to take it back and carelessly tossed the sales receipt at her. Realizing she'd hurt him, she'd tried to appease him. They'd ended up in bed.

They'd kissed before, but never made love. It was the first time they'd been so intimate, as well as the last. But once was more than enough. They'd made a baby, a baby Mark refused to acknowledge.

"There's been no one else," she'd told him, horrified that he even suggested she'd been sleeping around.

"I don't care," he'd answered bitterly. "I don't want this baby. You can't keep it."

"You're just angry."

"I'm not angry. Because I know you'll do the right thing—"

"Right thing?" she'd challenged.

"Yes, the right thing. This baby isn't an option." It was then he'd confessed he was married. He'd said he loved his wife and he didn't want to hurt her and that if Meg kept the baby, it would ruin his life.

Ruin his life.

Her eyes burned, and she picked up the hairbrush, gritting her teeth to keep from crying out.

How dared he? How could anyone be so self-absorbed?

His life. What about their baby's life?

Meg dragged the brush through her hair until her scalp tingled and her arm grew weary, refusing to stop until her anger subsided.

Thank goodness she'd never loved him. For a short time, she'd imagined she did. He'd looked so much like Niccolo, his Greek mother giving him the same hard features and dark coloring, but he lacked Nic's strength of character, not to mention Nic's morals.

Nic would never sleep around. Nic would take responsibility for his child.

Meg stilled, the brush hovering in midair. She had to stop doing that. Had to stop comparing every man to Nic. It wasn't fair to other men, and goodness, it wasn't fair to her. She'd never meet the right man if she continued to hold Niccolo up as some standard for manhood.

A knock sounded on her bedroom door.

Meg set the brush down and opened the door. Francesca stood in the doorway, hands on hips. "I saw your light still on. I thought you might not be well. How are you feeling?"

"I'm fine."

"You left the party early."

"Niccolo didn't mind."

Five minutes later, just as Meg prepared to slip into bed, there came another knock on her door. She opened the door a second time.

Niccolo stood in the doorway balancing a cup and saucer and a small plate of cookies.

Meg didn't think she had the energy to smile, but her lips twitched anyway. "Housekeeping?"

"You're not funny."

"I'm very funny. You just have a terrible sense of humor."

His lovely mouth grimaced. "This was not my idea."

"Obviously. You know I hate warm milk."

"The point is, I will not be making a habit of bringing you bedtime snacks."

She didn't know why, but his gruffness compelled her to tease him. "Are you sure this wasn't your idea? You know I'm a sucker for cookies."

"They're biscuits."

"Cookies, biscuits, same thing."

"They're not at all the same."

"Like comparing apples and oranges."

"No, not like apples and oranges. Like a Merlot and a Cabernet."

"Of course. Wine. That's all you ever think about."

Niccolo's expression darkened. She'd succeeded in aggravating him. "Do you like quarreling with me?"

Meg smiled impudently. "Yes."

He muttered beneath his breath in Italian. "You test my patience."

"Then don't let me keep you."

"You're not keeping me. I'm choosing to stand here."

"That's right, you always have to win. Even if it's just a war of words."

"And you have to argue. You're still such a child."

Meg's stomach began to cramp. Perhaps it wasn't the Brie that had made her sick. It was Nic. ''Like I said, don't let me keep you.'' With that she slammed the door shut, ignoring the surprised expression on Niccolo's face.

Meg twitched in her seat, trying to keep still. She'd never been bored by a discussion on perennials in her life, but at the moment, she thought she'd scream if deadheading was mentioned again.

She closed her eyes, pressed her knuckles against her brow and forced herself to draw a deep breath and slowly exhale. One yarrow, two yarrow, three yarrow…counting yellow yarrow the way one would count sheep.

Some of the tension left her shoulders. Meg drew another deep breath and opened her eyes. She'd woken up feeling blue, and the blue mood quickly turned to irritation. All morning her nerves had been on edge, and Mr. Hunt's rather long-winded discourse on deadheading had just about driven her mad.

What she needed was action.

She had a hundred and one things to decide, plans to make, and this discussion on gardening chores was getting her nowhere.

What she needed was a new apartment.

She'd been living in a quaint one-bedroom flat across from Central Park for years. The apartment had a squeaky hardwood floor, antiquated plumbing and a charming little terrace with a breathtaking city view. But the apartment barely accommodated her bed and sitting room furniture, much less a crib and changing table.

Yes, she needed a bigger apartment.

She also needed a crib. A car seat. High chair. A layette, not to mention diapers, ointment, powders and so forth.

Babies certainly required a lot of gear.

No wonder her old college friends had complained about babies being expensive. Meg would need a small fortune to outfit the baby's room, much less pay for child care while she met with clients.

She couldn't blame anyone but herself. She'd slept with Mark knowing the risks. He'd used a condom, but things did happen and, well, things *had* happened.

A nerve pulsed at Meg's temple and she pressed two fingers against the spot, trying hard to stay calm, to sit still.

The truth was, becoming a single mother terrified her.

It was such a huge responsibility, such a crucial role, she couldn't help being afraid. Meg had made her share of mistakes and she knew she'd make them as a mother. Her baby deserved the very best, but what if Meg wasn't good enough? Strong enough? Loving enough? What if she said the wrong thing, forgot the right prayer? What if…

''Margaret?'' Mrs. Hunt leaned forward to clasp Meg's hand. ''Margaret, dear, are you all right? You're looking quite pale.''

She was fine. She was just a little nervous. But that was only to be expected. Even for a modern woman, having a baby was quite a big deal.

Niccolo glanced at his watch. The winery co-op council meeting should have wrapped up just after lunch. Instead it threatened to last well into mid afternoon. He shot a quick glance at his watch. He had another hour before he'd have to excuse himself.

The local wineries had formed a co-op to promote northern California wines. The council was in the final stages of planning and implementing an international advertising campaign highlighting Napa's outstanding red wines.

The television and print advertisements would feature the Italian film star Sonia Carlo sipping a California Cabernet. It was hoped her celebrity endorsement would create excitement in the foreign markets.

At last the discussion came to an end, and Nic politely excused himself, knowing he didn't have much time if he wanted to make it home to take the conference call with his father.

Yet after reaching his car, he realized he'd left his cell phone behind. With a soft oath, Nic returned to the building and crossed the cool, dark lobby, pungent with the smell of oak, sulfur and fermenting grapes. When he was a boy he'd thought the smell too sour and raw. Now it was comforting. Like coming home.

Opening the door to the wine-tasting room, Niccolo heard Maggie's name mentioned. He froze, sure he'd been mistaken. But the vintner at the far end of the table repeated himself.

"That's right. I saw her myself. Maggie Buckner is back, and from what I heard, she's in some serious trouble."

CHAPTER THREE

NICCOLO froze, his hand on the doorknob. Maggie, his Maggie, in trouble? No, he hadn't heard right. Maggie was doing just fine.

"That poor family!" Another grower spoke. "They've certainly had their share of trouble. The last thing John and Eileen need is more heartache."

Niccolo felt rooted to the spot. He knew he should open the door and interrupt. He knew he should intervene. But he couldn't move. Couldn't bring himself to speak.

"They said she wasn't drinking," a woman said. "They tested her at the police station."

"But that doesn't mean she wasn't driving recklessly," one of the men interrupted. "I don't know another teenager that pierced more body parts than Maggie Buckner."

"It was just her ears. She had a whole row of studs up and down her ear."

The gossip infuriated Niccolo. He knew people in small towns liked to talk, but this was ridiculous. He opened the door and stepped into the room, but no one saw him. They were too busy wagging their tongues.

"Why didn't her parents do something?" the vintner from Copper Cellars demanded. "I'll tell you why. They couldn't. Maggie had John and Eileen over a barrel. If Maggie's in trouble, she has no one to blame but herself. If she cared about anyone but herself Jared would be alive today—''

"That's enough!" Niccolo's voice sliced through the room. "It's been years since the accident. Why can't you leave her alone?"

The growers gazed at him, white-faced and uncomfortable.

A moment ago voices had filled the tasting room. Now silence lay like a suffocating blanket. Finally, one of the growers spoke. "Niccolo, it was just talk. No harm was meant.''

"I'm tired of this. I'm tired of you using Maggie as a topic for discussion.''

"Don't be mad, Nic—"

"I'm not mad, I'm furious. You've never cared a whit about Maggie other than labeling her difficult and a troublemaker." His voice rang in the hushed room. "By the way, Maggie *is* in town. She's my guest. She's staying at my house while she works with the Hunts on their garden renovation."

His chest tightened, his anger turning on himself. This was his fault. They blamed Maggie because they didn't know the truth. He should have spoken up years ago, put the matter straight. Instead he'd bitten his tongue and looked the other way. "And one last thing," he added, his voice throbbing with emotion. "Maggie's not in trouble. If she was in trouble, I'd be the first to know."

The sun was setting when Meg pulled into the Dominici driveway. The ten-hour workdays were putting a strain on her nerves. Today her headache threatened to reduce her to tears. She desperately craved rest and a quiet, dark room.

Francesca met her at the door. She anxiously knotted her apron. "Niccolo is waiting for you by the pool."

"I'm not interested in a swim."

The housekeeper's forehead furrowed. "I don't think he's thinking of a swim, either."

Meg heard the warning in Francesca's voice. "Has something happened?"

"I've told him nothing."

"Francesca—"

"He returned from a winery meeting in a black mood."

"What happened?"

"I don't know, but I warn you, something's eating at him."

Meg sighed, already exhausted. She wasn't prepared for a scene with Nic. He was the strongest, most stubborn man she'd ever met. If he had a bone to pick, he picked it clean. She stepped out of the villa's cool interior onto the broad steps leading to the pool. The setting sun cast long red-gold rays across the water's surface, reflecting onto the sweeping stone deck and illuminating the massive Italian clay pots filled with dwarf citrus trees. The heady perfume of lemon blossoms hung in the air, a favorite fragrance of Meg's since she had been a girl. But it was impossible to enjoy the scent now, not with her anxiety about Niccolo's mood.

She spotted a towel stretched across one of the chaise longues, but she didn't see Nic.

Relief briefly washed over her. He must have returned to the house for something.

Her shoulders dropped, and she took a deep breath.

What on earth had happened at the winery meeting? How could it involve her?

Slowly Meg walked along the edge of the pool. The garden had always enchanted her. She responded to the luxurious use of blue tile and stone, the garden a fanciful interpretation of life in ancient Rome. More massive pots, clinging vines, small citrus trees. The enclosed garden was a perfect balance of light and scent and sound.

"I thought you trusted me."

Meg started, surprised by the grate of Nic's deep voice. She turned toward the sound, a small shiver coursing down her spine. She shouldn't let him unnerve her. He couldn't do anything to her. They were adults. Equals.

Nic sat beneath a market umbrella, his face hidden in the shade. "You should have come to me if you needed help." Disappointment tinged his voice.

"I don't need help," she answered sharply, defensive.

He pushed up from the chair and walked toward her. His casual shirt hung open, unbuttoned to reveal his bronzed chest and the hard, flat muscles in his abdomen.

Meg inhaled quickly, taken aback by his blatant virility. He'd never been shy, but he'd never been so confident, either.

"I hate hearing others talk about you."

She felt a lump form in her chest. It threatened to seal her throat.

He glanced at her as he walked past her. "Because they do talk, Maggie. They enjoy your escapades."

"I don't know what you're talking about."

"No?"

"No." She barely managed to get the word out, her voice strangled, her chest tight like a vise. He couldn't know. He couldn't have found out.

But he would, sooner or later.

The intensity in his golden eyes held her captive. She swallowed hard, lifted her chin. "Is there a point to this, Nic? I'm not in the mood for games."

"And I've never played games, *cara*."

She bristled at his tone. He made her feel sixteen again, and it was all she could do to keep from rolling her eyes. "So what do you want?"

Niccolo smoothed the towel on the chaise longue. "I want you to sit down here—" he patted the chaise "—and tell me what you're trying so hard to hide."

"I'm not trying to hide anything."

"Lie number one."

"Nic!"

"I'll ask you again. What are you trying to hide?"

"Nothing. I'm here to do a job. I'm doing the job. That's it."

"I don't believe you."

He wanted to fight. He was trying to be insulting. For a split second she considered telling him the truth. It would shut him up. Stun him to silence. Because of course Nic would be furious. She would have committed the ultimate sin.

But she wouldn't tell him. It wasn't his problem. She refused to let him interfere. "I'm going back to the house. I don't have to put up with this."

His expression changed, his fierce features softening. "*Cara*, I don't want to quarrel. Why can't you sit down and let us talk? You once told me everything."

"I was naive."

"We were friends."

"Friends don't judge each other."

"Who said I'm judging you?"

"You will."

"So you do have a problem." His eyes gleamed, then he smiled triumphantly.

It was a game to him. He didn't care about her. Didn't care about her feelings. He just wanted to be right. So typical. "That's charming, Nic."

His eyebrows met in the middle. Fine lines were etched on either side of his mouth. He was clearly losing patience. "Maggie, sit."

"As enticing as that sounds, I'll pass."

"Why?"

"Because I am not a dog and I do not respond to doggie commands."

"Doggie commands?"

"Sit. Stay. Roll over." She crossed her arms, glaring at him. "For a man with an excellent command of seven languages, your communication skills are hopeless."

He looked equally irritated. "I do not speak this way to everyone, just to unreasonable girls who do not listen."

"Ah, that's where you've made your first mistake. I am not a girl. I'm twenty-eight. Which leads me to your second mistake. Despite your medieval upbringing, women do not have to listen to you."

"That's illogical."

"Just like I'm unreasonable."

"Yes!" he said, his voice like thunder. "You're impossible. You drive me to distraction."

A breeze rustled the leaves of the trees, freeing a curl from her ponytail. Her chest burned, aching with bottled-up emotion. "Then leave me alone. I'm not who you want me to be. I'm not who you think I am.''

He closed the distance between them and took her by the upper arms. "That's not true. You're my Maggie."

"I'm not. I'm not your anything."

The expression in his golden eyes was pure pain. He held her so firmly that it felt as if his fingers would sink into her very bones. "Don't say that," he rasped. "I've lost Jared. I won't lose you, too."

A current of electricity surged through her, and Niccolo's eyes narrowed, his gaze dropping to her mouth. Her lower lip quivered as if he'd run the tip of his finger across the sensitive skin and Meg pulled back, terrified. *He meant to kiss her!* No. She couldn't let this happen.

His dark head dropped, blotting the last lingering rays of sun. Dragging her closer against him, he let her feel the hard, taut length of him. "I will not lose you," he muttered thickly against her lips. "I swear it, Maggie."

Then his mouth covered hers, hard and fast, expressing possession.

She closed her eyes, a shiver coursing down her spine. He smelled of oak and citrus, red wine and sunlight. As his lips parted hers, her knees went weak. He tasted even better. His lips, tongue, caressed hers. His warmth penetrated her bones, melting her into him.

She wanted to resist, but couldn't. It was exactly as she feared. She wanted him, oh, she still wanted him!

The kiss deepened, and his hands gentled, sliding up her arms to cradle the back of her head. She shivered against him and felt his body harden, making her aware of his desire. Just as suddenly his head lifted and he stared into her eyes.

Breathlessly she gazed at him, hope and desire filling her heart. But just as quickly as he'd drawn her to him, he thrust her away, the warmth in his golden eyes fading, the light gold flecks hardening, the passion dying.

He realized what he had done. He regretted the kiss. He hadn't meant to kiss her. It had been an accident, an error of judgment. Which should have made her happy. Niccolo had always held himself up as a model of decorum. Now he'd proved himself just as human as she was. They were even. A kiss for a kiss. Mistake for a mistake. Equals.

Stupid tears burned at the back of her eyes, but she covered her chaotic emotions with a quick laugh. "Trying to teach me a lesson, aren't you? Well, Nic, that's one way to silence the critics."

His jaw tightened, and he swallowed. It took him longer to recover his composure. "I didn't intend to do that. I was just trying to make a statement—"

"Oh, you did. No one has ever tried to kiss me into submission before."

"I'm quite serious. I'm trying to do the right thing."

"Which is what you've always tried to do." She managed a small, tight smile yet her heart continued to race and her legs felt unsteady, her body still traitorously warm from the kiss. She forced her chin up and a note of bravado into her shaking voice. "But there are some things you can't fix, and there are some people you can't change."

"I don't understand."

Her resolve was cracking. She could hear it inside her head as clearly as if it were an iceberg roaring as it broke in two. "No, you don't want to understand. There's a difference!" she retorted, worn out from sparring and overwhelmed by his kiss.

If he was determined to know the truth, she'd tell him. It wasn't as if she'd be able to hide the facts much longer. She was beginning to show, and soon everyone would know what she'd been trying to keep secret. "Nic, I'm pregnant. I'm expecting a baby early next year."

She didn't think Niccolo could look more shocked or more disappointed.

"Do your parents know?"

Of course that would be his first question.

Respectability, accountability, social conventions. These were always his first concerns. She wished he didn't care so much about what people thought. It was what was in people's hearts that mattered most.

"I've told my mother," she answered after a brief silence. "I plan to tell Dad when they return from the trip."

"You didn't want to ruin his vacation."

"I know he'd worry."

Niccolo shook his head once, expressing disbelief. "You don't think your mother is worried?"

This was the hard part. Meg knew she didn't have to answer to Nic, but she also knew Nic wouldn't leave the subject alone. It was better to get the truth out. Get it over and done with. "Mom thinks she's coming home to a wedding."

Nic could say more with his eyes and jaw than anyone else. His jaw tightened, the tiny muscle popping, accenting the hard angle of bone and golden skin. "There's no wedding?"

"No."

He stared at her through narrowed eyes, his black lashes fanning his high, bronzed cheekbones. His hard expression didn't change. The only sign he gave of his mounting fury was the pulse beating at the base of his throat. She stared at the tiny rapid pulse, fascinated. He was upset, very upset.

"Why isn't there a wedding?" He bit out the brutally short syllables.

"Because."

His head jerked, his gaze leaping to hers. "Because?"

Her nerves screamed, the tension so tight she felt as if her muscles had been pulled on a string, turning her into a dangling puppet. She shook her head, her voice failing her. He wouldn't understand. No matter what she said, no matter what she told him, Niccolo would not understand.

His fierce golden gaze bored straight through her. "Where's the baby's father?"

"The baby doesn't have a father."

"Don't tell me. It was a miraculous conception."

His sarcasm stung. She felt herself flush, overwhelmed by an onslaught of emotion. "I'm not the first woman to have a baby on her own."

"No, and you probably won't be the last. But there's no glory in being an unwed mother."

"There's no shame in it, either."

"No?" One of his black eyebrows lifted. His softly spoken word hung between them, mocking her.

Again he was reminding her of the past, pulling

her skeletons from the closet and shaking them in her face. He had a memory like an elephant, and he'd never let her forget her many mistakes, like the six-inch-high platform shoes she wore the summer she turned sixteen, the lime-green streak she put in her hair one Sunday morning when her parents were at church, the night she hot-wired a neighbor's work truck and went for a joyride that took out the rear end of the truck and put five stitches in her temple near her hairline.

Meg clenched her hands into fists, fighting desperately to hang on to her pride. "The baby might be an accident, but I'll be a good mother."

Niccolo shook his head again and walked to the table. He lifted one of the crystal decanters and poured himself a drink.

She waited for him to say something, but he didn't speak. He merely swirled the amber liquid in his crystal tumbler and stared across the patio toward the pool. The sun glimmered on the water, reflecting the sky and scattered clouds.

"I want this baby," she said quietly.

"Just like you want everything," he retorted before lifting his glass and taking a swallow.

She felt as if he'd slapped her. Her heart dropped. Her mouth went dry. "What does that mean?"

He tapped a finger against the crystal, making the tumbler ring. "It means you're still just a little girl, unwilling to accept responsibility for your mistakes."

"Who are you to pass judgment? You're no paragon of virtue, Niccolo. You've had lovers since you were seventeen, some of them twice your age."

"It's different."

"How so?"

"There are different standards for men and women, *cara*. Surely, even you know that."

"You're medieval."

"I'm telling the truth." He took another sip from his glass. "If you don't love him enough to marry him, what were you doing sleeping with him?"

"It's none of your business."

He slowly, deliberately set the glass down before turning to face her. His expression was grim, his golden eyes dark, intense. "It is now."

How could she be pregnant?

No, he knew how, that much was obvious—his jaw tightened angrily—but how could she have been so careless? If she was going to sleep around, she should have been prepared. Sex without protection wasn't just irresponsible, it was dangerous.

Although it was well past midnight, Niccolo poured himself a second cup of espresso and sat at his desk with his reports on the new Merlot. The vats were tested at regular intervals to measure acidity during the fermenting process, and this year's Merlot was proving to be especially temperamental. But the percentages and graphs might as well have been written in invisible ink. Niccolo stared at the sheets of paper and saw nothing.

Nothing, that is, but Maggie.

He was so disappointed in her that he couldn't think straight. Maggie, pregnant.

Her father, a salt-of-the-earth man, would be extremely unhappy about the news. Decent, hardworking, plain speaking, John was well respected by valley growers and ranchers. Everyone knew how close he'd been to his only son, just as everyone knew that John Buckner didn't have much patience with his rebellious daughter.

As a teenager, Nic had heard John Buckner say more than once that Maggie was a disaster waiting to happen. John didn't dislike his only daughter. He just didn't understand her.

Later, as Jared approached college age, he confided in Niccolo that he dreaded heading to college and leaving Maggie at home alone. He'd tried to be a buffer between his father and Maggie. Jared hated to make waves. Maggie was a veritable storm.

A storm was right. And John Buckner was going to be livid about the baby.

Nic pushed the paperwork across his desk, unable to concentrate. He shouldn't worry about Maggie. It wasn't his place to save her skin. But someone had to care enough about Maggie to intervene. Ever since Jared's death her parents had seemed too grief-stricken and overwhelmed to try. Her teachers hadn't had the time nor the inclination. People in town had just gossiped. That left him.

If he'd had more courage a long time ago Maggie might have suffered less. He shouldn't have allowed her to restage the accident scene, shouldn't have let her accept all the blame. Maybe if he'd been stronger then, Maggie and her parents would have a different relationship today.

Perhaps he and Maggie would be different people today.

Rubbing his closed eyes, Nic resisted remembering the accident. That Christmas Eve had become such a terrible memory that he shied away from recalling the details. Instead he'd begun to deny the truth, allowing him to bury the pain.

But Maggie hadn't been at fault that night. Jared had been at the wheel. Jared had been drinking.

And so had he.

Niccolo opened his eyes and gazed across the room, noting the plaques and honorable mentions his wines had won at international expositions. As a winemaker he was a success. But as a man?

Nic abruptly pushed away from the desk and stood.

He couldn't change the past, but maybe he could set the record straight. He'd tell Maggie's parents the truth about the accident, and maybe Maggie would finally have a chance to develop a real relationship with her father.

Meg dashed out the front door and down the villa's flagstone steps before Francesca spotted her. She would not let herself get detained this morning. Breakfast with Niccolo was about as relaxing as running with the bulls.

Keys jingling, she hastily unlocked the rental car's door. With a toss, she sent her briefcase sailing onto the passenger seat, and she slid behind the steering wheel as if sprinting in a race. Reaching for the door, Meg suddenly discovered she couldn't close it.

"Like a thief in the night," Niccolo taunted.

Meg's heart nearly leaped from her chest, and she jumped, scared to death. "What?"

He held the door firmly, knowing she'd be unable to close it. A cool smile tilted the corners of his lips. "Sneaking away, *cara*?"

Something in his silken voice made her stomach

plummet. The fine hairs on the nape of her neck rose, her skin prickling with keen awareness. He hadn't even touched her and yet her body quivered from head to toe. "I have to go. I'm late."

"It's not even seven yet."

"I know, but I have so much to do. I must get to work right away."

"Lie after lie," he drawled, cocking his head to better study her. "You've become quite an accomplished storyteller."

"Be quiet, Nic," she snapped. "This is getting awfully tedious." Impatiently, Meg turned the key in the ignition, starting the car. Thankfully the engine vroomed with impressive noise. She had to raise her voice to be heard above the roar. "Now please step away before you get hurt."

"Hurt? Now there's a thought. Run Nic over. Exciting headlines for tomorrow's paper."

"Good grief! Can't you let me go?"

"No." He leaned inside the car, his face inches from hers. "And as much as I enjoy listening to you gun the engine, I think you're better off inside, eating breakfast. You can't afford to skip meals. It's not fair to the baby."

"The baby will get something downtown. The baby likes deli food."

"Francesca already laid a place for you at the breakfast table."

Meg's foot worked the accelerator. She deliberately gunned the motor a couple more times. "What was that? What did you say? I can't hear you!"

Nic's lips flattened over his teeth, and his black hair fell forward across his strong brow. He looked distinctly tyrannical. A fierce Italian nobleman from the fifteenth century. He didn't care about rules. Didn't give a damn for polite conversation.

"Don't push me."

"Don't you push me!" she contradicted.

Grimly he reached over her, his forearm brushing her breasts, and grabbed for the keys.

Fear, pure instinctive fear, rocketed through Meg. The only thing she could think about was saving herself. Niccolo was furious and he'd give her hell. No way was she going to stick around listen to another of his righteous tirades.

Adrenaline flooding her veins, she slapped at his hand, her palm smacking him so hard that hers stung and drew sharp tears to her eyes.

Niccolo pulled back, stunned. "You little—"

Meg didn't need to hear the rest. His thundering voice told her all she needed to know. With split-second timing she slammed the car door closed, locked it from the inside and shifted into drive.

Her hands shook as she rolled down the window a half inch. "Sorry, Nic," she shouted. "I'd love to talk but I just don't have the time right now. See you tonight!"

CHAPTER FOUR

IF SHE thought she'd gotten away with something, her brief flirtation with freedom ended at noon when Niccolo showed up at the Hunts. He drew the elderly couple aside and spoke with them quietly for a moment. Before Meg could act, Niccolo was escorting her from the house to his red convertible sports car, his fingers viselike on her arm near her elbow.

Niccolo's classic 1962 Ferrari Spider roadster roared down the deserted road toward the highway. Meg sat rigidly on the supple leather seat, too furious to speak. How dare he show up at her job and collect her as if she were a child at school!

Niccolo shot her an amused look. "Breathe. You're starting to turn blue."

"Don't talk to me!"

"I'm doing this for your own good."

She clutched her notebook in her lap, resisting the urge to toss it at his head. "You had no right," she complained. "We were in the middle of an intensive discussion."

Nic shifted, driving swiftly through northern California's rolling hills. The golden landscape whirled past the convertible like the backdrop on an old movie set. "Sorry."

Sorry? That's all he could say? He'd broken off an important discussion, hauled her to the car and drove the back roads faster than a racing driver. Sorry definitely wouldn't cut it.

He cast a sidelong glance at her. "You should wear white more often. It suits you."

Now he was going for the charm. Anything to disarm her. "It's winter white," she retorted coolly, catching a glimpse of her cashmere suit jacket and navy trousers. She wore everything long and loose these days, wanting comfort instead of style as her waist began to expand.

"Anyway, it looks good on you. Perhaps it's the color in your cheeks today. Your face glows."

With anger. Meg caught a tendril of her hair as it whipped in her face. "Can you put up the top, please?"

"But it's lovely out, *cara*. Relax. Enjoy the sun."

"I'm not on vacation," she answered sharply, her chest rising and falling with quick, short breaths. She struggled to put her anger into coherent sentences. "Turn around and take me back."

"Take you back?"

"Now. *Please.*"

"I'm sorry. I've made plans for us. I thought we needed some time together—" his golden gaze raked her "—some time alone."

Time together? Time alone? It was the last thing she needed. Time with Nic was like time in a torture chamber. Each conversation felt as if it took place on a bed of nails. "Nic, I was working. You can't just show up and drag me away."

"But I did."

"That's not the point. This—my life—it isn't an episode of 'The Flintstones.'"

He sighed and shook his head. "How tragic. If you were raised in Italy, you would have a knowledge of music and art instead of cartoons."

Meg slapped one hand against her head in mock horror. "Yes, go right ahead, make fun of American education. Mock my lowbrow culture. Cartoons instead of opera. Video games in place of books. Hamburgers and fries rather than haute cuisine. Isn't that right?"

His smile was lazy enjoyment. "Yes, *cara*, that about sums it up."

She caught the twitch of his lip and realized he'd enjoyed baiting her. This was his way of getting back at her for driving away from him this morning.

Meg settled herself more comfortably in the roadster's seat. She glanced at Nic's profile, noting the fine lines fanning from the corners of his eyes and the grooves along his mouth. He looked older, more handsome than he did at twenty-two. Maturity suited him. Somehow she sensed he'd be even better looking at fifty.

Her anger melted. It was impossible to stay mad at Nic. But then he knew that. When they were younger he'd say something to hurt her feelings but then he'd smile, tease her, and she'd end up forgiving him.

She plucked another curl from her cheek and tucked it behind her ear. "So what did you tell the Hunts?"

He shrugged and shifted down, taking a tight corner. "I told them an emergency came up." He cast her a sidelong glance. "Personal matter, a family thing."

"Nic, the Hunts are my biggest, most important clients. I can't afford to lose them."

"Don't worry. Your big, important client will not fire you. I hosted their big fund-raiser at the winery last year. The Hunts raised a quarter of a million dollars that night. The Hunts—'' he drawled their name for emphasis, his golden eyes mocking ''—are still indebted to me.''

She didn't know whether to be irritated or amused. No matter what he did, Niccolo came out smelling like a rose. She turned slightly, looking at the rolling hills. ''Where are we going, anyway?''

''To the coast. I thought we could get a bite of dinner. Talk without interruption.''

Torture without interruption. More of his inquisition. ''I'd rather work,'' she answered dryly.

''I'm sure you would,'' he answered. ''You were quite anxious to go this morning.''

She felt her lips twitch, a bubble of laughter forming inside her. ''Mm,'' she murmured, trying to keep from laughing.

''You slapped me,'' he added.

''Your hand.''

''You slapped my hand.''

Her cheeks ached with the effort to not laugh. Her eyes began to burn. She felt them start to water. ''It was a gentle slap.''

''My hand was red for nearly an hour.''

''You must have sensitive skin.''

''Fine. Next time I'll haul you over my knee and give you a not-so-gentle slap on your bottom. We'll see who has sensitive skin then.''

Meg suddenly lost the urge to laugh. Her heart skipped a beat. ''You wouldn't.''

He cast a sardonic look in her direction, daring her to provoke her. ''Try me,'' he murmured with evil intent in his warm golden eyes. When she didn't answer, he chuckled quietly. "Don't look so shocked. It wouldn't be the first time you were spanked."

"Yes, but that was by my *father*," she answered, mortified. She could feel the blood rush to her cheeks, her face burning. "I'd never let a man spank me."

"Oh, come, Maggie, you can't be such a prude. You're a woman of the world. You must have indulged in your share of erotic games."

"Spanking is not an erotic game."

"Oh?" His soft laughter taunted her again. "I suppose it depends on who is doing the spanking."

She had a vision of herself over Nic's lap, her bottom up, exposed to the air, and she shuddered. It would be humiliating and horrible, and she'd never let it happen, never in a million years. Yet the insides of her thighs trembled and her lower belly clenched, as if anticipating the torture and the pleasure.

Niccolo would be a practiced lover. Of that she was sure.

"I'd like to change the subject," she announced frostily, as if to deny the heat in her limbs and the warmth spreading at the apex of her thighs. She couldn't want him, couldn't desire him. She'd thrown herself at him once and she'd never make the same mistake again.

His golden gaze assessed her, lingering on her mouth and the heightened color in her face. "Of course, *cara*. This conversation is too tame. Love, sex, erotica…it's all rather dull. Why don't we talk about gardens instead?"

"Very funny."

"I'm sure you have an opinion on the ideal height

for a mature hedge. Or tell me, what is the perfect perennial for a garden in the wine country?''

"Save the sarcasm. Just turn the car around. I want to go home.''

"Home. Is the villa home?''

"You know what I mean.''

"No, I don't know what you mean. I don't even know who you are anymore, *cara*. You're pregnant, alone, fabricating lies to your mother about make-believe weddings so she won't worry.'' He reached out and ejected a CD from the car stereo. "Maggie, would you please select another CD?''

How could he switch gears like that? Ridicule her and then ask for a new music selection? "I don't want music,'' she answered, "I just want to return to work.''

"There's a disk there, in the console. Could you please hand it to me?''

She did as he asked then turned to look out the window. Pressing her palm against her mouth, she fought to hold back a stream of insults. He was impossible. He wasn't listening to a thing she said. Obviously, he didn't care.

They were heading west, and the open golden hills were giving way to scattered groves of oak, scrub brush and pine. She fidgeted in her seat, crossing her arms only to uncross them again.

"Maggie, I've come to a decision.''

His serious tone made her sit up a little straighter. All hint of laughter was gone from his voice. Glancing at him, she noted his dark, brooding expression. "About what?''

"About a mistake I made years ago.'' He looked

at her sharply, glints flashing in his golden eyes. "About that Christmas Eve."

It was all he needed to say. Ever since Jared died, it was the way they referred to the accident. *That Christmas Eve.*

Butterflies tumbled in her stomach. Frightened, she waited in silence for him to continue.

"The way I behaved that night, and since then, it's reprehensible. I allowed you to take the blame—"

"I insisted."

"I was older. A man." He shook his head once, his mouth twisting bitterly. "I was wrong, and it's time for me to set the record straight."

"No."

"It was his accident, Maggie, not yours."

"I don't know what you're talking about."

"You know exactly what I'm talking about."

"I was driving. I was goofing off. I crashed into the tree."

"Jared was driving. I was in the passenger seat. You were in the back seat." It sounded as if he was spitting glass, each word, each vowel short and sharp, cutting straight through her heart.

"I don't remember."

"Cut it out. You know exactly what I'm talking about, but in all these years we've never discussed that night, never discussed your decision or my stupidity in letting you switch places with Jared."

"He was my brother!"

"And my best friend, but that doesn't mean he was perfect. Maggie, your parents—"

"If you tell them, Nic, I'll never speak to you again."

"When you leave here Friday you probably won't speak to me again, so where's the danger?"

His sarcasm made blood surge to her face. He sounded so cold, so determined. Panic gripped her. Nic couldn't do this. He couldn't break his vow. He'd promised years ago to stick with her story. He'd agreed that her parents would be devastated if they'd known Jared had been drinking.

"My dad idolizes Jared," she said, her voice small and faint. "Jared's memory is precious to him. If you tell them, you'll destroy my father's memory of him."

"But what about you, Maggie? What about *your* relationship with your father?"

"It's fine. We talk once every two weeks. I call on Sunday, he tells me about the ranch, I tell him about my work, we say we love each other and then we hang up."

"Maggie, he thinks you killed Jared."

It felt as if Nic was scratching his nails down a chalkboard. The skin on her spine crawled. Her stomach cramped hard. "He's forgiven me," she whispered.

"What I did was wrong. I let your parents blame you. I let the entire town blame you. It was a selfish, cowardly thing for me to do."

"I begged you."

She saw the muscle pop in his jaw, saw the anger and self-loathing flare in his eyes. "Jared would never have let you shoulder the blame. Jared would have fought tooth and nail to protect you."

Her shoulders hunched. She tried to block the sound of Nic's voice. This conversation was excruciating. She couldn't believe that she and Nic were having it in the first place. "It was Christmas Eve," she whispered, "he was just having fun."

"Yes, it was Christmas Eve. We were having a great time being together again. Jared was in fine form, too, joking and laughing and telling us stories about his year away at school. But Jared had been drinking. I'd been drinking, too."

Niccolo looked at her, sorrow darkening his eyes. "Maggie, I failed you and I failed Jared—"

"That's not true. You did what I asked you to do. I have no regrets. It was horrible that he…" She drew a rough breath. "Died. Why make it worse for Mom and Dad? Jared was the oldest. He was the ideal son. Eagle Scout. Student body president. Straight A student."

She reached up and wiped the dampness from her eyes. "Heck, he even saved a drowning kid one summer when he was fifteen." Her voice quavered and she wiped another tear. "The river was flooding, remember that summer? And that boy couldn't get out. So Jared jumped in. He didn't think twice. He just jumped in and pulled the boy out."

She looked at Nic with tears in her eyes. "He was a hero, Nic. He was my hero. I couldn't let everything good he did die with him."

They stopped for a late afternoon coffee in Bodega Bay. "You'll have decaffeinated, of course," Nic reminded her as the waitress approached.

Things had been unusually strained between them since Nic had brought up the accident and Jared's death. Nic had dropped the subject and they'd lapsed into silence.

Now they were seated at a small table overlooking

the rugged coastline. The picture window revealed wispy blue sky and an endless expanse of water.

Meg hadn't planned on ordering coffee, but Nic's authoritative tone made her want a cup. "The latest research says that small amounts of caffeine won't hurt the baby."

"You already had a cup at breakfast. You don't need another." He scanned the small menu before suggesting she try the fruit juices or one of the blended frozen yogurt drinks.

How like Nic. He relished his power and wielded authority like a barbarian nobleman. "Sorry," she said lightly, knowing her glibness would irritate him. "I'm not a smoothie aficionado."

"Fine. Order milk." He snapped the menu shut and looked at the waitress. "I'll have an espresso."

Meg smiled at the waitress. "A cup of coffee, please."

"Decaf," he added firmly. He gave her a hard look. "And she'll have the half sandwich and salad combination."

The waitress glanced at Meg before looking at Nic. "Would she like tomatoes and sprouts on her sandwich?"

"No sprouts. Tomatoes and lettuce."

The waitress, with a puzzled glance, departed. Meg stared at Nic, incredulous. "You can't order for me," she said.

"But I just did." He shrugged and unfolded his napkin, incredibly graceful for a man of his power and size. "You need to eat. The baby needs you to eat. You're far too thin."

"Niccolo, this is not your baby."

"Obviously. If I'd got you pregnant, I'd remember."

Heaven help her, what a thing to say! She clenched her knees together, feeling dreadfully exposed.

"And then," he continued, leaning forward on his elbows, stretching his shirt taut across his broad shoulders, "I'd drag you to the nearest priest and make you take my name and make you wear my ring."

More heat surged through her middle, stirring her senses. She resisted the coiling of desire, unwilling to contemplate marrying Nic. "Ah, lovely. A moral de' Medici!"

He smiled faintly but there was no humor in his eyes. "Why didn't you use protection?"

She felt herself blush, the heat surging through her cheeks. "That's a rather personal question."

"I want to know."

"Nic—"

"Were you so swept away by the moment that it slipped your mind? Or do you practice unsafe sex—"

"No!" Her fierce denial silenced him. Breathing hard, she struggled to gain control of her chaotic emotions. Nic had a way of getting under her skin. "I don't—didn't…" She shook her head, miserably aware of her stupidity. "There was a problem with the…condom."

The look he gave her was one of incredulity. "I've never had a problem with a condom in my life."

From the heat in her cheeks, she knew she was turning bright pink. This was far more than she needed to know about Nic's sex life.

"I wasn't the one wearing the condom, Nic," she

retorted, humiliated by his look and tone. "I didn't realize there was a problem."

Nic grunted and leaned back, drumming his fingers on the tabletop. "Fool."

"What?"

"Your friend—"

"Mark."

"Mark was a fool." Nic's brow creased with fury. "A real man takes the time to make sure protection *works*." He must have noticed her disbelieving look. "Maggie, this area we're talking about, it's quite sensitive."

She felt flushed from head to toe. She reached for her glass of ice water and took a gulp.

But Nic wasn't finished. "A condom isn't rocket science. A man knows when something isn't right."

"Okay." She swirled her glass, spinning the ice in the chilly water. "Got it. Thanks for the biology lesson, Nic."

To her surprise he began to laugh. The warmth in his voice drew delicate shivers across her skin. "You're laughing," she accused him, looking up and meeting his gaze.

"I have to, Maggie. I've never met anyone like you."

"That's a compliment, I'm sure," she retorted, glimpsing the waitress heading their way.

Meg made room in front of her for the salad and sandwich. Suddenly she felt ravenous. Her mouth watered as she glimpsed the moist turkey and avocado sandwich.

She'd never tell Nic, but sometimes she did think he knew exactly what she needed.

CHAPTER FIVE

"TELL me about the baby's father," Nic said, unexpectedly as they walked along the sandy shore after leaving the restaurant. A crisp breeze blew, and the waves churned, short and choppy, white foamy crests forming on each wave.

They hadn't gone a hundred yards down the beach, and already Nic was at it again. "No."

"Why not?"

She couldn't help laughing. Niccolo didn't give up. She'd never met anyone so persistent in her life. "Because it's pointless," she answered with a brief shake of her head. "There's nothing you need to know."

He bent and picked up a smooth piece of driftwood, the breeze catching his linen shirt, billowing the olive green fabric like a sail. "Humor me."

Humor him. That's all she'd been doing since arriving in Healdsburg.

He must have noticed the wry twist of her lips because he chuckled softly and with a swift fling of his arm, Nic tossed the driftwood to sea, the weathered piece flying high until it came splashing down.

Meg glanced at him from beneath lowered lashes. His hard, chiseled features appeared more relaxed. Creases fanned from his eyes, but these were faint smile lines, not lines of anger.

She still found it hard to believe she'd thought Mark resembled Nic. Maybe Mark was dark, and handsome in a smooth, nonoffensive kind of way, but he could never rival Nic's strength, nor his formidable power.

"What would you like to know?" she asked, hoping her tone sounded suitably casual.

"What does he do, to start with?"

She didn't think it would hurt to disclose Mark's occupation. It wasn't as if Niccolo could track Mark down based on a first name and a profession. "He's an investment banker in New York."

"I take it he's successful?"

"He's doing all right for himself."

"Attractive?"

If you like tall, dark and handsome. Meg squirmed inwardly. "He's not bad."

"A ringing endorsement."

"Nic, what do you want me to say? The condom slipped because the sex was so great?"

Nic glanced at her, eyebrows rising. "Was the sex great?"

"No!" The admission slipped out before she could help herself. Blood surged to her face. She felt utterly foolish. What a ridiculous thing to confess, and to Nic, of all people!

Covering her tracks, she hastily added. "I mean, it was fine. Perfectly fine—"

"Perfectly fine?" he interrupted, his gaze riveted on her. She wasn't sure if she heard incredulity or revulsion in his voice. "That's the best you can say? This man, your *lover*, got you pregnant. I'd hope for a little better than fine, *cara*."

"Oh, come on, Nic. Be realistic. Not everyone has great sex. Some people click. Some people don't. And some people…" She drew a deep breath, wondering how on earth he'd gotten her to say this much. "Some people have so little chemistry they shouldn't even dream of being together."

"That's not why you and Mark aren't together, is it?" Nic's frown deepened, his tone severe. "Maggie, surely you're not throwing away a relationship because it lacks chemistry?"

Throwing away a relationship? She almost laughed. There never had been a relationship. Just her misguided notions about men and romance and sex.

"Nic, you should see yourself. You look exactly like Miss Herrington when she was scolding the class for not completing the five-paragraph essay on time."

"Wasn't she the teacher who kicked you out of class?"

"I didn't put the stink bomb in her desk. That was Charles. But she didn't believe me."

"Maggie, we're not talking about Miss Herrington. We're talking about Mark."

Which was exactly what she didn't want to discuss. Nic and Mark were light-years apart. Two different breeds of men. No matter how many questions Nic asked, he'd never understand about Mark, and he'd never understand what Maggie saw in Mark in the first place.

"But I didn't give Charles the stink bomb, either," she answered as if he'd never spoken, desperately trying to divert his attention. "You know, Nic, that's all hearsay."

"You're incorrigible, Maggie Buckner. I'm trying to have a serious conversation with you and you can't even give me a straight answer." He caught her amazed expression. "What? You didn't think I'd know you were trying to sidetrack me?"

"No, I can't believe you know a word like incorrigible in English. I don't even know the word in English."

"Maggie."

She heard the indulgence in his voice as he said her name and felt a small thrill course through her. She shouldn't care what Nic thought of her and yet, perversely, she did. He was the one person whose good opinion mattered.

And whether she liked it or not, she still desperately wanted him to think well of her. Nic wasn't just part of her past. Her feelings for him were more intense than ever. She longed to have someone agree with her, someone support her decision. If only Nic could be on her side!

He reached out, caught her hand in his and drew it to his mouth. Pressing a small kiss to the back of her fingers he said, "Surely, Maggie, you know that passion is fleeting. Real relationships are based on friendship and trust. Don't let this chemistry be the obstacle preventing you from marrying Mark. Think of the baby, Maggie. Think of being a family."

His lips sent delicious shivers up and down her spine. She touched the tip of her tongue to her upper lip, wondering how on earth she could still be so attracted to him. He made her want things no man had ever made her want. He made her crave more warmth, more touch, more skin.

"This…it's not—" She broke off, finding it difficult to think. Niccolo's mouth was so warm against her fingers, his lips making her skin feel like velvet. She pulled free of him, jamming her hand behind her back as if she was putting out a fire. She had to keep Nic at arm's length. She couldn't let him keep touching her, melting her reserve, warming her body so that she hummed with need.

"It's not a chemistry thing," she answered indignantly, her voice quavering faintly as blood drummed in her ears. "I'm not that shallow."

No? she mocked herself. *You're standing here aching for Nic to take you in his arms again, aching for him to kiss you senseless. You don't even need an excuse to forget your pride!*

"So what is it?" He turned her to face him, his hands on her shoulders, his palms flexed against her skin. Slowly his thumbs caressed her collarbone, drawing lines of fire wherever he touched. He might as well have taken a felt pen to her chest, marking her as his.

The slow circling of his thumbs was like a drug. She stared at him, transfixed, her body turning to liquid, her breasts aching, full and heavy. The heat of his hands burned through her silk blouse. She felt her nipples harden, press taut against the cups of her bra and flimsy blouse. She felt so obvious, her desire so transparent.

"I'm not shallow," she repeated, suddenly longing for more from him.

"You do love him, then!"

The rough intensity in Nic's voice surprised her. Her head jerked up, and she stared into his narrowed eyes. He waited for her answer, and her mind raced, trying to decipher just where he was going with this conversation.

And then it struck her. Nic, lovely, old-fashioned,

moral Nic, wanted to believe that Meg's mistake had been an act of passion, an act of *love*.

Love. If she loved Mark, Nic would understand. He might feel more benevolent regarding her mistake.

"Yes," she whispered, balling one hand behind her back.

"Then what can possibly be more important than giving your baby a father? A family? Maggie, what's keeping you two apart?"

"Nic—"

"Don't lie to me, Maggie. We've been through too much together for you to start lying now."

She stared helplessly into his face, needing more than ever to have him on her side, to have him be her friend. Her parents were distant. Mark was definitely not available. Folks in Healdsburg had always criticized everything she'd done. If only Niccolo cared.

If only she could trust him again.

"Talk to me, Maggie."

She drew a deep breath, praying for courage. "He's already married," she said quietly.

"What?"

His voice sounded like ice. Frighteningly smooth and yet hard, brittle, sharp. Shiver after shiver streaked down her spine. "Mark's been married for nearly ten years."

Nic's hands fell from her shoulders. He took a step backward. He looked at her with horror.

Please, don't look at me this way! Please understand, Nic.

"Tell me this is a joke." His voice rasped. "Tell me this is one of your bad attempts at humor."

A lump swelled in her throat, threatening to seal it. "I wish I could."

"Oh, Maggie!"

She flinched, her shoulders lifting to ward off the harsh censure in his voice. Didn't he understand how much she needed him? Didn't he realize how alone she felt?

Niccolo took another half step away, rubbed his jaw and turned to her, completely nonplussed. "You had an affair with a married man?"

"It wasn't exactly an affair—"

"Please, don't mince words. Mark, this man, he's been married nearly ten years?"

Slowly, she nodded, her body almost numb.

"Then he must have children?"

"Two," she said in a small voice.

"Maggie!"

"I didn't know he was married, Nic. I didn't know until it was too late."

Nic didn't answer her. Didn't look at her. He kept rubbing his jaw, his dark lashes hiding his expression. After what seemed like eternity he said, "Don't you even bother to find out anything about the men you sleep with?"

She jerked as if he'd struck her. "New York's not a small town. People don't know each other—"

"Then what were you doing sleeping with a stranger?" Nic snarled, his jaw thick, his hands clenched at his sides.

Meg felt a moment of fear. "I broke it off as soon as I learned the truth, but by then I was already pregnant."

"He won't leave his wife, will he?"

She dropped her gaze, humiliated. "No. Mark says he loves her—"

Nic's harsh laughter silenced her, the words dying on her lips. "Mark sounds like a truly upstanding man." He gritted the words out, digging his heel into the sand. "Just the kind of man you want to father your children, Maggie. You should be proud. Damn proud."

She shriveled inwardly, ashamed of herself despite her resolve. Nic had effectively reduced her to the size of a pea. No, less than a pea. A bug. A flea. Something incredibly small and lowly to be squashed beneath his heel.

Her lips parted in protest, some kind of defense on her tongue, but she didn't speak. There really was nothing to say. Nic was right, of course. Mark wasn't the kind of man she would have picked to father her children. She'd always believed that man would be strong, compassionate and ethical.

Ethical. Like her father. Her father, the last in a long line of California ranchers, was a man of his word. People liked him because he was honest and straightforward. He didn't play games. If he offered his help, he gave it.

Maybe that's one reason her dad and Niccolo got along so well. Niccolo might be considerably more wealthy, but they were cut from the same cloth.

Her mouth pursed at the irony.

Her father always did the right thing. Just like Nic. Unlike Mark.

Unlike herself.

She suddenly saw herself through Nic's eyes, and her stomach dropped. No wonder he treated her like a child. He saw her as impulsive and emotional, an immature woman who refused to take responsibility for her actions.

That wasn't who she was. He didn't know that she'd pushed herself to become financially independent as soon as she left home. She'd struggled to make her own way rather than turning to her parents for help. There were times when she lived in New York that she'd felt utterly alone, and yet instead of worrying her parents with her loneliness, she'd buried herself in her work, devoted extra time to making new friends. She hadn't set out to fall in love with a married man. He'd been someone she met at the Smithsonian Museum. He'd been attentive and attractive, and she'd found him interesting.

But that was neither here nor there. Her good intentions didn't matter, at least, they didn't matter to Nic and they wouldn't matter to her father. He'd be as livid as Niccolo, and even more disappointed.

The pain inside her was almost more than she could bear. She'd decided years ago to rely on no one, and yet relying on no one meant she had no one to turn to. She was twenty-eight, reasonably successful, financially solvent, but she was most definitely alone.

Now, for the first time in years, she couldn't bear to be alone. She needed her family, needed her friends. She needed to know that her baby would be part of a community that would love her and cherish her baby's growth.

It was agonizing to admit, but she needed help. She desperately needed support.

She needed Nic.

"Niccolo—"

Abruptly he held up a hand, silencing her. "Don't talk to me." His voice was harshly unforgiving.

With a wave of his hand, he dismissed her, then turned and strode to the car.

Something broke free inside her chest, and she nearly screamed.

He'd never walked away from her before. He'd never abandoned her in her life.

Relentless waves of pain swept through her. Wave after wave of fear and grief and loneliness. He didn't understand that she'd always needed him. He didn't understand that he was the one person in the world who made her feel safe and sane and special. He was the man she adored.

He didn't know, and if he did, he didn't care. He continued to walk away, the wind whipping his shirt, his long legs carrying him toward the stairs and the parking lot.

No, no, no. He couldn't walk away from her now. Couldn't turn his back on her. If he believed in her, she could do anything.

Meg slipped off her leather heels and ran after him, chasing him across the sandy dunes to the rickety wooden stairs. The moist salt air sparkled in her hair. Fine droplets clung to her skin.

Panting, she caught up with him by the stairs. Meg grabbed the back of his shirt, nearly tugging the olive green linen fabric from the waistband of his chino slacks. "Nic!"

He didn't shake her off but he didn't turn around.

"Nic, please—"

"What? What do you want me to say? Good luck, Maggie, have a great life, Maggie?" Fury and pain throbbed in his voice, his Italian accent growing more pronounced. "Is it my approval you want, *cara*, while you toss your life away? Should I say, 'Well done, darling,' and cut you a check for your baby's savings account?"

"Stop it!"

"Is it a baby shower you want? Or a crib for the side of your bed?" He came down a step, caught her wrists and dragged her level with him. "Are you in need of children's storybooks or Irish linen for the christening gown? Maggie!" He nearly roared her name, his golden eyes turning amber with pent emotion. "What do you want me to do? What do you want me to say?"

He'd been shaking her, a shake for each question. By the time he'd finished she was crying.

"Just be my friend!" she begged.

His hands fell away. "Your friend?" He drew a ragged breath, pushed his dark hair from his brow with an unsteady hand. The ocean waves thundered in the background, wave after wave crashing on the shore. Clouds gathered.

The air smelled so strongly of salt that Meg's nose burned.

"Your friend?" he repeated. His tone changed, and there was a peculiar expression in his eye. "Just like I was your friend all those years ago when I let you take the blame for Jared's mistake? When I stood by and did nothing? When I looked the other way despite the fact that you were in way over your head?"

She stared at him, transfixed. She'd never heard him speak with so much anger and passion, and yet he was utterly coherent.

"Is that the kind of friend you need, Maggie?"

He barked a laugh, the short, acerbic sound so raw and savage it made her chest ache. "Someone like Mark, right?"

The breeze caught her hair, blew the curls around her face in wild disorder. Nic stared at her, his brow furrowed. "No. No, Maggie, I can't be your friend." There was sympathy in his voice, sympathy and a note of pained tenderness.

She'd lost.

She'd lost him, lost everything. Unconsciously, she'd counted on him, believing he'd be there for her to help her, support her as she became a single mother. In the past Nic had been the first one to take her side. But no more. She'd lost his respect. She'd lost what little they had shared.

Meg couldn't speak, her pain so intense that it hurt just to breathe. She wanted to say his name, wanted to touch him, find him, somehow save them, but her throat closed and her heart twisted. She was too stricken to put thoughts into words.

Please, Nic. Please, Niccolo.

"Maggie, you told your mother that she would come home to a wedding. And she shall."

Niccolo drove swiftly, steering with one hand while rapidly punching numbers into his cell phone with the other.

"Carolyn, Niccolo Dominici here. Listen, I need your help. Can you pull something together for me? It's rather short notice, but I'm thinking of Saturday, just over a week from now. About a hundred guests, give or take a few. Sit-down dinner. Black tie. Elegant food, the best of everything."

He frowned, listening, and then with a caustic

glance at Meg, said, "Actually, yes, it is a special occasion. I'm getting married."

Meg pressed one knuckled fist against her mouth, listening in horror. Niccolo couldn't be serious.

"Yes, the reception will be at the villa. The ballroom, of course, and perhaps cocktails and appetizers in the garden."

"Hang up," she ordered. "This is ridiculous!"

He ignored her and described the wines he planned on serving, adding something about importing a dozen cases of the finest French champagne. Meg couldn't believe he was seriously considering arranging a wedding. Not just any wedding, *their* wedding.

"Nic!"

He raised a finger to his lips, shushing her.

Her fingers itched to snatch the phone from his ear and toss it out the window. "Nic, I'm serious."

He shrugged and continued with his conversation. Meg rolled her eyes, crossed her arms and glanced at the passing scenery. The car was eating up the miles, flying down the freeway, but they weren't heading to Napa.

Nic hung up and prepared to dial another number.

"Nic—"

"Not now, *cara*, I'm busy."

"You're wasting your time."

He punched in the rest of the number. "*Amore*, yes, it's Niccolo. How are you? Excellent. I have a favor to ask you. Would it be possible to stay open late? Yes, for me. Actually my fiancée. You hadn't heard? Well, it's happened quickly. She's an old family friend. I think you'll like her. We should reach the city around eight. See you then."

Nic hung up again.

"Where are we going now?" she demanded.

"Into the city. We'll buy your bridal gown and accessories tonight."

"An off-the-rack gown? How common." Meg couldn't help making the dig. She was exhausted, tired beyond belief, and Niccolo's little game was not sitting well with her.

He named a well-known designer, then shot her a dark look. "Not so common."

"Does he do wedding dresses?"

"He should have something formal and elegant." He cast her another dark glance. "And as we both well know, it doesn't have to be white."

Meg's stomach suddenly cramped. She bit her lip, resenting Nic, hating the nausea. She'd been feeling fine until he started his bully routine.

"You better stop the car," she warned, her stomach heaving, her head beginning to throb.

"You can't run from me."

"Fine. But pull over or I'll be sick in your pristine vintage Ferrari."

The drive into San Francisco was more like a snail's crawl in snarled, congested traffic through the foothills and across the striking Golden Gate Bridge. The traffic downtown was equally sluggish, and Niccolo's bad mood grew blacker. By the time they reached the boutique, he was white-faced and thin-lipped. His hard cheekbones pressed against his skin, and his strong jaw jutted in wordless fury.

Inside the store, Niccolo watched, silent and hawk-like, as she tried on dress after dress, only to reject each gown with a careless wave of his hand.

Nic finally picked a gown out of a design book,

the sheath sleekly sophisticated with a daring slit up the back. "In white," he said shortly, with a cool curl of his upper lip. "My Maggie looks lovely in white."

By the time Niccolo had settled on the dress, it was nearly midnight, and Meg drooped with fatigue.

Without consulting her, Niccolo drove them to a small, exclusive hotel at the top of Nob Hill where they were immediately ushered into an elevator and swept to the top floor.

Theirs was a penthouse suite, two bedrooms with private baths opening off an elegantly chic living room decorated in gold, pale yellow and cream. Meg took six steps into the living room before sinking in exhaustion onto one of the matching caramel-colored sofas covered in the softest buttery leather.

Her head fell back on the down-filled cushion. She closed her eyes and drew a deep breath.

She felt Nic approach, became aware of his presence before she heard him drop his keys on the marble coffee table.

"Can I get you something?" he asked, politely formal, as politely formal as he'd been all evening.

"No." She paused, opened her eyes, her gaze briefly meeting his before she looked away. "Thank you."

He said nothing, nor did he move. He stood in front of her, staring at her. She knew he was disgusted with her. She felt his long, slow scrutiny as his gaze traveled the length of her, resting first on her face, then her breasts, her hips, her legs. It was a look of ownership, of possession. He was assessing his goods, taking stock of this new fiancée of his.

"Satisfied?" she whispered, a knot of emotion forming in her chest.

"As satisfied as I can expect to be."

She would have smiled if she could. "You're a very hard man to please, Mr. Dominici."

He didn't answer, turning on his heel to open a tall mahogany sideboard lined with bottles and glittering glasses.

She watched him draw out two crystal snifters from the top shelf, along with a bottle of liqueur. He broke the seal on the bottle and poured a tiny mouthful into one snifter and a very liberal measure into the other.

He returned with the glasses, leaning over to hand her one.

She could smell the potent liqueur. Brandy. Oranges. Grand Marnier. "I can't drink," she said.

"One sip. A toast."

Her eyes burned, and she blinked. "Just what are we toasting, Nic?"

Her soft voice sounded as bruised as her heart felt. She and Nic had been through so much together, but what he suggested, what he was pushing them into, was incomprehensible. She might be attracted to him, might fantasize about making love with him, but that was a far cry from marrying him.

"To us," he answered sardonically, lifting his glass. The crystal snifter glittered in the soft, incandescent lighting. The amber-colored liquid swirled in the glass. He stared at her over the rim of his glass, his lower lip curled, his eyes hard. He looked cold and cruelly determined. It crossed her mind for the first time that perhaps she didn't know Nic as well as she'd thought. If he was capable of forcing her into marriage, he could be capable of any number of things.

Meg suppressed a shiver. "Us?"

"Of course, it's all about us now."

The careless laughter in his voice stung. He was taunting her, mocking her naïveté and innocence. The grittiness in her eyes grew worse. She blinked, trying to keep the tears from forming. "You'll destroy our friendship, Nic. You'll take what we are, what we've been, and change it forever."

The corner of his mouth lifted. "That has already happened. It took place years ago when I let you pretend you were driving the night of the accident. It changed when I stood by and let your father's heart harden against you. It changed when people in town gossiped about you and I turned a deaf ear to the slander. It did change, just as we changed. So you see, *cara*, we're not really risking all that much."

"But marriage?" She choked. "I know I'm not the wife you wanted."

His eyes narrowed, his hard jaw tightening grimly. He subjected her to another slow, objective perusal. "No," he coolly admitted, "and apparently I'm not the man you wanted."

CHAPTER SIX

"WAKE up. You have a doctor's appointment in an hour."

Meg rubbed her eyes, propped herself on her elbow and focused with great difficulty on Nic's silhouette in the doorway. "A doctor's appointment?"

"Downtown, in an hour."

She stared at him blankly. "I'm not sick."

"It's with one of San Francisco's leading obstetricians. I thought it made sense to have him check you over and get some blood work done."

"Blood work? Whatever for?"

He smiled thinly. "Maybe I want to see what I'm getting."

"What about an ultrasound? That'd give you more ammunition."

"Excellent suggestion, *cara*, I'll ask Dr. Collins to schedule one of those, too."

He wasn't joking. He was serious! Her insides felt like they were icing over. "You have no right to make appointments for me, Niccolo."

He dismissed her with a shrug. "Somebody needs to. You're not taking care of yourself."

"Nic, I'm thin, I'm not anorexic!"

He shrugged and leaned against the door frame. "That's neither here nor there. I think we should get a professional opinion and have a check done on your iron levels. You don't want to jeopardize the baby's health by being anemic."

He made her sound as if she were being irrational, and yet there was nothing irrational about not wanting him to dictate to her.

She had her own physician in Manhattan. She'd already had two prenatal appointments, including one very thorough workup. Her blood work had come back just fine, and even though she'd hadn't gained much weight, her doctor assured her that was fine for the first trimester. Some women gained a healthy amount right away, others put on weight during the second and third trimesters. It all depended on body type.

"I'm taking prenatal vitamins with *iron*," she answered tersely, sitting up and pressing the sheet to her bare chest. "If you'd like to see my medical chart, I can request that a copy be sent to you."

"That's not necessary. I'm sure Dr. Collins is happy to start his own file."

"Perhaps I should have Mark fax his pedigree papers?"

Nic's cold smile faded. "Get dressed. Now."

She shivered inwardly, shocked by his tone, but she would never let him see how much he unnerved her. "I'm not going."

"You are going." He turned, disappeared into the adjoining suite and reappeared with a small tray. Niccolo slid the tray in front of her. "Coffee, not too strong, enough for one cup."

"You're so amazing."

"Thank you."

Her mouth pursed as she bit back the retort that she didn't mean it as a compliment, but as an insult. He was amazingly egotistical. Amazingly domineering. Amazingly sure of himself.

Meg pushed the tray aside. Clutching the sheet tighter, she slid her legs over the edge of the bed, groping for a bathrobe. "Somehow I think you care less about my health than you do about the baby's possible birth defects."

Niccolo paled, looking almost ashen beneath his golden tan. "Nonsense."

"Is it? You're marrying me out of obligation. You're promising to raise my child as a Dominici. Of course you want a medical workup. You want to make sure your adopted daughter or son meets your snooty standards."

He froze, his immense shoulders stilling, his powerful body tensing.

She'd said too much. She knew it right away.

Scathingly, his gaze dropped to the rise of her breasts peeking from the sheet, and to the shadow of her cleavage. With another caustic perusal, he dismissed her, his expression cold and utterly disgusted. Niccolo turned and walked out, closing the door firmly.

With her heart in her throat, Meg slipped her arms into the hotel's white terry-cloth robe and tied the thick sash firmly about her waist. She waited for Nic to return, but he didn't. After several minutes she poured her coffee, the single cup Nic had mentioned, sat cross-legged on the bed and sipped the coffee in between worrying her lower lip.

She shouldn't have said such a thing to Nic. She owed him an apology, but the words stuck in her throat. He just made her so angry. He pushed all the right buttons every time.

Sighing, she encircled the cup with both hands,

clutching it for warmth as well as courage. She might not agree with this doctor's appointment, but she couldn't ignore Nic. Then there really would be hell to pay.

Meg swung open the door, tightened the sash on her robe and tiptoed into the living room.

He was at the desk near the bay window, on the phone. He briefly glanced at her before returning his attention to the call. After several minutes he hung up. He looked at her but said nothing.

"What if the baby did have a birth defect?" She jammed her hands into the robe pockets. "What would you do then?"

"Get help. Inquire with specialists." He leaned back in the chair and ran a hand through his dark hair. "Some defects can be mended in utero."

Some of the ice thawed around her heart. She felt like a heel. "What if the defect was quite serious? What if nothing could be done?"

He stared at her long and hard, his black brows lowered, his expression incredulous. "Maggie, this is your baby we're talking about. Not a thing. Not a monster. A baby. What do you think I'd do?"

His gaze held hers. She felt him pull her in, swallow her whole. "Mark didn't want the baby," she answered in a small voice. "He insisted on an abortion. He made an appointment with a clinic in New York and said I had to go, or he'd—" She couldn't finish. The words were too horrible to speak out loud.

"He'd what?" Niccolo demanded savagely.

"Drag me there himself."

"You're making this up!"

She shivered and turned away. "I wish I was."

"How could you love such a man?" His voice

dripped disdain and disgust. "How can you be so desperate to please a man that you'd—"

"But I didn't!" She whirled around. "Obviously, I didn't get an abortion. I left New York. I came—" She almost said *home*. Hastily she substituted. "Here."

Nic's lip curled. He looked at her as though she were the lowest form of life. No one but Nic made her feel so worthless. Meg blinked, hating herself for caring so much about his opinion.

"I know this baby is healthy," she said, lifting her chin, her eyes burning, hot and gritty, "but even if he or she wasn't, I'd never abort the baby. Never in a million years."

"So, we do have something in common."

Nic sighed and ran his fingers through his hair again, ruffling the dark black waves. It struck her for the first time that he looked weary, bone weary. "This marriage," he said slowly, thinking before speaking, "it's not going to be easy. It won't be impossible, it's just not…natural."

"No." She laughed shakily, hugging the terry-cloth robe tighter. "It's definitely not natural."

"But that doesn't mean we can't make it work. We just have to try harder."

"Niccolo, don't you think this has gone far enough? You've made your point."

"Made my point? *Cara*, this isn't football."

"Obviously, but I thought you'd back off from the marriage discussion by now. You're not really going to go through with this."

"Oh, yes, *we* are."

"Niccolo, marriage isn't like starting a business. We're talking about sharing lives, becoming intimate.'' Meg regretted the blush that swept her face, making her feel ridiculously immature, but she had to see this conversation through to the logical conclusion.

''And?''

Perhaps Nic didn't really mean a *marriage* marriage. Maybe he was thinking of something less personal. ''Maybe I'm misunderstanding you. Maybe you mean something in name only, an arrangement—''

''That would be convenient, wouldn't it?'' he interrupted curtly, his expression hardening, his mouth pressed into an immobile line. ''You have your baby, you have your safety net, you have freedom to take lovers on the side.'' He shrugged. ''Sorry, Maggie, I'm not that altruistic. Our marriage would be *real*.''

Shocked, she could only stare at him while a thousand disjointed thoughts raced through her head. A real marriage. Naked, beds, sex. Niccolo making love to her. Niccolo—

She jerked her head up, met his gaze. He smiled faintly, eyes gleaming, as if he knew exactly what she'd been thinking.

Before he could say another word, she returned to her room, shutting the door behind her.

Meg sat on the hotel bed, arms encircling her bent legs. She wished she could curl up and disappear. Her life was careening wildly out of control. It was one thing to become a mother. It was another to marry Nic and become *his* wife.

Niccolo's wife.

The very thought made her shiver. Nic wasn't the man she thought he was. He was harder, fiercer, more determined than she'd given him credit for. If he said their marriage would be real, he meant it.

Her heart thumped double time as she tried to imagine life with Niccolo. What kind of lover would he be? She knew he wasn't lacking in experience, but would he be tender or aggressive? Generous? Selfish?

Suddenly she pictured his hands, his mouth, and warmth flooded her limbs. No, he wouldn't be selfish. Far from selfish. If anything, he'd drive her wild.

Meg dropped her head, resting her cheek against the back of her hand.

But was that reason to marry Nic?

The door opened. Niccolo stood in the threshold. "Why aren't you dressed?"

She glanced at him, toes curling into the soft comforter tossed across the bed. "This will never work. We don't—"

"Love each other?" He completed the sentence for her.

Meg slid off the bed. "No, we don't, and a loveless marriage would be miserable."

"Not necessarily. We know each other, we understand each other, I'm sure we'd enjoy sex together."

Why did he have to keep talking about sex? It completely unnerved her, made her feel incredibly inexperienced. Niccolo would know all sorts of things, and she would... A blush scorched her cheeks as she pictured herself naked in his bed.

She'd be putty in his hands.

Rivulets of desire chased away her fear. Hunger coiled in her belly, and her nipples tightened expectantly. If only Nic would stop moving toward her. If only she'd stop skittering around the bed. He was like a tiger about to pounce, and she felt no bigger than a mouse.

Nervously, Meg touched the tip of her tongue to her upper lip, acutely aware that she was naked beneath the robe.

''Cat got your tongue, Maggie?'' he softly taunted, closing in on her.

Her gaze darted right and left, seeking an escape, but the bed blocked her on one side and Niccolo stood on the other. For a moment she considered scrambling across the mattress but cringed at such a childish retreat. Trapped, she could only stand up to him. With far more bravado than she felt, Meg threw back her shoulders and braced her hands on her hips. ''Excuse me, I'd like to dress. Would you kindly get out of my room?''

Nic leaned forward, placed an arm on either side of her shoulders and gazed into her upturned face. ''If you want to dress, dress. I'm not stopping you.''

She smelled his citrusy sandalwood cologne and a hint of spearmint on his breath. He'd shaved already, and his jaw appeared impossibly hard, his face bronzed angles and planes that made her fingers itch to touch him. Furious with herself for even thinking such a thought, she unleashed her anger at him. ''It's a little hard to strip with you holding me captive.''

His eyes lit up at the word *strip*. They grew brighter at *captive*. Meg silently cursed herself. ''Mm, now there's an idea. Bondage. So you do like erotic games.''

Heat surged through her, her face burning with chaotic emotions. ''You're disgusting!''

''Liar, liar, pants on fire,'' he softly taunted, reaching out to stroke her feverish cheek. ''You rather like the idea of me playing erotic games with you. After all, you started them ten years ago when you slid across my lap in nothing but a schoolgirl skirt and a very sexy, very lacy garter belt.''

''I was stupid.''

''You were curious.'' His finger drew an invisible line from her cheek down her neck, across her breast-bone and up with tantalizing brevity across the tip of one nipple. ''And the truth is, you're still curious. I see it in your eyes every time I come near you. I feel it in your body every time I touch you. I hear it in your breath—''

''What nerve! What an ego! You're so incredibly full of yourself, Niccolo Dominici, you actually believe I'm still in love with you.''

''Not in love,'' he corrected, tilting her chin. ''But in lust.''

''No.''

''Yes. But it's not one-sided, Maggie. I'm just as enamored with you. You think I'm marrying you simply out of the goodness of my heart? Far from it. I want you. It's that simple. But I'll put a ring on your finger, make it legal, and then I'll enjoy you. Again and again and—'' his voice dropped a pitch ''—again.''

''I am not attracted to you, and I will not let you just use me like some common—''

''Be careful,'' he warned, hushing her with the tip of his finger. ''Be very careful, Maggie. Do not cast stones. You're in a precarious position, and I find your modesty act a bit overwrought.''

''How dare you!''

His eyebrows lifted. ''Maggie, you slid across my

lap at sixteen, your bare bottom on my lap and in my hands.''

She bristled, hands balling into fists, but before she could speak, he continued. ''You lay around the pool in swimsuits so skimpy they barely cover your…assets. You've slept with just about anyone, including married men—''

To hell with him! Let him burn in hell and rot his soul and—

She clenched her hands, longing to throw a quick jab. What she wouldn't give to bloody his perfectly straight, perfectly lovely Italian nose. ''For your information, I've been so busy with my career that I've dated very little!''

''No, you don't date. You indulge in affairs.''

''Not affairs. One relationship.'' She interrupted again, her temper blazing, blood roaring through her head, making her ears buzz. ''One relationship with one man. *One*, Nic. Not legions. Not dozens. Not two. One.''

''And he was married.''

''I made a mistake.''

''That's always your excuse, isn't it, Maggie?''

Bastard. He was quite a bastard. Scalding tears filled her eyes, but she gritted her teeth and blinked hard to keep them from falling.

Nic yawned and with a glance at his watch reminded her of the doctor's appointment. ''You've wasted a half hour. We've got twenty minutes left. I advise you to go shower and dress now. You need the time. You're not the wash-and-go type.''

Red-hot fury surged through Meg. ''Get lost!''

''What's wrong? Did I hit a sensitive nerve?''

So this was how it was going to be. Niccolo would

marry her, give her baby a name, but he'd humiliate her every chance he could, reducing her to something sordid and cheap. Her gaze met his and held. She'd never felt so much anger and hate for one person as she did just then for Nic. He wasn't just cold, he was harsh and cruel.

"I'll never marry you," she said, her voice strangled, her chest rising and falling with great gasps of air. "Being your wife would be pure torture. *Yes, Mr. Dominici. No, Mr. Dominici. How high, Mr. Dominici?* Forget it. I'd sooner put a hole in my head than put your ring on my finger!"

He clapped politely, a lazy smile curling his upper lip. "Well done, *cara*, you have a gift for the dramatic. Perhaps when the children are older and you've some time on your hands, you can audition for the community theater."

"Why are you treating me like this?"

His smile never wavered, his golden eyes gleaming. "Like how, *cara*?"

"Like I'm cheap. Like I'm beneath you."

"You're not beneath me, not yet. But on our wedding night, now that's another matter."

Her stomach cramped, and resentment burned within her. She would not stand here and take his insults. "There won't be a wedding night. I'm not going to marry you."

"Of course you will. It's been decided."

"It's been undecided. I will not marry you. Not now. Not ever. Don't you understand?"

"You've just wasted another minute. You don't want to see Dr. Collins in that bathrobe, do you?"

"Are you listening to me?"

"I heard what you said, but I don't think you've thought this all the way through."

"What's there to think through?"

His gaze met hers, hard and unyielding. "I see. So that's your final decision?"

She didn't answer, and after a moment, Niccolo turned and walked out of the bedroom.

She followed him to the door, watching as he reached into the living room closet and took his suit coat from the hanger. Nic swung the coat over his shoulders, sliding one arm into a sleeve, then the other. He eased the coat over his shoulders and smoothed his lapels flat. "I hope you've thought this through, *cara*. Considered the implications."

"Implications?"

"The implications of telling your parents the truth. Telling them what really happened the night Jared died." His grave expression changed, a light appearing in his golden eyes, a small smile curving his mouth, making him look quietly victorious. "What else did you think I meant?"

"This has nothing to do with Jared's death."

"Oh, but it does, my Maggie. You see, if I'd stepped forward and told the truth years ago, I think you'd have a different relationship with your father today. Indeed, I think you'd be a different person today."

"That's ludicrous!"

"Is it? You've spent more than a decade trying to forget the past. At least ten years carving a new identity for yourself. Obviously, the past causes you great pain." He checked his coat pocket for his wallet and reached into another for the valet parking ticket. "Anyway, that's a matter of opinion, and we're wasting time. What I'm offering you is marriage. I'm offering you and your baby emotional stability, financial security and respectability.''

Of course, respectability. Everything always came back to appearances with Nic.

Nic continued, unfazed by the anger in her eyes. ''But I'm not making threats and I won't hold you hostage. If you want to leave, you know where the door is. But if you leave now, know this. I shall never make my offer again, and I promise you, I will tell your parents the truth about Jared and the problems he'd been having with his drinking his last year at college.''

She froze, suddenly very, very tired. She hadn't thought he knew. They'd never once talked about the drinking before. ''You...knew?''

''I knew he'd been having problems for awhile, and I knew his university was close to suspending him. I interceded, offered to help Jared get counseling. They put him on academic probation instead.''

''Did you get him counseling?'' she asked, her voice faint to her ears.

''No.'' The bitterness in Nic's voice stung her. ''I drank with him on Christmas Eve and then let him climb behind the wheel. I might as well have killed him myself.''

Maggie turned a chair around and sat down rather heavily, her legs not quite strong enough to support her. ''No. That's not true,'' she whispered, reaching up to rub the back of her head, her soft curls loose, disheveled. ''Jared insisted on driving. He kept making a joke about someday competing in the Indy 500.''

Nic's mouth quirked, one corner lifting, and yet

there was only sorrow in his eyes. "Jared knew how
to make us all laugh. He could be delightfully persuasive. But then, alcoholics generally are."

"Don't call him that."

"What? An alcoholic?" She winced, and Nic
shook his head. "But Maggie, he was. Instead of
getting him help we—I—looked the other way." He
drew a ragged breath. "But I won't look the other
way again. I'm here, Maggie, and I'm going to do
the right thing by you. Now we don't have time to
waste. I suggest you dress."

But still she hesitated. "You can't tell my parents
about Jared. Not ever."

"I won't. As long as we stay married, the truth
will remain here, buried, my secret. Our secret." And
he tapped his chest, just above his heart. Pain filled
his golden eyes, etched itself in lines around his
beautiful mouth. "But it's up to you, Maggie. It's
your choice."

She and Niccolo didn't speak in the doctor's waiting
room. Nic pretended to read a magazine, and Maggie
studied the framed prints on the wall, examining the
still lifes as if they were great works of art.

Everything in the waiting room felt artificial, from
the lavender and rose-colored upholstery on the sofas
to the stiff arrangements of silk flowers on end tables.
Long-stemmed pink flowers and purple hydrangea.

Fake.

Fake flowers. Fake ambience. Fake engagement.

"Mrs. Dominici?"

The waiting room door had opened. A nurse with
a clipboard stood in the doorway.

Meg glanced around, as if a Mrs. Dominici would

appear. Nic stood up, gestured for Meg. "Come," he said.

Come. Sit. Stay.

"It's not Mrs. Dominici," she explained. "It's Margaret Buckner. *Miss* Margaret Buckner."

The nurse glanced at the chart, confused. "Ah, I'm sorry, we have you down as Maggie Dominici."

Nic's fingers wrapped around her arm just above her elbow. "She'll be Mrs. Dominici very soon," he replied smoothly, propelling Meg forward.

"How wonderful," the nurse remarked. "Where's the wedding going to be?"

"Napa."

Meg's stomach cramped. He made it sound so easy. A wedding in Napa. One hundred guests. Cases of champagne.

The nurse smiled at Niccolo with wide-eyed fascination. Meg shouldn't have been surprised. Nic affected every woman like that.

"Oh, I just *love* Napa," the nurse said, gushing. "All those darling bed-and-breakfasts, and the wineries are to die for. Do you have a favorite winery?"

"Dominici." Nic's expression gave nothing away.

"Like your name!" The nurse suddenly colored. "Oh, are you related to the Dominici wine makers?"

Nic inclined his head, and Meg ground her teeth.

With another bright smile in Nic's direction, the nurse gestured down the hallway. "We'll be going this way. But first Mrs. Dom—I mean, Miss, uh, Buckner—we'll need to weigh you and get a urine sample. Mr. Dominici, will you be coming with us?"

"Yes," he answered.

"No." Meg spun to face him. She placed two fingertips on his chest and pressed him back. "This is where I draw the line, Nic. This is my body and my appointment. Any information you want to know, you can find out after the examination is over.''

He smiled at the nurse and completely ignored Meg. "Of course I'm coming. I want to know *everything* about our baby.''

CHAPTER SEVEN

NICCOLO dropped Meg off at the Hunts. She spent the rest of the afternoon sitting in a shady corner of the garden sketching plans. Except for serving her a glass of lemonade and discreetly inquiring about the family emergency, the Hunts left her alone, eager for her to continue work on the proposed renovation.

Meg was grateful for the chance to make progress on her drawings and attempted to focus on her sketches, but the events of the last twenty-four hours weighed heavily on her mind.

Not everything was bad. Like today's ultrasound. It had been absolutely wonderful. Miraculous, really. To see the baby inside her, to watch the little heart pump, see the tiny legs kick. The baby had been active, wiggling this way and that, and Meg's heart had leaped to her throat, silent tears filling her eyes.

Her baby.

The ultrasound revealed what she already knew. The baby was healthy and strong. Meg might not be gaining weight quickly, but her baby appeared well-nourished, moving constantly during the ultrasound.

Niccolo had been there, of course. He'd been silent at first as the doctor pointed out the four chambers of the baby's heart, highlighting the vertebrae of the spine and the formation of the arms and legs. But when the baby appeared to pop its thumb into its mouth, Nic took two swift steps forward and touched the monitor in awe.

Just remembering made Meg's eyes fill with tears. She couldn't remember when she had last felt so emotional. Everything was affecting her strongly. The baby. Memories of Jared. Niccolo.

Especially Niccolo.

Picking up her pencil, she tried to force herself to concentrate on her project, shutting out everything but the peaceful garden and the dancing shadows cast by the tall poplar trees.

But as the afternoon drew to an end, dusk creeping into the garden, muting the garden's brilliance, Meg felt a rush of worry and dread.

It was one thing to become a mother. But another to marry Niccolo. Unless he cared a little. That would change everything. Their marriage wouldn't seem so overwhelming if there was more to it than duty.

Duty.

The word stuck in her throat, echoed gratingly inside her head. It was the kind of word that made Meg want to run. Indeed, all her life she'd shaken off that which was expected of her and done the exact opposite.

Duty.

It was the worst reason for a man to marry her. The absolute worst reason to spend her life with Niccolo.

But even as she struggled with the pretense of the marriage, a carnal hunger for Nic, to be possessed by Nic, ricocheted through her, flaming her senses. She was shameless, truly, to want Niccolo this way. She knew what he thought of her, and yet somehow, in his arms, his mouth against hers, she felt more alive than she did at any other time.

*   *   *

Francesca was lighting the candles on the table when Meg arrived at the villa. "Dinner will be served at seven," she informed Meg.

Meg nodded, hesitating in the hallway to watch the housekeeper finish lighting the candles. She noted the three place settings on the imposing dining room table. Francesca never had dinner with Niccolo in the dining room, so there must be a guest joining them tonight.

"Who's coming for dinner?" she asked.

"Father Rivera. Niccolo's priest." Francesca leaned forward to adjust the wineglasses, lining them up precisely. She then straightened one of the gilded chairs. "Change quickly, Maggie. Father should be here any time."

Meg hadn't expected any great display of affection from Niccolo in front of the family priest, but neither had she expected him to be so chillingly aloof. Nic ignored her during dinner, failing to include her in his conversation—which he conducted mainly in Spanish for the Andalusian priest's benefit—nor did he make eye contact.

It was as if she didn't exist.

Meg was surprised by the depth of her hurt. Somehow, after the ultrasound appointment, after the day they'd spent together, she thought Niccolo was serious about making a go of the marriage, making it work, making them a family. But if this cold silence was his idea of family, well, he could take his marriage proposal and put it in a not-so-nice place.

Niccolo suggested an after-dinner walk, and the three of them strolled the estate's extensive grounds, pausing frequently so Father Rivera could sniff the late roses, all the while sharing with them his thoughts on marriage and the sanctity of the vows.

Meg's insides churned as Father Rivera talked, and she felt Nic's tension grow. Glancing at him from beneath her lashes, she noted his darkening expression, his brow lowered, his eyes narrowed and brooding. And still he didn't acknowledge her.

He didn't have to tell her he didn't like marrying her; it was written all over his face, emanating from every pore in his body.

Her hurt gave way to anger. It was ridiculous for him to sulk. This marriage hadn't been her idea. If he didn't like it, call it off.

They finished the slow circle through the garden and returned to the front steps of the villa. It was late, the moon shining dimly above, and after blessing them both, Father Rivera said good-night, then slowly made his way to his car.

Meg had somehow managed to keep a smile pasted on her face through the garden tour, but she'd had about enough of Niccolo's frigid demeanor. "We make a delightful couple, don't you think?"

Niccolo glanced at her and frowned. "We're fine."

"You don't think we lack any…warmth?"

"Father's a priest. He'd prefer us to behave discreetly. Or would you rather have him know the truth? That I'm marrying you only to give your baby a proper name?" Niccolo smiled, baring his teeth. She thought he looked distinctly wolflike. "I think not, Maggie. He's a dear friend of the family's, and there's really no reason to shock him."

She couldn't have said a word at that moment even

if she wanted to. She felt the blood drain from her face. "We were once friends."

"We still are, *cara*. Otherwise I wouldn't be jumping through hoops."

"I didn't ask you to jump through hoops."

"No, you didn't ask, because you don't think." Savagely, he turned and walked away.

Meg followed him into the winery cellar. Cool and dark, the cellar smelled pungent, ripe with fermenting grapes, the stone walls lined with dozens of massive oak barrels.

She spotted Nic climbing one of the barrels, and she circled it. It was nearly ten feet tall and dwarfed her. "We need to talk."

"We'll have plenty of time to talk after we're married," he answered, twisting a cap off and drawing a sample.

The wedding! It was just days away. "Nic, I know how seriously you take these vows. I also know this isn't what you want for yourself."

He sniffed the sample, then let a drop fall onto his tongue. Wincing, he said, "I'm willing to compromise."

The word *compromise* sounded sour in his mouth, much like the wine on his tongue. She didn't like the comparison, but it fit. "You've never compromised about anything. Why do it now?"

Nic screwed the barrel cap on and crouched, his muscular legs pulling his denim jeans taut across the thighs. His long black hair brushed his collar , a lock falling across his temple. "Looking to weasel out?" he softly asked.

Weasel out? "A lovely phrase, if I ever heard one."

He shrugged. ''You're the one running scared.''

''I'm not running anywhere. I'm asking if you're having second thoughts.''

Nic stood up, jumped off the barrel. ''Listen, *cara*, you're wasting your time, and you're wasting mine. This wedding is going to happen. Now if you'll excuse me, I have work to do.''

He brushed past her, grabbed his cellular phone from his back pocket and quickly dialed a number.

''Nic, this conversation isn't over,'' she called after him.

Still walking, he turned, glancing at her over his shoulder. One of his black eyebrows raised, as if to mock her.

''Hello, Papa? Yes, Nico here,'' he said, switching to Italian and turning, effectively dismissing her.

Obviously, the conversation *was* over.

Niccolo managed to fill every minute during the next few days with business meetings, winery tours and public-relations planning sessions. He didn't have a minute to spare for her.

''Deal with them.'' That was all Nic said about the steady stream of visitors in and out of the villa anxious to discuss the coming wedding. The caterer, the florist, the musicians, the party rental company. The various businesses kept showing up, then returning with another list of details, questions and specifications.

The party rental company needed exact measurements to create a custom white canvas tent. The florist, on discovering that Meg was a landscape designer, wanted to know her favorite flower. The caterer wanted to be sure that Meg liked seafood, because three of the appetizers featured shrimp, scallops or crab.

And all Meg wanted was to escape to the Hunts and try to forget that this elaborate wedding would soon take place.

In the week before the wedding, as Meg labored over massive blueprints, Niccolo's shadow fell, darkening the plans and making it impossible for her to work.

"Why don't you have a cell phone?" he demanded irritably, dragging a hand through his black hair. "I couldn't reach the Hunts, couldn't contact you, and so I had to drop everything to drive over here."

"I'm sorry."

"Everybody has a cell phone."

"Not me." She pushed her sunglasses up, resting them on the top of her head. "What can I do for you, Nic? I'm assuming you have something on your mind?"

"Be home by six. We have an appointment with my lawyer."

Her heart did a strange flutter. His lawyer. That didn't sound good. "Do I need my lawyer present?" she asked sweetly, reaching for her sunglasses and placing them back on her nose.

"No. Not unless you're planning on presenting me with a prenuptial of your own."

A prenuptial agreement. Of course. Niccolo wouldn't leave any stone unturned. She drew her lips back, praying it looked like a smile. "I'll be there."

"Don't keep me waiting."

"Can't do that, can I? I'd hate to see you lose your sunny disposition."

* * *

Meg returned to the villa early enough to shower and change before dinner. Tonight of all nights she wanted to feel confident, and looking polished would certainly help make her feel more pulled together.

Ignoring the trepidation weighting her limbs, Meg slipped into black satin underwear, rubbed a scented lotion over her arms and legs, then fastened a black bra behind her back.

She wouldn't let Nic intimidate her. She wouldn't let him dictate to her, either.

Meg stepped into black silk trousers and pulled a long blue silk tunic over her head. The broad bands of gold embroidery at the neck, cuffs and hem made her feel elegant, if not just a little bit exotic. Rather Egyptian, she thought, twisting her hair up and pinning the curls into a sleek, sophisticated chignon.

Blue lapis and gold earrings, a gold bangle on her wrist. Meg stood back and checked her reflection, grateful that the royal blue tunic hid her pregnancy. She wanted to look poised, not maternal, not when she might possibly be called into battle.

A knock sounded on her door. "Niccolo is waiting for you," Francesca announced through the door. "He's in the library."

The library? The last time Meg met Niccolo in the library she'd dabbed perfume behind her ears, fastened the beautiful new lace garter belt around her waist and stepped out of her cotton underwear.

Her full lips twisted wryly. A repeat scenario would not take place tonight.

Meg pushed open the library's massive oak door and stepped into the dark-paneled room. Her gaze swept over the fire glowing in the hearth, the brass lamp on Niccolo's reading table, the walls covered in leather-bound books. Everything looked the same, even the leather couch by the fire.

"You look lovely," Nic said, rising from his desk.

His friendly tone disarmed her, and the unexpected compliment flattered her, sending heat creeping into her cheeks. "Thank you."

The sleeves of his white linen shirt were rolled back, revealing strong bronzed forearms. He looked deceptively relaxed. Meg knew better. Niccolo did nothing by chance.

"Where's your attorney?" she asked, praying her voice sounded steady.

"He's been delayed at the office. We should expect him in an hour."

An hour? So long?

Nic moved from behind his desk to lean against it, the leather belt in his dark trousers accenting his narrow waist and the powerful length of his muscular legs.

He studied her slim figure, his gaze slowly wandering from the top of her head to the heels of her shoes. "If I hadn't seen the ultrasound last week, I wouldn't believe you're pregnant. It'll be interesting to see if you carry your second child so well."

Meg's throat sealed closed. "Second?"

"Ours, of course."

Ours. She swallowed with difficulty, her nerves jangled, her mouth dry. With a shaky step, she moved toward the hearth, putting another foot between them.

She couldn't help thinking he'd planned this. The lawyer had never been scheduled to show at six. Niccolo wanted to knock her off balance. It had been one of his business tactics—befriend the competition then move in for the kill.

"I'll want several," he added, a taunting light in his golden eyes. "Most Italian men do."

"And Italian women agree?"

"Oh, yes, most definitely. They enjoy the attention of their husbands. You see, *cara*, Italian men are supremely proficient lovers."

"Oh, please!"

"Please, what?" he answered, his deep voice dropping lower, his inflection suddenly husky. "Please show you?"

Meg moved another step back, crossing her arms over her chest, discomfited by the warmth in his voice and the gleam of possession in his eyes. He'd prepared her for a legal transaction, then turned personal.

She caught Nic's smoldering gaze and blushed.

Very, very personal, indeed.

Meg walked the perimeter of the room, careful to maintain a discreet distance from Nic.

"You like my books?" he drawled, intently watching her.

She feigned an interest in the floor-to-ceiling shelves. Truly, she'd never known anyone to own such an extensive library of antique books, particularly books devoted to the history of commerce and the role of Italy in early medieval trade. But of course Nic's library wouldn't just be a room lined with books. It was his retreat.

"Is there a book you're looking for in particular?"

His mocking voice drew her attention, yet the dangerous gleam in his eyes made her heart thump harder. Her nerves scraping like fingernails on a chalkboard, she felt terribly on edge.

She had to calm down. Needed to focus her energy, try to control her emotions. Blindly she stared at the framed map above the fireplace, which highlighted Spanish and Italian trade routes in the sixteenth century.

"It's an intriguing map," he said from behind her.

Rivulets of tension zigzagged through her. She felt her shoulders tighten. Her spine was exquisitely sensitive. "I've always been fascinated by this room," she answered with forced brightness, knowing she couldn't stare at the map forever.

Reluctantly, but aware that she had no choice, Meg turned to face him. "It's a beautiful room."

"You used to find my love of antiques peculiar."

"I didn't grow up with antiques. In our house, really old meant nineteen-fifties collectibles." She smiled faintly, amused by her former lack of sophistication. "Yet this is magnificent."

"I'm pleased you've...matured."

She pretended not to see the quirk of his mouth. He so enjoyed baiting her. It had become his favorite pastime.

Nic leaned against the desk, arms folded over his broad chest, pulling the white collar open and giving her a glimpse of the bronzed plane of his chest. "How long has it been since you were last here?"

"More than ten years," she said in a rush, not needing to count them.

"That's right. Isn't this the place you attempted to seduce me?"

"Actually, we were on the couch," she answered with bravado, smiling a dazzling smile, refusing to let him know how humiliating she found the memory.

"I stand corrected." He left the desk, moved to the leather couch and sat down. "This is where we were," he added, sliding his palm across the dark brown leather as slowly and lovingly as if the couch were wired with nerve endings.

Meg stared at his caressing hand, mesmerized by the tanned length of his fingers, the width of his palm. For a split second she longed to feel his hand on her, his palm cupping her breast, fingers grazing her nipple.

A frisson of warmth sparked within her. She felt him, was aware of him, in every nerve in her body.

Niccolo's eyes met hers and held.

It was as if he knew she was attracted to him, as if he could read exactly how she felt. Just like one of the books on his shelf...

Meg broke from his gaze, turned to face the fire and lifted her hands to the flames. They trembled as she held them up.

"Come here," he quietly commanded.

She resisted the quiet entreaty in his voice, hating the shiver that slid up and down her spine. "No."

Going to Nic would be like throwing herself in the flames. He'd burn her. Destroy her. She couldn't control her feelings around him, which made him the most dangerous man she knew.

"Maggie, I want you to come to me."

There was less entreaty in his voice, more force. He wanted her to obey him. He wanted to prove a point, to demonstrate that she still found him impossible to resist.

Her shoulders lifted, hair rising on her nape. She

found it very hard to say no to him. But then he knew that.

"Ah," he said after a moment, "you're afraid."

"I'm not."

"You are. Otherwise you'd come sit with me."

"Maybe I don't want to sit."

"Maybe you're afraid I'll make love to you."

Her lashes closed, her body drooping even as the most carnal craving shot through her. He tangled her up, catching her in a convoluted web of dread and need. He was right, of course. She was afraid he'd make love to her. She was afraid of the strength of her feelings.

If he touched her, she'd want more, so much more than a simple kiss, a brief caress. He'd unleash her most primitive passions.

Wishing to protect herself, she grasped at the first thing that came to mind. "But you don't want me," she answered sharply. "You've never wanted me. You told me quite clearly that you don't fancy me."

"Things change." He circled his hand on the leather cushion again, rubbing the surface with the tips of his fingers. "Remember, *cara*, we've changed."

"You haven't!" she answered with a trace of bitterness.

"Oh, yes, I have."

His voice vibrated within her. Her belly clenched, her inner thighs tensing. He was seducing her already, seducing her with words, teasing her mind, making her want him without even a touch.

"And you've changed, too. Once you weren't afraid of anything, and yet look at you now. Cowering in front of my fireplace."

"I'm not cowering!"

"Quaking, then." He laughed softly at her indignant expression. "I think you're afraid because you're no longer in charge. You've lost control."

"Your conceit is amazing!" Her voice sounded panicked even to her own ears.

"You will come to me." His eyes dared her to argue. When she didn't speak, he lifted a hand, extended it to her. "I know you, *cara*, and I'm waiting."

"You'll be waiting all night."

"Fine."

His eyes held her captive. She couldn't move. Couldn't speak. He stared at her, taunting her, making her painfully aware of the change in both of them.

He was right. They weren't the same people.

Her heart seemed to slow, stop, change tempo. Then suddenly, helplessly, she found herself moving toward him. She stopped abruptly in front of him, as if she couldn't possibly take another step. Her pulse raced, but her bones felt as if they were dissolving, turning her into warm, sweet honey.

Niccolo captured her wrist in his hand and drew her down on the couch. "No, that's not quite right," he murmured. "You were on my lap, isn't that so?"

With a precision that would have impressed a surgeon, Niccolo lifted her onto his lap, parted her knees, then pulled her snugly forward, high on his thighs.

White heat exploded deep inside her. With almost clinical detachment, Niccolo parted her knees wider, heightening her awareness, and Meg writhed inwardly, shamelessly carnal.

She'd let him do anything to her. She'd beg him to do everything.

"Nic, no, this—" She broke off as his palms slid up the insides of her thighs, the heat of his hands burning through the flimsy silk of her trousers.

"What was that?" he murmured, his golden eyes darkening with desire.

She had to go. She had to leave this very second or she'd never escape with her pride intact. Yet she couldn't bring herself to speak, too fascinated by the play of his hands along her hips, lifting her, cradling her, until he held her bottom.

He lifted her, adjusting her, placing her immediately above the rise in his tailored trousers. She gasped at the press of his erection and the sharp bite of his zipper against her most tender flesh.

His eyes bored into hers, and with a deliberate move, he took her knees in his palms and opened her wider still.

Meg gasped, felt her head go light. Rivulets of sensation screamed through her, her thighs tensing, her body quivering.

"Is this how it was, Maggie?" he murmured, still watching her intently, analyzing her response to each of his actions. "You were on my lap, like this, yes?"

CHAPTER EIGHT

WITH a rock of his hips, he pressed against her thin silk trousers, his erection penetrating part of the delicate fabric. She felt the tip of him against her, felt the heat and urgency of his desire. She was afraid to breathe, afraid to move, precariously positioned against the thrust of his rigid shaft.

"Now what?" he asked, his eyes narrowing, his black lashes lowering.

She could only shake her head, her brain dazed by the exquisitely intense sensations. Years ago she'd climbed on his lap, anxious to seduce him, longing to prove she was a woman. She'd failed, and Niccolo had never forgotten her childish lovemaking. Now he was showing her just what she'd missed.

She bucked slightly as one of his thumbs traced the seam of her silk trousers, running along the line of her most private place.

"Stop," she ordered, grabbing Niccolo's elegant white shirt, her thighs tightening, her body responding despite her attempt to shift off him.

"Why? This is what you wanted that night, isn't it?" He cupped her through her thin trousers, heightening her warmth, the palm of his hand pressed to her mound. Ripples of sensation rocked her, wave after wave of need. His palm moved up, down, teasing the tiny, tightened bud engorging with blood.

It was what she wanted. It was exactly what she

wanted, but she'd never admit it, not when he played with her, toyed with her, mocking her need.

Her tongue felt heavy, thick. She forced herself to speak. "I regret that night with all my heart," she said bitterly, almost overwhelmed by the effort to defend herself.

"So do I," he retorted with a harsh laugh. "I should have taken you then, given you what you wanted."

"Go to hell!"

Nic laughed before reaching up to clasp her face in his hands and draw her mouth to his. "If I go, you'll go with me," he muttered against her lips before his mouth crushed hers.

She welcomed the harshness of his mouth, welcomed the punishing pressure of his lips. At least this was strong, fierce, consuming. For days she'd felt strung out, tensely nervous. But this…this anger and passion she at least understood.

Meg answered his kiss with equal ardor. No longer was she a girl. She was now a woman. At least her relationship with Mark had taught her one thing, that she didn't want just sex, she wanted this, this torrid, volatile hunger she felt for Nic.

The kiss deepened, intensified, his lips parting hers with a hunger he couldn't hide. Meg only knew that she wanted more, needed more, and she clasped his face in her hands, lost in him, overwhelmed by his warmth and the smoothness of his strong jaw in her hands.

His tongue played against her lips, flicked her teeth before drawing her tongue into a slow, seductive dance. She leaned against him, her breasts pressed to the hard contours of his chest, her hips grinding against his lap. She felt him everywhere at once, yet nothing gratified, nothing answered her tremendous hunger.

Suddenly Niccolo lifted his head. He appeared as shaken as she felt. He gazed into her face, his golden eyes darkened to amber. ''I should have taken you up on your offer a long time ago.''

His laughter shocked her. Before she could move, he lifted her off his lap and dropped her onto the couch next to him. ''That was delightful,'' he drawled, recovering his composure far more quickly than she. ''I thought you'd be passionate, but you're...beyond passionate. You're wild.''

His words, the taunt in his voice, were like a stinging slap on her already bruised ego. Meg scrambled off the couch, disgusted with herself and hating him with every fiber of her being. Nic wasn't just cruel. He was pure medieval malice. Hard to believe that men like him still existed in the twenty-first century.

She pointed a finger at him, jabbing it in midair. ''Do not touch me again. Do not come within six feet of me. And if you do...''

''What, Maggie?'' There was no anger in his voice, just lazy amusement and pointed curiosity about what she'd say. ''What will you do?''

''I don't know. But I promise you, you won't enjoy it.''

He stood, crossed to where she stood and gazed at her. ''Oh, I wouldn't be so sure, my love. I have news for you. When it comes to the physical, when it comes to the senses, I'm just as base, just as desperate and just as carnal as you.''

Base, desperate, carnal.

She felt his words and the mockery in his voice

all the way through her. Truly, he held her in low esteem. In his eyes she was loose, promiscuous. He'd never respect or love a woman like her.

She couldn't bring herself to speak. Her chest was tight with wretched emotion. She shouldn't have come home. Shouldn't have dreamed she could return.

Nic kissed the side of her neck, then trailed one fingertip from her earlobe to her exposed collarbone. She shivered at the fleeting caress.

He kissed her again, gauging her reaction. "I want you to realize that our marriage won't be without its rewards," he said huskily. "You might not love me, *cara*, but you will love what I will do to your body."

"Niccolo!"

"*Margaret.*"

It was the first time in her life he'd ever called her by her given name. Meg swallowed painfully, her mouth so dry it felt as if she'd swallowed a fistful of cotton.

"Yes," he added, passion still smoldering in his golden eyes. "You will love what I do to you. You might glare at me. You might say you hate me. You might try to defy me. But thank God you're not indifferent to me."

With that he straightened, and adjusted his fine white linen shirt, looking crisp and coolly elegant. One wouldn't have known that anything intimate had transpired between them. "My lawyer has arrived. It's time you met him and we took care of this important bit of business."

The lawyer was far younger, and more attractive, than Meg expected. She'd pictured a middle-aged attorney with a thick Italian accent. Instead the tall, blond, athletic-looking Carl August turned out to be one of Niccolo's university friends. Niccolo mentioned that Carl specialized in corporate law, mainly mergers and acquisitions.

It was on the tip of her tongue to say that their relationship was not a merger and she definitely wasn't an acquisition, but thought better of it at the last second.

Over dinner Niccolo told stories of his boyhood in Tuscany. How he and his brother romped through the olive groves, played chase in the vineyards and generally made nuisances of themselves for staff and family at their four-hundred-year-old ancestral home. Meg ground her teeth. Niccolo waxed poetic, his descriptions as vivid as though he were reading a travelogue.

After dinner Francesca poured coffee in the living room before leaving them alone, discreetly closing the tall arched doors behind her.

Niccolo immediately dropped his genial manner. Setting his espresso cup down, he turned to Carl, asking for the documents he requested be drawn up that morning.

"The terms of the marriage agreement have been spelled out," Nic said without a trace of emotion. "As my wife, you will share equally in my wealth, family estates and stake in the Dominici wineries. If anything should happen to me, you, and our children, will inherit everything."

"Our children?" she murmured, balancing the china cup on her lap. "What about…" She glanced in Carl's direction, wishing he wasn't party to this private discussion. "What about my baby?"

"Your baby?" Nic's eyebrows flattened. "There is only our baby. Our babies. We're to be a family, Maggie. There is no yours, mine, his, hers. I thought I'd already made that clear."

Carl slid another set of documents across the glass-topped end table. Meg picked the documents up and skimmed the first page. Her troubled gaze met Nic's before returning to the document. "But how can you adopt the baby? Mark—"

"He's already signed the papers."

Her head jerked up, and she stared speechlessly at Niccolo.

Nic nodded, his dark head gleaming in the soft light thrown by the wall sconces. "Carl flew to New York this morning. He traced Mark, took him my terms, and Mark accepted."

"Your terms?" Shock gave way to anger. "Just what were your terms?"

"Don't look so appalled. They were quite reasonable."

"Tell me you did not buy this baby!" The stapled set of papers fell from her fingertips to the table. "Tell me you did not offer Mark money!"

Nic's gold eyes glittered hard. He didn't answer.

She clenched her hands into fists. "You did not, Nic, you *could* not!"

His lips curled, reminding her of a leopard about to pounce. "Don't look so shocked, Maggie. You knew I was ruthless. You've known for years that I get what I want." He held up a hand as her lips parted, silencing her. "But before you defend your beloved, let me tell you he took it, Maggie. And he didn't just take what was offered, he demanded more. Significantly more."

"No!"

"Yes. Your noble, moral Mark was more than happy to give his son up—" he broke off, contemptuously shaking his head "—that's right, *son*, to the highest bidder."

"Don't!" She screamed the word, clapping her hands to her ears and staggering to her feet. "Don't ever say you bought this baby. This baby was never for sale, and I don't want to know what he took, or what you paid."

She drew a deep, tremulous breath and dropped her hands to her chest, pressing them to her heart as if she could control the ragged thudding. She couldn't believe this was happening, couldn't believe Niccolo would do this to her, to the baby. "How could you, Nic?" she challenged.

A nerve popped in his jaw, and his eyes narrowed to slits. "I did it to protect you. And our son."

Son. He'd said it a second time. Through the film of tears clouding her eyes, she looked at him. "How do you know it's a boy?"

"The ultrasound. I could tell. It was…he was—" Nic's eyebrow arched "—unmistakably a boy."

She hadn't seen and she hadn't asked. She'd been too preoccupied with proving to Nic that the baby was healthy, that she was healthy, to ask about the baby's gender. Perhaps unconsciously she hadn't wanted to know, leaving it as a surprise.

A son. Maybe someone wonderfully funny and kind like Jared. Or someone cruelly self-serving like Nic.

"Let me see the papers," she demanded tersely, imperiously extending her hand.

Wordlessly Carl handed them to her. She felt Nic's

gaze as she examined the set of documents in which Mark gave his consent for Niccolo to legally adopt the baby. There was no mention of financial remuneration, no wrangling over terms. Just dry legal verbiage.

Ignoring Niccolo completely, she looked at Carl. "Is it true? Did Mark accept money from Nic?"

The attorney glanced at Niccolo before nodding briefly, his expression blank. "I don't think it's accurate to say he took money for the baby, but yes, there was a financial transaction."

A financial transaction. Incredible.

Meg turned to Niccolo. She stared at him with undisguised dislike. She had obviously never known him or grasped how ruthless he could be.

"You might think you've bought the baby from Mark, but you haven't bought me. I am not, and will never be, for sale."

Meg heard the front door close. With a glance out her bedroom window she saw the attorney disappear into his car. At last, he was gone.

Now she'd have her say.

Meg opened her bedroom door and marched down the sweeping staircase. Niccolo was in the living room, standing before the elaborate marble mantel, staring into the fire.

Livid, she prepared to launch into a furious attack on his underhanded tactics. But before she could speak, Niccolo struck first.

"Well, well, that was quite a show."

Her mouth opened, shut. She was silenced by his sarcasm. *Wait a minute,* her brain protested, *I'm the one that's angry. I'm the one that has a bone to pick with you.*

But again, without giving her a chance to speak, he rebuked her.

"How can I help protect you and the baby if you insist on behaving irrationally? Stomping in and out like an irate five-year-old only makes you look foolish."

"Now, wait a minute, Niccolo Dominici. Sending an attorney to meet with the competition might be fair business tactics, but it's not acceptable when dealing on a personal level. You had no right to contact Mark. You had no right to pursue the adoption without discussing it with me first."

"What do you think I was doing tonight?" He smacked his forehead in disbelief as he turned to face her. "I was trying to have a discussion with you."

She laughed hollowly. "Semantics aside, a prenuptial agreement is not a discussion. Adoption paperwork is not a discussion. Intimidating me with your attorney is *not* a discussion."

The corners of his mouth twitched. "Carl is not an intimidating lawyer."

"Maybe not to you, because he's your old college buddy and your personal attorney. Niccolo, don't you understand what it felt like for me? I was alone in there. I was alone and you had my back up against the wall."

He was silent a moment, thinking. "You're right." He looked truly apologetic. "I'm sorry. I should have talked with you first."

"Thank you." She sank onto a soft suede-covered ottoman and covered her face. Her body curled. Her shoulders shook.

Suddenly Nic crossed to her side. "*Cara*, please don't cry." He ran his hand across the back of her head, smoothing her hair beneath his fingertips. His touch was gentle, comforting, more comforting than it had been in days.

"I'm not crying," she said, her voice a croak. She lifted her face to him. "I'm laughing. I'm laughing at how utterly ridiculous this all is. The very idea of us marrying is absurd. Niccolo, we don't see eye-to-eye on anything. How can we make a marriage work?"

His golden eyes stared into hers, his gaze so intense she couldn't look away. "You want what's best for the baby, yes?"

"Yes."

"You want to be sure that Mark doesn't ever hurt the baby the way he's hurt you, yes?"

"Yes."

He caressed her cheek with the back of his hand. "Then you see, *cara*, we do see eye-to-eye on two of the most important issues in your life. And if we can see eye-to-eye on these issues, I'm sure we'll agree on others."

She longed to clasp his hand, to hold it to her cheek forever. When he was gentle like this, when he was loving toward her, she felt so safe and so certain of her feelings.

He drew back, shoved his hands in his trouser pockets. "We should finish up with the contract. Get it signed and returned to Carl."

And suddenly she knew he was right. If anyone could protect the baby from Mark's selfishness and vindictive manipulations, it was Niccolo.

Meg took the documents from Nic and signed at

each of the indicated lines. Returning the pages to Nic, she felt almost immediate relief. For the first time in months she knew she'd done the right thing. Niccolo would do everything in his power for this—their—baby.

The wedding grew nearer. Between long hours spent working at the Hunts and Niccolo's many business appointments, she and Niccolo spent little time together. The first night she had dinner alone, Meg felt rather pleased. But quickly she discovered she truly missed his company.

She tried to tell herself she just felt lonely, but that wasn't it at all. Meg wasn't lonely. She simply wanted Nic. She liked the way he charged a room, making it feel brighter, warmer. She liked his laughter, the lines around his mouth, the glints in his eyes. She liked the way he said her name, the indulgence in his voice. He could be so hard, so unyielding, and yet he could also be tender and protective.

She missed him, missed being with him, and even if they weren't marrying for love, they were united in their desire to do what was best for the baby.

How could she not love a man who desperately wanted to do the right thing? Maybe morals weren't supposed to be sexy, but morals and Niccolo were beginning to drive her crazy.

Unusually restless, Meg wandered through the villa. She didn't want to work and wasn't interested in turning on the television. She could read, but that didn't really appeal, either.

She wanted to see Nic. Perhaps Francesca knew when he'd be back.

"He's in the tasting room." Francesca answered Meg's inquiry with a nod, and pointed her finger.

"He's meeting with someone?"

"No. He's just been having his dinner there." Francesca shrugged, focusing on the shopping list she'd been making. "If you're going there, will you take him his coffee for me?"

He'd been avoiding her, Meg realized, dismayed. He'd been dining alone, intentionally keeping his distance.

Meg balanced the cup and saucer as she walked down the back steps, across the terrace and past the tennis court to the tasting room.

She found him perched on a stool, studying a spreadsheet. He was dressed casually in jeans, work boots and a snug black T-shirt. He looked up as she closed the door, his eyes lighting, and then almost immediately the light died and his features hardened, losing all warmth.

She saw the change and felt it just as clearly inside her. "Your coffee," she said, nervously placing the cup and saucer in front of him. She didn't know why she suddenly felt jittery. She wished she didn't care so much about his feelings, but she did want him to like her. She did want him to enjoy being around her.

"You didn't have to do that. I could have come up to the house."

Something small and tight turned in her chest. "When? After I'd gone to bed?" She'd meant to sound flippant, instead she sounded hurt.

It was an idiotic thing to say. Emotional. Immature. "That didn't come out right. What I meant is that I've…missed you. Your company, I mean. And I just wanted to say hello.''

Grooves deepened on either side of his mouth. His smile looked strained. ''Hello.''

She felt like she'd swallowed a brick for dinner. ''Well, I guess that's that.'' She forced herself to sound cheerful and horrendously upbeat. ''Maybe I'll see you Saturday because, heavens, we're getting married then!''

She was babbling. She knew she was babbling, but she couldn't seem to stop herself. She let herself prattle on as she inched her way to the door.

It had been a mistake to come here tonight, a mistake to seek Niccolo out. She should have stayed in her room, minded her own business. Instead she'd deliberately put herself in his path, wanting him.

Wanting him.

Something tiny and electric surged through her, and from the look in Niccolo's eye, he saw it, too. Or he felt it, because suddenly he was on his feet and walking very slowly toward her.

''I was doing us a favor,'' he said, his voice deep, rich, softly accented. ''I thought it might help.''

''Help?'' she squeaked, drawing back a step, watching in silent fascination as he dragged the waistband of his T-shirt from his jeans.

''Something happens when we're alone together. You feel it. I feel it.''

''No.''

''Yes, and stop right there. Don't make me use my doggie commands with you tonight.'' Then he smiled at her, a real smile, with warmth and laughter glowing in his beautiful golden eyes. His smile made her feel as if they were sharing a private joke, and she loved the sweetness and the intimacy.

But Meg couldn't smile because her body quivered and her legs were turning to jelly.

"How brave are you, Maggie?" he whispered, drawing closer still.

"Not so brave," she answered in a breathless rush.

"Brave enough to play a little game?"

The gleam in his eye burned hotter and brighter. The gleam sent a frisson rippling through her belly. She touched the tip of her tongue to her upper lip. "What kind of game?"

"A children's game. One we used to play as kids."

"Truth or Dare?"

He nodded, eyebrows lifting. "Should I go first, or will you?"

Her mind scrambled, she searched for something to ask him. Suddenly she remembered Sonia, the actress, and Meg blushed even as she blurted her question. "Have you and Sonia Carlo ever been... intimate?"

"You didn't ask me, 'Truth or dare?' But I'll take the question." His mouth curved into a rueful smile. "No, I've never had sex with the lovely Miss Carlo. It's always been just an innocent flirtation."

He took a step toward her. "Truth or dare, *cara*?"

She swallowed hard. "Truth," she answered in a small voice.

"Why did you want to seduce me that night when you were in high school?"

"I—" she touched her tongue to her lip again. "I thought I loved you."

"You thought?" he asked, his expression puzzled,

perhaps even a little disappointed. But she wouldn't give him a chance to dwell on her answer.

Quickly, she asked, "Truth or dare, Niccolo?"

"Truth."

"When you threw me off your lap that night in the library—"

"When you were sixteen or just last week?"

"Last week," she answered breathlessly, struggling to finish the question before she turned chicken. "You looked so cool, so controlled. Did you really feel that way on the inside, or were you just putting on an act for me?"

He laughed softly. "You're asking very pointed questions."

"Truth, Nic."

"I wanted you, *cara*. I wanted you with every bone in my body, and then some." His lashes lowered, briefly fanning his cheek. "But Carl was scheduled to arrive, and I—"

"You what?"

"Was trying to make a point."

"Which was?"

"That I could make you want me just as much as I wanted you."

Warmth and excitement flooded her. She knew this was just a game, but she felt her heart race, her body deliciously awake.

"Truth or dare, *cara*?"

His voice sounded so silky. "Truth," she answered, suppressing a shudder.

"How many men have you been with?"

Heat burned her cheeks. "One," she answered, holding up her finger. "Just Mark."

He started to ask another question, but she cut him off. "My turn, Nic. Truth or dare?"

His golden eyes bored into her. "Dare."

The word came out harshly. She felt his tension, felt her own. Something was happening here, something that had nothing to do with playing a game.

"I dare you to take off your shirt," she whispered.

He drew his T-shirt over his head, leaving his sculpted shoulders and chest bare. She sucked in a breath at the sight of his smooth, taut, burnished skin. Slowly he dropped the shirt at his feet.

"Truth or dare, Maggie?"

"Dare."

"I dare you to come here, Maggie, and touch me."

She closed the remaining distance between them, lifted her hand but left it hovering in midair. "Where?" she breathed.

He took her hand, placed it on his chest. She felt his heart, the strong, fierce tempo, and still holding her hand, drew her palm down so she caressed the contoured muscles in his stomach and pelvis. "Your turn," he murmured, keeping her fingers flat against his taut belly.

His skin felt like satin over sinew. He was wonderful, strong, smooth. It was impossible for her to concentrate. "Truth or dare?" she breathed.

"Dare."

The huskiness in his voice was pure seduction. She pressed her fingertips against the firmness of his flesh, entranced by his beauty and warmth and playfulness. She'd never imagined that Niccolo could be like this.

"Come on, Maggie, give me a dare."

She lifted her head, gazed into his face. She wanted him. Wanted him. Wanted him.

"I dare you to make love to me."

CHAPTER NINE

THERE, the words were said. She couldn't take them back. Couldn't pretend they hadn't been spoken.

"Dare accepted." He captured her hands, lifting them above her head. "But I warn you, Maggie, you're going to have to wait a long long time for your turn, because this dare won't be rushed, and I won't be easily satisfied."

Excitement inspired a hint of panic. Maybe she should have suggested a different dare. Maybe she should have chosen something...safer. "Can I change my mind?"

"No." He backed her up one step at a time until her backbone bumped against the wall. Leaning past her, he shut the door. She couldn't help staring at him, fascinated by the play of light across his taut stomach, each muscle smoothly curved, light and shadows undulating across his smooth golden skin. He was all man, and beautiful. Her Niccolo. The man who'd stolen her heart so many years ago.

"There," he drawled, "that should give us some privacy."

Heat flooded her limbs. He made it sound wicked and wonderful at the same time. But just as suddenly she panicked. It was one thing to play a children's game. Quite another to make love on the winery's tasting room floor.

What if they did make love and he was disappointed? What if she really wasn't what he wanted? Meg didn't think she could bear another rejection.

Ducking beneath his arm, she tried to scramble for safety. But Nic moved just as quickly, and kneeling, he cornered her on the carpet.

"I thought you were brave," he said, crouching above her, trapping her body between his legs.

"No. Not anymore."

His teeth flashed, not quite a smile, and with humiliating ease, he dragged her lower so her hips lay just under his. The crush of the Berber carpet tickled her nape, pressed through her cotton top. "Then I'll have to teach you that, too."

Teach her that, too. A shiver danced up and down her spine.

"Hello, love," he drawled.

"Since when have I been your love?" And yet even as she said it, she felt a ripple of excitement, a craving for his strength and a taste of the sensual. She wanted to feel his mouth and his tongue, be driven wild by his hands, surrender to the rawness of her own desires

"I've never met a woman that likes to argue as much as you do," he said, lowering himself to his elbows, bracing himself just above her breasts.

The ripple within her widened, deepened. She shivered and he smiled faintly, aware of the tension in her rigid limbs, in her shallow breathing.

He kissed her mouth on a slant, his lips covering only a portion of hers. It was a maddening kiss, light, teasing, and when he kissed her again the same way, his tongue flicked the corner, tormenting her with the kiss's brevity.

She couldn't stand the teasing nature of the kiss.

Her mouth, her body, her senses screamed for more. Meg wound her arms around his neck, forcing his head lower, drawing his mouth to hers.

A hoarse sound came from Niccolo, primitive and raw. His arms tightened, and a knee slid between her legs, parting them as he kissed her in earnest, his tongue stroking her upper lip. As her legs parted to accept his strength, her mouth opened to him with a soft, strangled sigh.

Nic's body hardened against her, his arousal thrusting against her still flat abdomen, and she melted from the inside out. The evidence of his desire thrilled her. His arousal fueled her own. Lifting her hips, she blindly sought more contact.

Briefly his head lifted, and Meg murmured an urgent protest. Niccolo smiled faintly, kissing the side of her mouth and then her chin. "You look so disappointed."

She didn't have to say anything. He knew. His kisses dropped lower, his mouth moving to the curve of her breast. She throbbed inwardly, muscles clenching, blood pooling. His teeth closed around one exquisitely erect nipple, and she gasped.

Nic suckled her breast through the fabric of her blouse. Brilliant light exploded inside her head even as the core of her ached, wanting more, needing more.

"You've turned my world upside down," he whispered against her mouth. "I'm confused, Maggie. I don't know what to feel anymore."

It crossed her mind that this would be a good time to pull back and regain some control. If ever two people needed to talk, it was them. But Meg had waited so long to be in his arms, to feel him against her, that she ignored the voice of reason and curved herself against him, thigh to thigh, hip to hip, breast to chest. The loneliness of the last five months, the emptiness of her dating relationships, the separation from her parents seemed to ball inside her, combining to form a great, consuming need.

She needed Nic. She needed his love. Not on their wedding day, but right now.

"Are we still playing the game?" she whispered, blood pounding, body pulsating, her limbs liquid with need.

Niccolo lifted his head and gazed deep into her eyes. His breath was ragged. "We're past games, Maggie. This is just you and me."

It was the answer she wanted, the answer she hoped to hear. *Just you and me.*

Niccolo didn't have to love her, at least not yet, but of course someday she hoped he would. But for now, if he knew who she was, if he wanted her for herself, then making love was right, and very real.

His hand slid to the waistband of her gabardine slacks, unfastened the button and opened the zipper. The cool air against her bare skin made her muscles contract, followed immediately by the slow caress of Niccolo's hand.

She shuddered as he cupped her hipbone, his fingers like a rain of fire on her bare tummy. He found the apex of her thighs and brushed the curls protecting her sex. Her body trembled, her inner thighs clenching. With delicious intent, Nic parted her thighs to trace her most delicate skin, discovering her heat and eager dampness.

Meg reached for him, impatient with his jeans, wanting to feel the smooth polish of his skin. As she tugged at the buttons on his jeans, she heard voices outside the winery window. Stiffening, Meg looked at Nic. Nic sat up, pulled her to a sitting position.

The door swung open even as they scrambled to cover themselves, but Meg's fingers felt numb, and Niccolo smoothed her blouse and dragged his fingers through her chaotic curls.

"Maggie? Niccolo?"

God, her parents! They'd returned early from their trip.

As Francesca served plates of fruit and cheese, Niccolo's golden gaze sought Meg's over the rim of his espresso cup. She knew her cheeks still glowed, and desire clouded her brain, making it hard for her to think.

"We couldn't stay away," Meg's mother was saying, smiling her thanks at Francesca before turning her attention to the young couple. "Once we'd received Nic's telegram, the cruise lost its luster. I'm hoping there's something I can do to help, some little detail needing handling."

"Most things have been settled, but you're right, Eileen," Nic said, nodding, "there are always small things that get overlooked until the last minute."

They talked at length about the wedding, Niccolo unusually animated as he shared with her parents the wedding plans. He'd hired a string quartet for the cocktail hour and a fabulous dance band for dinner. A dozen uniformed wait staff would pass the trays of appetizers before serving the five-course seated dinner.

"You're spending a fortune, son," John Buckner said quietly, shifting in his armchair. "Traditionally, it's the bride's family's responsibility to foot the bill—"

"I want to do this," Nic interrupted gently but firmly. "It's my gift to Maggie. It's important to me."

In the end her father caved in. Meg was glad to know she wasn't the only one who couldn't say no to Niccolo.

Francesca appeared in the doorway, signaling to Nic, letting him know he'd received a call. Nic excused himself, and Meg and her parents discussed the wedding plans yet again.

Niccolo returned twenty minutes later, and Meg immediately sensed something had happened to change his mood. Just a half hour earlier he'd been nearly ebullient as he discussed the wedding. Now he listened, utterly detached, his expression shuttered, his words, when he did speak, terse.

By the time her parents left, it was well past midnight. Niccolo silently walked with Meg up the staircase, and she struggled to think of something to say. Hard to believe that this cold, distant man was the same one who'd almost made love to her hours earlier on the winery floor.

As she paused outside her bedroom door, she wished he'd take her in his arms again, display just a little of the warmth and affection he'd shown her earlier.

Instead he held himself stiffly, making a point of keeping his distance. "If I don't see you in the morning, we'll meet for dinner. Don't forget we've invited your parents to join us."

"I won't."

"I'll leave it to you to settle the arrangements with

Francesca. You should be taking that responsibility over, anyway. Just let her know the number of guests, the time dinner is planned and the menu you'd like served. Francesca will take care of the rest.''

Meg nodded, feeling the gulf widen between them. She wondered yet again what had happened to change his mood. He'd been fine until he'd left to take the call. It couldn't have anything to do with her, could it? It wouldn't be Mark....

No. That was ridiculous. It was a winery problem. Something to do with business.

Niccolo's mood was much improved by the next evening. He wasn't exactly talkative during dinner, but he listened closely and smiled at the anecdotes her mother shared.

''Sounds like a good trip,'' he said, filling her mother's wineglass before passing the bottle to her father. ''I hope Maggie and I will enjoy our honeymoon half as much.''

Honeymoon! Meg sat up straighter. This was news to her.

''My family owns a small private island off the coast of Naples. It's been in the family nearly a half century. A simple place, but there's something about the light and intensely blue water that makes it dazzling this time of year.''

Honeymoon, she repeated silently, unable to think of anything but lovemaking. Finally, she and Nic would be alone together. Finally she'd know him in every sense of the word.

''You haven't said a word, Maggie,'' her father said.

"She's just overwhelmed. Brides usually are," her mother replied. "I remember how nervous I felt," she added with an affectionate smile at her husband, then Meg. "I could hardly eat or sleep the last couple days, so much in love."

"Yes," Nic drawled, leaning back in his chair, grooves deepening alongside his mouth. "So much like our Maggie."

Perhaps the others didn't catch his cynical tone, but Meg did, and she held her breath for a moment, surprised by the sarcasm. What was bothering him?

Was he having second thoughts about the ceremony? New regrets? Well, it wasn't too late to cancel the ceremony. All he had to do was speak up!

"Nic, I want you to know that Eileen and I couldn't be happier about this wedding." John Buckner sat forward, broad tanned forearms resting against the table's edge. "You've always been like a son—" his voice broke on the word *son,* and for a second he struggled to find his voice "—to us. I know you're also expecting a baby early next year, and I want to thank you for doing the right thing."

The right thing. The exact thing Niccolo had said. Her dad and Nic were more alike than they knew.

Nic's golden eyes met hers, and he regarded her steadily. Suddenly she realized they were all looking at her, waiting for her to speak. "Nic's been wonderful," she said in a strangled voice.

"I have to admit, I was a little surprised at first," her father added. "Nic didn't strike me as the kind of man to not take precautions, but as your mom said to me, mistakes happen, and now that I've gotten used to the idea of a baby, I'm looking forward to being a grandpa. We haven't had a little tyke around the place in years. Not since you and Jared..." His voice drifted off and again he struggled for words, this time unable to finish the thought.

Pain seemed to radiate from her dad. His broad shoulders slumped, his body almost doubling with the grief he'd never come to grips with. Guilt assailed Meg.

Leaning forward, she touched her father's muscular forearm. Even at sixty-two, he had the rugged build of a rancher, the lean strength of a man who'd spent most of his life working the land, yet his grief was almost more than he could bear. "I'm sorry, Dad."

His fingers closed over hers.

"Please forgive me," she whispered.

His shoulders shifted, and slowly he lifted his head. His blue eyes, the same vivid blue as Meg's, met hers. "You didn't mean any harm that night," he said quietly, and yet his voice broke, reminding her of his still broken heart.

"Daddy, I'd do anything to bring Jared back. I would."

Almost gingerly he touched the back of her head and then her cheek. His deep voice shook. "I know."

She gripped his hand tightly. "I loved him, too."

Meg didn't see the frustration in Nic's eyes, nor the grief in her mother's.

Abruptly, Niccolo stood. "This isn't right," he rasped, his complexion pale, his jaw jutting forward. "I can't let Maggie continue doing this—"

"Nic, *no*." Meg struggled to her feet, trying to put distance between Nic and her parents.

"Maggie's not at fault," he said, ignoring her.

She caught his shirt sleeve. "You promised me," she whispered desperately. "You *promised*."

"I was wrong to promise," he retorted grimly.

Her father pushed back his chair. "What do you mean, Nic? What's this about?"

Nic stared into her face for a moment, his gaze searching hers, before pulling free. He turned to face her father. "Jared and I were drinking that night. Drinking pretty heavily." He shot a quick glance at her before continuing. "Maggie took the keys because we were in no condition to drive. She was trying to protect Jared. Trying to do what you'd want her to do."

The dining room was utterly silent when he finished speaking. No one moved. No one spoke. The only sound was the soft pop of an ice cube as it melted in one of the crystal goblets.

Her father picked up a fork. He stared at the bright, polished silver tines, fingers clenched around the handle.

Meg's heart beat wildly.

He set the fork down, the silver making a ping as it bumped a china dessert plate. "Why didn't you say something before?"

Niccolo smiled bitterly. "Because I was a coward."

Tears filled Meg's eyes. "No, Nic—"

"Yes," he interrupted harshly. "For years I've let you blame Maggie, and I'm ashamed of myself, ashamed of my immaturity and selfishness. Maggie should never have been blamed for the accident. If anyone's at fault, it's me. I was the oldest. I'm responsible."

In that moment, she fell in love with him all over

again. What he was doing was painful for him, for all of them, and yet he was determined to right a wrong.

John Buckner looked at his wife and then at his daughter. His blue eyes were puzzled, his voice rough with emotion. "Why didn't you tell us, Maggie?"

Her stomach cramped. "I couldn't. I..." Her gaze clung to her father's, begging him to understand. "I know how much you loved Jared."

His vivid blue eyes filmed, the tears turning the brilliant blue to aquamarine. "No more than I love you," he replied hoarsely. "Never more than I loved you."

Wrung out, Meg showered, changed into her striped nightshirt and fell into bed. But sleep eluded her. Her mind raced, and her emotions felt dangerously out of control.

An hour after turning out her light, Meg heard footsteps on the stairs. Niccolo was still awake. Hurrying to her door, she glimpsed him heading down the darkened hall to his suite of rooms.

"Nic!"

Her whisper carried, and he turned.

Slowly he walked the length of the hall. "What's wrong?"

"I can't sleep."

"Too much in love?" he drawled, a black eyebrow rising.

He sounded as if he hated her, and yet she saw something else in his face, pain and tenderness. He might not yet know it, but he needed her as much as she needed him. Wordlessly she took his hand in hers and drew him into her dark bedroom. "Stay with me," she whispered, softly closing the door behind her.

"I don't understand."

"Yes, you do. Stay with me tonight. Let's finish what we started."

"The game?"

She couldn't read his expression in the dark. Couldn't see more than the shadows of his face, the brief flash of his teeth. "Why not?"

"You dared me to make love to you."

"I did." Her voice dropped, her inflection deepening.

She felt his hands slide across her shoulders, fingers grazing her shoulder blades then meeting at the back of her neck. He drew small, slow circles on her nape before dragging his hands into her hair. His fingers twined in her long curls, imprisoning her. His mouth descended, and he kissed her with bottled emotion, his lips crushing hers, parting hers, his tongue probing the inside of her mouth, demanding a response.

Her body gave in to him. She curved to meet him, soft where he was hard, warm where he was rigid. Instinctively she knew this was what they needed. Skin, sinew, strength. Already there had been too many words spoken.

He carried her to the bed and dragged her cotton nightshirt over her head. Cupping her full breasts, he suckled one nipple and then the other. She moaned, arched against him, her hands grappling with his belt and the shirt tucked into his trousers.

He helped her undress him and then his hard naked body stretched against her, a knee parting her thighs, a hand moving across the soft swell of her belly to her intimate warmth. She was damp, soft and ready. She wanted him inside her, a finger, his penis, *him*, but he wouldn't give her the satisfaction.

Her legs parted wider, and she slid her hand down his strong torso to his lean hips. She grasped him in her hand, stroking him with the urgency she felt building within her.

The ache was almost intolerable. She needed his heat and length, needed to be filled by him. She caught his face, kissed his lips, breathing him in. He smelled of oranges and spice, of moonlight and wine. No one but Niccolo could smell so divine.

He drew her hands from his face and kissed the length of her, discovering erogenous zones she didn't even know existed. Ear, base of throat, the hollow under her arm, the curve beneath her breast. By the time he reached her inner thighs she was a trembling mess.

He kissed between her thighs, his tongue tracing her delicate lines and her warm, damp core. She pressed against his head, begging him to stop, wanting him to enter her instead. Yet he wouldn't back off, his tongue playing against her bud and then thrusting at her dampness.

She couldn't control the frantic tension building within her body, the coiling, tight and sweet, making her fingernails dig into his shoulders. Her legs buckled at the knees, and the sole of a foot arched against the tangled sheet.

"Please, Nic," she gasped, and he suddenly pulled himself up, kneeling between her quivering thighs.

"Will this hurt you?" he whispered roughly.

"No."

"And the baby?"

"No. He'll be fine."

Without another word, he drove himself into her, answering the empty ache inside her body. He filled her, covered her body with his, his groan so soft she almost didn't hear it.

Nic's hands clasped hers, his fingers pressing between hers, and he slid her arms above her head until his chest stretched taut, nipples grazing her swollen, aching peaks. Slowly he thrust into her, extending his body, driving deep, and then he withdrew only to thrust hard again. Then, as her hips began lifting to meet his body, he moved faster, his thrusts coming faster, his hips rocking deeply into her.

It was the most exquisite sensation she'd ever felt. She felt hot and raw and primal and she wanted even more. She wanted him harder and faster until she couldn't think another thought.

The quiver inside her body quickened, sharp, silver desire turning in on itself, balling into something bigger, hotter, brighter. She felt more alive than she'd ever felt before, and as Niccolo thrust, she arched against him, hands pressing against his weight. Suddenly she was no longer in control of herself. Her body controlled her.

She knew what an orgasm was. She thought she'd had one before, but that—that was nothing like this explosion of mind and body and senses. As she writhed in Nic's arms, she heard his guttural groan, and with a last, fierce thrust, he strained against her, drawing her to him as if he was afraid she'd disappear.

Breathing raggedly, still buried within her, he shifted them to the side. Reaching out, he brushed a dark curl from her damp cheek, tucking it behind her ear. Aftershocks coursed through her, ripple after ripple, and Niccolo kissed her swollen, sensitive mouth. "Do you know what we've just done?"

Her mouth felt dry, her body boneless. "Made love."

"No. I've made you mine," he answered, cupping one of her breasts, letting the weight of it rest in his callused palm. "There will never be anyone else."

He kissed her jaw, her chin, the base of her neck. His tongue flicked across her distended nipple, his breath warm, her skin tingling. "Soon I shall have you every which way I want you. You will be my wife. You will belong to me. No one but me."

Dazed by the intensity in his voice and the erotic warmth of his mouth on her breast, she couldn't protest.

"Tell me you understand," he commanded.

She felt his fingers drag through her hair, fanning her curls behind her head. "I understand."

She couldn't see his face, but she felt his fierceness, his muscles taut. "Who was your first, Maggie? Who took away your innocence?"

"Don't do this, Niccolo."

"Answer me."

Sighing, she kissed his shoulder, her lips moving across the smooth bundle of muscle. "You would have been."

"I should have been," he answered darkly, thumbs sweeping over her cheekbones like a sculptor examining his work of art. He kissed her again, this time with a softness she didn't expect, tenderness and hunger in the quest of his tongue, in the pressure of his hands as they molded her to him.

"You must promise me something."

"What?"

He pushed another curl from her warm, flushed face. "Promise me you'll never see Mark again, nor will you ever have contact of any kind with him."

"Nic, he's not a threat—"

"That's not the point. He's part of the past. I don't want to fight with his ghost. I want you to choose me."

"And I do!"

"Then promise me you'll have no contact with him. I need to trust you, Maggie. I need to know you trust me. Do you understand?"

"Yes."

He flipped her onto her back and kissed her once more, his tongue sliding across the inside of her lower lip. Helplessly she arched against him, hands caressing his broad, solid chest. She felt the ache start up, the desire coiling tighter than before. How could she want him so soon?

They made love again, this time more frantic, their hands and mouths and bodies searching. Meg felt as if she'd waited her entire life to be close to Niccolo, and she couldn't get enough.

He drove her to another shattering climax, his orgasm beginning at the end of hers, and Meg held him as he bucked with the intensity of it. He cried out her name as he came, and Meg had to bite her lip to keep from whispering she loved him.

They collapsed together, Meg falling asleep still wrapped in Nic's arms. She slept deeply, dreamlessly, until she woke and discovered her drapes drawn and sunlight pouring through the tall arched windows.

Saturday morning, her wedding day.

CHAPTER TEN

THE wedding, planned as it was at the last moment, came off flawlessly.

Meg had never seen anyone half so dashing as Niccolo in his elegant tuxedo. The sharp collar on the white shirt, the black bow tie, the lapel on the tuxedo highlighted his beautiful cheekbones and perfect mouth.

That mouth that kissed her senseless made her yearn for the sun and the moon and the stars. She loved his mouth. Loved him.

Last-minute jitters made her press her bouquet against her straight white skirt. The long silk sheath fit snugly, so snugly that Meg was afraid she wouldn't be able to walk, much less sit down. But the stylist the salon sent with the dress performed a miraculous conversion, opening a small hidden seam in the back and hooking an overskirt in a dove gray satin on her hips. Meg loved the gray overskirt against the white silk. With the Dominici jewels sparkling in her dark hair, left long and loose per Niccolo's request, she truly felt like a bride, a bride very much in love, a bride anxious to marry the man of her dreams.

They said their vows in the small stone chapel on the edge of the winery property. The chapel had been built in memory of Niccolo's grandfather, and when the Dominici family visited Napa, it was there they held their family services.

Meg gazed into Niccolo's golden eyes, and her voice was firm as she promised to love, honor and obey him. But as she said *obey* Nic's black eyebrows lifted, his lovely mouth quirked, and she felt a frisson of feeling. This was almost too incredible.

But more than anything, she wanted the marriage to work, and she was determined to make Nic proud of her. He might not love her romantically, but he did care about her, and he was attracted to her physically. That much she had discovered last night. All they needed was time to settle in together and the opportunity to become a real family.

The orchestra played until the early hours of the morning. The guests dined and danced, dined and danced yet again. The tiered wedding cake tasted even better than it looked, and everyone cheered when Niccolo slid the garter off Meg's slim thigh and tossed it to the eligible bachelors crowding close.

Meg was gratified by Nic's attention. He didn't let her out of his sight for more than five minutes the entire evening, clasping her hand in his as they made the rounds of the tables, visiting with each of the guests, accepting congratulations and kissing after appropriate toasts.

The evening was so perfect she almost believed they were really in love.

Almost, that is, except for the snugness of her gown at her waist, and the strange little flutter she felt in her abdomen. It was like the wings of a butterfly, a brief tickle inside her skin.

Covering her stomach with her hand, she looked at Nic in surprise.

"What's wrong, Maggie?" he asked, lowering his head to her ear. "Are you not feeling well?"

"I'm fine."

"Then what is it?"

"It's the baby. I felt him." She smiled, delighted and shocked and on the verge of tears. "He moved!"

Nic tilted her chin up and pressed his mouth to hers. His kiss was infinitely tender. "I think he's giving his approval," he murmured. "We've done the right thing, Maggie. We're doing what's best for our son."

But she needed reassurance, and reaching up, she touched his face, feeling the warmth of his skin and the hard curve of his cheekbone. "Are you happy?"

"Yes." He turned his face, kissed her palm. "I know we've done the right thing, and that makes me happy."

Not that he was happy about marrying her, but that he was happy about doing the right thing.

It hurt her pride, but there wasn't much she could do. She knew the terms at the outset. Niccolo was Niccolo. She could not change him. She could only hope his feelings for her would grow, and grow quickly. Just like the baby.

At midnight they boarded Niccolo's private jet at the business airport in Santa Rosa. Although Niccolo frequently flew his own planes, he'd handed controls over to one of his commercial pilots for the all-night flight.

They arrived on the small private island before noon. Meg slept most of the way, curled into her leather fold-out chair, although Nic indicated she was welcome to use the tiny private bedroom at the back.

Meg showered at the villa, changing from her traveling suit into a long sarong skirt and matching light-weight top in her favorite color, periwinkle blue. She started to pin her hair up before remembering how much Niccolo liked it loose. She let it drop, the rich curls cascading down her back. After all, it was her honeymoon.

Downstairs, Nic met her on the massive columned veranda. He handed her a bubbly orange juice. "Don't worry," he said, "no alcohol. It's just seltzer water."

He escorted her to lunch, and they sat in a gorgeous pagoda made of glass with a breathtaking view of Naples and the surrounding coast. "This must be heaven," she said, awed by the startling turquoise water, perfect azure sky, verdant green and lemon yellow of the villa.

She knew the Dominici family was wealthy, but the sheer opulence of the Italian villa left her speechless. This was extravagance on a scale she'd never known.

He smiled faintly, enjoying her wonder. "No, *cara*, heaven is what's going to happen later." His husky inflection left her in no doubt of his meaning.

She felt a blush sweep her face, turning her cheeks pink. He made her want things no nice girl should want, and the very intensity of her longing made her sidestep the issue. "Will we see any of your family while we're here? They didn't make it to the wedding, and it's been years since I've seen any of them."

"I was disappointed they couldn't come, but it was short notice," he answered, pouring more of the bubbly juice into her glass.

"And we won't be going to Florence this trip?"

"Unfortunately, no. My father has business plans, and Mother is busy with her fashions and parties."

She didn't want to make an issue of it, but she couldn't let the subject drop, either. "They know, don't they, about us?"

"Yes, of course."

She didn't know why she couldn't drop it. The fact that they might be upset about the wedding was a new and unpleasant thought. "They're pleased, aren't they?"

His golden gaze met hers, his lips curving ruefully. "It's a bit of a surprise, Maggie. But they'll adjust. They know how close we once were."

They finished their meal in near silence. Over coffee Niccolo reached for her hand and drew her fingers to his mouth. He pressed a kiss to her fingertips, and then another to her palm. "Don't look so sad. This is our honeymoon, *cara*."

"I know. But I feel selfish. I've been so caught up in all the wedding plans, and my feelings, that I didn't ever stop to think about your family."

"My brother is thrilled. You met him once. Remember how well we all got along?" She nodded. Nic continued, "And my parents, well, truthfully, they wanted a big society wedding for their youngest son, but they don't dislike you. How could they? I chose you for my wife."

He made it sound so simple. She tried to smile, wondering why she suddenly felt like weeping. It had to be the pregnancy making her teary.

He sucked the tip of her finger, his mouth and tongue wakening the hunger inside her. "Now if you're done eating, there's something I'm dying to taste again."

*   *   *

She couldn't count the number of times they made love that week. The days and nights blurred into an intoxicating cocoon of sensual pleasure. He kissed every inch of her body, made love to her with his lips, tongue, hands. He stripped her of her remaining inhibitions, unleashing a passion she'd always kept buried.

"You're so incredibly beautiful," he murmured, his voice husky. It was their last night on the island, and they'd spent hours in bed, curtains open to capture the ocean breeze and the distant lights dotting the coastline.

Slowly he traced her soft, swollen mouth with a fingertip. "Just the curve of your lip promises pleasure. It is a perfect mouth, a mouth for love, a mouth for sex."

Then he kissed her again, this time with a bittersweet hunger that brought tears to her eyes.

"I don't want to go back," she whispered, holding him tightly, afraid to let go. "Can't we stay here forever?"

He drew his fingers through her hair, untangling the long, dark curls. "You'd grow tired of me, *cara*. You're easily bored."

Her heart tightened in a spasm of pain. How could he say such a thing?

She'd loved him since she was twelve, when she was a girl, skinny and fearless in braids and denim overalls. Back then Niccolo Dominici was her brother's new friend, a handsome dark teenager visiting from Florence. An Italian boy-man with eyes like gold and a smile that made her feel funny on the inside, empty and yearning, and she hadn't understood the longing, or the desperate emotion.

Tears filled her eyes. She pressed her knuckled fists against the smooth, warm skin of his back, needing him as if she were a drowning woman hanging on to a life preserver.

As if Nic felt her love and longing, he clasped her head, holding her close, without words.

It was, she thought, her heart in her throat, the happiest she'd ever been, and yet she knew better than anyone that happiness was fleeting.

On the flight to the States, Niccolo announced they'd be stopping in New York for a day. He had a meeting with Dominici family members living on the East Coast, and he thought Maggie should be there when the movers arrived to pack her apartment and send everything to their Napa Valley home.

Shyly, Meg let Nic into her small apartment. She hadn't been home in three weeks, and her plants were wilted on the terrace. Mail lay in front of the door, and the red light on her answering machine indicated she'd received twenty-three messages.

The moving company was scheduled to arrive in half an hour. Meg bit her lip as she glanced around her small but snug apartment. It might have been better if she hadn't returned. She'd never been very good at leaving or saying goodbye.

As if he could read her mind, Niccolo enfolded her in his strong arms. "It's all right," he said, kissing her upturned face. "Your things will find a new home. It'll be an adjustment for both of us, but soon you'll be settled in."

"You're right, of course. I've just grown attached to the city. I love the secret gardens and the energy of Manhattan."

"Then perhaps we should buy a place here."

She took a step back. "That'd be too expensive!"

"Maggie, I have plenty of money. Don't you worry about the finances." He chuckled softly, kissed the top of her head. "Actually, it's a good idea. Your design firm is headquartered here. They've already told you that they'll need you here for monthly meetings, and I frequently make trips to the East Coast."

"Wouldn't a hotel be cheaper?"

"Not if we're traveling with the baby. He'll want space to play. Which reminds me, when we get back to Napa you see about getting the nursery done. It's never too soon to have everything ready."

The movers arrived. Just before leaving, Niccolo reminded her that his meeting would go late, but he hoped to join her at the Ritz-Carlton for dinner by eight-thirty, nine at the latest. Then he kissed her and excused himself, aware that his limousine waited downstairs, ready to whisk him to his meeting in Connecticut.

"Well, well, Margaret. You're moving up in the world, aren't you?"

Meg stiffened at the sound of the voice. *Mark.*

Revulsion coursed through her as she turned toward the doorway. The movers had been carrying boxes and furniture up and down and had propped the front door open. "What are you doing here?"

"Your building manager said you'd be moving out today. Lucky I caught you before you left."

"Get out, before I call the police." She made the threat before she remembered the phone, along with nearly everything else, had already been packed.

"Don't get all excited. I'm not here to fight. I'm sick of fighting. That's all I ever do with my wife anymore." He stumbled to the plastic-wrapped couch and sat down heavily, covering his face with his hands. "God, my life's a mess!"

She refused to feel sorry for him. "That's your doing, Mark."

"I know. I know. You don't need to remind me." He rubbed his face with his hands, like a kid in desperate need of sleep. "My wife's talking about a divorce."

"I don't blame her!"

He looked at her over the tips of his fingers. "We have three kids together. Three great kids. They don't deserve to go through this."

Her chest tightened. She did feel badly for the children. Then she remembered her baby, remembered how he'd tried to strike a bargain with Nic. "Why did you ask Niccolo for money?"

Mark shrugged. "I'm broke."

"You're not. You drive expensive cars, live in the swankiest neighborhood—"

"All on credit." He smiled thinly. "Margaret, I'm in the hole so deep I don't see light anymore. I haven't made money in years. Oh, I go to work, but I'm scared to death to trade. A trader who doesn't trade loses his accounts. Mine dried up ages ago."

"Your wife doesn't know?"

He shook his head, a rueful expression shaping his features. "She likes living in the lap of luxury, and so I let her spend."

Meg slowly sat on a chair opposite him. "What were you doing with me, Mark?"

He rubbed his hands together and looked at her

from beneath his lashes. "Escaping." When she didn't answer he added, "When I was with you I forgot my problems for awhile. You're so beautiful and so...alive. When we were together I felt almost like a man again."

She hadn't wanted to care about his problems, hadn't meant to feel anything but anger and disgust, yet his despair moved her. She couldn't imagine living with so much unhappiness. "You are a man," she said gently.

"Not if we lose our home," he said, still rubbing his hands.

"You're behind in mortgage payments?"

"Six months. They gave me until this Friday to come up with the money. But I don't have that kind of money. And no one is going to give me a loan." He glanced at Meg, his eyes red-rimmed. "Heck, I wouldn't give myself a loan."

Meg smiled even as hot tears scalded the backs of her eyes. "Maybe Nic can help you again."

Mark shook his head. "I already asked him."

"When?"

"Two weeks ago Thursday. I called in the evening, asking if he'd perhaps extend me some more credit." Mark winced. "Actually, I begged, but Mr. Dominici still said no."

"How much do you need?"

He named a sum that made her gasp. What had he done with Nic's original payoff?

"I know." He turned dark red. "It's a small fortune."

It was a small fortune. It was everything in her checking and her savings accounts combined.

She looked at Mark, then at the huge diamond and

sapphire ring Nic had placed on her finger during the wedding.

She'd never want for anything again. She knew Nic. He'd always provide for her and the baby.

But Mark's children. His *other* children…

Her hand shook as she reached into her purse and withdrew her checkbook. Niccolo wouldn't approve of her doing this. But she wasn't doing this for Nic. She was doing it for her baby, for the half brothers and sister her baby would never know.

She handed him a check. "I hope this helps."

He stared at her so long and hard that she felt a lump grow in her throat. His red-rimmed eyes blinked. His mouth worked. He cleared his throat, the sound raw and hoarse. "Thank you."

"You're welcome," she answered gently, and she meant it.

After Mark left, Meg panicked. What had she done?

What hadn't she done?

She'd emptied her savings, broken her promise to Nic and given money to Mark. Nic would be furious.

She'd have to tell him. She just didn't know how.

Sick with anxiety, Meg paced the suite at the Ritz-Carlton, her high heels sinking into the plush carpeting. She'd dressed for dinner but knew she'd never manage to eat.

Niccolo unlocked the door to their suite at five minutes before nine. His gaze swept her figure, resting possessively on her figure before returning to her pale, composed face. "You look beautiful."

She was wearing an off-white wool swing coat and a short slim skirt, pale hose and taupe-colored heels. The skirt showed off her legs. The swing coat hid the swell of her tummy. Despite the designer labels in her clothes, she felt hideously naked.

"Thank you." A lump formed in her throat.

"Anywhere special you'd like to go for dinner?"

"Back to the island?"

He missed the thread of desperation in her voice. Smiling, he shrugged off his overcoat, dropped it on a chair. "I wish we could."

She felt her eyes burn, her throat close. She couldn't cry. Couldn't break down in front of him. Fighting for control, she grasped at the first thing that came to mind. "How did your meeting go?"

"So-so," he answered, looking more weary than she'd seen him in days. "Family business isn't always good business. It's hard not to step on each other's toes."

Of that she was sure.

He walked to the elegant suite bar, poured himself a drink. "Want one?"

"I wish."

"Sorry." He opened a chilled bottle of mineral water for her, carried the drinks to where she stood at the window.

He handed her the glass. As he lowered his head to kiss her, she noted the fine lines fanning from his eyes and the strain etched near his mouth. His lips brushed the side of her neck. "I missed you today."

He sounded almost apologetic, as if he'd admitted to a weakness. "There's a tragedy." She attempted to sound teasing.

He answered by taking her in one arm, drawing her firmly against him. He cupped her bottom with his palm. She felt his strength, and something else.

"You're shameless," she told him, standing on

tiptoe, kissing his chin. "Sex, sex, sex. That's all you ever think about anymore."

"Not true. I think about you."

If only that were true!

Suddenly she knew she couldn't tell him about Mark's visit. He didn't have to know. It wasn't as if Nic needed to be bothered with it. It was her money. Her decision. She didn't have to explain anything.

Nic tilted her face to his and kissed her, his lips firm, warm, searching. "Let me just check messages and then we'll head out."

Nic listened, then snapped his cell phone shut. Slowly he turned to look at Meg. His features were contorted, his lip curling in disgust. She waited for him to speak, but he didn't. He simply stared at her through narrowed lashes.

"Bad news?" she whispered.

"Your bank called."

Her heart slammed into her ribs.

"It seems the check you wrote to Mark didn't clear. But the bank honored it anyway, as a courtesy to me." Nic made a rude, rough sound in the back of his throat. "I don't know who's a bigger fool. You or me."

He was crushing her heart in his hand. "Nic, don't say that."

He turned away, dragging a hand through his thick, inky hair. "Where did you meet him?"

"I didn't *meet* him anywhere. He showed up at the apartment this afternoon. I asked him to go…"

"But he wouldn't. He got rough. Made threats."

"No."

"But you gave him money."

Her stomach heaved. "He's broke. His family could lose their house."

"I know. He came to me again, shortly after he signed the adoption papers. I told him under no circumstance would he receive another penny from me."

"He told me that, too."

Nic's head shot around. The look he gave her was one of disbelief. "But you wrote him a check anyway?"

She didn't answer.

Swearing softly, Nic poured himself another drink, downed it with a single flick of his wrist. "I told you to let me handle this, and you promised me you would. You agreed that there'd be no contact. Maggie, you gave me your *word*."

"Nic, you don't understand what it's like to be poor. Mark's drowning in debt. His wife is about to leave him. The children—our child's half siblings—need a place to live—"

"Don't tell me you feel sorry for the bastard!"

She swallowed hard. "He needed help. Someone had to help him."

"But not you! Not *my wife*."

"It's just money, Nic."

Nic slammed his glass down, the ice cubes clinking. "You don't get it, do you? This isn't about money. It's about trust. And commitment. You made a promise to me but you had no intention of keeping it."

"That's not fair!"

"It's more than fair. It's dead-on." He swore softly, ruffled his dark hair. His golden gaze skimmed her before dismissing her with a low, bitter laugh. ''My God, you've turned my life inside out.''

''I won't give him more money.''

''No, you won't, because you won't see him ever again, and I'll make sure you have no more contact with him, even if I have to keep you at the villa under lock and key.''

CHAPTER ELEVEN

NIC didn't speak to her on the thirty-minute drive to the airport. He read a business newspaper and looked over correspondence.

The Fokker jet was waiting at the airport. The pilot stepped out, shook Nic's hand, greeted Meg and took their luggage from them, stowing it in the back of the sleek white-and-burgundy-striped jet.

Twenty minutes later they were in the air, and Niccolo again immersed himself in paperwork, running numbers on his calculator, working on his laptop computer, everything but acknowledging her.

Meg closed her magazine an hour into the flight, unable to concentrate on the glossy celebrity photos when she felt so disturbed. She slipped the magazine into the side pocket on the leather lounge chair and looked across the mahogany table where Nic sat working, head bent, black hair gleaming in the overhead light. "Can we please talk?" she murmured.

"I've got work to do."

"It's midnight, Nic."

"If you're bored, sleep. I've got a company to run, a family up in arms, and grapes suffering from a new root fungus. I don't have time to baby-sit."

Blood rushed to her cheeks. "Baby-sit?"

He lifted his head, just barely, his contemptuous gaze meeting hers. "You're like a little child that must constantly be minded. Frankly, it bores me."

His words hit her like two humiliating slaps. Right.

Left. She gripped the arms of the lounge chair, fiercely fighting tears. How could he change from tender lover to arrogant brute in less than three hours? "Nic, I know you don't understand why I felt compelled to help him, but I did, and I don't regret my decision."

"Even now, knowing how angry I am, you'd do it again?"

His glittering gaze held her. "Yes," she whispered, her heart thumping painfully.

"My God, how could I even think this would be a real marriage, much less a real relationship?"

"You're blowing this out of proportion!"

"Maggie, this man, this married man, got you pregnant and then pressured you to abort the baby. When I approached him about adopting the baby, he demanded money. Less than two days after receiving a fortune, he calls me again, wheedling for more. He's a pathetic excuse for a man—"

"Maybe," she interrupted hotly, "but I won't kick him while he's down!"

"No, you'll just support his corrupt life-style." He stared at her long and hard, his features rigid, like a mask. "I did not marry you so you could indulge your lover and squander our financial resources. In case you didn't understand it before, when you married me, you pledged to love, honor and obey. I would say you've already failed on all three counts."

Stunned by his vindictive diatribe, she could barely find her voice. "You make me want to hate you."

"Good. It'll help keep things simple."

Her mouth was dry, her throat as parched as if

she'd swallowed cotton. "Our honeymoon was beautiful. Why are you ruining it now?"

His cynical laughter sent chills racing down her spine. "You ruined it this afternoon when you met with Mark. He knew the terms. He agreed to them, signed on them, accepted funds already. There was no reason for you to involve yourself. Instead of turning to me, you did exactly what you wanted, even though you knew I'd disapprove."

He looked at her with such coldness and contempt that she felt he was someone she didn't know. It was as if he'd turned a switch, shut down his emotions. The closeness between them was totally gone.

"I don't trust you anymore, Maggie, and frankly, I don't like you very much, either."

She didn't speak to him again during the flight. His harsh rejection left her numb and speechless. On one hand she understood his anger. But on the other, it frightened her that he could withdraw so completely.

They arrived in Healdsburg in the middle of the night. Wordlessly Nic showed her to the master bedroom, depositing her luggage at the foot of the opulent bed.

"But this is your room," she protested.

"Our room," he corrected. She felt a moment of hope. Perhaps there could be some reconciliation. He dashed her hope in the next breath. "We're married, and we'll appear united. However, for now I'll take one of the guests rooms at the end of the hall. I'll tell Francesca you're not feeling well."

He turned at the door. "Except when we entertain, I won't be sharing meals with you. I think it's better to distance ourselves—"

"Yourself, you mean," she interrupted in a passionate burst, finding it impossible to remain quiet or contain her hurt. "I don't need space. I don't want to be apart from you."

"You should have thought of that earlier."

She couldn't bear him to be like this, not after their beautiful wedding and the paradise-perfect honeymoon. She knew what it was like to be loved by him.

Meg went to him, put her arms around him, pressed herself to his chest. "Please, Niccolo, please. Let's not go to bed like this. I can't bear to have you angry with me!"

He held himself rigid. His muscles felt like steel bands beneath her fingertips. His harsh expression didn't relent. "I can't be with you now, Maggie. I'm sorry."

"No, *I'm* sorry. Forgive me!"

He pushed her arms down, propelled her back a step. "I'm tired. I'm angry. I can't talk to you about this anymore. I'm sorry things have turned out this way, but maybe it's for the best."

Her eyes clouded with tears. "Why don't you just divorce me and get this sordid deal over?"

"Because it's not an option."

Of course. Niccolo took his vows with utmost seriousness. He'd never act in passion. "What will we tell my parents?"

"There's nothing to tell. We're married. We're home. The honeymoon—" he hesitated, shrugged most eloquently "—is over."

Truly, she thought dispiritedly, climbing into bed alone fifteen minutes later, the honeymoon was over.

For the next week he slept down the hall in the guest room Meg had used. She heard him come and go at night, saw the light shine beneath his door, but she never spoke to him.

They never shared the same meal, table or room. Niccolo walked out when she walked in. He averted his eyes, drawing back his body, as if she were tainted or possibly contagious.

Meg returned to work at the Hunts', grateful to have the chance to escape the villa. She liked focusing on something other than Nic and her disastrous marriage. Work helped her forget the internal chaos, but only a little, and as one week stretched into two, her anger turned into quiet, silent sadness.

Francesca pretended that nothing was amiss. She chattered cheerfully with Meg, going out of her way to fix her special snacks and fresh fruit drinks. But Meg's appetite was gone. She ate for the baby's sake, and not much more.

Two weeks turned into three, and still Nic avoided her. Once, downstairs, passing the library, she bumped into him as she walked, her head buried in the morning's paper. Nic caught her arm as she reeled backward.

"Nic!" she said in surprise. His hand on her arm felt strong, achingly familiar, and his skin smelled heavenly, like sweet ripe grapes, earth and sunshine.

He righted her and stepped back. But it was the silence that followed that completely unnerved her. He looked at her as if she were a stranger. No tenderness in his eyes. No warmth in his expression.

"How are you?" she asked, folding the paper and tucking it beneath her arm.

"Fine. And you?"

"Fine."

He nodded, yet his mouth frowned. "Have you seen the doctor lately? You're looking thin again."

"I'm supposed to see him tomorrow."

"Do you want me to drive you—" He stopped himself, didn't finish the sentence. His jaw tightened, a nerve popping against the tautness of his skin. "I shouldn't have offered. I already have…something… scheduled."

It was a fib. He had nothing scheduled. He didn't want to be with her.

She forced herself to smile even though her heart ached, the pain almost too intense to bear. "Mom's going with me," she said, creating a fib of her own. But maybe her mother could go with her. They could make a day of it. Have lunch. Do some shopping.

"Good. I'm glad you won't be driving alone." Then he walked away, moving quickly as if she'd already detained him too long.

As Meg watched his hasty retreat, tears burned her eyes. A lump the size of her fist sealed her throat. Niccolo, she was beginning to realize, had no intention of forgiving her.

The next month passed in an exhausting blur. The baby was indeed getting bigger, and Meg's back began to ache from all the hours she spent sitting. To compensate for the long hours at the Hunts, she enrolled in a prenatal exercise class at a local fitness center.

But despite the instructor's constant exhortations to clear the mind, to forget everything but breathing, Meg couldn't banish Nic from her thoughts.

She remembered the honeymoon off the coast of Naples, remembered the eroticism of their time together. Nic had made love to her with tenderness and passion. There had been an urgency in his hands and mouth, a driving force in his sinewy body. She knew he found her desirable, and yet there was more to it than sex and orgasms. Nic held her as though she were infinitely rare, fragile and beautiful.

In his arms she felt…loved.

Weeks continued to pass, and Niccolo remained as distant as ever. As if sensing the discord, her parents made fewer visits, trying to give Meg and Nic time to sort things out for themselves. Meg didn't have the heart to tell them that the extra time and space only made her lonelier.

One Friday, Nic left a scrawled message for Meg that he'd be away for the next several days.

It was late afternoon, and the weekend loomed ahead endless and empty. She couldn't bear being alone another minute, and she picked up the phone, called her mom and asked if she could join them for dinner.

Her mother was delighted, and Meg changed into a sweater and maternity jeans before driving to the ranch.

Golden sunlight washed over the white Victorian farmhouse, highlighting the last of the fall roses. The leaves on the maple glowed red, burgundy and gold. A grapevine wreath hung on the front door.

Home.

And for the first time since Jared had died, there was no pain, no remorse, nothing but warmth. Maybe she and Niccolo would never sort their problems out, but at least Niccolo had made it possible for her to come home again.

Her mom had made Meg's favorite meal, pot roast and mashed potatoes with glazed baby carrots. A fire crackled in the old brick hearth, and after leaving the table, they sat in the family room and played a competitive game of Scrabble. Throughout the game her parents kept the conversation going. They talked about the baby, the crops her dad was considering rotating, her job and the prediction of no rain that month. But they didn't talk about her marriage or her husband.

As Meg finished drying the dessert dishes, her father cornered her in the kitchen. His forehead creased. His toe tapped nervously. "You all right, Maggie?"

She folded the damp dish towel and set it aside. It had been the nicest evening she'd had in a very long time, and she refused to spoil it now. "I'm fine, Daddy."

He stared into her eyes, looking for a sign, for a clue to her emotions, but he didn't find what he was looking for. "I hope you know we love you, Maggie, and we're proud of you. No matter what happens in your life, you can count on us."

Meg wrapped her arms around him. His cheek grazed hers. He smelled of spicy aftershave. Never had she needed a hug as badly as she needed it just then. "Thank you."

"Hang in there, Maggie. I know it seems tough right now. But things always work out in the end."

This coming from a man that had lost his beloved son. Tears filled her eyes. "I love you, Daddy."

"I know you do, baby."

Niccolo seemed to travel constantly. And when he did return he appeared so quietly that half the time

Meg didn't realize he was back. Then, before she could have a word with him alone, he was gone. Board meetings, business meetings, overseas investors, media relations.

The meetings were real, she knew. From what she'd read in the newspaper, the mysterious fungus affecting the red grapes threatened to ruin half the state's vineyards. Niccolo's name consistently appeared in the news reports. He was in the thick of the battle, spearheading funding for research, educating vintners, struggling to calm investors.

She understood on one level but felt totally cut off at another. She'd always known he loved the grapes. His passion for them was nothing new. Only it hurt more now, being his wife and yet being no one, living in his house and yet shunned by him.

She struggled with her emotions, resisting the urge to cry. Tears were useless, she curtly reminded herself, not about to turn morbid in her pregnancy's last trimester. Crying wouldn't repair her damaged relationship with Niccolo, and the baby certainly didn't need the negative emotion. What the baby needed was a nursery, a sweet room to make him feel loved.

Meg ordered a delicate wallpaper and border, and yards of pretty French fabric. With extra time on her hands, she decided to hang the paper herself. Every night, after returning from the Hunts, she ate dinner and changed into her work clothes, a white T-shirt and loose denim overalls.

The work went slowly, but she found it gratifying. After a week laboring in the spacious, high-ceilinged nursery, she'd nearly finished the walls and had one border left to install.

Perched on top of the tall wooden ladder, Meg carefully lined up the border with the thick ceiling crown. Concentrating on keeping the paper straight, she didn't hear the door open.

"What in God's name are you doing?"

Nic's thundering voice startled her, and she nearly fell. Grabbing the ladder to steady herself, she dropped the strip of border tacky with wallpaper paste.

"Look what you did!"

"What I did? I'm not over seven months pregnant balancing on ten-foot ladders!"

"Well, there's no reason to sneak up on me. I'm doing quite nicely without your interference," she retorted, struggling to peel the border off her denims without ripping it.

"I'll give you the count of three to get off that ladder."

"I'm not getting off." Her narrowed glance took in his elegant dress shirt and dark trousers. "Don't you have somewhere important you're supposed to be?"

"One," he said, crossing his arms over his chest and beginning to count.

If he wanted a fight, she'd give him a fight. "Two," she added helpfully.

His glare deepened. "Three. Get off now, before you break your neck!"

"Wouldn't you like that? It'd take care of your most unpleasant commitment."

"Maggie, I'm warning you—"

"Why should I listen to you?" she demanded, tossing the tacky border into the paste bucket hanging from the ladder. "It's been weeks and weeks since our honeymoon, and you've said less than ten words to me. I wake up alone. I eat my meals alone. I go to bed alone. I'm trapped here. And you don't care. You're too wrapped up in your work and your stupid grapes!''

She'd shocked him to silence. It was as if she'd taken the Lord's name in vain. *Stupid grapes.* His mouth hung open. He snapped it shut.

He crossed to the ladder in less than four steps. Reaching up, he unceremoniously hauled her down, holding her against his chest until her feet hit the ground.

Crushed to his chest, her nose buried in the open collar of Nic's white dress shirt, Meg breathed in his cologne. It was her favorite. Citrus and sandalwood.

She closed her eyes, undone by the very smell of him.

He squared her on her feet but didn't immediately let her go. ''Those grapes,'' he said shortly, ''pay our bills.''

She felt his warmth and strength from head to toe, but they only infuriated her. Now it was *their* bills. As if she was part of his life! ''This isn't about money, it's about you. About me. Those grapes matter more to you than anyone or anything.''

''What a typical female response!''

She jabbed her finger into his chest as hard as she could, hitting his breastbone cleanly. ''Sorry, Nic, this time I hit the nail on the head. Dead-on, I might add!''

He pushed her hand away. ''I'm dealing with an industry crisis, and you cry about not spending enough time together!''

''Enough time? Try *no* time.'' She made a circle

with her thumb and pointer finger. "Zilch. Zip. None. But that's what you wanted. This is your way of getting back at me. You're punishing me for making a decision on my own."

"A bad decision."

"It wasn't bad, not if you are Mark's kids."

"My God, Maggie, are we ever going to be rid of Mark?"

He had a point. She knew it. But that didn't excuse his horrible behavior. Worn out, Meg sat on the last rung of the ladder, letting her hands rest on her knees. "I don't know, Nic. All I do know is that this marriage isn't working."

"I won't divorce you, if that's what you're asking."

She laughed softly, without humor. "No, I'm not asking for a divorce. I'm just telling you the truth. This isn't working. And sooner or later something will give."

"I don't have time for this."

"No, you'll never have time. You've got your work waiting for you."

"You make it sound like I have a choice!"

"You do. This disease, even if it kills some of your new Sangiovese grapes, won't bankrupt you. Wines, particularly your new California Chianti, are just a fraction of the Dominici wealth."

"True. My family can afford to weather a crisis like this. But most small wineries can't, and I won't stand by and let my friends and fellow vintners lose everything while I sit up in my big marble villa counting my gold bars."

"No. You'll just leave me in the big marble villa while you chase your precious dream."

"This isn't your dream?"

"No! My dream was us. Us together. Becoming a family." She couldn't stop herself. The words poured out in a rush of feeling. "At least, that's what you told me we'd become. That's what you made me believe would happen."

"What a waste of time!" Niccolo threw up his hands in disgust. "I'm not going to stand here and argue with you. Stay off the ladder. I'll hire someone to finish putting up the wallpaper. And find something else—preferably less dangerous—to keep yourself occupied tonight."

She wanted to shake him. He wasn't listening to a thing she said! "But I don't want to keep myself occupied. I want to be with *you*."

"Hanging wallpaper?"

"Just this last section of border."

"I have a business dinner, Maggie!"

"So, miss the cocktail hour. Skip the appetizers. You can go right after. I'm sure you won't miss the important part of the discussion."

For a moment she thought he was going to relent. His jaw softened, and a small pulse beat erratically at the base of his throat. He reached out and fished a glob of wallpaper paste from a loose curl.

"I would love your help," she added, her voice breaking on the word *help*, "but most of all, I'd just love to be with you for awhile."

In his eyes she saw a longing that matched her own, and she realized with a jolt that he missed her maybe even as much as she missed him. But he wasn't going to bend, and he wasn't going to forgive. Niccolo and his pride.

"Truth or dare?" she whispered, willing him to

play with her. Willing him to move beyond his anger and their feud.

Nic hesitated, swallowed, then turned away. His voice was hoarse when he spoke again. "I can't, Maggie. I have to go. Just stay off the damn ladder, all right?"

CHAPTER TWELVE

Too guilty to focus on the business discussion, Niccolo toyed with his butter knife. She was right, he knew she was right, and that only aggravated him more.

He'd been treating her abominably. If it were anyone but Maggie, he would have forgiven him or her by now. But since it was Maggie…

Nic gave his head a small shake, flipped the butter knife onto its blade.

Well, if he wanted to push her back into Mark's arms he was certainly doing a good job. She didn't hate him yet, but she would soon.

He remembered how she begged him to stay, remembered the softness in her eyes, the need in her voice. But instead of listening, instead of caring, he'd walked away. Quite the noble thing to do, hmm?

His cellular phone rang, and it was Francesca. She sounded hysterical. "Slow down," he insisted, leaving the table to take the call in the restaurant's quiet hallway.

Francesca could barely get the words out. Maggie was hurt. She'd gone into labor. An ambulance had been called.

Nic left the restaurant immediately, forgetting to even excuse himself. His heart pounded as he drove the forty miles at record speed. Ten miles from the hospital the freeway turned into a logjam, traffic snarled for miles, red taillights shining as far as he could see.

He was trapped, trapped with his guilt, trapped in the traffic, trapped when Maggie truly needed him.

But then, she'd needed him for a long time, and he'd shut her out anyway, telling himself his work commitments were pressing, pretending that his vineyards were more important than she was. As if his grapes, even his Sangiovese, could ever rival Maggie!

God, what a rotten husband he'd been so far.

Feeling utterly helpless, Nic dialed the hospital's number and requested information on Maggie's condition. But the hospital wouldn't divulge any details over the phone.

"I'm her husband, for pity's sake!" he snarled. *A lousy husband,* a voice rang contemptuously in his head. *Just like you were a lousy friend.*

"I'm sorry, Mr. Dominici, hospital policy. I can tell you that your wife is in her room resting now."

Resting. But what about the baby? "She's pregnant. Is the baby all right?"

"I'm sorry, hospital policy—"

"Yes, I've got it. Thank you."

He reached the hospital three hours after he left the dinner meeting. His nerves were shot, and his mind raced, imagining a hundred horrible scenarios.

After checking in at the nurses' station, he was immediately shown to Maggie's private room. She'd been sleeping, but she stirred at the sound of the door opening.

"Nic!" she whispered groggily, her long dark curls loose over her shoulders, her cheeks pale. She tried to lift her head but lay back, overwhelmed by the effort.

"Did you…have you…?" His voice roughened. "The baby?"

"Fine. So far. The contractions have finally stopped." She managed a wry smile. "Sorry about interrupting your meeting. Wasn't my intention."

God, had he really made her believe his business was more important than her health? Or the baby's life? But thank God Maggie had tried to joke with him. It gave him hope.

Her bright blue eyes met his, and he walked closer to the bed, his heart in his mouth. She looked so small with the medical equipment around her, an IV drip line, a big-screened monitor. "What's that?" he asked, nodding at the green screen.

"A fetal monitor. They're keeping tabs on the baby. Making sure my contractions don't start again."

He smoothed her dark silky curls from her forehead. "I'm sorry, Maggie, I'm sorry for putting you through hell recently."

"You're positively medieval. You know that, don't you?"

"It's one of my faults."

"You make it sound like a virtue."

He smiled rather weakly. Then he caught sight of her wrist. It was bruised and swollen, dark blue smudges circling the slender bones. "So what exactly happened?"

"I was hanging the rest of the border—"

"You were on that ladder?" He saw her small nod. "Even after I told you—"

"Old habits die hard."

"Yes. I know." And he did know. He'd spent two months trying to get her out of his system, with miserable results. He rubbed the back of his neck, gazed at her wide blue eyes and pale face. "I'm not going to change you, am I?"

"No." She reached up and touched his face, her fingers tracing his lips. "But I love you so much the way I am, I hope you won't ask me to change."

"You love *me*?"

"Of course. Why else would I marry a brute like you?"

His lips pursed. "Because I made you."

"Since when have you made me do anything I don't want to do?" she demanded.

Suddenly the rocks he'd stacked around his heart shifted, exposing his feelings. He wanted her, loved her, needed her. "You're impossible."

"I know. You've said that since I was twelve."

She looked so utterly vulnerable, yet beneath the fragile exterior lay the heart of a tiger. "Tell me again about the baby. The doctors have run tests? They're sure he'll be okay?"

"I'll have to take it easy for a few days, maybe a couple weeks. Otherwise, there's been no serious harm." She sniffed, and suddenly tears trembled on her thick black lashes, her eyes darkening to sapphire. "I shouldn't have been on that ladder. I knew it was reckless, but I was so angry with you!"

"My fault," he said, sitting on the edge of the bed and gently drawing her into his arms. She curved against his chest, held on to his coat. "Don't cry," he murmured, kissing the top of her head and smoothing the curls from her damp cheek. "I can't bear it. God help me, Maggie, but I'm a miserable man without you.''

She'd imagined the words, imagined him saying them. He couldn't have meant them. Could he? She looked at him, lightly touched his mouth. ''Say it again, please.''

His mouth curved, a mocking smile. ''What? That I'm lost without you, the most miserable man in the world when you're not with me?''

''Go on.''

''That saving your skin means more to me than saving my silly grapes?''

''They're not silly grapes.''

''No, they're *stupid.*''

Her nose wrinkled. ''Sorry.''

''I deserved it. I've treated you terribly. And really, all I wanted tonight was to be with you. Hanging wallpaper.'' He grimaced, his mouth contorting. ''Dominicis don't hang wallpaper. But to be honest, nothing sounded better than getting the baby's room ready with you.''

''Then why didn't you stay?''

He didn't immediately answer, and then he sighed, deep, heartfelt. Painful. ''Pride.''

''I thought so.''

''Forgive me, Maggie. Forgive me for being arrogant and prideful. Foolish and unthinking. Tonight when I was stuck in traffic, I thought I'd go crazy, worrying about you, worrying about the baby. *Our* baby.''

''You really care about us?''

''Care? Maggie, I've been obsessed! I've worried constantly that you'll change your mind, return to Mark, move back to New York.''

"You didn't exactly make me *want* to stay."

"No, I'm sure I wouldn't win any awards for hospitality."

"Or congeniality."

His mouth curled. "You're enjoying this, aren't you?"

"Yes. You look lovely eating humble pie."

He laughed softly. When he spoke, his voice was husky. "Maggie, what am I going to do with you?"

"Love me," she whispered, clasping his head and drawing his mouth to hers. At the warmth of his lips, she felt a wave of intense need sweep through her. She'd forgotten what it felt like being nestled in his arms, forgotten the peace she found with him.

"I might not show it very well, but I do love you, Maggie. I love you so much my heart hurts."

"That's a lot of love," she gently teased, holding on to him as if she'd never let go. "So what happens now?"

"I take you home where I can wait on you hand and foot—"

"*You* wait on *me*?"

He grinned shamefacedly, his expression boyish, his golden eyes gleaming. "All right, Francesca waits on you hand and foot, and I adore you from afar."

"I don't think I like the sound of that, either. I want you close, very, very close. I don't think I can bear sleeping in the master bedroom one more night without you."

"You won't have to. I'm not sleeping anymore now that I'm out of the bed."

"You do have comfortable beds," she said with mock seriousness.

"Yes, but it's the irresistible wife that interests me." He kissed her lightly, tenderly, careful not to hurt her or the baby. "I love you, Maggie," he murmured against her mouth. "I love you more than anything, and I can't wait until the baby comes. It'll be wonderful to finally be a family."

"Do you really mean that?"

"With all my brutish heart." He kissed her nose, her brow, her temple. "And I've been thinking about names for the baby. How does Jared sound to you?"

Her heart leaped, and her throat closed. In that moment she realized Niccolo knew her better than anyone in the world.

She struggled to smile through misty tears. "Perfect," she whispered, wrapping her arms around him. "It sounds absolutely perfect."

Summer
Temptations

Lori Foster
Kristine Rolofson

On sale 4th June 2004

Available at most branches of WHSmith, Tesco, Martins, Borders, Eason, Sainsbury's and all good paperback bookshops.

PENNINGTON

Catherine George
PENNINGTON
Evidence of Sin

MILLS & BOON

BOOK TWELVE

Available from 4th June 2004

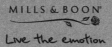

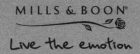

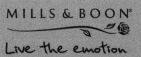

A TASTE OF FANTASY *by Isabel Sharpe*

One Last Fling

Lawyer Samantha Tyler just wants some fun. And who better for a steamy fling than sexy photographer Jack Hunter? She's sure he can give her everything she wants without the risk of emotional entanglement, but when she becomes his model, Samantha realises there's much more to Jack than his considerable talents…

THE DIVA DIARIES *by Karen Anders*

Jenna Sinclair has to find a set of scandalous diaries, and her plan is to seduce her way inside Sam Winchester's home, retrieve them and get out… It all seems to be working, until Sam offers her the best sex of her life – any way she wants it. And soon Jenna finds herself telling him exactly how – with him, right now! But could she lose more than just the diva's diaries?

On sale 4th June 2004

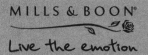

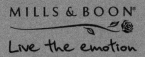

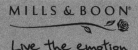